I, ELIZA HAMILTON

I, ELIZA HAMILTON

SUSAN HOLLOWAY SCOTT

KENSINGTON BOOKS
www.kensingtonbooks.com

KENSINGTON BOOKS are published by

Kensington Publishing Corp.
119 West 40th Street
New York, NY 10018

All Kensington Titles, Imprints, and Distributed Lines are available at special quantity discounts for bulk purchases for sales promotions, premiums, fundraising, and educational or institutional use.

Special book excerpts or customized printings can also be created to fit specific needs. For details, write or phone the office of the Kensington special sales manager: Kensington Publishing Corp., 119 West 40th Street, New York, NY 10018, attn: Special Sales Department, Phone: 1-800-221-2647.

Kensington and the K logo Reg. U.S. Pat & TM Off.

ISBN-13: 978-1-4967-1252-3
ISBN-10: 1-4967-1252-8
First Kensington Trade Paperback Edition: October 2017

ISBN-13: 978-1-4967-1253-0
ISBN-10: 1-4967-1253-6
First Kensington Electronic Edition: October 2017

10 9 8

Printed in the United States of America

PROLOGUE

New York City, New York
August 1804

Y ou know who I am.

As much as I would wish it otherwise, I cannot ignore the attention, not now. The sudden rush of interest and recognition as I step from my carriage, the bows and curtseys that quickly give way to the whispered explanations and curious stares with no respect for my mourning or the veil I hoped would keep the keenness of my suffering to myself.

Nor does it matter that I have my youngest children with me, Little Phil on one side and Betsey on the other, both clinging tightly to my hands and skirts. How can I guard my babies when strangers crowd so close? How can I defend them from those who would steal away not only our home, but also the sweet legacy of their father's love? What can I do, when I am all they have left in this world?

Yet I will be brave and strong for the sake of my children. *Our* children. That is what my husband would have wanted, and what I must do to honor his love. I must give no credence to the lies and calumnies his enemies continue to spread against him, and do my best to combat their slanders. I haven't faltered before, and I won't now, no matter how sorely tested I might be.

Love is not easy with a man chosen by Fate for greatness. My Alexander was such a one, a man so bold and brilliant that all others dulled in his company, just as the brightest comet that shoots across the night sky will make the other stars fade meekly in its trail. Yet he was so much more than what the world saw. I knew the rare kindness and gentleness he gave to those he cherished most, and the heartfelt tenderness that I miss more sorely than any words can describe.

I was not born as clever as my sister Angelica, nor so beautiful as my sister Peggy. I don't possess the gentle serenity that graced my friend Lady Washington, the regal elegance of Mrs. Jay, or the hospitable ease in company of Mrs. Madison. Yet I maintain I am the most blessed among women, because I alone had the love of my dear husband. He was mine, and I was his, and even through death our love will bind us forever together.

But that is what you don't know of me, isn't it? Not the scandals and the lies and the rumors, but the truth—not only of my Alexander, but of me, Eliza Schuyler Hamilton.

CHAPTER 1

The Pastures
Albany, Province of New York
November 1777

Iwas twenty years of age when I met Lieutenant Colonel Alexander Hamilton.

To be truthful, at first I found little that was memorable regarding him that evening. Because our country was mired in war and my father was a major general of the Continental Army, our house was frequently overrun with young officers, and I was hard-pressed to recall one from another.

But no: I shouldn't say that about Colonel Hamilton. He did immediately distinguish himself from the others, though not necessarily for reasons he might have wished.

Before he arrived, my family and our guests were gathered in the front parlor, as was our custom before we dined at The Pastures, our home here in Albany. Evening came early in November, and the candles were already lit, their glow soft against the yellow wool flock-papered walls. Papa was standing before the fireplace, where the heat of the fire would ease the perpetual ache of old wounds and gout in his knees for all that he was only forty-four, while my mother sat in the mahogany armchair beside him, her silk skirts spread gracefully around her as she greeted their guests. My younger sister Peggy and I stood waiting near one of the windows, dressed for evening with silk flowers in our hair and prepared to be charming and agreeable. We knew our roles with company. Our parents were proud of their reputation for hospitality, and Peggy and I were as much part of it as the rich meal and imported wines that would be served at table.

Yet we were also a home suffering beneath a cloud of disgrace. Although my father had served his country and his men with courage and efficiency, his political enemies in Congress had plotted against him, and after the fall of Fort Ticonderoga this past summer—a blow to the cause that even he could not have avoided—he had been removed from his command of the Northern Department. Papa had requested a court-martial to clear his name, but his request thus far had been ignored, and the fact that his replacement, General Horatio Gates, had employed Papa's forces and tactics to defeat the British at Saratoga had been especially bitter for Papa. He had considered his career for the Continental Army to be done, and he'd given up wearing his uniform. Although he spoke little of it to us, we understood the depths of his disappointment, and as a family we defended his reputation however we could.

Little wonder, then, that Peggy and I met the arrival of the aide-de-camp from the army's commander-in-chief with wariness, if not open suspicion. Was he bringing further humiliation to our poor father? Was he the bearer of more ill news from the army, more disgrace to tarnish our family's name?

Colonel Hamilton himself did little to dispel our suspicions. When his name was called by one of our footmen, he remained standing alone in the room's arched doorway for a moment too long, appraising the room and all of us in it, before striding forward to present himself to my parents. It was rude, that pause, especially to my father, still his superior in rank, and it clearly appeared to be born of a surfeit of confidence and perhaps an arrogant desire to be noticed. As unmannerly as such a gambit might be, however, it was also effective.

"Look at that cocky fellow!" Peggy said to me from behind her spread fan, adding a shocked little hiss for emphasis. "You know who he is, don't you?"

"Colonel Alexander Hamilton," I said, letting contempt curl through my pronunciation. He wore the elegant blue uniform of an artilleryman, with buff facings, brass buttons, and buckskin breeches, yet it fit him ill, the wool coat hanging loosely about his frame, the cuffs threadbare, and the green sash of an aide-de-camp slung across his chest like an afterthought. No wonder, really: he was slight for a soldier, slender and boyish, with a wind-burned face and reddish-gold hair.

"I cannot fathom why he is here," Peggy said. "Aside from the fact, of course, that Papa invited him to join us, but then Papa invites everyone. They already met together this afternoon. What could Colonel Hamilton possibly have left to say? One would think a gentleman officer would have declined such an invitation under the circumstances, simply to be respectful."

I sniffed with disdain. "I doubt Colonel Hamilton has considered respect."

Peggy nodded, her gold earbobs swinging against her cheeks. "But Papa is smiling at him, and so is Mamma."

It was true. Our parents were conversing with the young colonel as if he were the most honored of guests. On the other hand, appearances could be deceiving where Papa was concerned. Our father was so much a Christian gentleman that if he chanced to step upon a den of copperheads in the forest, he'd bow and beg their pardon for having disturbed their rest with his boot.

"You can't deny that the colonel's a favorite of General Washington," Peggy continued, clearly persuading herself as much as she was me of the colonel's character. "Perhaps he's brought good news from His Excellency, not bad. Papa said Colonel Hamilton has come to Albany on an important military errand, which must be a great honor for a gentleman of his years."

"And how many years has the colonel seen?" I asked wryly. "Fifteen? Sixteen?"

"Hush," Peggy scolded. "Colonel Hamilton is twenty. Nor does he have a wife, which you know is why Mamma is now greeting him so warmly."

That went without saying. Although Peggy and I had always been expected to wed gentlemen from among the wealthy Dutch New York families much like our own, the war had changed everything. The times had become so unpredictable and unsettled that no one was marrying anyone (except, of course, my older sister, Angelica, who had impetuously eloped with an Englishman the year before). All the gentlemen from Albany who ordinarily would have considered courting Peggy or me had joined the army instead, and thus Mamma wasn't above widening her nets for our matrimonial sakes. Twenty in an unmarried woman was a great deal older than twenty in a bachelor, and Mamma made sure that presentable young officers were always welcome at our house.

Including, it appeared, Colonel Hamilton. I cautiously continued my own appraisal, still unwilling to abandon my earlier grudge against him. I supposed he was considered handsome, with regular features and a manly jaw. But he also possessed a longish nose that he held raised like an eager hound sniffing the air for a scent, and so intense a gaze that he was almost scowling as he listened to my father. Yet he *was* listening, respectfully, and not attempting to force his own opinions on Papa the way so many other young officers did. That was in his favor; perhaps he had brought Papa good news, and reluctantly my opinion of him rose a fraction.

"Papa said Colonel Hamilton was attending King's College before the war interrupted his studies," Peggy was saying. "He must be vastly clever. I wonder what his prospects might be."

While I knew Peggy meant his prospects for inherited property and wealth (considerations we'd always been taught to value), I could only think instead of the colonel's prospects for survival in the army, and the war. I'd already seen too many gentlemen march away to battle and not return, and from unhappy experience I'd learned not so much to harden my heart, as to guard it against sorrow and loss. Given his size and stature, I doubted Colonel Hamilton's prospects in this way were very promising at all.

Yet even as these gloomy thoughts filled my head, the colonel bowed and turned away from my parents. His gaze met mine, and held it. He bowed in acknowledgment. At once my face grew hot— what lady wishes to be caught boldly staring at a gentleman?—yet like a deer trapped frozen in a lantern's light, nothing could induce me to look away. His eyes were an unexpected blue, as bright as the summer sky, and at once bold and enticing, with more than a bit of sly humor besides.

And it was that humor that finally released me, too, for as soon as I saw the smile that began to play across his lips, I suddenly was able to shake myself free of his spell. I was no longer captivated; I was mortified. I'd already been shamed, but I needn't be laughed at as well, and swiftly I looked away before he'd find further amusement at my expense.

Flustered, I wanted nothing to do with the colonel now. To my relief, one of my mother's friends came sailing toward me on waves of taffeta and indignation, and for once I gratefully gave myself over to listening to her complaints about how the cobbles in the street before her house had made her carriage late.

At dinner, too, I was mercifully spared. We were short of ladies that night, and at the table I was surrounded by older gentlemen and gloomy talk of the war. Colonel Hamilton, however, had been granted the choicest chair beside my father, and whenever I dared glance their way, the two seemed thoroughly fascinated with each other's opinions. I wasn't exactly jealous, but I did wonder what they discussed, and how much more interesting their conversation must be than those around me.

After dinner the party returned to the sitting room, where I played several pieces on the fortepiano and Peggy and I sang together, as we always did. Polite applause followed our performance, and as I rose from the bench, I knew the evening was mercifully nearly done. Soon carriages would be sent for and our guests would say their farewells, including Colonel Hamilton. Soon he would be gone, and with luck I'd never see him again.

But tonight luck was with him, not me. I'd scarcely stood from the fortepiano's bench when he appeared beside me.

"I must thank you for the pleasure of your songs, Miss Elizabeth," he said, bowing in a way that neatly blocked my escape. "You rival Calliope herself."

I busied myself with the sheet music to hide my discomfort. "You are too kind in your praise, Colonel Hamilton, too kind indeed."

He had appeared small when he'd stood next to my father, but here beside me I had to raise my gaze to meet his. Now his smile seemed warm and genuine, and without the mockery I'd been so certain I'd seen earlier, which confused me even more.

"So you know my name, Miss Elizabeth," he said, "even without an introduction. I am honored."

I blushed again, and hated my cheeks for betraying me.

"You are a guest in our home, Colonel Hamilton," I said briskly, squaring the edges of the sheet music into a tidy stack. "I would be remiss not to know your name."

But he was looking past me, to the window behind the forte-piano. "Your father told me I should admire the view from here, from the southeast."

Of course, the view was familiar to me, but I turned about any-way, seeing it anew through his eyes. Our house overlooked the part of Albany set aside for grazing cattle, with an unimpeded view of the surrounding lands. Above the dark hills, the night sky was pierced by only a handful of stars and a shivering new moon. As if to answer, the lanterns on the sloop tied to my family's dock in the river offered their own meager light, reflecting and dancing across the inky water.

"Your father is a fortunate man," the colonel said softly beside me, his hands clasped behind his waist as he considered the land-scape. He didn't say it as a mere pleasantry, but as a definitive state-ment, and with a touch of wistfulness that clearly encompassed far more than the view alone.

"Papa chose this site himself for the house," I said, deciding to ignore whatever strange mood possessed the colonel. "He is so par-tial to how the lands slope away to the river that he won't permit the shutters to be closed against the windows at dusk. That's the North River, as we call it, though you likely know it as the Hudson, having sailed along it from New York to Albany."

"But I didn't," he said, turning to look back over his shoulder to me. "I rode directly from Valley Forge. Sixty miles, some days."

I frowned, skeptical. That was hard riding for any man. "Sixty miles in a single day?"

"For five days," he said, smiling again to take away any hint of boastfulness from his claim. "When His Excellency's orders re-quire haste, they must be obeyed. Duty forbids me from saying more, Miss Elizabeth."

"Recall that I'm the daughter of a soldier, Colonel Hamilton," I said. I liked his smile, and I realized I wanted to hear more from him. "Discretion, even secrecy, are imperative for the security of the country. I know to respect the confidence of your orders."

He nodded, his expression stoic, while the candlelight from the sconce to his left turned his hair bright as flames around his face. I might not be entitled to learn the reasons for General Washington having sent him racing here at breakneck speed from Pennsylvania, but I could see the toll that that haste had taken upon the colonel. Now I saw the weariness around his eyes, and understood why his clothes hung loosely about his shoulders. To ride nearly three hundred miles in five days meant he'd barely paused to sleep, let alone eat. I respected him all the more for it.

"I can tell you that His Excellency regrets the accusations that have been made regarding your father, Miss Elizabeth," he continued, still lowering his voice so none of the others might overhear. "There's no secret to it. Congress should not dictate military decisions tainted by politics. Nor does His Excellency find General Gates a particularly trustworthy successor."

"He isn't," I said, indignation welling up on my father's behalf. "The country, and the army with it, deserves much better than General Gates's self-righteous conniving. The man has merely reaped the success of what my father worked so hard to put in place. He has shown no regard for honor, or for the brave men from this state who fought for the cause of liberty, and not for him. Yet he was praised as a hero after Saratoga, an honor he'd no right to claim. None at all!"

The colonel's jaw tensed and he frowned, as if there was much he wished to say but couldn't. "You speak with passion, Miss Elizabeth."

"Pray do not forget that I am a Schuyler, sir," I declared fervently. "I know the cost of liberty, and victory besides."

He cocked a single brow with interest. "Those are brave words for a lady."

"Brave words born of truth, Colonel," I said, "and from what I have witnessed. Ill and in pain, my father insisted on his duties where others would have taken to their beds. When all others were fleeing Saratoga and the coming British, my mother bravely went toward them, to our farms and property there. With her own hand she set fire to the entire season's crops, acres of wheat and corn, to keep from feeding the enemy. Still, General Burgoyne and his officers commandeered our house in Saratoga as their own, and when they had drunk all my father's brandy and plundered my mother's goods, they burned our house, our barns, our mills to the ground for sport before they surrendered to General Gates."

It had been a shocking, sorrowful day when the news of that destruction had reached us. Our family had spent more time in that house in Saratoga than this one here in Albany, and I'd only but the sweetest memories of sleeping with our bedchamber windows open in the summer. I'd hear the breeze in the trees, and gathered berries in the fields, and danced with my sisters out of doors beneath the stars. Now that home and the trees and the berry fields were burned and blackened by war and my father's name cast into disgrace, and with it all had gone much of my childhood innocence, too.

Yet the colonel said nothing in return, and I feared I'd prattled on too much. Many other families had lost their homes to the British, and most did not have a second house in which to live, as we did. Doubtless I sounded spoiled and indulged, a rich man's daughter and nothing more. I tried to smile, tried to explain, tried to make light of what still hurt.

"There was an old tabby-cat at the house who always slept with me on my bed," I said foolishly, unable to help myself. "Her name was Sally, and she had only one eye and a crooked tail, but she was the sweetest cat. The servants told me that one of the officers thought she was an ugly nuisance in the house, and had her thrown into the river to drown. And when afterward those same Englishmen—Burgoyne and his men—came to stay here in this house for ten days as prisoners-of-war, Papa obliged us to be as gracious to them as we would to any guest. He called it the fortunes of war, and said we must do it for the sake of liberty. Yet each time I dined with the English officers, or sang songs for them, all I could wonder was which one of them had drowned poor Sally in the river."

I bowed my head, looking down at the ivory fan in my hand. I'd only made things worse, not better, and I blushed again from misery.

But the colonel wasn't laughing at me. "Nothing about this war is easy."

"Not for you," I said ruefully. "You risk your life in battle, while I weep over a cat."

"No," he said firmly, so firmly that it startled me. "It's not the cat alone that is causing you distress, is it?"

Taken aback, I shook my head warily, unsure of what he intended. "I don't see what—"

"But you do, Miss Elizabeth." There was a fresh intensity to his expression. "None of us can deny that this war has turned all our lives upside down. The old dreams of our future are gone. Nothing is as it was, and nothing is the way we'd always expected it would be. But this new country that we have claimed as our own will be better, braver, more glorious than anything the world has dared imagine."

Other officers, including my father, spoke of the war in droning, practical terms of cannons and maneuvers, casualties and regiments. But none of them spoke like this, about dreams and glory, nor with this fervor. I understood now why Papa had been so intrigued with the colonel's conversation at dinner: his manner was that exciting, and contagious, too.

He leaned toward me, a fierceness in his blue eyes. Although I knew I should step back and away from him, the way I should with any man who was too forward with me, I didn't. Despite the fact that the rest of my family and our guests were not ten feet from us in the drawing room, my conversation with Colonel Hamilton had made me forget them all, and turned this window corner into a place so private that we might have stood in another house entirely.

"I knew from the first that you understood, Miss Elizabeth," he continued, lowering his voice like a conspirator. "I heard it in your speech, and see it in your face now. You understand the sacred rights of mankind, and perceive the injustice of how those rights have been taken from us. You crave liberty, and have no more patience with injustice or tyranny than I."

"I do, Colonel Hamilton," I said, pleased that he'd imbued me with such patriotic qualities instead of flattering me with compliments on my eyes or my complexion, the way most gentlemen would. "But I also know that these dreams and glories exact a terrible price."

He nodded solemnly. "They do indeed. That is why each time I am called to battle, I accept that 'Liberty or Death' is no empty, vainglorious slogan for me. If I die, I do so knowing that I have helped secure our country's dearest freedoms."

"How terribly melancholy!" I exclaimed. "A most noble sentiment, but consider how your loss would affect your poor mother, your sisters."

"I am quite without family, Miss Elizabeth, or even a true home of my own," he confessed. "My father left my mother at an early age on the Caribbean island of Nevis, and after she died I came alone to New York for my studies. I can be that most perfect soldier, free to sacrifice myself without thought of those I must leave behind."

I shook my head, unable to accept his grim explanation. Surrounded as I had always been by my own large and loving family, I couldn't conceive of being so utterly alone in the world.

"I–I shall add you to my prayers, Colonel Hamilton," I said. "I'll pray for your safe delivery in battle, and for God's blessings upon you as you triumph over our enemies."

"I am honored by your kindness," he said gravely, and bowed as gracefully as any French courtier might. "I cannot think of anything that would give me greater pleasure, Miss Elizabeth."

"Eliza," I said impulsively. "My friends call me Eliza."

"Then I shall call you Betsey, to set myself apart from your other friends." He smiled again, and added a disarming little nod that made me smile in return. "Now that you've honored me once again with a pledge of friendship, Betsey, I shall remain always in your debt."

Too late I realized I shouldn't have smiled with such encouragement, or let him misinterpret my good wishes. I hadn't intended to pledge friendship, and no lady ever wished to have a gentleman in her debt. But before I could demur, my sister Peggy suddenly appeared, popping up like a sprite beside Colonel Hamilton.

"Mamma wishes you to come bid good night to our guests, Eliza," she said pointedly, seizing me by the arm to make sure I understood. Which of course I did: I'd been too long alone in the colonel's company, and Mamma—or worse, Papa—had noticed. "Pray excuse us, Colonel."

She didn't wait for me to speak, instead pulling me forcibly away from him and from the room. As soon as we were in the hall, I shook my arm free of her grasp.

"I don't require you to yoke yourself to me like that, Peggy," I said crossly. I followed her—not willingly, but because I knew I must. "That was rude of you, and you know it."

Peggy pursed her lips and raised her brows, a face full of smugness that I never liked to see.

"Then you can tell that to Mamma and Papa," she said. "I was only obeying their wishes, which is more than you were doing."

"I was doing nothing wrong," I said defensively, though I knew that wasn't quite true. "I was discussing the war with Colonel Hamilton."

Peggy made that face again, but by now we were in the front hall, and I slipped into my place beside my mother. One by one, carriages were drawing up before our house and our guests were taking their leave. As usual, my parents bid each of them farewell in turn, with many promises of good wishes and returning calls.

Last of all came Colonel Hamilton. I didn't note what he said to my parents, because I was concentrating so hard on saying nothing foolish myself.

"Good night, Colonel Hamilton," I murmured, all I dared say as I dipped a slight curtsey.

"Good evening, Miss Elizabeth," he said. He bowed, and moved on to thank my mother.

And that was all. Four words, my full name, and perfect propriety. I should have been relieved (if, in honesty, a bit disappointed), except for how he looked at me as he spoke. His eyes crinkled at the corners and the slightest of smiles played upon his lips, as if together we shared the greatest, most amusing secret in the world. It was only there for the instant that he stood before me, and gone before he'd turned to my mother. Even as I hoped no one else had taken notice, I smiled swiftly in return, unable to help myself.

Soon afterward, one of the footmen closed the door behind the colonel, the last guest of the evening. At once my mother began giving brisk orders to the servants so that the house would be put back to order, while my father tested the lock on the front door, the way he did every night before retiring. Peggy turned to climb the stairs to bed and I began to follow, believing I'd escaped.

I hadn't.

"Eliza, a moment," Papa said, and reluctantly I paused. Peggy stopped, too, eager to listen, but a curt nod from Papa sent her on her way up the stairs and out of hearing.

I turned to face him, my hand on the twisting newel post. Because I remained standing on the bottom step, we were nearly eye to eye.

"Colonel Hamilton is an agreeable young gentleman, isn't he?" he said.

"Yes, Papa," I said warily.

"A young man with great promise," Papa continued. "Intelligent, perceptive. Resourceful and persistent, too, to hear His Excellency tell it."

I nodded, wishing for all the world that I'd been able to flee upstairs with my sister.

"You appeared to enjoy Colonel Hamilton's company, Eliza," he said, not a rebuke, but a statement. "He's a charming fellow, is he not?"

"He is," I agreed uneasily. Papa had never been one for guile or trickery, but I couldn't see where all this was leading us. "We spoke of the war."

Papa smiled. "I expected so," he said, "for war is much on his mind, as it would be for any officer. Although speaking of war is hardly the way for a gentleman to win a lovely young miss."

"He wasn't trying to win me, Papa," I said, rankling a bit at that "lovely young miss." Among the three of us sisters, Peggy was the beautiful one and Angelica the most clever. I was somewhere in the middle, exactly where I'd been born, pretty enough and clever enough. But Papa insisted on praising my appearance whenever he'd the chance, as if repetition were sufficient to make me over into Venus herself. He meant well, I know—he always did—but still I wished he'd recognize my other qualities, too, the ones my sisters didn't possess, such as how well I could ride a horse, or how skilled I'd become at managing the household affairs with Mamma.

"Gentlemen don't always make their intentions apparent at first," Papa continued. "I saw the attention he paid toward you."

How many times this night had I blushed? "I assure you, Papa, that our conversation was entirely innocent of—of any intention."

Papa's smile faded. "I am glad of that," he said more seriously. "I wouldn't want you to consider an attachment to him."

"Oh, Papa!" I exclaimed with dismay, my cheeks growing warmer still. "After a single conversation?"

"I am serious, Elizabeth," Papa said. "Colonel Hamilton is a young officer with much to recommend him. I liked him very much. He is entirely devoted to the cause and to this country. Perhaps *too* devoted. According to His Excellency, the colonel is brave to the point of being reckless in battle—the first to engage and the last to leave the fray."

Sadly, I couldn't argue with Papa, not after all Colonel Hamilton had said to me earlier. Liberty or death, indeed.

"I've seen it before in other young officers," Papa continued, "and to my sorrow I'm certain I shall see it again. While courageous, even admirable, such men do not have long lives as soldiers. He'll return to Pennsylvania tomorrow, and I fear that will be the last we'll see of him. I would be surprised if he survives to his next birthday."

"Yes, Papa," I agreed softly. I wished that what he'd said wasn't true, and I wished even more that we all lived in different, more peaceful times.

"Yes." There was sadness and regret in Papa's face as he doubtless remembered all those other brave young soldiers, now lost, who'd served with him. "You can understand why I caution against him, Elizabeth. There are plenty of other young gentlemen in the world for you. Perhaps they may appear less dashing or less handsome, but they will be steady by your side, and love you more than glory or fame. That's what matters most. It's late now. Time for you to find your bed."

He kissed me on the forehead, and added a fond pat to my shoulder as I turned and slowly climbed the stairs. He was a wise man, my father, and wanted only the best for me. I knew that. I was always grateful for his wisdom and guidance, as any daughter would be. He'd been right: most likely I would never again meet Colonel Hamilton in this life. Forgetting him should be easy enough, just as he would forget me.

But still, I added him to my prayers that night, exactly as I'd promised, and as I drifted to sleep I thought of how he'd smiled when he'd called me Betsey. . . .

CHAPTER 2

Morristown, New Jersey
January 1780

I think every family must have a habitual matchmaker—a sister, aunt, or grandmother (for of course matchmakers are by nature female) who devotes her every waking minute to contriving the perfect pairings for those she loves best.

In our family, the title belonged to my aunt Gertrude Cochran, my father's sister. She was herself happily wed to an amiable and well-respected physician, Dr. John Cochran, who was currently serving not only as the personal physician to General Washington, but also as Surgeon General of the Middle Department, as appointed by Congress. In her way, my aunt was serving, too, traveling with her husband wherever the army might take them. Most recently they had settled in to winter headquarters in the town of Morristown, in New Jersey, not far from the city of New York.

From my aunt's letters, this was not nearly as odious—or arduous—as one might think. While my mother had shuddered and feared that Aunt Gertrude must be huddled against the winter winds in some mean tent, in truth she and Dr. Cochran had been granted a pleasant house with every convenience for their use. They were situated not far from His Excellency's headquarters, and were often invited there to dine and share in other entertainments. I'd several friends who were already in Morristown, too, ladies who were staying with relations and happily being courted by at least a half dozen gentlemen. It all sounded quite merry, and my aunt wrote long letters describing assemblies, suppers, and musicales, all attended by gallant young officers.

If her letters were contrived to make me envy her situation, they achieved that goal. Over the last months, the major conflicts of the war had shifted from the northern states to the south, and while this brought more security for my family, it also meant there were fewer and fewer visitors both to our house and to Albany. Last April, my father had finally been exonerated of any wrongdoing in the court-martial he'd requested, but even so, he'd resigned his commission, left the army, and once again taken his place as a delegate to the Continental Congress in Philadelphia. No longer did officers, gallant or otherwise, come to call at our house, and Peggy and I both chafed at the lack of gentlemanly company. When Aunt Gertrude wrote to invite me in December to visit her in Morristown, I nearly leapt at the offer.

In perfect fairness, I must add that there was one more enticement to my aunt's invitation. Among the dozens of officers she'd mentioned in her letter, one name had stood out as sharply as if it had been doubly inked: Colonel Alexander Hamilton. Whether because of my prayers on his behalf, God's grace, or the colonel's own innate good fortune, he was not only still alive, but prospering as a trusted member of General Washington's staff—the General's Family, as it was called—in Morristown.

During the two years since the colonel had called at our house, there had been no further words shared between us other than the ones I have described here. We'd exchanged no letters, nor sent messages through others. I knew better than to behave so boldly, and besides, I was sure he'd far more demanding things to do for the sake of the army and the war. He'd become a hero of numerous battles, decorated and lauded for his bravery, daring, and resourcefulness under fire. And yet as soon as Colonel Hamilton had learned of my aunt's connection to me, he'd asked at once for her to relay his regards, and his fond memories of our only meeting.

She'd done so in her very next letter to me, and had in all the letters that followed. Further, she'd added so much praise for the colonel—his wit, his courage, his handsome face and form—that I'd blushed at her audacity. Aunt Gertrude was not only a habitual matchmaker; she was a brazen one, too.

I was flattered. I was intrigued. I'll admit to nothing more, even now. I was by nature more practical than many ladies, and I didn't believe in the kind of instantaneous love that poets praised. I had liked Colonel Hamilton, and I'd thought often of him, and yes, I'd kept him in my prayers each night for the past two years. Apparently, he had liked me, too, at least well enough to confess it to my aunt. Now, in Morristown, he and I could discover where that affinity might lead us.

To my great surprise, my parents were nearly as eager as I for me to join my aunt—so eager that I suspected Aunt Gertrude had shared her schemes for me and Colonel Hamilton with them as well. The favorable impression that my father had first formed of the colonel had continued to grow with reports of his diplomacy and intelligence from General Washington himself, reports that balanced the more frivolous praises from my aunt. The colonel had become the general's most skilled aide, and his most trusted as well. Whatever my parents' reasoning, they agreed that I should go, and when Papa departed Albany to return to Philadelphia soon after Twelfth Night, I traveled south in his company, with the plan that I would be left off in Morristown.

Although none of us realized it then, that winter would be the worst in memory, with bitter cold and numerous storms that froze rivers and harbors solid and buried roads thick in snow and ice. Our journey was slow and arduous, by sledge and by sleigh. Although the campaigns of both armies had ceased for the winter season, the country was still at war, and Papa took care that our driver followed only the safest (if indirect) routes through territory held by the Continental forces.

There was another reason to be cautious. Although my father had resigned his commission, he remained a close friend and advisor to General Washington as well as a member of Congress. The British knew this, and there'd been sufficient rumors of a possible kidnapping that we were granted a military escort for our journey.

Not a day passed that our progress wasn't hampered by fresh snow or ice, yet still we pressed onward. As a soldier, Papa was accustomed to this kind of hardship, and lost himself in reading letters and dispatches from the other members of Congress as if he were home at his own desk. I was woefully not as stalwart, no matter my resolve. Fresh coals in my foot warmer turned cold beneath my skirts within an hour, and even bundled beneath heavy fur throws, my fingers and toes were often numb with the cold. It wasn't possible to divert myself with needlework or reading; all I could do was concentrate on keeping warm.

In the midst of my misery, I thought often of how Colonel Hamilton had made this journey in five days during October. Now, in January, it took Papa and me nearly three weeks to cover the same distance.

We finally arrived in Morristown late in the afternoon on the first of February. The weak winter sun was low and rosy in the sky, making long shadows across the snow. I sat up straight and looked about me as the weary horses slowly pulled our sleigh through the small town, eager for a glimpse of the exciting encampment that Aunt Gertrude had promised.

I didn't see it. Instead Morristown had a weary, pinched look, and none of the bustle and purpose that I'd expected. The snow in the streets was dirty and trodden, and the few soldiers we passed were hurrying hunched and bent against the cold. To my surprise, there were no women or children abroad at all. Although the houses were agreeable, some had their shutters closed on the lowest floors as if the inhabitants were in hiding, while others showed more the appearance of public houses than private homes, with a general lack of care and tidiness that no good housewife would admit.

"Where is everyone, Papa?" I asked, my words coming out in little clouds in the chill air. "Aunt Gertrude said there were thousands of soldiers here, yet I've seen fewer than a dozen."

"The majority of the men aren't stationed here in town, but to the north, in a place called Jockey Hollow," Papa said as he, too, glanced about the quiet street. "Some of the higher-ranking officers have secured quarters in private houses for themselves and their families, with His Excellency and his staff in Mrs. Ford's mansion at the end of town."

I nodded, for that made sense. "But if the soldiers are elsewhere, then where are the townspeople? I know it's cold, but there should still be people about at this time of day. There would be in New York or Albany."

"But neither of those are Morristown," Papa said, his voice

somber. "I suspect your aunt has painted this place like some merry Vauxhall frolic, but that couldn't be further from the truth. The townspeople don't want the army here at all, and have no compunctions about showing their disdain by keeping their distance, as you have noticed."

His frankness startled me, for though he was still closely involved with affairs of the war, he seldom confided these matters to me.

"How very uncivil of them," I said warmly, "and unpatriotic, too."

Papa grunted. "They have their reasons," he said. "Nor would I question their patriotism. The last time the army camped here three years ago, the soldiers brought smallpox with them, and many from families here fell ill and died. Since then, His Excellency has ordered that all men be inoculated so they no longer carry the contagion, but the fears among the people remain."

Their fears were understandable, too. Smallpox was a terrible evil that claimed young and old alike, and while inoculation was growing in popularity, there were still many more superstitious folk who would rather risk the disease itself. No wonder they kept within their homes.

"But for this camp, disease is the least of the worries," Papa continued without any prompting. He wasn't looking at me, but staring straight ahead past the driver's back, his profile sharp against the banks of snow, and his mouth grimly set. I wondered if he even remembered I was beside him.

"The soldiers themselves are already suffering," he continued bluntly, his voice edged with anger, "and winter still has months to run its course. There are insufficient shelters, leaving men to weather these snowstorms with no more comfort than a tattered blanket. His Excellency does what he can for them, but there isn't enough food, firewood, or cabins, and most of the men haven't been paid in months. Some have deserted for home, and others have turned to thieving. It is a constant challenge for the officers to maintain morale and discipline."

No, there hadn't been a word of any of this in Aunt Gertrude's letters. I sank a little lower beneath the piled furs that kept me warm with my hands snug inside my muff, and with guilty remorse I thought of soldiers shivering through the winter without proper shelter, without fires for warmth or food in their bellies. What right did I have to feel the cold, or complain of it?

"Where *are* the army's provisions?" I asked. "It's still early in the winter. Surely supplies are not already exhausted. If the men are in want, why hasn't Congress addressed their needs?"

Papa frowned, and lowered his chin into the thick collar of his greatcoat like a turtle closing into its shell. "It is not so simple as that, Eliza."

"Why isn't it?" I asked, genuinely troubled. I wasn't being difficult; I simply wished to know. Surely there was a way to remedy this appalling state of affairs. "You're a member of Congress yourself, Papa. If it is known that our soldiers are hungry, why isn't food being given to them?"

"That's no concern of yours, nor should it be," he said, more sharply than I'd expected. "It will be addressed by Congress, and they will be made to understand."

He gave my knee an awkward, muffled pat with his gloved hand. "I shouldn't burden you with my worries. That's not why you've come all this way, is it? No, your purpose here is to be a companion to your aunt through a difficult winter. I'm sure you'll be a cheerful and virtuous presence and a comfort to all those here who need it most, as any good Christian woman would."

"I shall do my best, Papa," I said, an easy promise to make. Being cheerful, virtuous, and a comfort to others had been ingrained into me and my sisters all our lives by our mother.

He nodded, though I sensed that his thoughts were already elsewhere.

"I'm sure your aunt has told you that Colonel Hamilton continues as His Excellency's primary aide-de-camp in Morristown," he said gruffly, "and that he has asked after you. You do recall the gentleman, don't you?"

We'd been traveling together for three weeks, yet it had taken Papa until now to speak those words to me. But because I'd been half expecting this from the beginning (and even long before), I managed to keep my voice even and my reply measured and truthful.

"Aunt Gertrude did relay the colonel's compliments to me, yes," I said carefully. "And yes, I have not forgotten him. But he has never written to me directly, Papa, nor presumed upon our acquaintance."

Papa frowned, his brows drawing tightly together beneath the cocked brim of his hat.

"I would expect that as an officer, Colonel Hamilton has been far too occupied with his duties to write love letters," he said. "It's your aunt who has been the presumptuous one in regard to the man."

"You liked Colonel Hamilton when he called on us two years ago," I said, daring greatly. "You said he had great promise, and you said he was intelligent, resourceful, and courageous."

"And you, daughter, have an excellent memory." He shifted on the sleigh's seat to face me. He had tied a scarf around his black beaver hat to keep the wind from carrying it away from his head, yet long wisps of his hair had pulled free from the ribbon around his queue to whip in the breeze beside his weathered cheek. I don't know why I took notice of his hair at that moment; perhaps my thoughts would rather have concentrated on his unkempt hair than on the seriousness of our conversation. "So the colonel did catch your eye when he last visited us. I thought as much."

My cheeks warmed, even in the cold air. "One evening's acquaintance is scarcely enough to judge him, Papa," I said. "He made himself agreeable to me, that was all."

"You needn't be so coy with me, Eliza," he said. "I knew within moments of meeting your mother that I would marry her."

"Papa, please," I exclaimed. My parents had never made a secret of the warm devotion and love they held for each other, and although they had been wed for nearly twenty-five years, the nursery on the uppermost floor of our house was still frequently required for another new little brother or sister. Yet it made me feel uncomfortably rushed to hear my father speak of me and Colonel Hamilton in the same fashion. "It's far too soon for that."

He shook his head, making it clear that he believed my objections to be nothing more than over-modest rubbish.

"Such matters are inclined to move more swiftly during times of war, Eliza," he said. "I realize that your aunt may be as enthusiastic as Cupid himself, especially where Colonel Hamilton is concerned. It cannot be denied that he has certain impediments, however. The man has no fortune or family, and his origins are questionable at best."

"I know his family wasn't Dutch, like ours," I began, "and I know he wasn't born in New York, but—"

Papa cut me off. "It's not where he was born, Eliza, but how," he said. "His mother left her lawful husband to live sinfully with her lover. That man was Hamilton's father. He is illegitimate, a bastard, and all the world knows it."

All the world might have known his parentage, but I hadn't, and in confusion I looked down to my lap. I'd never known anyone who'd been born outside a lawful marriage, and although it was shocking, I was still unwilling to abandon Colonel Hamilton.

"But that is not his fault, Father," I said earnestly. "None of us has the ability to choose our parents. That is God's will, not ours. I was fortunate in my birth, and he was not, and he should no more be blamed for that circumstance of his fate than I should be praised for mine."

"What republican sentiments for a lady, Elizabeth," Papa said, so dryly that I couldn't tell if he agreed with me or not.

"They're Christian sentiments as well," I said firmly. "You cannot quarrel with that."

"Nor with you, daughter," he said more gently. "Permit me to continue. You should know that regardless of Colonel Hamilton's lack of a respectable family, I remain impressed with his zeal, his courage, and his determination. By his own merits, he has achieved far more than he should have by rights of his low birth, and I've little doubt he'll continue on that path. He will do well in this world. He already has. He has won the favor of His Excellency, and therefore mine as well."

"Then you—you do not find him objectionable?" I asked uncertainly.

"Not at all, Eliza," Papa said. "If you discover that the fellow continues to be agreeable to you, why, then, I want you to understand that neither your mother nor I would object if he presses his suit. I would not object at all."

I bowed my head, my thoughts spinning. That was as good as a blessing, better than I'd expected. But I understood what Papa wasn't saying, too: that I was twenty-two-years old, that he worried for my future, that he was relieved that a reasonably acceptable man was showing interest in me, and that he didn't want me to waste away as a spinster.

I didn't want to perish as a spinster, either. But it had been over two years since I'd last seen Colonel Hamilton, and even that had been for only a few hours' time. After so many months, I wasn't sure I could even recall his face, handsome as it had been, with real clarity.

Yet I *had* liked him; he'd impressed me in all the ways that mattered most. That was what I remembered, that he'd been so different from other gentlemen. He'd been special.

If I'd married someone from Albany or New York as had always been expected of me, a young gentleman who was from a family similar to my own, I would know exactly what my life would be. I would oversee a large house in the country and another in the city of New York, with children and servants and a respectably dull and dully respectable husband. It would all be predictable and safe and without a whit of excitement, and the longer I considered such a life, the less appeal it held for me. Yet even after only one meeting, I knew that life with Alexander would always be exciting, because *he* was exciting.

So yes, I'd liked him. But as much as I respected my parents' wishes, I wanted this decision to be mine, not theirs, and I wanted to be sure.

Papa, however, misread my silence.

"Of course, I wouldn't expect you to go against your heart, Elizabeth," he said with another awkward pat to my knee. "If your mother and I are mistaken and he doesn't please you, then you're sure to find many other fish in the sea, yes? Above everything else, we wish you to be happy. There will be officers by the score here at this encampment, and perhaps there will be another who will better—"

"He didn't die, Papa," I said, my head still bent. "Colonel Hamilton wasn't killed in battle or by illness or anything else. You and I both feared he would be, and yet instead he was preserved."

"He's lucky that way," Papa said easily, an explanation that I expected was popular among soldiers. "Some men simply are."

"Perhaps Colonel Hamilton was kept from danger for a purpose, Papa." I looked up to meet his gaze. "Perhaps he was meant to do great things, for this country, and nothing will stop him until he does."

Papa only smiled indulgently.

"I suspect the colonel would agree with you, Elizabeth," he said, glancing past me to the houses we were passing. "Ahh, finally, there are your aunt's lodgings. I cannot wait for the comfort of a good fire, can you?"

To mask my disappointment, I busied myself with arranging my cloak, as if preparing for the end of our journey. I should have known better than to say such things about Colonel Hamilton to Papa. It wasn't that Papa couldn't understand. It was more that he wouldn't. In his head he'd already decided that Colonel Hamilton would be acceptable as a suitor for me, and that was the end of it. The subject was done.

Mamma claimed proudly that Papa's ability to make up his mind quickly and progress forward to the next decision was why he had been a successful general, and perhaps it was. My opinions were of no consequence, because his thoughts had already moved elsewhere, doubtless to the confidential meeting he would have with General Washington later in the evening. How could my humble opinions rival that?

I smoothed my gloves and sighed, and resolved to let it pass. But I could understand now why my sister Angelica had eloped rather than battle with Papa about her own choice of a husband.

The horses had stopped before a clapboard house, with candles already lit within against the dwindling daylight and smoke from the fires that my father so craved curling from the chimneys. The house belonged to Dr. Jabez Campfield and his wife; Dr. Campfield was an army surgeon who had agreed to quarter my aunt and uncle during the winter encampment. In a town where lodging was at a premium, the arrangement between the two medical gentlemen had become both gracious and convenient. Still, as was the case everywhere in Morristown, we would be a crowd in the house, with not only Dr. and Mrs. Campfield and their young son, their servants, and the doctor's two apprentices, but my aunt and uncle, their two sons, their servants, and now me as well.

Aunt Gertrude must have heard the horses, for we hadn't yet

climbed from the sleigh before the door to the house flew open and she came out to greet us herself, heedless of the cold. Before long we'd been swept inside and my father was blissfully before the fire he'd craved. Soon after, we all dined together—my father, my aunt and uncle, and Dr. and Mrs. Campfield—and after so many meals among strangers in the drafty common rooms of inns and taverns it was a great pleasure to be among family and friends. But Papa didn't linger at the table, excusing himself as soon as the cloth was drawn and leaving for His Excellency's headquarters a half mile away.

I, too, retreated to my bedchamber to oversee Rose as she unpacked my trunks. Mamma had made a loan to me of Rose, one of our Negroes, to act as my lady's maid and to dress my hair for me while I was here in Morristown. Rose and father's manservant had only just arrived, having traveled more slowly in the sledge with our baggage, and she was now beginning to shake out my gowns. I joined her, trying to decide what of my belongings to unpack and which to leave for now in the trunks. As was to be expected, my room was small for all that Mamma had insisted I needed to bring with me.

We'd scarcely begun before Aunt Gertrude joined us. My aunt resembled my father, with the dark eyes and long nose of their family, as well as the same practical streak. But while in years she was the older sibling, she had always seemed much younger to me. This was perhaps because after being widowed and then remarrying, she'd surprisingly become the mother of two more sons, now aged nine and three, the younger born when my aunt was fifty-three.

"So many clothes, Eliza!" she said with unabashed approval as she sat in the ladder-back chair that was the only one in the room. "But you're wise to have brought them, my dear. Wartime or not, the young ladies here dress to captivate the officers. The competition will be very fierce."

I laughed uneasily, and sat across from her on the edge of the bed. I hoped she was exaggerating. I didn't possess the necessary cattiness for ballroom skirmishes with other ladies, and I didn't enjoy them.

"I cannot imagine that the competition will be very heated when the men so outnumber the ladies."

"Yes, yes, they do," my aunt admitted, picking up a mother-of-pearl fan edged with sequins from my trunk. "But there are men, and there are gentlemen, and then there are the *best* gentlemen, if you take my meaning. My, this is a pretty thing!"

She spread the fan and held it over her mouth, mimicking a coquette.

"It's French," I said, not really interested in the fan. "Which gentlemen do you mean, Aunt?"

"There are the ones to be avoided at all cost," she said, clicking the fan shut blade by blade. "The gentlemen who are intemperate, for whom strong drink is their mistress. The gentlemen with fiery tempers, and the ones who play too deeply at cards. The gentlemen who seek a mistress for the winter, not a wife for a lifetime. The worst, of course, are the married gentlemen who conveniently forget their wives and children at home when they come to winter encampment, and act as if they were bachelors. And then there is Colonel Hamilton."

Rose was holding a folded bundle of shifts and stockings, waiting for my decision. I nodded, grateful for the distraction, and pointed to the small chest of drawers beside the window.

"Why would you mention the colonel with those other ill-favored gentlemen?" I asked as carelessly as I could. "Or has he earned a place among them whilst here in Morristown?"

"I don't believe General Washington gives him sufficient time to be a wastrel, even if he wished it," my aunt said. "The colonel is as fine a gentleman as can be, Eliza, but I will be honest with you: he has not been pining alone beneath the moon and waiting for you to arrive."

I blushed, for that was painfully close to what I'd been imagining. It wasn't that I had *expected* him to be as chaste as a monk in his cloister while away from me. I'd no right to hope for that. But in my thoughts I'd always pictured him as stoic and solitary, his heart pure and devoted to liberty. I realized now how foolish this was, and how unrealistic, too, which only made me feel more the perfect fool. After all, the colonel was young and handsome and a soldier, and soldiers were notoriously free with their affections; my aunt's catalog of rogues in the camp was likely entirely accurate.

To my relief, my aunt continued without noticing my discomfort.

"Since he has been in town this winter, the gossips have claimed the colonel to be hopelessly in love with at least three different ladies," she said. "Or rather women, not ladies, for I should not describe any of them that nicely. Along with the colonel's other qualities, he does have the reputation of being something of a gallant—but then, what young man isn't?"

"They all do," I said, striving to echo her nonchalance. Striving, but not entirely succeeding, though again she took no notice.

"Exactly so," my aunt said, nodding sagely. "But I do believe he is intelligent enough to realize the difference between a passing infatuation at a camp assembly, and the honorable and loving life he might have with a lady like you. In that brief meeting in Albany, you must have pleased him with your kindness, your intelligence, and, of course, your beauty. He would not have asked after you if you didn't."

"No, he wouldn't," I said faintly.

"No, indeed," my aunt said shrewdly. "Nor would I have invited you to come here, either. But I tell you all this with a purpose, Eliza. If you decide that the colonel is the gentleman for you—or even if you wish the opportunity to decide—then you must act. You are a prize, yes, but he will not wander your way willy-nilly. You must plot and wage a campaign to capture the colonel's heart, and be prepared to defend your prize once it is yours."

This was a far different conversation than the one I'd had earlier with Papa. He clearly believed that Colonel Hamilton would in fact be mine for the taking, like an apple that dropped from the tree into my hand of its own accord. Aunt Gertrude, however, expected me to climb to the highest branches of the apple tree, reach for the fruit, and tug it free if I wanted it.

And yet I found I preferred Aunt Gertrude's perspective. Fed only by a memory and an impression, I had come this far through snow and ice. I needed to learn if Colonel Hamilton was not only special for this country, but special for me. If he proved he was, if love grew between us, then I would do whatever I must for the sake of that love. In a land full of soldiers, this would be my battle.

And I would win.

"Lady Washington is eager to meet you, Elizabeth," Aunt Gertrude said as we rode together in a sleigh to the general's headquarters the next morning. "Bound as we are in our little community, we all welcome a new face, especially one as pretty as yours."

"It will be an honor to meet her," I said, with one hand holding my wide-brimmed hat from blowing away. Dr. Campfield's house was less than a mile from headquarters, so our drive wouldn't be long. For a change, the sun was bright on the snow and the sky a brilliant blue overhead. The air was clear and sharp, and on such a day it was difficult not to be in fine spirits. I had risen early to bid farewell to Papa, returning to his duties with Congress in Philadelphia, and now the centerpiece of my day was being presented to His Excellency's wife. I *would* be honored—and a bit intimidated—to meet her, for she was the first lady of the country, and widely regarded as worthy of that title.

I'd dressed with great care for this presentation. I wore a blue silk Brunswick jacket, close-fitting and edged with dark fur, and a matching petticoat, both quilted with a pattern of diamonds and swirling flowers. My gloves were bright green kidskin, and on my head I wore the one extravagant hat I'd brought, the sweeping brim covered in black velvet and crowned with a profusion of scarlet ribbons. I had a weakness for tall hats, for I felt they added height to my small stature, and kept me from being overlooked in a crowd. Aunt Gertrude had assured me that Lady Washington was a lady of fashion, and that before the war, she'd ordered the finest of everything from London. She would appreciate the effort I'd made in her honor to dress with fashion and taste, even in the middle of a military encampment.

But I'd other reasons, too. The general's aides-de-camp were quartered in the same house, and followed the general's orders from his office. There was an excellent possibility that I might encounter Colonel Hamilton—or so Aunt Gertrude had assured me—and I wished him to take note of me.

"It seems that we are all crowded together with the Campfields," she said, "but I assure you that there are far, far more people squeezed into headquarters. The General's Family, his Life Guard, officers and messengers and diplomats of every color coming and going day and night so that Mrs. Ford must wonder what has become of her household. That's a true lady-patriot for you—giving over her fine house to His Excellency and half the army, it seems, and living below in two rooms with her own brood of children. There's nothing more melancholy than a young widow, poor lady, but she honors her husband's memory and patriotism in the best way possible."

"How many aides-de-camp does His Excellency employ?" I asked.

"A half dozen, I believe," Aunt Gertrude said. "They are all part of what His Excellency refers to as his military family, and a close-knit family they are, too, with him of course as the father. But Colonel Hamilton is the one held in highest regard, with the most responsibility. I wonder that His Excellency could accomplish half of what he does without the colonel by his side. That's Mrs. Ford's house, there, the large white one before us on the hill."

It would have been difficult to overlook. The house was large and imposing, nearly as large as our Albany house, and by far the largest that I'd yet seen in Morristown. It was two stories with tall chimneys at either end, and an ell to one side where I guessed the kitchen stood. The doorway was elegant indeed, with a prettily arched door flanked by rich carvings and pilasters, and a half-moon window above and two more on either side. Nearby were a number of rough log huts that quartered the general's Life Guard, his most trusted soldiers in charge of protecting him, and to the rear of the house were several more log buildings, squat and temporary.

But what I noticed first was the bustle of activity around the house, like a bee skep surrounded by swarms of the busiest of bees coming and going. Soldiers and horses, wagons and sleds and sleighs, and all of them moving briskly on the army's business. The cold air was filled with the sounds of orders given, of barked conversations, and the jingle of harnesses and the creak of wooden wheels over the packed snow. There were several small fires with men clustered about them for warmth, and bright flags on staffs that proclaimed that this was in fact the army's headquarters.

We climbed down from our sleigh before the house, and I followed my aunt up the steps to the sentry. Among so many dark cloaks and uniforms, I felt like a gaudy parrot in my bright clothes. I also felt acutely female in the midst of so many men, and though I held my head high and pretended to take no notice, I sensed every eye upon me as I stood there on the whitewashed steps, my skirts swaying in the breeze and the bright ribbons of my hat dancing around my face. I might be short, but no one was overlooking me now.

The sentry recognized my aunt, and mercifully we were soon ushered inside the house. But the wide hallway was likewise filled with men as well as the same bustle, with a scattering of tradesmen and waiters hurrying among them. The Washingtons' personal servants stood out among the others, for they were all Negroes, and wore the red and white livery of Mount Vernon, His Excellency's mansion in Virginia. Yet every man, white and black, stepped aside to open a path for my aunt and me to pass, bowing and lifting their hats to us as well. It was respectful, I suppose, especially since I was sure that the word had moved swiftly among them that I was General Schuyler's daughter, but I was still happy to be ushered up the stairs to the door of the single room that formed the Washingtons' private quarters.

A neatly dressed black woman in a linen cap (doubtless another of the Washingtons' servants, who had traveled north with them) told us Lady Washington would receive us in a moment. My aunt sat on the bench beneath the hall window, but I preferred to stand, glancing into the room across the hall. Once another bedchamber for the Ford family, it now appeared to be an officers' barracks with a half dozen small camp beds, each with its own low-arched linen canopy, and the owner's belongings stacked neatly beneath. To me it looked more like a children's nursery than a room for grown gentlemen, and I craned my neck a bit farther from curiosity, amusing myself by imagining the men all tucked snug beneath their coverlets for the night.

"Miss Elizabeth?"

It had been over two years, but I recognized that voice immediately. Startled, I turned about, and there before me was Colonel Hamilton.

He stood with a sheaf of papers beneath his arm, doubtless important orders and letters from His Excellency's desk, and tucked into the top buttonhole of his coat was a gray and black pen cut from a turkey's quill. He'd aged since I'd seen him last, more manly, his blue uniform more neatly tailored and his boots polished and gleaming. His hair was sleeked back in a tidy queue that couldn't quite contain its fiery red-gold, and his gaze was keen with the intelligence—and the warmth—that I remembered. To me he looked like a man who carried great responsibility and trust with ease and confidence, exactly the sort of man a commander-in-chief would rely upon. But then, I'd sensed that when we'd met before, an intangible quality that made me long to trust him as well.

I cannot say how long it took me to make this studied appraisal, for it seemed as if time itself had ceased to matter as I stood before him. Yet somehow I managed to recover my wits, and dipped a quick but graceful curtsey to him even as he bowed to me, and to Aunt Gertrude as well.

"Good day, Colonel Hamilton," I murmured. "I trust you are well."

"Very well, Miss Elizabeth, very well indeed," he said, and I realized he'd been studying me just as I'd been doing with him. "And you?"

"Quite well," I said, smiling, "and grateful that my journey here is done."

"Oh, I'm sure of that," he said. "Travel is never easy at this time of the year. But changes of scenery and diversion afforded by travel must agree with you, Miss Elizabeth. If I might be permitted, I'd say that you are looking not only quite well, but even more beautiful than I recall."

"Thank you, Colonel," I said, not objecting at all. The bright colors of my attire had done what I'd hoped, and I pointed playfully at the pen in his buttonhole. "I admire your turkey-standard."

He frowned, not understanding at first, and then sheepishly pulled the pen from the buttonhole. "I fear that it's the standard of my lowly position here as a clerk," he said ruefully, twisting the quill between his fingers. "Hardly the field of glory, is it?"

Too late I recalled how much he'd longed for battle, and chafed beneath his current duties for the general.

"The fields are all covered in snow at present, Colonel," I said softly, repairing my unfortunate jest as best I could. "It's hardly the season for glory, and I am sure that the work you do here for His Excellency is of great importance. Spring will come soon enough, and opportunities with it."

"You are kind, Miss Elizabeth," he said. His gaze locked with mine, the warmth of it wonderfully intense, and I thought this the finest compliment I'd ever received from a gentleman.

To our right, the door to Lady Washington's room opened, and her servant reappeared to usher us inside.

"Excuse us, Colonel," said my aunt as she rose and came to stand beside me, "but as you can see, Lady Washington expects us."

"Of course, Mrs. Cochran," he said, stepping back to let her pass, yet still looking at me.

My aunt smiled broadly. "My niece is residing with me at Dr. Campfield's house, Colonel, between here and the town."

"I know it well, Mrs. Cochran," he said with a small bow to her while still not looking away from me.

"If His Excellency can part with you, Colonel, we would welcome you for a dish of tea," my aunt said with what I thought was remarkable boldness. "In the evening, perhaps, after Dr. Cochran and Dr. Campfield have finished their final rounds. I'm sure they would welcome your conversation."

I'll credit my aunt for discretion, for that was neatly done, and I glanced quickly at my aunt in gratitude.

Colonel Hamilton smiled, and from the amusement in his eyes it was clear he, too, realized how deftly my aunt had put a gloss of respectability on her invitation. I'd be there, of course, and the colonel knew it, too, but this way none of us could be accused of being too forward.

"I shall be honored to join the gentlemen, Mrs. Cochran," he said, bowing. "I shall do my best to attend this evening, if my duties permit."

My aunt nodded in acquiescence and looped her arm into mine to draw me away with her. "We shall hope to see you then, Colonel Hamilton."

"Good day, Colonel Hamilton," I said, sorry to be leaving but realizing it was necessary.

"Good day, Mrs. Cochran, Miss Elizabeth," he said, bowing. "And perhaps Miss Elizabeth would enjoy the conversation of the medical gentlemen as well?"

I smiled over my shoulder as we entered the room. "Perhaps, Colonel," I said. "Perhaps."

CHAPTER 3

I'd thought that Aunt Gertrude had been speaking lightly when she'd invited Colonel Hamilton to call upon us to converse upon the health of the army with Uncle John and Dr. Campfield. I thought it was more polite subterfuge, for the convenience of all parties. I thought it was understood that the colonel would be calling upon me, not the surgeons, and from the colonel's parting words to me at headquarters that afternoon I was certain he believed the same.

If he did, then we both were sadly, even woefully, mistaken.

Before the evening had fair begun, I learned to my dismay that Aunt Gertrude expected me to receive the colonel in the parlor, a small room made even smaller with the presence of Dr. and Mrs. Campfield as well as my aunt and uncle, all seated in a half circle of chairs before the fire. There was a chair reserved for me at one end of the row, and another for the colonel at the opposite end, with the two of us separated as far as was possible in the small room.

Nor would I have an opportunity to play or sing to display my talents, for Mrs. Campfield possessed neither a pianoforte nor a harpsichord. Instead Aunt Gertrude handed me a skein of rough-spun wool and a set of knitting pins with the suggestion—a suggestion I'd no choice but to obey—that I begin making Monmouth caps for the poor soldiers who had none against the cold. I told myself it was the proper thing to do, that such caps were much needed and would be welcomed, that I'd be selfish to think of myself first, yet still I couldn't help but be disappointed.

How could the colonel and I ever become better acquainted in such dismal circumstances? How was this supposed to attract a gentleman who'd had as many sweethearts as there were days in the month?

But I'd dutifully begun to cast on stitches on my needles when the colonel was announced. I looked up eagerly, for he'd arrived with a punctuality that I soon learned was his by nature. His blue uniform was freshly brushed and his boots polished, his buff-colored breeches immaculate, his hair carefully combed and his jaw newly shaved. He wore his dress sword, too, appropriate for both a warrior and a gentleman, and which was likely at his side to make me forget that I'd seen him earlier with the turkey-feather pen. It was clear that he wished to make the best impression possible on me, just as I'd tried to do the same for him.

Yet as a soldier, he understood rank and precedence, and greeted each of the others in the room first with perfect civility. I was reminded of how respectful he'd been to my father when he'd come to our house, and this, too, impressed me, perhaps even more than his dress sword. By the time he finally reached me, I was smiling warmly and happily. I never was able to play the coy coquette, no matter how it might have helped my cause.

"Good evening, Miss Elizabeth," he said, bending slightly over my chair with one hand resting on the pommel of his sword. "Once you gave me leave to call you Betsey, but I wouldn't presume—"

"Of course you may call me Betsey," I said quickly, so quickly that I winced inwardly at my own lack of guile. "You're not presuming, not at all."

He smiled, too, and I basked in the charm of it.

"Very well, Betsey," he said easily, as if he'd been calling me that all our lives. "What are you making?"

"I'm knitting a cap for a soldier in need," I said, holding up my needles with only a few dozen stitches cast on. "I've just started."

From the corner of my eye, I saw my aunt lean forward to draw the colonel's attention.

"Eliza is known for her charitable acts, Colonel Hamilton," she said, more loudly than was necessary. "In Albany, she and her mother stitch clothing for the poor, and will offer comfort and food to any needy person who appears at their kitchen door. She hasn't been here in Morristown but a day, and yet already she has found a way to ease the suffering of the men in the camp."

I could have groaned aloud from embarrassment. The part about Mamma and me making clothing and feeding unfortunate folk at our back door was true, but the rest was pure invention, and I rather wished my aunt hadn't invented it.

But the colonel only nodded solemnly. "I have heard considerable praise of the Schuyler ladies, yes," he said, answering my aunt, but looking directly at me. "There are few things to be held in higher esteem than a lady who is both kind and generous."

I hastily lowered my gaze to the pitiful beginnings of the cap in my lap. I felt doubly, even triply, obligated to finish it now, plus a score more besides. I gathered the needles in my hands and resumed my knitting.

"You're very kind, Colonel Hamilton," I murmured without looking up from my work. "My mother has set the most perfect example for my sisters and me, and we all strive to emulate her goodness."

"She is a true paragon for us all," Aunt Gertrude said, though I couldn't help but notice that her own hands were occupied with a china cup filled with tea. "If you please, Colonel, there is a chair for you beside my husband, who is most eager to learn of His Excellency's latest plans for the care of the soldiers."

My uncle's chin jerked up swiftly like a schoolboy caught dozing at his lessons.

"Yes, yes, Colonel," he said, patting the railed back of the empty chair. "Come tell me the news from headquarters."

Oh, this was so patently transparent! If there were any news about the welfare of the soldiers, then my uncle, as the army's surgeon general, would already be well aware of it.

"Yes, Colonel Hamilton," I agreed with half a heart. "The chair beside my uncle is meant for you."

My dismay must have shown on my face, for the colonel leaned forward again toward me, lowering his voice in a confidential tone.

"Please, Betsey, you must call me Hamilton," he said easily. "Military ranks have no place between friends. Is that so much to ask?"

It was, and we both knew it. It was one thing for him to use my given name, but another for me to address him in such a jocular, even masculine, manner.

"If all your other friends address you as Hamilton, then I shall call you Alexander," I said boldly, and with equal boldness I let my gaze linger with his. I was purposefully echoing what he'd said to me, long ago in Albany, and I did so to show him I'd not forgotten our very first conversation. I said nothing further, nor did he. It didn't seem necessary, not then.

Yet if I'd realized that those were to be the only words we exchanged for the rest of the evening, I would have spoken more, much more, and I'd no doubt that he would have, too. My aunt made certain that that didn't happen, however, keeping Alexander (for I'd now given myself permission to use his given name even in my thoughts) seated between her and my uncle until the case clock on the wall struck ten. Dr. and Mrs. Campfield rose instantly, and my aunt and uncle with them, signaling the end of the evening. The poor colonel was left with no choice but to make his farewells and leave, and that was that.

"Am I never to have a conversation alone with Colonel Hamilton?" I lamented to my aunt once the Campfields retired upstairs for the night. "How am I to become acquainted with him if all I do is listen to him discuss the quality of the soldiers' provisions with my uncle?"

"The colonel did have a quantity to say on the subject, didn't he?" My aunt began gathering up the tea and coffee cups and saucers to take to the kitchen, Mrs. Campfield having already sent her servants to bed. "My, that fellow can talk! You can tell he studied the law. There's no other profession where he'd be paid for the length and breadth of his speeches."

I collected the last cup from where my uncle had abandoned it upon the mantelpiece and followed her into the kitchen.

"I wouldn't know how much Colonel Hamilton had to say," I said, "because he wasn't permitted to say more than a half dozen words to me."

"You'll have time enough for that, Eliza," Aunt Gertrude said with maddening calm. "This was for the best."

"But how?" I cried with frustration. "He will not return if all we offer him is a tedious evening."

Aunt Gertrude raised her brows. "Oh, it was not so bad as that. You're nearly half done with that knitted cap."

"Aunt Gertrude, please," I pleaded. "Knitting for the soldiers is important, to be sure, but it's also important that Colonel Hamilton and I—"

"Hush," she said mildly. "I shall tell you what is important, niece, and I will be blunt, so that you will listen. You and I have already discussed how Colonel Hamilton is a charming, handsome fellow accustomed to having young women and a few older ones as well smile and sigh over him, much as you did tonight. He is accustomed to that occurring without much effort or responsibility on his part, and he is also accustomed to those same women obliging him with their favors in return."

"I know that, Aunt, and I—"

"I doubt that you do," she said. "Do you know the colonel's reputation about Morristown for what can indelicately be called whoring? I've heard him likened to a tomcat, and no wonder."

I flushed, and made a small strangled sound in my throat. It was not the vulgar words coming so unexpectedly from my aunt's lips that startled me, but the thought of the gallant colonel engaged in what the word described. To be sure, I wasn't entirely certain what whoring entailed, yet I knew what a whore was, and could guess the rest.

My aunt sighed. "I didn't intend to shock you, Eliza," she said. "But if you believe you wish to marry a soldier, then you must be aware of what transpires in a military camp. The ways that men choose to assuage their boredom, their passions, and even their fears of battle and dying have been the same since the ancients, and it's no different here at Morristown."

I listened reluctantly, and realized that she was most likely right. Now that I was here at the site of the encampment, I did need to be less blind as to the lives of soldiers, and perhaps to those of men in general. I'd always prided myself on being practical, and there could be no more practical thinking than this. Surely my mother would have agreed. I'd never seen her flinch from the less pleasant realities of life, and she was as perfect a lady as was imaginable. She'd always followed the army with my father, sometimes into the very face of the enemy, and I suspected she'd witnessed far worse things than mere "whoring."

But I myself was young in experience, and still didn't quite wish to tarnish the golden gleam of near-perfection that I'd granted Alexander. I raised my chin a stubborn fraction higher, determined to be as forthright and direct as my aunt.

"Forgive me, Aunt Gertrude, but I do not see the sense to this," I said, striving to sound reasonable and not petulant. "If the colonel is as much a—a rogue as you say, then I should think that a dull evening here would send him directly back to his—his—baser pursuits, and we'll never see him here again."

"If it does, Eliza, then you are well rid of him," my aunt said. "If he is that easily discouraged, then you'll know the measure of his character, and you will do well to begin looking elsewhere. He must prove himself worthy of your company, and that he is ready to put aside his bachelor's pursuits for your sake. You are the prize, Eliza, not the colonel, and you must not forget it."

"But how can I—"

"Hush, and listen," she said. "In addition to your own delightful person, you will bring all the Schuyler family's wealth, influence, and resources with you to your bridegroom. All Colonel Hamilton has to offer is his own promise. Your father agrees with me in this, too. Oh, I know he is impressed with Colonel Hamilton because General Washington holds him in high esteem, but not so far that he'd ignore propriety where you are concerned."

"It's not a question of propriety," I began, even though I knew that's exactly what it was. "I'm not a child, Aunt."

"No, you are not," she agreed, her voice as even now as it had been at the beginning of our conversation. "For if you were a child and not a young woman of marriageable age, then none of this would be a consideration. Good night, Eliza, and sleep well."

I'd no choice but to retire to my bed in despair, convinced my aunt's heavy-handed plan had ruined my future. The next day we made more calls together, visiting other officers' wives who had come to the encampment to be with their husbands, and I presented the letters of introduction from my father to several of his army acquaintances, including the Prussian General von Steuben.

We passed many officers and soldiers, but not the one I most longed to see. Was it mere coincidence, I wondered anxiously, or was Aunt Gertrude's grim prediction already coming true? Although neither she nor I mentioned the colonel again, he loomed over the day like a silent presence, always in my thoughts if not in my conversation.

Yet to my amazement (and relief), he called at the Campfield house again that evening, and the evening after that as well, proving my fears unfounded. He endured every one of my aunt's trials with good humor and grace, and certainly more than I did. Each night we were permitted to exchange a few more sentences, a few more smiles, a few more glances that seemed to express so much more than words alone. As much as I chafed under my aunt's restrictions, Alexander's persistence pleased me, and I felt honored by it.

Perhaps he truly did consider me the prize that everyone claimed I was. Perhaps he was as ready as I for marriage, and lasting love. With the innocence of my situation, it all seemed very easy, and very romantic, too. He was charming, and for the first time in my life, I was eager to be charmed.

"I do believe it's going to snow again." My aunt glowered upward at the heavy gray clouds gathering overhead, as if a doleful look would be enough to change the weather. "Haven't we had enough for one winter?"

"We'll be back at Dr. Campfield's house before it amounts to anything," I said, likewise looking upward. Cold as it was, I didn't mind. I'd spent too much time this winter trapped drowsing beside the fire, and I relished this opportunity to be out of doors, to walk briskly across the small town and breathe deep of the clear, cold air.

Although my uncle was the surgeon, not my aunt, she still would consult him for a friend with aching joints, or a neighbor's child with a rheumy eye, and if the remedy to the affliction were a simple one, she'd carry it herself. Colonel Eckford's wife had been plagued by a persistent cough, and earlier this afternoon my aunt had brought her a soothing tisane to ease her discomfort. While the two of them had talked, I'd amused the three Eckford children, singing nonsense songs and dandling the littlest on my knee.

"Snow or not, aunt, you must admit that the days are growing longer," I said. "Little by little, and soon enough it will be spring."

But my aunt only sniffed loudly, daubing at her nose with the handkerchief she'd pulled from inside her muff.

"Spring, indeed," she scoffed, pausing before the window of a small shop. "You are ever the optimist, Eliza, aren't you? I wonder if this shopkeeper has any dark thread left in his stock. Your uncle promised he'd try to send for some from New York as soon as he could, but in the meantime the buttons keep popping willy-nilly from his waistcoat."

"Miss Elizabeth!"

I knew that voice, and I knew its owner. Swiftly I turned just as Alexander came striding across the street toward me, dodging a horse-drawn sledge in his haste.

Could there be a more welcome surprise? I'd grown so accustomed to seeing him by the firelight that he dazzled me here, even on this gray day. His dark blue cloak billowed around his shoulders in the breeze, and the same breeze made the white silk cockade on his black hat flutter like an out-of-season butterfly. Because his face was ruddy with the cold, his eyes were even more blue by contrast, and his smile—ah, his smile would have melted every last flake of snow in Morristown.

"Miss Elizabeth, good day," he said formally, bowing to me and touching his hat just below the cockade, then making the same salute to my aunt. "Mrs. Cochran, madam. How fortuitous that I find you here! I was just on my way to Dr. Campfield's house with this."

He pulled a letter from inside his waistcoat and handed it to me. I didn't open it, but held it in my gloved fingers: a single sheet, folded and sealed with dark green wax. Part of me wished to prolong the delight of receiving a letter from him (letters from gentlemen, especially from gentlemen like him, being a rarity for me), while another part of me feared the worst, and dreaded reading whatever ill news the letter might contain. I smiled still, but I could feel the uncertainty in the curve of my lips.

"I regret that because of my duties, I won't be able to attend you this evening," he said. "His Excellency is giving a dinner for several visiting dignitaries, and my attendance is required. I didn't wish you to worry when I didn't come."

To my surprise, his smile was tinged with uncertainty, too, though I couldn't fathom what should make him so.

"I wouldn't have worried," I said quickly. I meant to put him at his ease, but as soon as I'd spoken, I realized how flippant my words sounded, as if I wouldn't have worried because I wouldn't have cared—and that was very far from the truth.

I glanced downward, both from embarrassment and to compose my thoughts.

"That is, if you did not come, I would have guessed His Excellency had made some urgent demand upon your services," I said. "I would have understood, for your service to him is far more important, but I would also have been disappointed not to see you."

His smile widened, and the hint of uncertainty fell away from his face. "Would you?"

"I would," I said, declaring it soundly as my smile grew, too. "But none of that matters, Colonel Hamilton, because you are here now."

Beside me, forgotten, Aunt Gertrude cleared her throat loudly to remind us of her presence.

"Good day, Colonel," she said. "I was going into this shop in pursuit of thread, which I know holds little interest to my niece. Would you be so kind as to escort her back to Dr. Campfield's house?"

I caught my breath, astonished that she'd grant us this freedom after how we'd been watched so closely.

"Go, niece," she said. "Don't squander the colonel's time."

"I shall take the greatest care in the world with her, Mrs. Cochran," Alexander said gallantly—perhaps a shade too gallantly, for my aunt looked up toward the heavens, beseeching, and sighed with resignation.

"To the house and no farther, Eliza," she said as she opened the shop's door. "I shall follow after you shortly."

When the door closed after her, I grinned at Alexander, feeling a mixture of giddy freedom and solemn responsibility.

He must have felt it, too.

"I don't want you to fall," he said gravely. He crooked his arm and offered it to me. "The streets and paths can be treacherous with the snow, and I promised your aunt I'd look after you."

"I'm not so delicate as that, you know," I said, but I took his arm anyway, settling my fingers familiarly into the woolen sleeve of his uniform coat. "Consider all the ice along the hem of my cloak. I have been traipsing all over Morristown with my aunt this afternoon without any harm done."

"Brave and stalwart women," he said with approval. "What entertainment did you find for yourselves in humble Morristown?"

We fell into step easily, and I didn't mind how the narrow path cleared through the snow made us keep close together, the side of my skirts brushing against his boots. We walked slowly, not wanting to reach our destination too soon. The packed snow crunched beneath our feet, and my quilted petticoats, the hems as crusted with ice as my cloak, swung heavily around my ankles.

"We called upon Colonel Eckford's wife," I said, "and brought her a remedy for her sore throat. While she and my aunt talked, I amused her children. Not so grand a service compared to what you do each day, I know, but Mrs. Eckford welcomed it."

"I'm sure the children did as well," he said.

"They'd welcome any new face," I said. "They were quite wild from being shut inside so much with the cold weather. I pitied Mrs. Eckford."

"I would, too," he said, pretending to be stern. "Did you marshal the little rogues into line?"

"Oh, no," I said, smiling. "I like children too well to act the termagant with them. Besides, they reminded me of my own brothers and sisters, and what a tumbling, raucous lot my family can be."

He raised his brows with mock outrage. "General Schuyler permits that in his house?"

"I don't believe he'd wish it any other way," I said, thinking fondly of my family. "I know I wouldn't."

He nodded, as if this made perfect sense. "I hope one day to have the privilege of meeting them all. If they're anything like you, then it shall be the rarest of treats."

Another compliment, but an easy one to make me smile.

"You've already met Peggy, when you came to our house two years ago," I said, "and I'm sure the rest would all turn out for the chance to meet the famous Colonel Hamilton."

"I'm not so famous," he said, more seriously than I'd expected.

"You would be famous to them," I said. "Especially to my brothers. You'll meet them one day, and be able to judge for yourself. I cannot imagine my life without my brothers and sisters."

"I envy you that," he said. "I have—or had—only a single brother, and when our mother died, we were separated and sent along different paths, and he became lost to me."

"Now I've made you sad," I said softly, pressing my fingers into his sleeve in sympathy. There was so much of his history that I didn't know, and each time he did reveal another bit of his past, it seemed so steeped in tragedy and loss that I wondered how he could bear it. "I'm sorry. I didn't intend to raise up old memories for you."

He covered my hand with his own, and I felt the sudden intimacy of it even through our gloves.

"Don't be sorry," he said gently. "You only spoke the truth, as did I. Never be sorry for that, Betsey, or for the kindness that is so much a part of your nature."

Suddenly shy, I smiled and glanced down, but he took no notice, or pretended not to. He also kept his hand over mine.

"Do you intend to read my letter?" he asked, almost teasing. "Or did I labor over those words for nothing?"

I'd tucked the unopened letter into my muff, which was now slipped over my free arm. I'd have to take my other hand away from his to pull the letter free, and I didn't want to do that.

"Do those words reveal anything that I must immediately know?" I said, striving to sound as playful as he did. We had nearly reached the Campfield house, and I didn't wish this time alone with him to end. "Are they of such great and eternal importance?"

"No," he admitted. "The letter is as mild and dull as new milk, and only explains my absence this evening. But I assure you, it was still a challenge to write. I didn't know if your aunt would insist on reading it first, so there is nothing in the contents that could possibly disturb her."

"I was surprised that she didn't take it from me," I said. "That must mean you've won her trust."

Abruptly he stopped walking and turned to face me, linking his fingers into mine so that our hands were now clasped. He wasn't teasing any longer.

"Your aunt's trust is secondary to me, Betsey," he said. "What matters far more is whether or not I've won yours."

I gazed upward, searching his face before I answered. Light snow, lazy and scattered, had begun to fall around us, and the air was so cold that when the snowflakes landed on his dark cloak and hat, they didn't melt, but held their shapes like tiny, glittering jewels.

When I stood here with my hand in his, I longed to say yes without hesitation. He had thus far been a perfect suitor, devoted, charming, and gentlemanly. Why shouldn't I trust him the way he desired? Why couldn't I take that first step—or was it a leap?—toward love? Surely that was what my sister Angelica would have done, and had done when she'd eloped with Mr. Carter.

But I wasn't Angelica. I remembered my aunt's tales of Alexander's bachelor ways, and of his taste for unsavory company. . . .

"You've doubts," he said when I didn't answer, concern in his voice and his expression. Yet he didn't release my hand, nor did I pull away.

"You said before that I should never regret speaking the truth," I said slowly. "Do you believe that in regard to yourself as well?"

"Wisdom and truth, combined with beauty!" he exclaimed. "You are a rarity among women, Eliza."

"I'm likely a sorry sort of beauty," I said, "standing here in the snow with a nose red from the cold."

"I admire your nose, which is quite adorably red, and I prefer it along with the rest of you over a score of powdered, painted court beauties," he said, raising his voice loudly there in the street, and not caring one whit who heard. "I prefer your kindness and your conversation and your laughter. I especially like the way you tip your chin to look at me, the way you are doing at this very moment, as if you're weighing and considering each word I say for merit."

"Oh, that's not true," I protested. "That's not what I am doing."

"Isn't it?" he said without pause. "Then it should be, because I want you to judge me. I am not without flaws. I realize that. But with you as my guiding star, I will strive to be all that you desire. I want you to find me worthy. *That* is the truth, Eliza Schuyler, my truth, and I'll swear to it by any oath you please. I've never met another lady whom I could trust more than you. I would trust you with my honor, my life, and most especially my heart, and I pray with all my soul that you may in time feel the same for me."

My eyes widened and my heart raced, my entirety overwhelmed not only by the poetry of his words, but by the unbridled emotion and the sentiment behind them that captured me in its spell.

There could be only one answer.

"Yes," I said breathlessly. "So long as you continue to be as truthful to me as you promise, then I'll grant you my trust, freely, openly, gladly."

His fingers tightened around mine, and he raised my hand to his lips. The gesture was muted by our gloves, but it still seemed the most fervidly romantic thing I'd ever experienced. I sighed with the perfection of the moment, but as I began to tell him so, I glimpsed my aunt, bustling across the snowy path toward us.

"I can't stay here with you any longer," I said swiftly, pulling my hand away and thrusting it back into my muff. "My aunt is coming."

He didn't move. "The officers are sponsoring a series of assemblies with dancing. The first will be held next Wednesday evening. Say you'll come, Betsey."

I loved how he said my name. "You'll be there?"

"I will be there," he said, "waiting for you."

"I won't disappoint you," I whispered fiercely, my hand holding tight to his. "Not now, not ever."

It was as solemn an oath as any young woman my age could vow, and I meant every word of it. How was I to know how sorely my words would be tested over time?

CHAPTER 4

I attended that first assembly not with my aunt and uncle, but with a friend, Kitty Livingston. Kitty had persuaded (or more likely begged) her father to take a house in Morristown while the army was encamped there, even though their home of Liberty Hall was only twenty miles away in Elizabethtown. Kitty was only an acquaintance, but a distant cousin in the way of so many of us from New York, and I was delighted that she was in town for the winter, too.

That night we rode together with her parents in the second bench of their sleigh, our evening finery bundled beneath thick furs as we traveled across the wintery roads. We wore quilted silk petticoats beneath our gowns, and at our feet we each had a carved oak foot warmer filled with hot coals. The skies were overcast, and we all prayed the next snowstorm—for so it seemed inevitable that one would come—would hold until after the assembly. The sleigh's lanterns cast their wavering light across the snow banks on either side, and the tiny brass bells on the team's harnesses rang merrily in the cold night air.

Sharing my excitement, Kitty grinned at me, and snuggled a little closer both for warmth and in confidence. She was quick and lively and flirtatious in company, one of three sisters as was I, and always the first with fresh news from everyone and everywhere. I soon learned, however, that for the first time I was the center of tonight's fresh gossip.

"So tell me, Eliza," she said softly in a near whisper that her parents wouldn't overhear, our conversation further shrouded by the fur-edged hoods of our cloaks. "How is it that all the talk in the town and the camp is of you and Colonel Hamilton?"

"Then this place must be tedious indeed, if that is the best talk it can muster," I said, surprised. "Colonel Hamilton and I have supplied very little to your mill for tattle, Kitty."

"I've heard otherwise," she said. "In fact I've heard of little else."

I frowned, my hands twisting uneasily inside my muff. I didn't like being spoken of, especially since I suspected most of what was being said was embellished, if not outright tales. All I could do was hope to correct Kitty, a vain hope though it might be.

"Colonel Hamilton has called upon me at Dr. Campfield's house in the evening," I began, "and I've received him in the crowded company of my aunt and uncle as well as the Campfields. He has their approval, and my father considers him a worthy gentleman, too. Colonel Hamilton and I have walked together in the town, with my aunt ten paces behind us, and he and I have exchanged greetings in passing as he went about his duties near the headquarters. Oh, and he joined me at Sunday worship."

"Sunday worship?" she repeated, her voice rising in teasing disbelief. "Hamilton? I vow he's never seen the inside of a church, the wicked heathen."

"He did come with me," I insisted, "and it was by his own initiative, too. That's all that's happened between us, Kitty. There could hardly be anything less scandalous."

I wasn't exaggerating. Alexander's regard toward me had been so decorous and proper that, in the telling, it must have sounded almost boring, and without even a flicker of scandal. Yes, there had been times when I'd felt sure he was going to kiss me, but at the last moment he'd held back: he was that intent on proving himself worthy of me.

And to be entirely honest, I rather wished he hadn't. An honorable gentleman was all well and good, but if he'd shown me a bit— just a bit—of the rakish gallant that I sensed was within him, I wouldn't have objected. I wanted him to kiss me, because I wanted very much to kiss him.

But clearly Kitty didn't believe me, and smothered her laughter behind her gloved hand.

"Hardly less scandalous, Eliza," she whispered, "and perhaps infinitely more. You can't play the innocent with me, especially not when your dalliance is with Colonel Hamilton. Recall that he's long been an acquaintance of mine, and that we have no secrets between us."

"I assure you, there aren't any secrets for him to share," I protested, painfully aware of how she might indeed know more of him than I did. Kitty and Alexander had in fact been friends for years. When he had first arrived as a youth in our colonies from Nevis, he had attended Elizabethtown Academy in New Jersey, where he'd boarded with the Livingston family. To hear Kitty tell it (which of course she'd made sure I had), the schoolboy Alexander had been thoroughly moonstruck over her, yet she'd deftly turned his infatuation into a friendship.

"No secrets, no." Kitty paused now for emphasis, her upper teeth pressing lightly into her lower lip in a way that was unique to her, as if biting back what she'd say next. "No secrets, because where you are concerned, Colonel Hamilton cannot keep them. He wears his heart like another medal pinned to his coat, there for anyone who wishes to see how the name *Elizabeth* is engraved upon it."

"Hush, Kitty," I said, uneasy with her overblown foolishness.

"Then let me tell you this, Eliza," she said, leaning closer. "You know how the officers are in the habit of having supper together, and how after the cloth is drawn, they will sit for hours drinking and toasting until they tumble into their cups, and their menservants must come claim them."

"What of it?" I said warily. Such behavior among gentlemen was hardly unknown to me; my father's entertainments for his friends were often like this.

"What of it?" she repeated, unable to keep the triumph from her whisper. "Because I have it on the *best* advice that when the officers take their turns with a toast for each wife and sweetheart, our dear friend Hamilton raises his glass to you by name, and all the other gentlemen follow."

I listened, stunned. Having my name toasted in the officers' quarters would not please my aunt, but I found it undeniably thrilling to think that Alexander Hamilton would toast me as his sweetheart.

"You are sure of this?" I asked eagerly. "You know it for fact?"

"I wouldn't tell you if it weren't so," she said. "We both know that Colonel Hamilton has left half the women in New Jersey *panting* for his attentions, yet you, Eliza, are the one who has dazzled him. Though it's not surprising, is it? You're a perfect match for a man like him. You're a Schuyler, and you're rich, and your father's a friend of His Excellency's, and—"

"Why must everyone assume that he likes me only because of Papa and his money?" I whispered, my frustration spilling over. "Your family has power and wealth, too, Kitty, and no one says that of you."

Kitty gave a small, dismissive shrug to her shoulders that was also faintly pitying. "That's because no suitor of mine has been as impoverished and without a respectable family as Colonel Hamilton."

I don't believe she intended to wound me or insult Alexander, but her words still stung.

"Colonel Hamilton possesses qualities and virtues that are worth far more than mere wealth," I said warmly. "I value him for himself, not for his family or fortune."

She nodded and fell silent, and remained silent so long that I feared I'd spoken too much. I was almost ready to apologize when she finally spoke again.

"Oh, Eliza," she said softly. "You care for dear little Hamilton that much?"

"I do," I said so quickly that I startled myself. Yet it was true; I couldn't deny it, nor did I wish to.

"How fortunate you are!" she said wistfully. "How fortunate you are! I have yet to have such sentiments for any gentleman."

"That can't be true, Kitty, not of you." Kitty was a belle, a beauty, and always surrounded by admirers at every ball and assembly in a way that they never had been for me.

By the glow of the sleigh's lanterns, the edge of Kitty's hood shadowed her face, and all I saw was her half smile, a smile that had lost all its earlier humor. Carefully she lifted her hood back over her shoulders, and the light twinkled in the paste stars she'd pinned into her elaborately dressed and powdered hair, all icy-white as if she were a snow queen incarnate. She turned, and now I could see the entirety of her face, and the concern in her eyes.

"You asked me earlier to speak plainly, and I shall," she said, covering my hand with her own. "Take care of your heart, Eliza, and do not give it blindly. Perhaps I know Hamilton too well, and I know what he aspires to be. He is ambitious, and he is determined, and he won't let anything or anyone stop him."

"If you mean Alexander will achieve great things in his life, Kitty," I said, "then we agree, as friends should."

"Hamilton charms the world and makes friends with ease," she said, "but he also makes enemies, and the higher he rises—and he will rise high—the more hazardous those enemies shall be to you both."

"I don't believe it, Kitty," I said, the only proper answer to un-wanted advice, and pulled away my hand. "None of it, not of Alexander."

"Believe it or not, as it pleases you." She glanced down at her muff, avoiding my gaze. "His character is widely known among the other officers, and many of the other ladies here, too. But if your father isn't troubled by Hamilton's flaws and faults, then why should you be?"

"Papa isn't," I said quickly. "Nor am I."

"Then I'll never speak of the matter again." She darted forward and kissed me on the cheek, her lips cold. "Of all women I know, Eliza, I pray you'll be happy, no matter which gentleman you marry. Now come, let's dance, and break every heart we can."

A dancing assembly held by subscription (I'd heard the extrav-agant sum to be $400 a gentleman, but that was at the inflated rate of our then-near-worthless paper bills) and supported by thirty-four of the most esteemed officers of our army sounds like a grand affair. For us wintering in Morristown, it was. But if I had heard de-scribed the conditions of this self-proclaimed assembly whilst still in Albany, I would have laughed aloud.

Instead of taking place in an inn or private residence of the first quality, this assembly was held in a military storehouse built by the army near the Morristown Green. Now emptied of goods, the storehouse was as full of echoes as a barn, and like most barns, it had been built for rough service, without any amenities or decoration; I would venture it to be seventy feet in length, and forty in breadth. A pair of crude cast-iron stoves stoked with wood were the sole sources of heat in this cavernous room, and lanterns for light had been strung along the walls on a length of rope. Both the stoves and the inferior tallow candles in the lanterns smoked, and even this early in the evening there was a haze gathered just below the ceiling beams.

The stables for my father's horses in Albany were more elegantly appointed than this space, and yet the guests gathered here were as brilliant a company as any in our country. Most of the officers wore their dress uniforms, and the lanterns' light glanced off gold bullion lace, polished brass buttons, and medals and other honors.

Of course, we ladies were not to be outdone, and our gowns were like bright silk flowers of every color. Our hair was powdered and dressed high on our heads, and ornamented with silk flowers, ribbons, paste jewels, and even a plume or two. To be so expensively and stylishly attired in the middle of a war might seem to some to be wrong, even disrespectful, but as Aunt Gertrude noted, our finery could be wonderfully cheering to the spirits of the gentlemen in the army, and proof to the British that we refused to be subdued. We ladies were also in the minority, with more than three times as many gentlemen in attendance; there'd be no wallflowers tonight, that was certain.

I'd chosen my own gown with care, a brilliant silk taffeta that was neither blue nor green but a shimmering combination of both, much like a peacock's plumage. Being small in stature, I often wore vibrant colors so I wouldn't be overlooked in company. The sleeves and bodice were close-fitting and the skirts very full over hoops, as was the fashion then, and the neckline was cut low over my breasts, with a thin edging of lace from my shift. Around my throat was a strand of glass pearls fastened with a large white silk bow, and earrings of glittering paste jewels hung from my ears, my mother having wisely decided that the encampment was no place for fine jewels. Unlike most of the ladies, from choice I wore no paint on my face. I suspected my cheeks were rosy enough without it because of the cold and the excitement, and I also suspected that Alexander would be like other gentlemen, and prefer me without it.

At least he might once I found him. I scanned the guests eagerly, searching for the one face I longed to see above all others, but in vain. The assembly's subscribers stood in a line near the door to greet newcomers, and as I waited my turn I continued to look for Alexander. Other gentlemen appeared to ask me for dances and though I smiled, I turned them aside. Alexander was one of the subscribers, and he'd invited me as his guest. How could he not be here?

"Where's Hamilton, I wonder?" Kitty murmured beside me. "He's usually one of the earliest to arrive at these affairs."

"He'll be here," I said swiftly, as much to reassure myself as to defend him. "I don't doubt him."

Kitty smiled slyly over the spreading arc of her fan. "He'd do well to appear soon, or else some other gentleman will scoop you up, especially in that gown."

I didn't smile, because I'd no wish to be scooped up by anyone other than Alexander. We'd almost come to the end of the line anyway, and to my surprise the last person in it was Lady Washington, alone and without General Washington.

I had called upon Lady Washington several times since my arrival in Morristown, and she'd graciously taken a liking to me, and I to her. It would be impossible not to hold her in the highest regard: she was that rarest of ladies who could put anyone at ease in an instant, and make them feel like the oldest and dearest of friends.

She was of middle age when we met, still handsome if a bit stout, her large, dark eyes full of warmth and her speech soft with Virginia gentility. She was known for her rich taste in dress, and tonight she wore a dark green damask gown with a neckerchief of fine French lace and a magnificent garnet necklace with earrings to match.

"Miss Eliza, I am so glad that you have joined us," she said as I curtseyed before her. "How your beauty graces our little gathering!"

"Thank you, Lady Washington," I said, blushing with pleasure at her compliment. "You are most kind."

She raised her gaze, frowning slightly as she studied my hair.

"You are wearing the powder I gave you, yes? That slight tint of blue is so becoming to us brunette ladies."

"Thank you, yes," I said, my hand automatically going to my hair. She'd given me a box of her scented hair powder as a kindness, though I'd had to use a prodigious amount of it to dust my nearly black hair.

"You see I am wearing the cuffs you gave me as well," she said, holding out her plump, small hand toward me. The ruffled cuffs were of the finest white Holland with Dresden-work scallops, sent along with me by my mother as an especial gift for the general's wife. The cuffs were Paris-made, for although our country was under a strict embargo for foreign goods, my mother (like most ladies of the time) still had her ways of securing the little niceties of life from abroad.

"You must be sure to thank your dear mother again," Lady Washington continued, "and please tell her how honored I am to be remembered by her."

"I shall, Lady Washington," I said. I took this as my dismissal, and I bowed my head and began to back away.

But she had other notions, and took my hand to keep me with her.

"A moment more, Miss Eliza, if you please," she said. "Here I am prattling on and on, without recalling the one bit of knowledge I was entrusted to share. You note that my husband is not yet here, and I am acting in his stead. He and Colonel Hamilton have been detained on some military business, but they expect to join us as soon as it is concluded. The colonel in particular asked me to share his considerable regrets at being detained, and prays that you shall forgive him."

I couldn't keep from smiling broadly with relief, so broadly that Lady Washington chuckled.

"There now, I'd venture he has your forgiveness already," she said. "You may grant it yourself directly."

She was looking past me, and without thinking I turned to look in the same direction. The crowd rippled with excitement as His Excellency entered the room, towering over most other men with a stately presence that could command attention without a word spoken. Instead of his uniform, he wore a suit of black velvet, neatly trimmed with silver embroidery and cut-steel buttons, and in every way he epitomized how the leader of our country should look.

But I wasn't looking at His Excellency. Instead I saw no one but the gentleman behind him, slighter and shorter by a head and yet the only one who mattered to me. He was easy to find, his red-gold hair bright like a flame, and uncharacteristically unpowdered for this formal occasion. To my gratification, Alexander was seeking me as well, and as soon as our gazes met I saw him smile and un-abashed pleasure light his face, as if no other lady than I were in the room for him.

The general came forward to claim the first dance with Mrs. Lucy Knox, the wife of Major General Knox, and led her to the center of the room to open the assembly with the first minuet. The rest of the guests stood back from the floor to watch them dance with respect (and admiration, too, for together they cut an elegant figure), and as the musicians played, the general and Mrs. Knox—he so tall and lean, and she so stout—began the minuet's elegantly measured steps.

Yet Alexander hung back and I remained with him, away from the dancing and the other guests.

He took my hand. "Pray forgive me," he whispered, "I was with His Excellency, and the delay was unavoidable."

"Of course you're forgiven," I replied. "Your orders and your duties to the army and to the country must come first. I under-stand, and always will."

"You will, won't you?" he asked, his voice rough with urgency. "You'll understand, no matter what may happen?"

"Of course I will," I whispered, and it seemed more like a vow, an oath, than a simple reply. "Never doubt me."

He raised my hand and kissed the back of it, a bold demonstra-tion in a place so crowded with witnesses and ripe for gossip. But no one was taking any notice of us whilst the general was dancing, and I did not pull free.

Gently he turned my hand in his and kissed my palm. I blushed at his audacity, but it was far more than that. I felt my entire body grow warm with sensation, melting with the heat of his touch. This was what I'd wanted, what I'd longed for. When at last he broke away, an unfamiliar disappointment swept over me, and I felt oddly bereft.

If I felt unbalanced, then he must have as well, for his expression was strangely determined and intense. Within the General's Family he was called "The Little Lion," and for the first time I understood why. This was not the Alexander I'd seen this last fortnight sitting politely in Mrs. Campfield's sitting room. This was a different man altogether, and while part of me turned guarded and cautious, the larger part that contained my heart, and yes, my passions, was drawn inexorably toward him.

"Orders had nothing to do with why His Excellency and I were detained," he said to me, his fingers still tight around mine. "It was instead the matter of my future, my hope, my very life, and yet he will not listen, and refuses it all."

I glanced at the general, dancing as if he'd no cares in this world or worries for the next.

"Then tell me instead," I said.

"Come with me outside," he said, leading me toward the door. "We cannot speak here with any freedom."

Venturing outside alone in the dark with a gentleman was one of those things that virtuous ladies did not do. But for the first time in my life I didn't care what anyone might say or think. I fetched my cloak and he his greatcoat, joined him at the storehouse's rear doorway, and together we slipped outside.

"This way," he said softly, leading me behind the storehouse and away from where the sleighs and horses were waiting with their drivers gathered for warmth around a small fire. "No one will see us on the other side."

Most times when a gentleman and lady leave a ball or assembly, there is a moonlit garden with shadowy paths and bowers to welcome them. But here in Morristown, all trees and brush had long ago been cut by the army for firewood and shelters, and the only paths were ones trodden by others into the snow. There was no pretty garden folly or contrived ancient ruin; instead we stood beside the rough log walls of a military storehouse. The only magic that Alexander and I had was the moonlight, as pure and shining as new-minted silver spilled over the white snow and empty fields.

But that magic, such as it was, held no charm for Alexander now.

"The general still refuses to promote me for an active post, and will not consider a command for me to the south," he said, his voice taut with frustration. Despite the cold, he hadn't bothered to fasten his greatcoat, and the flapping open fronts only exaggerated his agitation.

"Oh, Alexander," I said, for I'd heard this from him before, though not with such vehemence. "Did you present your case for a field command to His Excellency again this evening?"

"I did," he said. He was pacing back and forth before me, the heels of his boots crunching over the packed snow. "He claims he cannot grant me a command without giving offense—offense!—to other officers who surpass me in seniority. Instead I must be mired here in endless drudgery without any hope of action or glory."

Dramatically he flung his arms out to either side, appealing to me. "Do you know how I passed this day, Betsey? Can you guess how I was humbled?"

I suspected there would be no acceptable answer to this question, not whilst he was in this humor, yet still I ventured one. "I should guess you were engaged in your duties as ordered by His Excellency."

"Oh, yes, my *duties*," he said. "Such grand duties they were, too. I tallied and niggled the expenses incurred for the feed of the cavalry's mounts, horse by horse. My *duty* was to count oats and corn and straw like any common farmer in his barn."

I sighed, my feelings decidedly mixed. I knew he was dissatisfied with his role in the winter encampment. Although he was the general's most valued aide-de-camp, he chafed under that honor and the duties with it, and longed for a posting where he'd see more active duty and combat with the enemy. I wished him to be happy, yes, but I also wished him to stay alive, and I dreaded the very thought of him in the reckless path of mortal danger.

He took my silence as encouragement, and continued on, his voice rising.

"The general would unman me completely, Betsey, and replace my sword forever with a pen," he said. "There is a sense of protection to the position, of obligation, which I find eminently distasteful. How can I be considered a soldier? Each day that I am chained to my clerk's desk is another that questions my courage, my valor, my dedication to risk everything for the cause."

This, too, I'd witnessed before. Alexander was a gifted speaker, and once he fair had his teeth into an argument, he could worry it like a tenacious (but eloquent) bulldog for hours at a time. His skill with words was a wondrous gift and one that left me in awe. But beneath my cloak tonight I was dressed for a ball, not an out of doors declamation beneath the stars, and I needed to steer him gently toward a less furious course before my teeth began to chatter.

"His Excellency knows you're not a coward," I said, tucking my hands beneath my arms to warm them. "Your record in battle has already proven your courage. But there are no battles to be fought by anyone in the winter season, and—"

"There are in Georgia, in Carolina," he said, the words coming out as terse small clouds in the cold air. "Laurens has written me of brisk and mortal encounters with the enemy."

I sighed again. John Laurens was another lieutenant colonel and former aide-de-camp, and Alexander's dearest friend in the army. Laurens had left the General's Family before I'd arrived, but I felt as if I knew him from Alexander's descriptions of his friend's character, handsomeness, and daring; he'd also been born to wealth and privilege as the son of the wealthiest man in South Carolina, accidents of fate that greatly impressed Alexander. His fondest reminiscences of Laurens, however, involved hard-fought battles, gruesome wounds, swimming rivers under enemy fire, and having horses shot from beneath them. These tales I found terrifying, even though I understood from Papa that this was how soldiers behaved during wartime. Little wonder that I also believed—though I'd never say so—that Colonel Laurens was responsible for much of Alexander's restlessness.

"You've told me before that those are random skirmishes," I said as patiently as I could. "Colonel Laurens admits that himself, does he not?"

He grumbled, wordless discontent. "He does, on occasion."

"And you've said yourself that they're risky ventures," I continued, "and of no lasting value to the cause."

He paused his pacing again, and tipped his head to one side to look at me. The moonlight caught the curl of his hair beneath the brim of his hat, like a flame against the dusky sky.

"Not when compared to larger, more organized campaigns, no," he admitted, finally sounding a fraction more reasonable. "Yet every action, large or small, has its use in deciding a final victory."

"But even the general accepts that there is a season for battle, and a season for rest." I kept my voice logical yet soothing, too, knowing from experience that was what would calm him. "The letters you now write for the general, the plans you make for the army for the spring on his behalf, are far more important than any random encounter in the Carolina wilderness."

"But there's no glory in it, Betsey," he said, his earlier impatience now fading into a sadness that touched my heart. "You know I'm a poor man, without family or fortune. I've made no secret of that with you."

"But consider how far you have come on your own," I said, "and how much you have already achieved."

"It's scarcely a beginning," he said. "I need to make my name for myself now, during the war, and that I can't do scrivening away at a desk. I cannot gain any measure of fame unless I return to the battlefield, and yet because I have no familial influence of my own, I will never be advanced to a higher command."

"You have friends," I said softly, trying not to think of what Kitty had told me earlier. "Important friends, in the army and in Congress. Friends who appreciate your talents, and regard you as you deserve. All will come to you in time. I'm sure of that."

"In time, in time, in time," he repeated in despondent singsong. "What if I can't wait, Betsey? What if *you* can't? I want to be worthy of you, and yet I have nothing of any value to offer you."

"Oh, Alexander," I said. "You have so very much to offer to me! You're brave and honorable and kind and clever, with a hundred other qualities besides. You have grand ideas and dreams that only you have the power to make real. You could never raise your sword against the enemy again, and still I'd be the one who wasn't worthy of you."

"My dear Betsey." He smiled, a weary smile, yes, but a smile nonetheless. "No wonder you've become so dear to me, and so indispensable, too. I do not think I could bear this winter without you. You're my very Juno, filled with the wisest counsel, combined with the beauty of Venus herself."

"You say such things." I smiled, too, but uncertainly. I knew he'd just paid me a compliment, but unlike Angelica, I'd no aptitude for scholarly endeavors, and I was never quite sure what he meant when he spoke of ancient goddesses.

"I do indeed," he said, finally coming to stand close to me. "And you are cold, aren't you? Let me warm you." He wrapped his arms around me and drew me close, folding me inside the dark wings of his heavy wool greatcoat. I went to him and snugged next to his chest as if I'd found my true home. I felt safe and protected with his arms around me and my cheek against his chest, and so contented that I could not keep back an unconscious sigh of pure joy.

He chuckled, and drew me closer. "Sweet girl," he said. "You thought you'd come here to dance, not to shiver in the moonlight with me."

I tipped my head back to see his face. I'd been so occupied with our conversation that I'd nearly forgotten about the dance, and with his reminder I was again aware of the music coming faintly from the assembly within the storehouse. The minuet was long past done. What I heard now was an *allemande*, and I wondered how many other dances had been danced since we'd left the assembly. By now our absence must have been noted—I doubt I'd ever escape Kitty's sharp eyes—but I didn't care. This time alone with him was worth any price.

"I've never seen a moon such as this," I said breathlessly, turning a bit in his arms to better see the sky. "It's like magic, isn't it? A full moon wrought from silver, there in the sky."

His hands had settled familiarly around my waist above the whalebone arc of my hoops, and just that slight pressure of his palms against my sides was making my heart beat faster.

"You should see how the moon glows in the sky over Nevis," he said. "There's no magic involved, but a phenomenon caused by the island being so close to the equator. It's every bit as bright as this, with the brilliance reflected and magnified by the sea below it."

"Truly?" I said, trying to imagine what he described. "You make it sound very beautiful."

"Oh, it is," he assured me, but the way he said it made me think perhaps it wasn't. "A sight worthy of the finest poets."

He fell quiet, gazing up at the moon. He almost never mentioned the island where he'd been born, and I longed to know his thoughts.

"Does this make you wish to return home?" I asked. "The moon, I mean."

"Nevis is no longer my home," he said bluntly, "and I never wish to return. If I'd remained there, I would by now be dead. It's the way of that place."

The sadness in his voice was heartbreaking. "But you're here now," I said. "Beneath an American moon, not a Nevis one." I turned around to face him again, and placed my palms lightly on his chest. My right hand rested over his heart, something I didn't realize until after I'd done it.

"You shall do wonderful things, Alexander," I said fiercely, gazing up at him. "I'm sure of it. You are a man born to do great things. I only pray that I'll be there to see you do them."

Suddenly he smiled, and so warmly that I forgot I'd ever been cold. "You pray a great deal, Betsey."

"I've prayed for you ever since that first night, exactly as I promised," I said, my fingers spreading over the front of his waistcoat. "My prayers have been answered, too."

"Perhaps mine have as well." He reached up to cradle my jaw with one hand, gently turning my face up toward his. "You're kind and generous and tender to a fault, especially where my wretched self is concerned. Have I told you that you're beautiful as well?"

"You have," I said playfully. "But I will listen if you choose to tell me again."

He chuckled. "You are beautiful, dearest, surpassing beautiful and unmercifully handsome, and I'll never tire of telling you that pretty truth. You have so addled my wits that the other night when I returned to headquarters from seeing you, I could not recall the password. Of course the sentry knew me, the dog, but he wouldn't let me pass until Mrs. Ford's boy rescued me with the proper word. That's all your doing, Miss Elizabeth."

I laughed, picturing him foundering at the front door before a grave-faced guard. "You cannot fault me for that!"

"I can, when it's the truth." His smile faded. "You speak of the future as if you can foresee what it holds. You're so wise, perhaps you can. Do you know how honored I'd be to have you beside me in that future, Betsey? To know you'd be with me always, as you are now?"

My heart was beating so fast that it was almost painful within my breast.

"I could wish for nothing more than to be with you like that, Alexander," I whispered. "Nothing." I was trembling, for I'd never spoken like this to another man, nor had I ever desired to. "I—I love you, Alexander Hamilton."

I wish I could have preserved that moment forever, how he looked at me with such boundless emotion and regard, as if I were the most worthy woman in the world.

"I love you, Elizabeth Schuyler," he said solemnly, and yet I was sure I heard a tremor to his voice to match my own. "My joy, my happiness, my love. Do I have your leave to address your father?"

I nodded, not trusting my voice. I suspect he didn't trust his, either, for he spoke no further.

Instead, he kissed me.

How dry and dull those words seem when writ on paper! How, in their simplicity, they lack the riches that Alexander's first kiss held for me! At first he barely touched his lips to mine in the kind of chaste salute that would have pleased even Aunt Gertrude. This kiss was an honorable pledge meant for marriage, the most sacred of sacraments for any woman, and as our lips came together, I realized his honorable regard and devotion for me. I felt cherished, and I felt loved.

But as glorious as that moment might have been, it would not long suffice for either of us. I will be honest: I'll include my own impatience, however unseemly for a lady that may appear, for in this as in so many things Alexander and I were already in perfect union. That first brush of his lips over mine was like a spark to overdry tinder, and at once the heat of desire washed over me.

In innocent eagerness, I pressed my lips more ardently against his, and at once he responded. He slipped his hand from beneath my jaw to the back of my head and tangled his fingers into my hair, and slanted his mouth over mine to deepen the kiss. My lips parted beneath his, and with a hunger I'd never realized existed within me I tasted him as he tasted me. The heat of his kiss burned me with its unexpected passion, and made me yearn to become his even more completely. I slid my hands around his shoulders to steady myself, and shamelessly stretched my body against his.

I am not certain how long that first kiss lasted, there in the silver-bright moonlight. It seemed both an instant, and an eternity, with the only certainty being that I did not wish it to end. Yet like all things, finally it did, when with obvious reluctance Alexander lifted his mouth from mine.

I opened my eyes, still dazed with heady bliss. He was almost frowning as he gazed down at me, his lips still parted and his breathing quick, as was my own. My thoughts were muddled: I was a lady born, a Schuyler, and not one of the slatterns who frequented the camp. I tried to push away from him, belatedly fearing he'd think ill of me for encouraging such freedom.

"I—I am sorry, Alexander," I stammered in confusion, my cheeks hot. "Forgive me for—"

"Hush," he said softly, placing his fingers lightly over my newly kissed lips. "It must be I who apologizes, not you, dearest Betsey, nor can I lay the fault on the moonlight. Even in your innocence, you have that power over me. You tempt me so much, when I must show more regard for the lady whom I pray will one day soon be my wife."

I smiled shyly, liking the notion that a lady-wife could be tempting, too, and pressed my lips against his fingertips.

"One day," I breathed, liking those words. "And soon."

CHAPTER 5

As magical as that night had been, I didn't see Alexander the next day, or the next after that. Winter stepped between us, as it did so often that year. By the time the assembly had ended and I was once again bound for home in the Livingstons' sleigh, that shining silver moon—our moon—had become obscured by thick clouds. Snow began falling before dawn, and continued to fall for the entire day and the next night, too. The skies remained as dark as if the sun had never risen, with the flakes falling so rapidly that all landmarks were lost in swirling white.

Every house, shop, church, and barn in the town as well as the army's encampment was blanketed by the snow, and the streets and roads were so thickly covered that by midday no outward signs remained that these passageways had ever existed. Even the very birds in the trees were quieted by the snow, and all around us was muffled in icy white silence.

Muffled, and cut off from the larger world around us, too. The snow was too deep and treacherous for man or horse to traverse, and I pitied the poor sentries standing guard in such weather. Everyone else kept within doors and away from the frost-iced windows, and did not venture far from their fires.

There was no question of Alexander calling upon me, yet still I was impatient to see him again. How could I not be? As I sat and knitted more caps for the soldiers, I imagined him in the crowded quarters of Mrs. Ford's house a mere quarter of a mile away, sitting at the long table that served as a desk for the aides-de-camp and continuing to write His Excellency's orders, transcribe his letters, coordinate his meetings, arrange his messengers, and perhaps even tally the expenses for the cavalry's horses. The work of the army's headquarters would not stop even in a snowstorm, though nothing could be sent until the roads again were passable.

Yet I also pictured Alexander later in the evening, after the general and the other aides had retired to their beds. Bent over his desk with a tallow candle for light, he'd be writing still, but at that hour the words would be his own.

And to my joy, they'd be meant for me.

Ever since my aunt had permitted Alexander to hand me that first letter, he had launched a veritable barrage of missives my way, so many that I could scarce keep up my replies. He was my soldier-poet, and oh, the sweet words that were in his arsenal for winning me! His letters were like him, brilliant and beautiful and rich with ideas and, yes, with love. Some were short, scarcely a sentence or two written in haste, and others were worthy of the greatest writers in our language. I cherished them all. In his letters, I was his dearest girl, his angel, his happiness, his charmer, but above all I was simply his Betsey, his Eliza. What more, truly, could I ask?

The storm's last flake had scarcely fallen when Alexander again appeared at our door, his greatcoat covered with snow and his face flushed with the cold. As can be imagined, I greeted him as warmly as if we'd been separated for months, not days. I'd never claimed to possess a sentimental nature, but it did seem that our fondness for each other had strengthened with that first kiss, as if the very moon herself had blessed our love. From that time onward, I could not imagine myself with another man as my one love and husband, nor did I wish to.

Over the next weeks, and whenever the snows and the General permitted, we stole as much time together as was possible. While we attended several frolics and wintery amusements such as sleighing in the company of Kitty and several of my other friends as well as various officers from headquarters, I preferred the occasions when Alexander and I could be alone together. Aunt Gertrude had decided that he had proven himself worthy of me, and relaxed her more stringent rules. I was now permitted to sit with him unaccompanied in the front room of the Campfields' house in the evening (though the door must be kept open), and to bid him farewell alone in the hall. When Lady Washington invited me to tea, she made sure that Alexander would be spared from his duties long enough to take a dish with me, too. I was allowed to walk with him along the narrow paths carved into the snow, and if during those walks a kiss or two was exchanged, no one took notice.

It was also during these long walks that I began to realize the extent of his restless brilliance. While we spoke of a shared future together, as every couple will, our conversations were also deeper and more philosophical than most. It was Alexander's nature to speak more than I, and I happily listened, for he'd more ideas in a day than most mortal men have in a lifetime.

Hand in hand, he told me his plans for the country's future, of the rare opportunities—and possible perils—that would await our land once the war was won (which even in that grim winter, he never doubted would happen). Unlike most young gentlemen I'd known who seemed obsessed only with the battles at hand, Alexander looked ahead. He thought of new ways of government and ruling and new notions of finance, schemes and contrivances so magnificent and grand and important that I listened in awe as he recounted them.

I couldn't begin to match his knowledge, but I did ask many questions as they came to me, wanting to understand the things that interested him most, and learn new things for myself as well. In turn my eager attention pleased him, and he said that the process of explaining these things to me helped clarify them in his own head. Although we didn't realize it then, we'd unwittingly fallen into the pattern of discussion that we'd continue for the rest of our lives together, and I dare to believe that in this way I encouraged him in his achievements.

We were also creating the kind of partnership that I'd always witnessed in my parents' marriage. Mamma had taught me that to be a loving wife and a thorough, supportive helpmate to my husband was the surest course to contentment for any woman, while Papa for his part had always regarded my mother with unerring kindness, devotion, and respect. That I had found the same qualities in a gentleman as charming, as witty, and as handsome as Alexander was to me the rarest good fortune in the world.

It became accepted throughout the town and the camp that an understanding existed between us. Other men no longer asked me to dance at the assemblies, and the former gossip of Alexander's rakish dalliances ceased, too, with his name now linked only to mine. As can be imagined in so small a community, this led to a great deal of good-natured jesting on the subject, and we both were accused of being love-struck and addled by Cupid's darts.

Neither of us could deny it.

Given all this, it was no real wonder that as the days grew longer and February slipped into March, Alexander and I agreed that it was time for him to write to my father. I was already well aware of how high Alexander stood in Papa's favor and had no doubt that he'd give his blessing to our union.

Alexander, however, had no such confidence, and labored long in composing this letter, which he rightly called the most important of his life. His uneasiness only increased when Papa didn't reply at once, but said he first must defer to my mother. Further, he announced that he'd taken a house here in Morristown to better survey the state of the army for his reports to Congress, and also to be nearer to me.

"Your father doesn't trust me, Eliza," Alexander said gloomily as we sat together one evening. "Instead of granting his consent, he's coming here to defend you against the friendless, penniless suitor who dares ask for your hand."

"Hush," I scolded gently. "That's not his reasoning at all, Alexander. You know his friendship with His Excellency, and how hard he strives to present the army's needs to Congress. It makes perfect sense for him to be here in Morristown now, as the plans are being made for the summer campaigns."

He shook his head and restlessly tapped the hilt of his sword.

"I don't deny that those things are part of his reasoning," he admitted. "But you know that the general is sending me to Amboy next week to negotiate the exchange of prisoners. I could be gone a fortnight, even longer, and I hate leaving you here with so much undecided. Why hasn't your father replied? Why is he taking so long?"

"Because he wishes to consult with my mother first," I said. "Among Dutch families, mothers have as much say as fathers in determining their children's marriages. He is in Philadelphia, while she remains in Albany, and you know how slowly letters travel at this time of year."

He grumbled wordlessly like a restive dog. "I can understand why Carter persuaded your sister to elope with him, if he was forced to suffer this same misery."

Although he hadn't asked for more coffee, I refilled his cup from the pot beside me. I'd already learned that small attentions like this helped to calm him when he was agitated.

"I've told you before that it was my sister's idea to run away, not Mr. Carter's," I said. "But she did so because my parents would never have approved of him as a suitor, and an elopement was their only path to happiness."

He raised the porcelain cup to his lips, inhaling the steaming fragrance of the coffee before he sipped it. "I cannot fault your parents. Though I myself like Carter, many regard him as the worst sort of slippery English rascal."

"He's never seemed a rascal to me," I said mildly. John Carter had first come to our house in 1776 as a commissioner appointed by Congress to audit the accounts of the army while my father in command of the Northern Department. Papa had liked him then, judging him to be thorough, fair, and hardworking, but he'd never considered him as a suitable addition to our family. I'd thought him pleasing enough, if a bit phlegmatic, yet Angelica had been intrigued by his clever intelligence. I'd known there was an attraction between them, but I'd been as surprised as anyone when they'd eloped, and I still silently marveled that he'd snared my fiery sister's heart. He was dark and intense, and known as a gambler, a gentleman who took great risks. He was rumored to be profiting from the war through various business arrangements that many thought weren't entirely honorable, and I think that the aura of wickedness and mystery about his past in England had also held a powerful allure for my sister. "And it's not his fault that he was born in England."

"He's an Englishman who fled his native land after an ill-fated bankruptcy," Alexander said. "I know his primary income comes from provisioning contracts, but I've heard he's also indulging in some tidy speculation that will either make him very rich, or very much in debt, which is bound to unsettle your father. In his eyes, matters must be going from ill to worse with you choosing a pauper. Though at least I have come to my poverty honestly, and as a gentleman should."

"*Hush*," I said again, and more sternly, too, for the coffee had not helped his humor as I'd hoped. "You are not at all like Mr. Carter. My parents have found you agreeable from the moment you first appeared on their doorstep, and you have only risen in their estimation since then. I'm sure they will bless our marriage, as sure as I am of anything under Heaven. What other assurance can I offer you?"

He glanced down at the delicate cup in his hand as if seeing it for the first time, and deliberately set it on the table between us. When he looked up again, I saw the deep sorrow in his eyes that he seldom revealed to anyone but me. I saw the loneliness of that long-ago boy who'd lost his parents and his home, and the aching fear of abandonment that haunted him still.

I dropped my knitting in the basket beside me and rose swiftly from my chair. I looped my arms around his neck and bent to kiss him, determined to make him understand the depth of my feelings for him. He answered by curling his arm around my waist and drawing me forward on his knees, and kissing me with an urgency that bordered on desperation. It was all done with haste and need, not grace, with my petticoats flurrying around my ankles, my knee bumping his sword awkwardly against the chair, and his half-empty cup rattling in its saucer on the table, yet we took no notice of anything except each other.

At any moment we could be discovered by another of our household, and we both understood that this bold display of emotion would have tested my aunt's new tolerance. We didn't care. He kissed me more deeply, his hand sliding along my leg beneath my tumbled petticoat as if by accident, until he'd reached the back of my bare knee above the ribbon of my garter. There he settled his palm quite happily, nor did I protest this impulsive caress; far from it. I'd already discovered how much I enjoyed the feverish pleasure Alexander's touch could inspire, and risking the discovery by others only made the enjoyment more thrilling. I'll admit that this was not the demeanor of a lady as I had been taught, and I had never granted such freedom to any other gentleman. But with Alexander, these freedoms, these kisses stolen and freely given, these small, teasing games were all part—an exciting part—of loving him.

"My own Alexander," I whispered breathlessly, my face close to his. "If you wish it, I'll wed you now, tomorrow, however and wherever you choose. We needn't wait for my parents at all."

"Oh, Eliza," he said ruefully, smoothing my hair back from my face. "Nothing would bring me more joy than to hold you in my arms as my wife. But as much as I long for that day, I won't ask you to make that sacrifice. You're Eliza Schuyler, and you deserve a proper wedding, surrounded by your family, and I wouldn't rob you of that."

Reluctantly I nodded, realizing how foolish I'd been to suggest such a giddy plan. Another elopement would break my poor mother's heart, and I wouldn't wish Alexander to be forced to face my father's wrath. The rashness of an unexpected marriage could even compromise his position in the army; His Excellency expected his officers—especially one as trusted as Alexander—to behave with measured decorum, and not to run off with a general's daughter.

"Perhaps it is for the best that we wait, but I wish it could be otherwise," I said wistfully. Still perched on his lap, I smoothed his neck cloth and straightened the collar of his coat with would-be-wifely concern. "There is so much that is unsettled in our lives because of the war, that if we could only be wed . . ."

I let the words drift off, because they didn't really need to be said. I'm sure he understood as well as I. The war was a constant pall over all of us, with no guarantees of what might happen next. When the army broke camp in the spring, all the wives and families of the officers from Lady Washington downward would return to their homes, and the men would head to battle. Alexander complained of being desk-bound as an aide-de-camp, but once the fighting resumed, he would be in as much danger as any other soldier. The reasons for waiting to marry were undeniable, yet still I feared that I could lose him before he'd ever truly been mine.

"In time, my angel, in time," he said softly. "I'll go to Amboy, and you shall remain here to welcome your father. We'll both have our orders, won't we? I'll be thick in tedious negotiations with the

British, while you'll be persuading your father of the wisdom of our match."

I tried to smile. "You've told me yourself that the negotiations aren't so very arduous, and how in the evenings you'll be expected to dine every night with the British officers as if they were your boon companions."

"That is true," he admitted. "The British like nothing more than to drink themselves into a stupor every night. I will endure it, of course, if it means I can bring even one more of our men back to our side. You know that Congress is responsible for paying the keep of our own men in British hands, and God only knows how much of our payment ever reaches the poor wretches. To have as many of them returned to their regiments before the spring would be a benefit to everyone."

"They couldn't ask for a better champion." It didn't feel appropriate to discuss prisoners of war whilst sitting on his lap, and I eased from his knee, intending to return to my own chair.

But before I'd turned away, he'd caught me gently by the wrist.

"Eliza," he said softly, in the voice that was deep and low and meant only for me. "Know that I will always be your champion first, above all others."

I nodded, and all my earlier disappointment melted away. As I smiled down at him, unexpected tears stung my eyes, and I hurriedly dashed them away with the heel of my hand.

"Don't weep, my love," he said, half teasing and half not. "My sorry self isn't worth your tears."

"But you are." My voice squeaked with emotion. "I'm crying because you make me so happy."

"Ah, then, tears of joy." He raised my hand to his lips and kissed it, lingering over the saltiness of my tears. "I vow to make those the only kind you'll ever shed, Eliza, at least on my account. The sweetest tears of joy, and no others."

I smiled, even as fresh tears slid down my cheeks. Such a beautiful promise to make, such a perfect vow from him.

How I wish it was one he'd been able to keep.

Soon after Alexander left with a small party for Amboy, a town on the Raritan Bay that overlooked Staten Island, and that served as the way station and ferry stop for travelers between New York and Philadelphia. It had also become something of an informal meeting point for the two armies, with our forces occupying Philadelphia and the British still holding New York. This was why Alexander had gone there to negotiate the mutual exchange of various prisoners from both sides.

Amboy was not far from Morristown, perhaps forty miles, but on account of the roads being rutted with ice, Alexander and his party required three long days to make their destination. I know this because he wrote to me as soon as he arrived, sending his love and informing me of his safe arrival.

I was, of course, delighted to receive his letter, and all the others that followed, for if I thought he'd written often to me when we were both together in Morristown, now, with a county between us, he seemed to have doubled his daily words.

He recounted the details of the negotiations, the officers he met and liked and the ones he didn't, what he ate and what he drank, and any sundry scraps of gossip from New York involving acquaintances of my family's. Forgetting (or choosing to forget) how far-reaching the Schuylers were in New York, he was simultaneously baffled and irritated by how my sisters Angelica and Peggy as well as I were mentioned in the nightly toasts of British officers. He also devoted much ink and paper to how thoroughly he missed me, and how much he longed to be with me again, and many small, private intimacies and endearments besides. No gentleman wrote a more devoted love letter than my Alexander, and no love letters were treasured more completely than I did his.

The only drawback to his literary devotion came with my replies. I couldn't keep up with him, leastways not at the pace which he desired. I had never been facile with a pen in my hand, nor did inspiration come easily to me, the way it did to him. My spelling could be various and my hand lacked grace, and too often in the time it took me to capture an anecdote or sentiment upon the page, the words would fly clear away from my possession like a bull through an open gate, never to be recaptured. These lines which you read here, in all their clumsiness, are sufficient proof of how much I labored over my missives to him. Whereas his letters could cover sheet after sheet, mine were seldom more than a single page in length, and every word hard-fought at that.

It didn't help matters that Papa arrived at his new lodgings in Morristown soon after Alexander had left. I bid thanks and farewell to my aunt and uncle and the crowded house of the Campfields, Rose packed up my trunks and belongings, and we shifted to the house my father had taken for the next few months. Yet I'd scarcely settled there before Papa announced that, as a treat, I was to accompany him back to Philadelphia, where he continued to hold his seat in Congress.

With the worst of the winter's snows and ice behind us, our journey to Philadelphia was uneventful. When I'd been younger, New York had always been the city that we'd travel down the Hudson River to visit, but being patriots, we had not returned there since the British had seized control of the main island in the fall of 1776. Although some of Philadelphia's citizens with Tory sentiments had fled, it was now the largest of our country's cities with wide streets, grand homes, and handsome public buildings and churches built mainly of brick.

There was much to entertain me while my father tended to his political business: plays and musical gatherings, teas and suppers held by friends old and new, sermons to heed on Sundays, shops to visit, and parks to stroll. Because of Papa, I received more invitations than I could accept.

There was another side to all this company and entertainment, however, and I found it both discomfiting and disrespectful. While in Morristown, where everyone I met was connected in some fashion to the army and to His Excellency, the talk had always been of the deprivations our troops endured, especially during this winter's storms and hardships, and how little support the general and men were receiving from Congress. But here in Philadelphia, the home of that same Congress, the conversation over tea and supper was of how the army scandalously squandered whatever was granted them by the magnanimity of Congress, and worse, how much His Excellency exaggerated the needs of his forces to squeeze more from Congress.

None of this was true. In fact, the truth was quite the opposite of these assumptions, and I didn't like how these fine, wealthy Philadelphian ladies made such free assumptions. I didn't like how they sat before their warm fires and whispered about soldiers who had spent the winter shivering in makeshift cabins, and soon would be heading off to risk their lives once again on the behalf of us safely at home.

I knew the truth, because I'd witnessed it myself, and I knew many of the officers they slandered, including the one I loved. I was my father's daughter to the core, and to his delight (and Alexander's, too, when I told him), I spoke up as often as I could in those elegant drawing rooms and parlors, and corrected as many ladies as I dared. It wasn't in my nature to keep still in the face of falsehoods. I doubted they believed me, as people who are misinformed seldom do, and I'm certain they considered me ill-mannered, but at least I had not given the impression of agreeing with them through silence.

Was it any wonder, then, that I soon tired of Philadelphia? What my father had intended as a pleasurable journey quickly came to feel more like a punishment, keeping me farther away from Alexander.

I missed him more than I'd believed possible. He filled my thoughts awake, and my dreams when I slept. I was certain I heard his voice and his laughter from the next room, or his footfall in the hallway. Whenever I glimpsed an officer in a uniform like his in the street, my heart beat faster until he turned, and I realized the man's face was not the one I wished most to see.

My only solace came in Alexander's letters, speaking to me across the miles. I replied as swiftly as I could, filling them with pledges of my own love and devotion. But instead of bringing him the same comfort I took from his letters, mine seemed only to make his doubts grow.

He took my brevity as a sign not of my lack of talent for letter writing, but proof that I was enjoying the pleasures of the city and forgetting him. It wasn't so much that he was jealous, or picturing me in the company of other gentlemen. Instead he worried that I'd had time to reconsider my love for him, and that I'd decided he lacked the qualities I required in a husband.

He tried to cover his fears with playful witticisms, but I wasn't fooled. Already I knew him so well, my dear Alexander. No matter how I reassured him, his uneasiness persisted in the saddest way possible, telling me he'd understand if I cast him away for being too poor. I was at a loss for how a gentleman who could bravely command a regiment in battle could feel this unsure of his own considerable merits. There was one sentence in particular that struck me with its truth, and reverberated within my heart—*"You must always remember that your best friend is where I am"*—and that made me long to fly to his side to reassure him both of his worth, and my love.

He was indeed my best friend, and all I wished was to be where he was.

On my last day in Philadelphia, I made one final call on a lady who sorely needed company. By rights Mrs. Peggy Arnold and I seemed fated to enjoy each other's company, we'd that much in common. We were close in age, and her husband, a major general, had served with my father, who held General Arnold in the highest regard for his bravery and military prowess in the northern campaigns.

But General Arnold had not fared as well in his most recent post as the military commander of Philadelphia, however, and had garnered so much ill will among the citizens that he had been compelled to resign. Worse still, he had recently faced a court-martial over his behavior while in the post, and though he'd been acquitted, the rumors continued to the extent that he had left the region until matters settled. He'd also been forced to leave Peggy behind, who had only just given birth to their first child, a son.

It was a sad story all around, and when Papa urged me to call upon her for the sake of good will, I happily agreed. How could I turn away from the opportunity to congratulate another lady on her safe delivery, and to welcome the blessing of her new baby into the world?

But when I called upon Mrs. Arnold, she appeared in low spirits, and to take little joy in her babe, who slept in a beribboned cradle beside her chair. Although she received me dressed in fashionable and costly undress—a pink silk jacket edged with fur over a quilted silk petticoat, a profusion of lace around her neck and elbows, and her hair lightly powdered—her eyes still carried the exhaustion of her recent confinement, and her entire posture drooped beneath the misery of her separation from her husband.

"Please forgive the meanness of my situation, Miss Schuyler," she said with a weary wave of her hand. "Until my husband summons me to our new home, I am forced to remain in this place as if I were a prisoner."

"Not at all, Mrs. Arnold," I said. Her description surprised me. The house was hardly mean, but pleasant and well furnished. Papa had told me that with her husband away, she was residing here in the home of a friend, and while I thought this an ungrateful way to repay the friend's hospitality, I was willing to ascribe it to the changeable nature of new mothers.

"Surely you must be in Heaven itself," I continued, "so long as you have this little cherub at your side."

He was a beautiful baby, with wisps of golden curls and full cheeks like his mother's. If I were in her position, I would indeed feel blessed to have such this perfect reminder of my husband and his love, especially in the middle of a war. I'd often wondered if Alexander's son would resemble him: would he inherit his father's golden red hair, his smile, his blue-green eyes that were as changeable as the sea?

"My darling little Edward," Mrs. Arnold murmured, and sighed as she glanced at the sleeping baby. "How fortunate he is that he knows not the persecutions his poor father has endured!"

"You must be brave, Mrs. Arnold, for your child's sake and for your own." As a soldier's daughter, I knew the importance of being stoic. "Your husband would wish that for you."

"Alas, my poor husband." She drew a lace-trimmed handkerchief from her sleeve and daubed prettily at her eyes. "He has so many enemies! It wasn't enough that he became a cripple in the service of his country. His enemies now hound him wherever he goes, and will not rest until he is completely ruined."

I was beginning to suspect her sorrows were for effect and that she might make a better actress on the stage than a general's wife, yet again I granted her the benefit of the doubt.

"Surely things will soon improve, Mrs. Arnold," I said. "Now that the court-martial is over and your husband is acquitted, he can again resume his duties with the army."

"You don't understand my husband's situation, Miss Schuyler," she said with another great sigh. "The acquittal means nothing. The villains in Congress and in the army will continue to plot against him and deny his hopes for promotion and reward. If only he had friends he could trust!"

"But he does," I said. "My father speaks of General Arnold as a hero, and he and His Excellency both wish to help your husband to restore his reputation as quickly as possible."

She sighed again. "You father is an honorable gentleman, yes," she admitted. "But if there were someone closer to His Excellency, someone able to sway him in favor of my husband, someone who was constantly in his company."

She looked at me expectantly, as if I alone possessed the answer. I am glad to say I didn't understand her meaning.

"The general is a wise and experienced gentleman," I began. "I'm certain he'll make a decision that shall benefit you—"

"I'd heard you share an intrigue with Colonel Hamilton," she said. "His Excellency's most favored aide-de-camp. That is true, yes?"

"No," I said quickly, blushing and thinking again of how unsettling it was to be the centerpiece of idle gossip. "That is, yes, Colonel Hamilton serves as a member of the General's Family at headquarters, and yes, I am honored to consider him a dear friend, but there is no 'intrigue' to our connection."

"Yes, yes," she said, leaning forward with more animation than before. "My husband has only the highest praise for Colonel Hamilton, for his intelligence and his cleverness, and his devotion to the general. But then, that is only to be expected, isn't it, considering Colonel Hamilton's illustrious patrimony."

I frowned. "I fear you're mistaken, Mrs. Arnold. Colonel Hamilton has achieved much, but through his own industry and the support of his friends, not his father, a Scottish gentleman long absent from his life."

"Your reticence is admirable, Miss Schuyler," she said with an archness that made me uneasy. "But you needn't be so discreet with me. The truth is widely known here in Philadelphia, and explains much of the general's fondness for Colonel Hamilton."

"I have told you the truth as I have heard it from Colonel

Hamilton himself," I said, ready to defend Alexander in whatever way necessary. "There is no other, Mrs. Arnold."

She smiled slyly. "But there is, isn't it? Everyone has heard how the colonel is the general's natural son, conceived while His Excellency was visiting the Caribbean long ago. They see the obvious resemblance in the same coppery hair, the same line to his jaw, and you cannot deny how His Excellency positively dotes upon Colonel Hamilton, favoring him as if he truly were the son he never sired with Lady Washington."

"Hush, madam, please!" I exclaimed, not so much scandalized by what she said as shocked that she'd repeat such ill-founded gossip. "Colonel Hamilton His Excellency's son! That goes beyond tattle to purest slander, and I will not hear another word. Good day, Mrs. Arnold."

I rose to leave, but she caught my arm.

"Forgive me, Miss Schuyler, I beg you," she said, her head meekly bowed and her voice so contrite that I heard the tremble of tears in it. "Please don't leave yet. If I spoke rashly, it was from my desperate desire to assist my husband in any way that I might. Please stay, Miss Schuyler, and help me to help my husband."

Reluctantly I sat, though I kept to the very edge of the chair. "How can I possibly help General Arnold?"

"By asking Colonel Hamilton to use his influence with General Washington on my husband's behalf," she begged. "All my husband desires is another command or post, another chance to serve and prove his worth. Is that so much to ask for an officer who has already given so much?"

I remembered how Papa had said that General Arnold had been so grievously injured at the Battle of Saratoga (so near to our own house) that he'd nearly lost his leg, and that he'd never fully recover from the wound to the point that he could ride or walk with ease again. That was indeed a sacrifice, and I relented.

"I can promise nothing," I warned. "But I will share your plight with Colonel Hamilton in the event that he has the opportunity to set it before the general."

"I cannot begin to thank you enough." Her face relaxed, and for the first time she seemed her age, a young woman of only nineteen years cast into a difficult situation with a new baby and an absent husband. "All I can offer in return are my wishes for your own happiness and prosperity."

"Thank you," I said, preparing to take my leave. "You do me honor, Mrs. Arnold. I wish the same to you and your husband, and your dear little son as well."

"Yes," she said, her thoughts clearly elsewhere. "Yes. I can also offer you and Colonel Hamilton some hard-won advice, for you to take or not, as you please. If Colonel Hamilton can show my husband this small favor, his kindness will not be forgotten. He is most obviously a gentleman and an officer of promise, and his talents shouldn't be squandered to his disadvantage. You have been at Morristown, Miss Schuyler. You have observed the despair and disarray of this country's army for yourself, and the confusion of its leaders. Sometimes we ladies must see more clearly, and act to preserve the gentlemen we love."

I thanked her one last time and departed. I did wish her well, for she seemed a lady in need of good fortune, as my father had said. It wasn't until later that day, as I took time alone with my needlework, that I considered more closely her last little speech to me. The longer I thought upon her words, the more disturbing I found them. She wished her husband to return to active duty with the army. So why, then, had she faulted that same army? Alexander already had the highest esteem of His Excellency. Why should she say he was squandering his talents by serving his country? And what exactly was she counseling me to do?

I shared my worries the next morning at breakfast with Papa, but he swiftly brushed them aside as being of little lasting consequence.

"As you saw for yourself, she is a lady in sore need of comfort and compassion," he said as he sipped his coffee. "Her father remains a Tory with sympathies to the Crown, and he was not pleased with her marriage to Arnold. His friends were equally surprised when he found favor with her, a wealthy lady almost half his age, and many continue to suspect her allegiances. She is caught between her loyalties to her father and her husband, poor lady, and tries to serve them both as best she can. You saw that yourself."

"I did," I said thoughtfully. Perhaps that was explanation enough for her curious speech; I couldn't imagine marrying a gentleman under such difficult circumstances. "She must love General Arnold mightily."

"I pray that she does, for she has sacrificed a great deal to be his wife," Papa said. "Although I do not wish to raise false hopes, I am already planning to speak to His Excellency regarding a post for General Arnold as commander of our fortifications at West Point. It would be a good position for him, and it would be wise for the army to have an experienced officer so many consider a hero in command of a prominent location. Governor Livingston—your friend Kitty's father—agrees with me, too."

"Do you believe His Excellency will also agree?" I asked, still unsure whether I should wish him to or not.

Papa sighed, holding out his cup to the servant to be refilled. He was always unwaveringly loyal to soldiers who had served with him; I recognized the trial this must be for him.

"I do not know, Eliza," he said. "This is not to be repeated, but I know for a fact that His Excellency was displeased by Arnold's behavior, acquittal or not. There's no doubt that the man was indiscreet, and took advantage of his post as military commander for his own profit."

"So he should not have been acquitted?" I asked. "He was in fact guilty?"

Papa's brows drew together and his expression turned as stern as granite in what my sisters and I called his "general face."

"He was found not guilty," he said. "That was the verdict of his fellow officers in the court-martial, and that is how it shall always stand. The verdict cannot be questioned. But the very fact that Arnold was compelled to defend himself grieved His Excellency, who expects his officers to act in a manner that is beyond reproach, as gentlemen should."

I nodded, and my sympathy for Peggy Arnold and her husband rose. I had always found General Washington to be a daunting figure, and if I were one of his officers, I'd never have wanted to earn any measure of his displeasure.

I thought this would be the end of my father's explanation, but to my surprise he continued.

"I have heard that His Excellency's unhappiness is the reason he plans to issue a formal reprimand of Arnold, which will make the West Point post more difficult," he said. "But likely Colonel Hamilton will be able to tell you far more than I."

"Should I tell him how—how disloyal Mrs. Arnold was in her speech?" I asked tentatively. I had been only vaguely aware of General Arnold's court-martial having happened in Morristown in January, shortly before I'd arrived. Alexander hadn't mentioned it, and I hadn't known enough to inquire for more details, or at least I hadn't known enough until now. "How she found fault with the army and its officers?"

"Oh, I shouldn't trouble him with it," Papa said. "I suspect that was Mrs. Arnold's own disappointment speaking, not any reflection of her husband's opinions. But I leave it all to your own judgment, Eliza. You may say what you please to Hamilton when you meet him next. He knows I will be returning you to Morristown tomorrow, yes?"

I nodded, Peggy and Benedict Arnold forgotten in an instant. I'd my own problems to resolve, and I took a deep breath, my fingers anxiously pleating the damask napkin in my lap.

"I'd hoped that by now you would have given Alexander and me your consent," I said, wishing my voice wasn't shaking with emotion. "It's been three weeks since he wrote to you."

Now it was Papa's turn to look uncomfortable. He helped himself to a slice of toasted bread from the silver rack on the table and placed it precisely in the center of his plate.

"You already know I hold Colonel Hamilton in high esteem for a young gentleman," he said, still looking down at the toast. "He has impressed me with his initiative, courage, and resourcefulness, all important qualities for a man to possess before I would entrust him with your future welfare."

My hope rose to giddy heights. "Then you will grant us your permission?"

"I have granted nothing as yet, daughter," he said with maddening patience. He took his time buttering the toast, making certain the yellow butter went exactly to the crusts on four sides, and no farther. "I would prefer that the colonel had a suitable income to support a family, but I also believe he will rectify that deficit by his own talents as soon as the war is done. So long as he loves you and you love him—"

"Oh, I do, Papa!" I exclaimed. I was too anxious to eat, and I waved away the dish of shirred eggs that the servant began to place before me. "And I am sure, very sure, that he feels the same love for me."

Papa studied me for a long moment, the silver butter knife still in his hand.

"I have never seen this—this enthusiasm in you, Eliza," he said. "You have always been a thoughtful child, even cautious, and this fervor is unlike you."

"But it *is* like me, Papa, or the woman I have become," I said. I felt as if he was raising unnecessary obstacles, and I couldn't understand why. "I am still your daughter, your Elizabeth, but I long to be Colonel Hamilton's wife as well. If I have changed, it is love, his love, that has changed me. I dare to hope that the change is for the better, too."

If he agreed, he didn't say. Instead he dropped a large, glistening spoonful of strawberry jam into the center of the well-buttered toast, again avoiding my gaze.

"I suppose this is how every father must feel when confronted with a beloved daughter's marriage," he said gruffly. "I cannot imagine our home without you in it, Eliza. You're our shining light, our cheerful Christian soul. Your mother depends upon you so much to help with the household and other children that I can't fathom how she will cope without you. I knew the day would come that you would leave us, but now that it has, it seems entirely too soon."

"Oh, Papa," I said softly. I hadn't expected this from him, not at all. "I won't be leaving forever. You know I'll be back, and often."

He smiled down at the jam, not at me. Finally he raised the toast from the plate and bit into the crust, chewing it deliberately before he replied.

"When you do return to our house," he said, "you will be as Mrs. Hamilton."

"I shall always be your daughter." I rested my hand upon his arm. "That will never change, not in this life or the next."

He grunted as he finished the toast, no real answer, yet one I understood. He'd been devastated when Angelica had eloped, and I guessed he was feeling a degree of the same sense of loss with my pending betrothal to Alexander. But I was twenty-two. I was ready to be wife and a mother as well as a daughter. I'd found a gentleman I loved beyond all others, and it was time we married and began a home of our own.

"Please, Papa," I pleaded softly. "Won't you give your consent? Won't you write to Alexander?"

Self-consciously he patted my hand on his arm, and I felt sure that at last he'd agree.

But he didn't. Instead he withdrew his arm from my hand, pushed his chair back from the table, and rose.

"You know I am in communication about Colonel Hamilton's proposal with your mother, Eliza," he said. "When she has made her final decision, then I shall write to him. But not before. Not before."

I knew better than to argue, though tears of disappointment clouded my eyes as I kissed Papa's cheek before he left for the day. Afterward I retreated to my room, and continued the letter to Alexander that I'd begun earlier. I wrote slowly, carefully, determined to give him no hint of my own misery.

> *My father praises your virtues daily, and speaks of the day when I shall return to Albany as Mrs. Hamilton. I whisper it, too, as often as I dare, to help make it a reality. I pray each night to be yours forever, my dear Alexander, my love, my love.*

I stared down at the words as the ink dried and lost its glossy wetness, then ran my fingertip across them. I didn't belong in Philadelphia any longer. It was time I returned to Morristown, and to Alexander.

My dear Alexander, my love, my love ...

CHAPTER 6

My father did not write his fateful letter to Alexander until April. Though I shall never know for certain, I believe that it was my mother who finally pushed him to write, and if it had been left to Papa, I would still to this day be a spinster waiting for his blessing, he'd become that loath to part with me.

The contents of the letter were simple enough—that he and my mother had accepted Alexander's offer to me of marriage—but my life, and Alexander's, were changed forever. With the weather and the roads improving, my mother made the journey from Albany to Morristown, and took up residence in the house Papa had rented. I was pleased that they wished to know Alexander better, and I was equally pleased that he in turn wished to know them as well. Having no family of his own, he was eager to become part of mine, and as often as he could be spared from headquarters he came to our little house. With his usual charm, quick wit, and perspicacity, Alexander discussed military matters with Papa and household economies with Mamma, and won them both so thoroughly that they became as happy to see him at our door as I was.

Best of all was the glowing happiness that came with being betrothed to Alexander. My parents insisted on us marrying at our home in Albany, and we all hoped that Alexander would be able to procure leave to do so before the summer campaigns began. Our joy in one another was boundless, and whenever we were together, we planned and plotted our shared future together as husband and wife, and dreamed of the children we would have and the house where we'd live.

But the unhappy truth was that we had increasingly less time to spend in each other's company. It was not from lack of interest, of course, but on account of Alexander's duties. By now he had become for all purposes the general's chief of staff, and was as indispensable as any single officer in the army could be. I do not believe there was anyone that His Excellency trusted more. As can be imagined, I was thoroughly proud of Alexander, but his role meant that he was constantly either at the general's side, or away executing a mission or order on his behalf.

Privately I thought the general took advantage of Alexander's great energy and ability to subsist on little sleep. Whenever he'd steal away a few moments to call upon me, he often looked weary, with circles of exhaustion beneath his eyes, and I thought he'd grown thinner, too, which he could ill afford. He could become preoccupied, his gaze turning blank in the middle of a conversation as his thoughts began to churn some problem or another. It was obvious he'd much on his mind, and I worried at the toll it was taking upon him. Yet I could hardly protest, since the very survival of our new country was at risk.

For even as spring was returning and the fields around Morristown were turning green with new growth and optimism, the Continental Army was foundering; nor had I needed Peggy Arnold to tell me so, either. Most of us in Morristown were aware of it, and that knowledge hung like a forbidding cloud over the entire encampment.

No one had expected the war to continue as long as it had, with seemingly so little achieved. There had been hints of mutiny in the snow-covered cabins of Jockey Hollow, from muted grumbling to out-and-out insubordination. Many of the men had enlisted in 1777 for a term of service of three years, and were well aware that their duty would be finished at the end of April.

"Already the men are beginning to drift away," Alexander said. It was early evening, and we were sitting side by side on a rough plank bench in the small yard behind my parents' house, where we'd have a measure of privacy, if few comforts. Whatever cheer the sun had given earlier in the afternoon was gone, and I'd wrapped myself in a thick woolen shawl, with Alexander's arm around me for extra warmth. Small ghostly patches of old snow still lingered in the shadows, dirty and tattered like worn lace, but at last the first shoots of green were beginning to appear in the sticky, muddy ground.

Yet the way Alexander was explaining it, spring was bringing little cheer to General Washington.

"Each morning's muster shows more men have vanished overnight," he continued. "Their guns are gone and their other belongings with them. They've had their fill of soldiering, and all that matters to them are new crops to be planted and sweethearts to kiss. Staying here another few weeks makes no difference to them, nor can I fault them for it."

"But if they're captured, they'll be charged as deserters, won't they?" As a soldier's daughter, I knew the unequivocal sentence for desertion—the most grievous sin in any army—was death.

"The general will have no choice if he wants to maintain discipline," Alexander said. "Yet most who flee are young, younger than I, and eager to return to homes they left as boys. They haven't been paid in months, at least not in money that has any value to it. Many are sick, and all are near to starving from the poor rations. They believe Congress and the populace despise them, and they're justified in that. And yet . . ."

He let the words drift off unfinished, but I could complete them as well as he.

"You've stayed," I said, tightening my fingers into his. "You're here."

"I'm an officer, Betsey," he said, "and on my honor as a gentleman I'm bound to be part of this until the end of the war."

I leaned my head against his shoulder. "It's more than that for you."

He sighed deeply. "I believe in this, all of this. The war, our country, our future, the men who have died in battle beside me and the children I hope to have one day with you. To abandon it now would be madness, and cowardice besides."

"That's why I love you," I said softly. "Wrapped there in a single sentence."

"It was three sentences, actually," he said wryly, "but the sentiment is the same nonetheless."

"You spoke it as one." Only he would parse the syntax of a passionate declaration, and how endearing I found it, too. "The rumors among the ladies are that a thousand men are set to quit the army by the end of April."

"If only that were all," he said. "The last report that I wrote for the general to Congress estimated that at least two thousand eight hundred will be gone as surely as the last of the snow. That's more than a quarter of our regular army. Yet Congress urges the general to send more troops south to Charleston, heedless of how we'd then be helpless to stop the British here in the north. How can we send what we don't to spare? There's little doubt that given the opportunity, the British would overrun New Jersey, and likely take back Philadelphia as well."

I remembered the blithe confidence of so many of the Philadelphians I'd met. They'd placed all their faith in Congress and ignored the warnings of military gentleman like Papa, and instead assumed that the British would never choose to recapture their pretty city of red brick and neat houses. I didn't want to imagine how wrong they could be proven to be.

"Are you certain the British are interested in Charleston?" I asked, preferring to discuss a city I'd never visited. "Even if so, they wouldn't begin to shift their forces until summer, would they?"

"Oh, my sweet Eliza," he said with a curious mix of fondness and despair. "In January, General Clinton sent an expeditionary force of both British and Hessian soldiers to the town of Savannah in Georgia, which is already in British hands. Some say it's eight thousand men, some say twelve. Either way, it's far more than we have. By all our best intelligence, Clinton has every intention of attempting Charleston by land, where the city is weakly defended. If he does, he'll likely succeed. He could be there by now."

Abruptly I sat upright, twisting about to face him.

"Is it so bad as that?" I asked.

"I've heard from Laurens as well," he said grimly. "Those skirmishes he's led, the attacks that he and others in the local militia have made against the British—it's all that our forces can do to keep them from Charleston."

"And how is Colonel Laurens?" I knew how close Alexander was to John Laurens, and though I'd yet to meet him, I prayed for his safety, too, for the sake of their friendship.

"Laurens is as strong as a bull and has more good luck than ten mortal men together," he said. "He's nigh invincible because of it. God, I wish I were there with him!"

"I'm glad you're not," I said fervently. I'd heard too much of Colonel Laurens's reckless form of heroism, and I was horrified by the prospect of Alexander lying dead on some distant southern battlefield while his bull-like friend charged onward.

"You needn't fear," he said, the familiar bitterness and disappointment welling up in his voice. "The general shares your opinion, and will not let me go with the others."

"The others?" I repeated. "You just told me that His Excellency had no troops to spare."

He sighed again; this conversation was too full of sighs, and worse, too full of the reasons for them.

"This is for your ears alone, Eliza," he said, lowering his voice even further. "At the Council of War this week, His Excellency and the other generals agreed that they would send the Maryland Line to join and support the Southern Army. They shall depart as soon as it can be arranged."

"How many men is that?" I asked.

"Two thousand," he said, the number a blunt fact.

I swiftly made the calculations. "If those two thousand soldiers are subtracted along with the twenty-five hundred expected to depart when their terms are done, then there will be scarcely more than five thousand remaining here."

"Other brigades should be returning soon from outpost duty, but yes, the Northern Army will be sorely depleted." He raised his hands and spread his fingers in an uncharacteristic gesture of resignation. "I pray we won't be tested. Those fools in Congress believe that the General exaggerates our needs, and that we can continue indefinitely without more men, guns, and other resources. With their lack of support, all the general can do is pray that Clinton will not decide to launch an attack on us from New York."

I shook my head in silent empathy. I had heard the same from

Papa, who was every bit as frustrated with Congress's denials as was Alexander.

"The general might as well march us all to Charleston," he said with increasing bitterness. "At least then we would meet our fate with a semblance of honor instead of wasting away to shabby noth-ingness here."

"Is that a possibility?" I asked anxiously. I knew all too well what he meant by the word *fate*; to him it was a more-noble eu-phemism for death.

"I don't know, Betsey," he said wearily. "I'm only a soldier. I await my orders, and I follow them."

I curled against his chest, desperate for some sense of security in the face of so many unfortunate tidings, and the way Alexander wrapped his arms around me meant he needed that same comfort, too. It was quiet in the little yard, too quiet, really. So many of the birds and wild creatures had perished during the harsh winter that the absence of their songs and cries was eerie.

I do not know how long we sat there together. The sky was over-cast, with clouds that masked the sun and stars and made for a muffling darkness that reflected our somber mood.

Alexander was first to break the silence. "Your mother has great plans for our wedding, doesn't she?"

I smiled sadly, though I didn't lift my head from his chest. So that was how it would be tonight: we'd pretend that we were an or-dinary betrothed couple, with no concerns beyond our wedding clothes.

"Mamma does," I said, mustering a semblance of good cheer. "She speaks to me—and you—of little else, as you've doubtless ob-served. She missed the fuss of a proper wedding with Angelica, and now she's bound to redouble her efforts on our behalf to make up for it."

He chuckled. "I suspect your father's not the only general be-neath your roof."

"We've often thought that," I said, only half in jest. "Mamma is the bravest woman you will likely ever meet. She has accompanied my father into the very face of the enemy, and has stood beside him against dangers that would make most men flee in terror. A wedding will be as nothing to her. There are few things in this world more efficient or determined than a Dutch woman. You stand forewarned."

"I shall have none but the greatest regard for your mother," he said. "I'm delighted."

"You say that now," I warned. "You may feel otherwise once you see the stacks of marked linens and barrels of porcelain and crystal that she vows are absolutely necessary for us to begin to keep respectable housekeeping."

"Somehow we shall make do," he said, lightly stroking my hair. "Imagine a battle royal of supreme tidiness between your Dutch grandmother and my Scottish one, aprons flapping and brooms flying."

I laughed, and he did, too, and the silence that fell afterward was warm and companionable, and reminded me again of all the reasons that I loved him.

"My dearest girl," he said softly, quietly. "You do know I won't be granted leave to go to Albany with you in June."

I took a deep breath. I did know. I'd known for weeks, from everything I'd heard and witnessed in the encampment and from what he'd already told me that the general would not be able to spare him from his duties, but to hear Alexander speak it aloud was the final blow to pretending I didn't.

"I do," I said, unable to keep the sorrow from my voice. "I wish it were otherwise, but I—I understand."

"Late autumn," he said, "or December at the latest. A wedding in the Christmas season would be a merry thing, wouldn't it?"

I nodded with my cheek pressed against his chest, not trusting my voice to agree. It wasn't simply postponing our wedding that upset me. Certainly, my mother could, and would, use the extra months for preparations.

It was how and where he'd spend the summer. He could well be ordered to join the Southern Army with the others. The general could finally relent, and send him to a regiment that would see battle. Even if he weren't killed or maimed outright, he could equally succumb to the myriad of fevers found in the Carolinas, fevers that could kill a man as surely as British guns.

How could I explain? I could so easily lose him before he'd

truly become mine, and I slid my hands inside his coat, striving to burrow beneath the layers of wool and linen to the warmth and the flesh, the bones, the sinews, and the heart of the man.

"We could marry now," I whispered with feverish urgency. "We needn't wait."

He groaned, even as his own caresses across my body grew more fervent.

"No, Eliza," he said. "I've given my word to your papa, and I'd not betray him—or you—that way."

"But he needn't know," I pleaded, my words tumbling fast over one another. "No one else would. We could pledge our love to ourselves now, with only God as our witness, and be bound by that until we stand before a minister. Think of it, Alexander. It would be our secret, and only we would know that we were already man and wife."

"Oh, my love, if only we could." Despite his words, I heard the rough edge of desire in his voice, and with the increasing freedoms he was taking with my person—freedoms that I made no attempts to stop. He kissed me deeply, and my heart fluttered with longing, believing that love had triumphed.

But I was wrong. With a muttered oath, he forced himself to ease away from me and rose from the bench, going to stand some feet away, his back to me as he struggled for control. I sat forlornly alone on the bench and waited, struggling as well, with my hands twisting in the corners of my shawl.

Finally he turned, and I saw the anguish in his face.

"My mother was not married to my father," he said. "I've never hidden that from you before. My mother loved my father and he loved her, and I've no doubt they made the sort of pledges to each other that you describe."

"Then why won't you—"

"I won't," he said, "because in the end, what mattered most was that they hadn't made those vows before a priest, or minister, or magistrate, or any other august personage that society demands. Not only did my mother suffer for it, but my brother and I were labeled as bastards, a sin that was no sin, but that shall always be pasted over my name. And I will not do that to you, or to our children."

I had no answer. He was right, and I knew it, and yet that rightness was not easy to bear. I felt myself wilting beneath its weight, huddling into myself as I sat on the hard plank of a bench.

He understood my misery and returned to me, gathering me into his arms with great tenderness.

I would not cry. I would *not* cry. "I know you will be brave and honorable wherever your duty may lead you," I said, my voice husky with emotion. "All I ask, God willing, is that you return to me unharmed, Alexander. Return to me, and be my husband."

He kissed me, or perhaps I kissed him. It didn't matter which. Until we could wed, this would have to be enough.

Good news will come in fits and starts, like the bright bursts of shooting stars in the night sky, but bad news is often relentless in its progress, one unhappy event after another. It seemed that Nature herself had even conspired against our cause. Even the most venerable and aged persons in the region declared this to have been the worst winter in memory, and no one quarreled with them. As grim as Alexander's fears for our army's future had been, the truth as it unwound that spring was far worse than even he could have predicted.

As expected at the end of April, those men whose terms had expired left, leaving gaping places in the lines that could not readily be filled. But there was more: the shortages of food had reached a true crisis, with the forage in the area long exhausted and months before the new season's crops could be expected. Men stole not only from one another, but left camp without permission to steal what they could from the outlying farms. No threats of punishment deterred them; they were that hungry.

When my mother had traveled from Albany, she had brought with her provisions from our farms. These we rationed out for our own use, and never left untended in our kitchen. In fact I suspected that the sentries that His Excellency had posted outside our house, day and night, were as much to guard our provisions as our persons, and from her own generosity of spirit, my mother made sure to give each of these men a share from our own dinner when his station was done.

The word that reached us in May from the Southern Army was nothing short of disastrous. As feared, the British had laid siege to Charleston by land and by sea. The Americans under Major General Lincoln fought bravely and for as long as they could, but they were grossly outnumbered and outfought. When the British cannon began to rain heated shot upon the city, causing fires to homes and public buildings alike, the army and the city had no choice but to surrender.

The British victory was more costly than anyone in the North had expected. Nearly five thousand Continental soldiers surrendered and were made prisoner, and the British also captured more than three hundred cannons, six thousand muskets, and several tons of gunpowder—a grievous loss in every way.

The British now had possession of the largest city in the south with the best harbor, and further, by their decisive actions, they had won back the allegiance of many of the citizens who'd wearied of the long war. As Alexander told me in gloomy confidence, General Washington himself could have gone to Charleston and met only defeat, the odds were so much against the Continental troops.

At the same time, there was misfortune in Morristown, too. In May, a number of the Connecticut troops fomented an out-and-out mutiny against their officers, citing the lack of pay, food, and respect from Congress. The mutiny was quickly put down, but a number of their leaders were sentenced to death. They were not alone in their infamy, either. Several other men were sentenced for crimes including repeated desertion and forgery, bringing the total of eleven criminals. Some were to be hung for their sins, and others shot.

The night after the executions, Alexander described the scene to me, though in such halting terms I was sure he left much out to spare my sensibilities. At the last moment beneath the gallows, General Washington pardoned ten of the men, but the worst of the lot, a man from a Pennsylvania regiment, was not spared, and died his dishonorable death. As Alexander said, it was one thing to watch a man die in battle, and another to see him die as a weeping, guilty miscreant at the forced hands of his military brothers. The execution shadowed the encampment and the whole town with it, as if any of us needed more darkness in an already dark year.

And yet even in the midst of these unhappy troubles there were scattered bright rays of light and hope.

Alexander learned that his friend Colonel Laurens had survived the siege of Charleston unharmed, but was now among the thousands of prisoners of war waiting to be exchanged and released. Unlike most of his fellow prisoners, however, he'd a wealthy and well-respected father laboring to secure his release, and with Charleston fallen, Alexander hoped that he would soon return to rejoin His Excellency's family.

In May the encampment was honored by several distinguished visitors from abroad, including the Chevalier de la Luzerne, Minister of France. His presence was seen as a sign that France would soon enter the war as our allies, and hopes began to rise at a giddy rate.

Nor were those hopes in vain. Soon after, another Frenchman arrived, Gilbert du Motier, Marquis de Lafayette, who also served as a major general in the Continental Army. Lafayette (for so everyone called him, ignoring his noble title) was another old acquaintance and compatriot of Alexander's, and much esteemed by His Excellency as well. The news Lafayette brought with him from the French king Louis XVI, however, outshone even the bonds of friendship: the French fleet was bringing six thousand much-needed soldiers to join the American cause against the British.

In honor of these visitors, His Excellency announced a military review and a ball in honor of the French ambassador. As can be imagined, we ladies rejoiced at the news of such a diversion, and rallied to create ensembles suitable for a ball there in the fashionable wasteland of Morristown.

I also took pleasure in again meeting Lafayette, who had once been our guest at The Pastures during the early days of the war. I'd no notion then that he was a close friend of Alexander's, or that the two would fight together with such distinction and bravery, especially at the Battle of Brandywine where the marquis had been wounded. I remained in awe that he could have achieved so much for the cause of a country that was not his own, and yet was still of the same youthful age as Alexander and I. I liked his enthusiasm and his vigor, and how he hoped that one day I might have the honor of meeting his wife and young son, now left behind in

France. He showed me painted miniatures of them, too: the marquise a sweet-faced lady of fashion, and his son a true little cherub of less than a year, named George Washington de Motier in honor of His Excellency.

For me, however, there was one more guest who arrived on a rainy, muddy, April afternoon of more importance, someone who in my eyes eclipsed all the French nobility combined: the much-admired Mrs. John Carter, or as I knew and loved her, my older sister, Angelica.

"I wish you had brought your children with you," I said as I followed my sister up the stairs of our house. I could see from how closely her riding habit fit that she'd regained her neat figure after giving birth to her second child the previous November. "I've yet to welcome little Catherine."

"You'd hear little Catherine before you would see her," Angelica said. "She's a dear little creature, but colicky as the wind itself, which can make her a trial. I cannot imagine traveling with her at this season, nor taking her from her nurse to come traipsing off to an army encampment. She's much better off in Boston with her brother and John. I shall bring her home with me this summer, and you shall meet her then."

This was a pretty story, but I suspected it was more likely that her husband had preferred to remain in Boston and avoid my parents. Although both parties had finally been brought to a reconciliation, it was an uneasy connection at best. I'd hoped that Angelica's naming the new baby after Mamma would lessen some of the tension, but that rapprochement wouldn't occur if Angelica didn't bring the child to Mamma for her blessing.

"How does Mr. Carter?" I asked. "Is he well?"

"John is always well," she said, "and always prospering. It is his nature to do so."

That was certainly true. One of the reasons that Papa disliked Mr. Carter was his uncanny ability to increase his fortune from the vagaries of the war, while most men had seen theirs decline. "You're brave to travel so far without him."

"It's only brave when a woman does it, Eliza," she said. "No one thinks twice of a gentleman making a similar trip. I made the journey in the company of several of John's associates, and never once felt frightened or ill at ease."

She paused in the doorway to survey the bedchamber under the eaves that had been mine alone until now. Her trunks had already been brought upstairs, and stood waiting on the floor to be unpacked.

"So I see we shall share a room once again, Eliza, and a bed with it," she said, walking the length and breadth of the small room in a few quick steps. "Will you share your secrets again as well, dear sister? Will you tell me everything in your heart, as you used to do when we were girls?"

She smiled at me and turned about quickly, making the petticoats of her scarlet riding habit flare dramatically around her ankles. But then, that was how Angelica did most everything, with drama and a perfect confidence that all others about her were watching. They did, too, for she was impossible to ignore. She was a fraction taller than I (or appeared that way) and handsome rather than beautiful, but it was her style, her wit, and intelligence that drew others to her.

When Angelica had showed promise as a child, Papa had obtained a tutor for her as if she were a boy, and she had learned to speak French like a Parisian, read Latin like an Oxford don, and could discourse with ease on male topics such as politics and economics. She had always aspired to be one of the accomplished ladies in London and Paris who attracted brilliant company to their drawing rooms, whilst I had always held humble aspirations, dreaming instead of a house filled with laughing children rather than philosophers.

I will, however, hasten to note that there was never any animosity between us, despite what scandal-mongers later whispered. We were as different as sisters could be, yet still we loved each other with the warmest bonds of our blood. Only a year separated us, yet Angelica had always played the role of older sister to the hilt— though to be honest, I'd been equally content to stand starry-eyed in her grandiloquent shadow.

But on that April afternoon, I gave no thought to any of that. I was only happy to have Angelica before me.

"Much has changed in our lives since you left to marry," I said, which was true. I had been nineteen when she'd eloped, and was twenty-two now, and at that age three years seems an eternity. "I cannot even recall what secrets we exchanged beneath the coverlet at night."

"Which proves how closely we kept them." She pulled off her black hat, cocked like a man's, and shook the raindrops from it as she sat on the edge of the bed. "But I care more for the present than the past, Eliza. Come, and tell me of the dashing and splendid Colonel Hamilton."

She stripped off her yellow kid gloves and straightened her gold rings, two on one hand and three on the other, another sign of her husband's wealth. She patted the coverlet invitingly, and I happily sat beside her.

"I've told you most everything in my letters," I began. I folded my hands in my lap, then consciously drew them apart. I'd forgotten how being in Angelica's company could make me feel a bit prim, and I was determined not to do it again. "Colonel Hamilton is handsome and clever and more charming than any gentleman I've ever met."

"Oh, Eliza." She clucked her tongue with mock dismay, and tipped her head to one side, her dangling gold earring swinging lightly against her cheek. "Mamma has told me that much. I'd hoped you would share something regarding the colonel that only you would know."

I nodded solemnly. It wasn't that I couldn't think of any of the special qualities that I alone saw in him—his kindness, his gentleness, his laugh, the way he'd caress my breast above my gown and how he'd kiss me until I was breathless, and a hundred other things besides. But I realized that to share these little endearments would take something from the love we shared. I now owed my allegiance to Alexander, not to my sister, and I volunteered nothing.

"That is all, Eliza?" she said, disappointed. "Is the gentleman so much a saint that he hasn't a single quirk or foible?"

Still I kept silent, with only the April rain drumming once against the window.

"Well, then, a saint he must be," Angelica said with resignation. "I shall be forced to judge him for myself."

That resignation made me feel guilty, and at last I spoke.

"Kitty Livingston says he is too charming by half," I said, "which leads him to make fast friends, but also lasting enemies."

"That's scarcely a flaw," Angelica said thoughtfully, shifting her weight to sit more thoroughly on the bed. She had a way of scowling that made her appear as if she were sitting in judgment, and to see that scowl now made me uneasy for Alexander's sake.

"I don't believe it is, either," I said bravely. "But Kitty said it, and she has known him longer than I."

"Yes, but Kitty Livingston is also something of a fool," Angelica said succinctly. "The fellow who makes no enemies usually has only boon companions in place of real friends. To have both enemies and friends proves the colonel to be a man of convictions and beliefs. He sounds quite intriguing."

"Oh, he is, Angelica, he is!" I exclaimed with relief. "I'm certain you will like him. I've spoken often of you to him, and he is eager to make your acquaintance, too. If he can be spared by His Excellency, he'll call here this evening, after we dine."

"I'm sure we shall become fast friends," she said, and smiled slowly, her dark eyes watching me shrewdly. "You're mad in love with him, aren't you, Eliza? It's painted bold across your face."

Her smile was so filled with affection that I realized all over again how much I'd missed her, and how glad I was to have her here now.

"I *am* mad in love with him," I declared boldly, borrowing her phrase. "I don't care if the whole of Christendom knows it, too."

"I'm glad, because the whole of Christendom will see it at once," she said. "I always kept your secrets, Eliza, but you never could keep one from me. Now bring on your pretty colonel, and let me decide if he is worthy of you."

CHAPTER 7

As eager as I was for Alexander and my sister to meet, circumstances—and the dignitaries from abroad—prohibited it for several days after Angelica's arrival. He was in demand at headquarters from the moment he rose in the morning until whenever His Excellency finally released him at night, which was late indeed.

One of Alexander's most valuable talents was his fluency in the French language. His late mother had spoken little else to him as a child, and as a result he could not only converse with the nuance of a native Frenchman, but also compose letters and other written documents with ease. Almost sheepishly, he claimed that he'd no real separation between English and French in his thoughts, and that one language was much the same as the other to him.

To me who spoke only English and a smattering of Dutch learned from older relatives and from church, Alexander's facility in French was a marvel, and another mark of his genius. To His Excellency, however, who likewise spoke only English, it was an imperative.

While the French ambassador had brought an interpreter with his people, wisdom dictated that each party have their own for the sake of impartiality. Alexander served as interpreter for the Americans. But the French interpreter proved more familiar with the strict English spoken in London palaces, and found our rustic version difficult to comprehend. Alexander was called upon to answer every conceivable question for the visitors, from describing the assorted rifles and muskets employed by our troops to explaining the humble fare that His Excellency was forced by necessity (and to his embarrassment as a host) to serve his exalted guests.

But Alexander was employed for a more somber occasion, too. Joining the French minister was Don Juan de Miralles, a gentleman of distinction from Spain who was likewise interested in the American cause. Alas, poor man, he was stricken with a severe biliary complaint that defied the best efforts of the surgeons to relieve, and after great suffering, he perished in his bed at the headquarters. In his last hours, Alexander was able to offer him words of comfort and sympathy in his native tongue.

When he described this sad scene to me later, I expressed my surprise that he spoke Spanish as well as French.

"It's not often of use here in New Jersey," he said with a cavalier shrug, as if yet one more singular accomplishment meant nothing. "When I was a boy, I took my first studies with the Sephardim children on our island, and from them I learned Spanish, and Hebrew besides. If His Excellency ever entertains an emmisary from the Levant, I'll doubtless be called into service then, too."

"Wasn't there a Christian school for you to attend instead?" I asked in my innocent ignorance.

"There was," he said evenly. "But because my parents weren't married, I wasn't permitted admission to the Anglican school."

I gasped with indignation on his behalf. "How un-Christian of them! To punish a child for the sins of the father!"

"Since my father was no longer in evidence, I suspect it was more the sins of my poor mother that they wished to punish," he said. "The Sephardim were considerably more forgiving."

As always whenever he revealed more about himself, I listened in fascination, and pity for the outcast little boy he'd once been. It was as much about how he spoke, however, as what he said: without any shame or regret, but simply as a matter of fact. Other men would have buried such a childhood behind half-truths or not mentioned it at all, but Alexander didn't do that. He swore that he cherished the truth, and there was no finer example of his honesty and lack of any perfidy than this. No wonder I loved him all the more for it.

While I didn't share all of his past with Angelica (that was his to tell, not mine), my proud description of his learned accomplishments only increased her impatience to meet him. I was every bit as eager, for I longed for these two whom I loved so dearly to be as pleased with each other as any true sister and brother might be. I felt sure it must happen, with even Fate conspiring by making their names so similar: Angelica and Alexander, both beginning with the same letter and with the same number of syllables.

Yet when at last they came together in the same place, it wasn't in our house, and it wasn't nearly as fortuitous as I'd hoped. Instead this fateful meeting occurred outside the chamber shared by His Excellency and Lady Washington, and where that good lady received her friends and acquaintances. Since I'd arrived in Morristown, I'd been honored to become a regular visitor. Each week, I joined my mother, my aunt, and Lady Washington as we sat with our handwork and conversed genteelly, pretending we were still in our own neat drawing rooms in our various homes and not in a military encampment.

It was my mother's idea to include Angelica, so she, too, might pay her respects to His Excellency's wife. Now my sister was not given overmuch to needlework, but she did wish to be presented to Lady Washington as the first lady of our young country. Angelica was also vastly amused at the notion of visiting headquarters, where the men so outnumbered us women, though she was also wise enough not to voice it to our mother. I was myself always conscious of that fact, and took extra care with the neatness of my dress because of it whenever I visited Mrs. Ford's house.

There was no mistaking my sister's love of an admiring male audience as she swept through the front yard to the house in her bright red habit. Angelica had countless ways to draw the male eye, small gestures and mannerisms that made her impossible to ignore, exactly as she wished. I couldn't begin to emulate her, nor, really, did I desire that kind of attention, but it was a wonder to watch her effect on most every soldier and officer we passed.

"How cheerful everyone is, Eliza," she said to me as we sat waiting on the bench outside Lady Washington's chamber. "From your letters, I thought all I'd see were long faces and grim miens, but everyone here is exceptionally agreeable."

"Hush, Angelica, not so loud," Mamma said mildly, not truly

scolding. "Recall how I cautioned you to be discreet. In these close quarters, everything you say here may be heard, and repeated."

Angelica smiled, unperturbed, as she smoothed the leather of her gloves. "I only said that everyone was exceptionally agreeable, and where's the harm in that?"

"There isn't any," I said, daring to agree with my sister over our mother. "Not at all."

Mamma only sighed and shook her head with the resignation of mothers with grown daughters. But I didn't care, for I was more occupied in glancing about at the usual crowd of officers, visitors, waiters, and servants that crowded the upper hall, hunting for Alexander. Word spread quickly through the house whenever I called on Lady Washington, and if Alexander could be spared from his duties, he'd appear as surely as if I'd summoned him myself.

Today was no exception. As soon as I saw his familiar golden-red hair (glossy with pomade and clubbed with a black bow, but not powdered) appear over the edge of the landing as he bounded up the stairs, I smiled, and I was smiling still as he hurried toward us. He was looking exceptionally handsome today, dressed in the new uniform he'd recently had made. His Excellency liked his Family to be as spruce in their attire as he was himself, and he'd grown so unhappy with the motley state of his aides' uniforms after the winter that he'd had a tailor brought to the camp from Philadelphia for a general refurbishing. Now Alexander stood resplendent in a new blue and buff coat with double gilt buttons and epaulets, fresh breeches and waistcoat of cream-colored corded dimity, and the light green sash of an aide-de-camp. He cut the very figure, and I could tell from the way that my sister drew back her own shoulders beside me that she'd taken notice, too.

"Mrs. Schuyler, your servant, madam," Alexander said as he bowed dutifully before my mother, always taking care to address her first.

He turned next to me, his eyes instantly so full of love that I felt it as surely as if he'd embraced me outright.

"Miss Elizabeth, my own," he said softly, taking my hand and lightly pressing my fingers. That was all he said, and all he needed to say. There was nothing sweeter to my ears than my name on his lips, and I loved that he wasn't embarrassed by showing affection to me here at headquarters the way many men would have been.

"We're here to call upon Lady Washington," I said, my own voice turning breathless as it did whenever he was near, even whilst delivering this most mundane explanation. I was so rapt in the simple pleasure of his nearness that I nearly forgot my sister's presence beside me, and would have, too, if she hadn't shifted pointedly beside me as a reminder.

"Colonel Hamilton, may I present my sister, Mrs. John Carter?" I said. "Angelica, Colonel Hamilton."

My sister held her hand up to him, and reluctantly he abandoned mine to take hers. But before he spoke, she addressed him first, and to my enormous surprise, she did so in French.

"*Enfin, enfin, le fameux colonel Hamilton!*" she said, her chin raised at the perfect beguiling angle. "*Je vous ai tellement entendu parler des lettres de ma soeur, que j'ai l'impression de vous connaître déjà.*"

He frowned, yet he answered her in kind, without the slightest hesitation.

"*Bonjour, madame,*" he said, bowing over her hand. "*Que je suis enchanté et honoré de faire la connaissance de la soeur de ma belle, bien-aimée Eliza.*"

I stared, speechless. I could comprehend his name and my own, but beyond that none of what they said meant anything to me. My sister was beaming at Alexander as if this were all delightful, while Alexander continued to frown politely, if such a thing were possible. What *had* she said to him? How had he replied? I'd never before given much thought to learning French or any other foreign language—I'd not the patience for it—but in that moment I would have given much to have been able to understand what had just occurred. Uncertainly I glanced from my sister to Alexander and back again, desperate for any clues as to the meaning of their conversation.

"*Je comprends tout à fait pourquoi ma petite soeur est si dévouée à vous, monsieur.*" Angelica delicately slipped her hand free from his and with her fingers smoothed a lock of her dark hair (which did not require smoothing) around her ear. "*Votre charme ne connaît aucune limite! Quelle chance—*"

"In English, Angelica, if you please," Mamma interrupted with a touch of irritation. "My grasp of French is slight, and not so firm as once it was."

"Pray forgive me, madam, I'd no intention of being so ill-mannered," Alexander said contritely as he bowed again to my mother. "When Mrs. Carter addressed me in that language, I returned her compliment without thinking. It was barbarously wrong of me—"

"It was wrong of *me*, Mamma, and I claim full blame," Angelica said, though with none of Alexander's contrition. "I should not have led Colonel Hamilton into that impolite snare."

Now I wondered exactly what he had said that required so much apologizing, that he called "barbarously wrong" and she described as "impolite," with my name in the middle of it.

"Forgive me, Mrs. Schuyler, I am the one, and not Mrs. Carter, who is entirely at fault," Alexander began again. I knew how much he valued my mother's good regard, and her rebuke, mild as it had been and in no way intended toward him, must have cut him to the quick. His usual ease in company had deserted him, and his cheeks had turned endearingly pink, the curse of his fair complexion. "There was nothing impolite in our conversation. That is, ah, I am certain—"

"No one is to blame for anything," I said quickly, rescuing him and absolving them both, even as my own confusion continued. "What pleases me is that you discovered so much in common worthy of conversation."

"What we have in common, my dear little goose, is you," Angelica said, looping her arm fondly into mine. "I told Colonel Hamilton that because of your letters, I felt as if I knew him already, and he in turn told me how honored he was to meet at last the sister of his beautiful, beloved Eliza."

I glanced quickly back to Alexander, my own cheeks growing warm. How could I have ever doubted him? "You said that of me?"

"*Ma belle, bien-aimée Eliza,*" he repeated solemnly, his gaze beseeching. "My beautiful, beloved Eliza."

"Ohhh," I sighed, overwhelmed to hear such a sentiment, in French and in English, here in the middle of the busy hall. "Oh, Alexander."

At once all was forgiven, if there was in fact anything to forgive, which there hadn't been. Even then, before we were wed, I found it nearly impossible to be unhappy with him.

True, it was hardly the first meeting I'd envisioned for my sister and Alexander, but when he called upon us later that evening, the general conversation proceeded much more smoothly, and without any French confusion, either. This could have been because my father was there as well, guiding matters with his usual forthright direction, or because both Alexander and Angelica had each resolved to do better. Whatever the case, by the evening's end they seemed quite amiable toward each other, and yet I wanted to be sure. I could barely wait until the rest of my family retired so I could ask him in private before we said our farewells.

"Did you like my sister?" I asked at once. "I know she surprised you earlier by addressing you in French, but I hope you can forgive her that."

He smiled. "Of course I can forgive her," he said. "She caught me off guard, that was all."

"But you do like her?" I asked again, more anxiously this time. We were standing outside the front door, on the worn old round millstone that served as the house's front step.

"I do," he said, though with a shade more reserve than I could have hoped. "She's charming company. Is her husband not with her?"

"Not here, no," I said. "Mr. Carter is a quiet gentleman, much occupied with his business. He also does not always see eye to eye with my father, and it is often better for all parties that she visits us without him."

He nodded, his face thrown into sharp shadow by the small lantern that hung outside the door.

"Mr. Carter doesn't see eye to eye with many men," he said. "You know I find him agreeable, but in some circles his habit of selling supplies to whomever will pay the most makes him as much loved as a usurer."

I sighed, for it could be difficult to defend Mr. Carter. "My sister says he does very well by the trade."

"I'm sure he does," Alexander said dryly. "He has that ability."

I nodded again, wondering how I'd been cast in the unsavory role of apologist for my brother-in-law. "Angelica says Papa was more unhappy with Mr. Carter's reasons for coming to New York on account of an unfortunate affair in London."

"I heard it was a duel," Alexander said. "With a member of Parliament. Not that I can fault him for that."

"Hush," I said softly, resting my palms lightly on his chest. I'd heard that rumor, too, but Angelica had brushed it aside with disdain when I'd asked her about it, so I doubted it was true. "I don't wish to discuss him any further. What I want to know is whether or not you believe you can be friends with my sister."

"Of course I can," he said, now without his earlier hesitation. "Mrs. Carter is witty and amusing, with thoughts of her own and the intelligence to defend them. She is well-read for anyone, man or woman. I never thought to discuss *Common Sense* and Thomas Paine before your father's hearth, especially not with a woman as handsome as your sister. It was quite remarkable."

"So you do like her?" I asked, daring to hope. I had sat by in silence and listened (and marveled, too, at the cleverness of their arguments) as the two of them had sparred in words, and in the end I hadn't been certain if Alexander had enjoyed the exchange or not. "Truly? It matters much to me that you do, Alexander, and that she likes you in return, almost as much as my parents' approval."

"I do," he said. "She will make a most diverting sister-in-law."

I wasn't certain that *diverting* was the word I would have preferred.

"She has many excellent qualities," I said earnestly. "You'll soon see how loyal she can be. She made this long journey to Morristown for my sake, just to make certain you were worthy of me."

He laughed, slipping his arms around my waist. "Ah, so here's the truth, then. You're more concerned with her verdict regarding me than mine of her."

"Alexander, please," I said. "Be serious."

"Very well, then," he said, making a show of composing his face into the picture of grim severity. "I liked your sister very much, and I look forward to learning more of her in the future. She's very different from you."

"She's much wiser than I," I said.

"She reads and studies more than you," he said, "but that makes her bookish and intellectual, not wise. You, my dear Betsey, are wise in the ways that matter."

I refused to believe he was serious. "She speaks French."

"Yes, she does," he said mildly. "But I'd wager a hundred dollars that she learned it not because French is the language of diplomacy and King Louis's court, but because it's also the language of flirtation and seduction."

He'd seen so much more of the world than I, to know such things! I was glad he couldn't see me blush, not only for myself, but for my sister.

"I don't know what Angelica said to you today, but she didn't mean it, not that—that way," I said. "It's simply her manner. She is accustomed to attention from everyone, gentlemen and ladies alike. She's been that way since we were girls."

"I understand that now," he said, pulling me closer. "But it's also proof that you're the wiser sister."

I shook my head, looking down at my hands on the blue woolen of his blue coat, the long rows of brass buttons winking dully in the moonlight.

"There's more to wisdom than a library filled with books," he said softly. "You're gentle and kind and patient, Betsey, and filled with reason and sound judgment. You're loyal and honorable, and you always consider others before yourself. Even when it's your selfish sister."

"She's not selfish, Alexander," I began, but how he tipped his head to one side proved that he was right.

"You would never leave our children behind, as she has done with hers," he said. "Not when they're so young, so fragile."

"No," I said wistfully, ashamed for Angelica's sake.

"Nor would you ever speak as freely to Carter as she did today to me," he said, leaning closer over me. "Not in French, or English, or any other language in creation."

"She's my sister," I repeated helplessly, hoping that would be explanation enough.

I don't believe he cared.

"*Mon sage petit hibou*," he whispered, brushing his lips over mine.

Breathlessly I turned aside. "What did you just say?"

He smiled. "I called you my wise little owl."

"An *owl*?" I wrinkled my nose, picturing the heavyset predatory owls who hunted mice in the barns at home. "I thought you said that French is the language of love."

"It is," he said, his voice low and dark as he pressed me back against the door to kiss me. "*Je t'aime au-delà de tous les autres, ma belle, bien-aimée, ma Eliza.*"

And without knowing a word, I understood.

As the days grew longer and warmer, the army—or what remained of it—began to return to life, like a great slumbering bear after a long winter. The soldiers drilled with more purpose, openly eager to challenge the enemy again. All of Jockey Hollow buzzed with rumors of when the camp would break for summer, and where the various regiments would be sent next to meet the British in battle. The next campaign could be a counter to the siege of Charleston to the south, through Virginia and Georgia. Each day brought more tales from Congress's meetings in Philadelphia, from spies across the Hudson in New York, from letters from Georgia and Carolina. All carried stories of more British troops arriving, of more guns, more cannon, for the sole purpose of finally bringing an end to the war.

The most popular rumor, however, had the Continental Army waiting until the French troops landed in Rhode Island, and then joining with them in an attack upon the city of New York, across the Hudson River. Part of this plan (or so it was said) also involved the defense of the fortifications farther up the river at West Point— which by curious coincidence was the same West Point that my father was urging as an appointment and fresh start for the disgraced General Arnold.

The only thing that anyone seemed to agree upon was that things would change, and soon, and that the war would begin anew. The British general Henry Clinton had completed his triumphal victory over Charleston, and was reported to be sailing back to New York with a large company of troops. Emboldened by this news, small groups of British soldiers from New York were already to be seen in New Jersey, launching small attacks on the populace that were meant to draw His Excellency out of Morristown earlier than planned.

So far these small attacks had been contained by local militiamen, but those of us still in Morristown became more and more ill at ease as the attacks grew closer to the encampment. Few civilians wished to find themselves in the middle of a campaign. One by one, the wives and families of officers who had wintered with us in hired houses packed up their belongings, bid their husbands and friends farewell, and began their long journeys back to their homes, scattered across every colony.

As a general's wife, Mamma had witnessed this before, and she was determined to stay with my father here at the camp until, as she said, she could see soldiers marching to battle from her front door. Lady Washington and Aunt Gertrude likewise took this forthright stance, the three older ladies standing confidently beside their husbands as our little community shrank around us. We now also had an additional sentinel at our house posted to guard both front and back doors, and Mamma and I did not go about the town without the company of at least one soldier. I'm not certain if this was an order from His Excellency, or a request by my father. Mamma, Angelica, and I understood, and we did not complain. Because of Papa, we would have made valuable prisoners had we been captured.

It went without saying that I, too, remained in Morristown, relishing every moment that Alexander could spare for me. I pressed him as much as I could for more information on the army's plans for the summer, but even though he wrote and read all of His Excellency's orders and letters, he couldn't offer any more definite news than anyone else did. It truly did seem that the army's movements were the proverbial game of cat and mouse. His Excellency possessed neither the men nor munitions to strike as he might choose. Instead he was forced to wait and watch, and then react to whatever the British did first.

Angelica remained with us until late May, long enough to attend the last assembly held in honor of the French ambassadors. But finally she, too, began to worry that she might become separated from her children for the entire summer, and made arrangements with her husband's people to return to her home in Boston.

We took one final stroll about the little town on day before she left. It was odd to see how much it had changed in the last weeks. The original owners of the houses that had been leased to the army had now returned to Morristown with their families, and were busily planting new gardens and making repairs to their properties after the long winter. To them, we represented the army and all its inconveniences and hazards, and they made no effort to acknowledge us except as unwelcome interlopers, soon to be gone. We missed the familiar faces that we'd come to know so well these last months, and the town that had earlier felt like another home now had nothing but strangers to it.

No wonder, then, that Angelica and I walked closely together on that last afternoon, our arms linked and our heads bowed beneath our wide-brimmed straw hats, and our guard following at a respectful distance behind. I was going to miss my sister mightily, and though we promised we'd soon meet again later in the summer at our parents' house, we were both acutely aware of how our plans could be overturned at any time by the war. Most of what we'd had to say to each other had already been said, and we walked largely in companionable though melancholy silence.

"With weather this fine, you should be home in time to see the roses behind your house bloom," I said as we passed a garden with bushes already in bud. "There were snow-filled days this winter that I doubted I'd ever see flowers of any sort again."

"Marry Hamilton," she said suddenly. "Now, as soon as it can be arranged. Don't wait any longer than you must."

I stopped walking to face her, and she stopped, too.

"Angelica, please," I said. "You know we're to wed in December, when he can arrange for sufficient leave."

"And I say to wait so long is to tempt the very Fates," she said, her expression uncharacteristically somber. "I've considered this with great care, Eliza, else I wouldn't have spoken now. Marry Hamilton now, while you can."

I sighed unhappily, for in my heart I agreed with everything she said. "Why do you torment me by saying such things now?"

"I don't intend to torment you," she said, resuming our walk at a slow and measured pace. "It's what the men are saying now, of how they cannot wait to go back to war and fighting, and—and I do not wish any misfortune to befall your dear Hamilton before you've become his wife."

"Do you believe I've not thought that for myself?" I was kicking my petticoats forward with each step, venting my fear and frustration on the new grass. "Each time I bid him good night I wonder if it will be the last. You know as well as I how perilous and sudden a soldier's life can be, and I worry constantly on his behalf."

She nodded, her face mirroring my own beneath the sweeping shadow of her hat's brim. In the last weeks, she and Alexander had developed a considerable regard for each other as a true brother and sister might, and exactly as I'd hoped they would. True, that undercurrent of flirtation that Alexander had first noted occasionally reappeared on Angelica's side, but because I knew it meant nothing, I took little notice of it, and he soon learned to deflect it with practiced ease. But that same regard meant that she shared my concern for his welfare, and that it was genuine.

"I worry for him, too," she said. "He is still so young a gentleman, with so much brilliance and promise but at the same time impetuous to a fault. As long as he remains an aide-de-camp to His Excellency, I suppose he's as safe as any soldier can be."

"But all he wishes is another command, and another chance to prove his bravery and courage with no regard for his own safety," I said, my voice breaking with emotion. "It need not even be in battle, Angelica. His blue coat could be spied by some lone British scout, and he'd be shot before he even realized it, and then—"

My sister handed me her handkerchief. "That is why you must marry him now, Eliza, to guarantee you'll have some measure of happiness, however brief."

"What, run off and wed as you did?" I asked, blotting the tears from my eyes. "You know I cannot do that, Angelica, not after I promised our parents we'd marry in Albany. Especially not now, when Mamma hasn't been well. I wouldn't break my word to her, or to Papa, either."

Angelica raised her brows. "Don't you realize the cause of Mamma's illness?"

"She says it's from having eaten so poorly, and I cannot disagree."

"She's told me otherwise," Angelica said. "She believes she's with child again. She came here to comfort Papa, and I suppose she has."

"Angelica, please," I said, shocked she'd be so frank about our parents. But the more I considered what she'd said, the more I realized it was true. My mother had given birth to fourteen children (seven of whom still lived) during her marriage, and by now all in our family recognized the signs of another imminent brother or sister. But Mamma was nearly forty-seven years old, a considerable age for child-bearing, and I prayed both she and the babe would survive the extended ordeal of pregnancy and childbirth.

"You shouldn't be surprised," my sister said, misinterpreting my reaction. "Mamma and Papa have always been ruled by their hearts and sentiments. Recall that I was born a scant five months after they wed."

Of course I recalled it. The dates of my parents' wedding and Angelica's birth were noted in both our family's Bible and our church's registry, with no effort ever made to alter them toward more respectability. I suppose that given the lofty stature of the Schuylers and the Van Rensselaers, they had simply stood above any whispers of scandal, high and haughty, and ignored it.

"They were much younger then," I said, striving for an explanation. "They both say they were much in love, too."

"Mamma was the same age as you are now," Angelica said. "Which is why again I press you to marry, even if in secret, before you return to Albany."

I stopped again, my cheeks scarlet. "You believe that I have already granted Alexander a husband's favors?"

She didn't blush at all. "I would be surprised if it were otherwise," she said bluntly. "Strong passions run in our family, Eliza, among the ladies as well as the gentlemen, and we're a remarkably fecund lot. Consider that my dear little Philip was born scarce ten months after I wed John."

"How you and Mr. Carter have been blessed is of no affair to me, Angelica," I protested.

"It should be," she said shrewdly. "I see it in your eyes whenever Alexander enters the room. Given his formidable reputation as a gallant with other women before he met you—"

"We haven't," I said, unable to bear her assumptions any longer. "I have granted him certain—certain liberties from the love I have for him, but not the last. It was his decision, too. Because his own parents were not wed, he refuses to risk the same shame for me, or for any child of ours."

"He said that?" She was clearly surprised, though without any good reason that I could see. "Alexander has many excellent qualities, to be sure, but I hadn't thought him to be a gentleman of such high and fastidious honor."

"Why shouldn't you think well of him?" I said in warm defense. The truth was that I'd been as eager in offering those liberties to my person as he'd been in claiming them: proof enough of how noble he truly was not to press for the final one. "Has he ever given you indication that he is anything less than a gentleman? Has he ever shown evidence before you of dishonorable intentions?"

"Have I ever accused him of those things?" she asked with maddening innocence.

"Even now you have done exactly that by implication!"

"Then may I offer my most heartfelt apology, Eliza, for it was never intended that way," Angelica said. "All I wish for you both is that your marriage, whenever it occurs, is a long and happy one."

Her apology was so abject and her manner so soothing that I'd no choice but to accept it, especially on the last day we were together. That was my sister's nature: as Papa said, she could be the first to jab a stick into a bee's nest, but she was also equally quick to calm the insult with a ladle of honeyed sweetness.

I gave one final sniff by way of acceptance, and returned her handkerchief, wet with my tears.

"I'm not entirely blind by love," I conceded. "I'll grant you that my Alexander is like every other man, and not without his flaws. He worries overmuch that he is beneath me, and can become impatient when he cannot achieve his goals as quickly as he wishes. He believes himself too slight compared to other more sizable soldiers, and he's not as pious as I might wish for the sake of his Christian soul. But he is honorable and generous and surpassing kind, and the most honest gentleman I've ever known. I know in my heart that he will never lie to me, and few other women can say that of the men they marry."

But if I expected Angelica to agree with me for the sake of sisterly cheer, I was sadly disappointed. Instead her face grew serious, even wary.

"Do not say that of him, Eliza, I beg you," she said. "That he is honorable and generous and kind to you I will not deny, but there is no mortal man who is entirely honest."

Although ordinarily my first reaction to this would be to fly to my love's defense, there was this time a cautionary directness to Angelica's manner that stopped me, and made me take note, even as I tried to divert it.

"Perhaps that can be said of your husband," I said, hedging. "But I don't believe my Alexander is cut of that particular cloth."

"But he is, Eliza," she said softly. "They're both brilliant, worldly men, and determined to make the most for themselves of what life presents. We wouldn't find them so fascinating if they weren't."

Still I shook my head, unable to reconcile Alexander's glorious dreams for the country with Mr. Carter's more mercenary trading.

But Angelica would not be deterred. "I cannot stop you from trusting him, Eliza, nor do I wish to," she said. "All I ask is that you not trust too much, and guard yourself. Oh, he may not lie to you outright, but I assure you that in the course of your marriage there will be omissions that he'll justify and half-truths that he'll dismiss. Some shall make you laugh and others, alas, may make you weep."

I made a great show of untying and then retying the long silk pink ribbons on my hat, snugging them close along the nape of my neck below the bottom of the cap, as if this deliberate tidiness would resolve the unsettling questions that my sister now raised. I remembered how Kitty Livingston had cautioned me regarding Alexander's ambition and habits, and now here was Angelica doing the same. I respected them both, and I'd be a stubborn fool if I didn't at least consider and weigh what they'd said.

And yet I thought also of the look in Alexander's eyes when he kissed me, how when he held me I felt as if I were the most cherished of women, how he said he loved and trusted me above all others. I remembered how he had sworn he'd only make me cry from joy, never from pain or sorrow, and I believed him now as I'd believed him then. Surely a vow such as that must account for something. Surely if he loved me as I knew he did, he would not lie or tell me half-truths, as Angelica predicted. He wished me by his side always, our lives combined into a single shared future.

No, not my Alexander.

I turned to head back to our house, the late afternoon sun now bright in my face, and I looked upward to feel its warmth on my cheeks.

"All I ask is that you take care, Eliza," Angelica said, falling into step beside me. "I pray that you and Hamilton will be the happiest and most blessed couple under Heaven, and all of this will fade away as an unnecessary caution, unneeded and long forgotten."

"Thank you, Angelica," I said, brushing aside my hat's ribbons as they blew across my shoulder in the breeze. "I will take care, as you wish, even though I don't doubt Alexander's love for me."

She nodded, but with resignation, not agreement.

"That's all I would ever dare ask of you," she said. "But remember, dear sister, that the easiest men for us to love are often the same ones who hurt us the most."

CHAPTER 8

Albany, New York
July 1780

It was Papa's decision that Mamma and I return to Albany in the middle of June. This was the same time that Lady Washington had chosen for her departure from the encampment, too, making it an obvious, and seemly, choice. Because Mamma was unwell, in her stead I oversaw the servants packing our belongings and (not wanting the owners of our hired house to think ill of our housekeeping) giving the house a thorough cleaning before we left it.

Most of all, I resigned myself to the inevitable separation from Alexander, with my only consolation coming from the fact that the army remained mired in Morristown, with no summer campaign as yet decided, let alone begun. Although Alexander was as restless as every other man still in the camp, I secretly rejoiced, grateful that the lack of fighting preserved him from danger.

Until, that is, the seventh morning in the first week of June.

Dawn came early, as it does in June, and already the sky was a brilliant blue with only the merest puffs of snowy clouds along the horizon. If I'd been home in Albany, this would have been a perfect day for the languid pursuits of early summer: a walk in the shade beneath the fruit trees in the orchard, or picking strawberries warm and sweet from the sun, or perhaps a row in a skiff on the pond.

But this was 1780, not 1770, and I wasn't at my parents' house, but instead in Lady Washington's chamber in headquarters. Early as it was, I'd known she'd be awake and already at her day's business; His Excellency himself never lay abed past dawn, and his entire Family took their cue from his habits. I'd been sent here by my mother, who was suffering mightily from her queasy belly. Two days before, Lady Washington had offered Mamma a special elixir of peppermint from her own recipe by way of relief, and from respect for Lady Washington's station and generosity, I'd come to collect the bottle myself instead of sending a servant.

While I waited for Lady Washington to decant the elixir in her closet, I sat beside the open window, halfheartedly watching the soldier who'd escorted me here and another man throwing a stick for a spotted dog in the front yard. The sentry at the front door—by now I recognized all of them, and they me—had told me that His Excellency was meeting in his office with his aides-de-camp. I'd hoped to steal a hasty moment or two with Alexander, but if he were already deep embroiled in the general's work of the day, then he likely wouldn't be free until this evening, if then.

As I watched, the soldier who'd been my escort suddenly turned, staring down the road with the stick now forgotten in his hand. Seeing him look, the other soldier turned, too, leaving the dog to dance impatiently between them. Now I, too, could hear the sound of an approaching horse, its rider spurring onward toward the house. The rider was dressed in the makeshift uniform of a New Jersey militiaman, and he'd ridden hard, and in great haste. The horse's sides were flecked with foam and the man's clothes were stained with gunpowder, grime, and sweat, and when he reached the house, he slid swiftly from the saddle, tossed the reins to a bystander, and ran to the front door.

I leaned from the window, curious to hear what news the man was bringing. Alas, he kept his voice too low for me to overhear, yet whatever he said to the sentries was important enough for him to be swiftly ushered into the house. The news likewise sent a ripple of excitement through the house, audible in the rise in men's voices, their hurried steps across the floorboards, and doors opening and shutting. The men out of doors were shouting, too, calling back and forth to one another as they rushed this way and that with fresh purpose, while even the dog, too, ran back and forth, barking loudly with the same excitement.

"What a prodigious racketing!" Lady Washington exclaimed as she returned to the chamber with the bottled elixir. "Whose dog is that?"

"I don't know, madam." I rose swiftly from the chair, determined to learn more. After so many months of inactivity for the army at the camp, the excitement was contagious, and I hurried across the room toward the doorway. "But a militiaman has only just arrived in great haste with some sort of news for His Excellency. Permit me to go learn more so that we might—"

"Thank you, Eliza, but such an alarm is neither necessary, nor proper," Lady Washington said. "We shall learn the news when the gentlemen decide to share it with us."

I stopped, but my excitement still raced on. Surely all those raised voices around us must be signs of celebration! "But what if there's been a great victory, madam? What if—"

"Hush, Eliza, and calm yourself." She didn't raise her voice, but the firm dignity of her tone made it impossible to ignore. "You're the daughter of a general, and you intend to marry another officer. You know as well as I that it is not our place to meddle in the military affairs. If the news pertains to us, then we shall be told in due time, and not before."

I dropped my hands to my sides, instantly sobered by her experience and wisdom, and feeling myself a young and giddy fool. Why had I let myself be carried away, and assume a victory—or even a battle or skirmish—simply because I'd heard the excitement of others? Papa had always cautioned us that this was precisely how wartime rumors began, born of half-truths, misread observations, and wishful thinking, and here I'd been no better than the rest. What sorry kind of wife would I make to Alexander, with thoughts as distracted as these?

Yet Lady Washington continued as if nothing at all were amiss, as if the men's voices growing louder and more insistent in the house and in the yard were only a mere inconvenience.

"Instruct your mother to take three drops of this mixed in a dish of weak tea," she said, pressing the little bottle into my hand. "She may sip the tea if that is less taxing to her, but she must finish it if she is to achieve relief."

She covered my hand with her own, not only to make sure that in my agitation I would not drop it, but also to comfort me.

"There is nothing to be gained by fretting and fussing over the matters we have no power to effect, my dear," she said gently, her plump, small hand remaining over mine. "We must be brave, and we must be strong. It's far better to place our faith and prayers in God, and our trust in the men whom we love to do what is right."

Her smile was warm but there was an undeniable tension around the corners, and I realized then that she knew exactly what was happening, and exactly what I had been denying to myself for Alexander's sake. I could hear the drums outside now, marshaling the troops to battle. Tears stung my eyes, and as I bowed my head over the bottle so she wouldn't take note, I thought of how our hands were clasped together around the bottle as if in prayer.

It was at that exact moment, too, that the chamber's door opened and His Excellency himself came striding into the room. I'd always found him a powerful, even daunting, figure, but to see him now, with his eyes flashing with resolution, he seemed the most impressive of leaders, and the one hero our foundering country needed most.

Yet at that moment, he clearly desired to speak to his wife, not to me. He frowned briefly when he saw me with her, then with gentlemanly grace even in a time like this, he managed to smile at me.

"Miss Schuyler, good day," he said. "I regret that I must ask you to return to your own quarters at once, and remain there with your mother until your father joins you later today. One of the men will see you there."

Acutely aware of how much of an inconvenience I must be, I curtsied and backed from the room. I don't recall what I managed to stammer to either His Excellency or Lady Washington; I only hope I was able to share my gratitude and my best wishes to them both.

But as soon as I was in the hall and the door closed behind me, I found myself in the middle of more chaos than I'd ever witnessed before in this house as the officers who'd lodged there prepared to leave. For once, no one paid any attention to me at all, and I was as good as invisible. Servants and waiters rushed back and forth as they collected bundles of uniforms, shirts, and stockings as well as leather bags and boxes. It became clear that they'd received orders not just for a single encounter with the British, but to gather their belongings for a campaign.

I was desperate to know more, to know what had happened earlier and what would happen next. Despite how Lady Washington had advised me to wait and be told, I couldn't, and I caught the sleeve of one of the passing African servants. Dressed in the red and white livery of Mount Vernon, he belonged to the Washingtons, and if anyone knew the latest news, it was always servants.

"A moment, if you please," I said. "Can you tell me what has happened?"

He nodded, and touched his forehead to me in deference.

"Yes, madam," he said, with the same eager excitement that nearly every other man, of every rank and station, was displaying around us. "They say there's five thousand of the enemy rowed over from Staten Island last night, madam. They say they landed in Elizabethtown, but that the Jersey brigade and militia took them on, and now master will finish the fight, and drive them back into the Hudson, see if they don't!"

He nodded again, clearly delighted at having been the bearer of such news. It was nothing that hadn't been expected, even anticipated, and yet still I felt the unwelcome shock of it. The British had invaded New Jersey, and the general was finally determined to engage them. There would be fighting, and bloodshed, and likely lives lost on both sides.

And no matter how hard I'd prayed to the contrary, Alexander would have his wish for another chance at the glory he so craved.

I had to see him before he left, to wish him well and give him my love. One more time, one more time . . .

Swiftly I glanced past the servant to the room that he had shared with the other aides-de-camp. The door was open, but there were no officers within, and only waiters dismantling and packing away the camp beds.

"Where is Colonel Hamilton?" I asked, my voice taut with urgency. "He must still be here, since His Excellency remains in the house."

The servant made a long face, aware that he hadn't the answer I sought.

"No, madam, Colonel Hamilton's already gone on orders," he said. "I saw him myself on his horse, madam."

I couldn't hold back a little cry of dismay, pressing my hand over my mouth. I nodded by way of dismissal, and let him continue on whatever errand he was bound. I shouldn't be surprised; given how much the general relied upon Alexander, he'd probably sent him ahead as an advance, with all the responsibilities that entailed.

But this meant that there was a very real possibility that I'd never see Alexander again. I wish he hadn't told me of how reckless and impulsive he was in battle, and I wished I didn't know of all the times he'd barely escaped with his life. None of those dangerous exploits in his past made this day any easier.

How did women like my mother and Lady Washington, both married for decades to soldiers, remain so stoic in the face of the risk to their husbands? Lady Washington had urged me to be brave and strong, and to place my faith in God and my trust in the man I loved. Wise advice, sage advice, especially since this would most likely be only the first day of many like it while married to Alexander. But oh, how difficult it was going to be to follow!

There was no reason for me to remain here. I wrapped the bottle with the elixir in my handkerchief, tucked it into my pocket for safekeeping, and made my way down the back stairs and from the house. I didn't know what had become of the soldier who'd brought me there earlier, nor had I any way to find him once again. The walk home was only half a mile; surely I could accomplish that unattended. I narrowly dodged two men with a trunk, and another who growled at me for being in his way. I felt small, insignificant, and very much in the way, and I quickened my pace to escape this place where I did not belong.

But amidst all those voices that meant nothing to me, one suddenly stood out, sweetly familiar and impossibly dear, calling my name. I turned back, and there was Alexander, striding down the house's steps toward me. I was too stunned to run toward him, too overwhelmed to move.

I'd never seen him in his full uniform with his sword and pistols, too, as martial as any warrior could possibly be. The gold buttons on his coat and the braid on his epaulets glinting in the June sunshine, and his tall black boots and black cocked hat with the black plume stood out in sharp contrast against the white house behind him.

He stopped directly in front of me, smiling, and I realized he was gazing at me as intently as I was with him. Strange to think we both wanted to remember this moment, as if a painter had captured it for us to hold tight and keep forever.

"I haven't much time," he said. "Lady Washington told me you'd been here, and I feared I'd missed you."

"But you didn't," I said. "I'm here."

Now I noticed the servant holding his horse near the door, how he was wearing spurs with his boots, and how his gloves were creased from the reins. He must have returned here to headquarters with a message for His Excellency, and now likely needed to head back to the front as fast as he could.

"Has anyone told you what has happened this morning in Elizabethtown?" he asked, and I nodded. Doubtless he could tell me more, much more, of fortifications and skirmishes and a thousand other military niceties, but I didn't want these to be the last things I heard from him.

"I know you must go there, too," I said, rushing my words to say them all before he left. "I know you'll be brave and honorable and—and everything else you must be for the sake of our country."

"My own Betsey," he said, his voice thick with emotion. "Then you know I've no choice but to go."

"You'll go because you cannot wait to fight with the others." I tried to smile, but my mouth seemed unable to turn upward the way I wished it to. "All I ask is that after this day, this battle, this war is finally done, you'll come back to me, because we have so much to do together. Will you promise me that, Alexander Hamilton? Just—just take care, and come back."

He didn't answer, but instead drew me almost roughly into his arms, lifting my feet clear from the ground, and we held each other so tightly I wished that we'd never part.

"I love you," he said, a promise warm against my ear. "My angel, my love."

"I love you, too," I said, "and I always, always will."

Another moment that went far too fast, and then he was gently easing himself apart from me. "I must go now."

"Go," I echoed sorrowfully, my open palm still on his breast. "May God be with you, my love, and keep you safe."

He paused and smiled. "You always pray for me, don't you, Betsey?"

"Someone must do it." Somehow I managed at last to smile through my tears. "I love you."

"Dearest love." He kissed me quickly, then backed away from me perhaps a dozen paces before he finally turned and walked purposefully toward his horse.

Left behind, I hugged my arms around myself, a sad mockery of his embrace, and no real solace at all. He swung himself easily up into the saddle, gathered the reins, and settled his hat more firmly on his head. He looked one more time toward me and saluted, and then turned, and was gone. I stood alone and watched him as long as he was in view, and longer beyond that, before at last I too turned away and began on my solitary way.

But to my surprise, this was not to be his final farewell to me that day. Later that evening, I sat sewing with my mother in our parlor. The events of the day weighed heavily upon us both, and when we did speak, we kept our voices low, as if unconsciously fearing that the enemy might somehow overhear us. With all of Papa's military experience, Mamma wished that he were here with us instead of in Philadelphia, while I missed Alexander's presence most sorely.

We still had our two sentinels from the army to watch over us, yet both Mamma and I jumped in our chairs and exclaimed with surprise when the knock came on our door. No one would call upon us at that hour of the evening, especially not on this night. Not trusting a servant to answer on a day such as this, Mamma herself rose and I joined her, and together we hurried to the door.

Standing beside the sentinel was a small mulatto man whom I recognized as another of the Washingtons' servants. In his hand was a letter for me, addressed in Alexander's unmistakable hand. My mother sighed with resignation and nodded, excusing me, and I rushed upstairs to read his letter in privacy. I couldn't imagine he'd had opportunity to write today, not on horseback, and not on the first day of a campaign, either.

I slowly and carefully cracked the seal and unfolded the sheet, the way I always did to prolong the pleasure of his letters. This time, however, there wasn't a letter, but a single line, written in obvious haste:

> *My dearest Betsey,*
> *I would have given you this myself tonight. Instead let it carry my heart to yours, and love your Hamilton as well as he does you. ~ AH*

He'd written that tender closing in letters to me before, a true lover's admonition, and again its tenderness brought tears to my eyes. He must have scrawled these lines this morning, when he'd believed he'd missed me at headquarters. The servant had become our unlikely Cupid, unable to carry Alexander's message until after his own duties were done for the day.

But this short note only served as a prelude to a smaller sheet, folded into a tight square within. This wasn't a letter, either, but a poem, and written out with care.

> *ANSWER TO THE INQUIRY WHY I SIGHED*
> *Before no mortal ever knew*
> *A love like mine so tender–True–*
> *Completely wretched–you away–*
> *And but half blessed e'ven while you stay.*
> *If present love would show its face*
> *Deny you to my fond embrace*
> *No joy unmixed my bosom warms*
> *But when my angel's in my arms.*

He'd never written a poem to me before. No one had. I read it again, then read it aloud, whispering the words to myself as I imagined hearing them in his voice. I smiled, and pressed my lips lightly to the page, and counted myself the most fortunate of women to love, and be loved, as I was by my Alexander.

* * *

At Papa's insistence, Mamma and I and our servants left Morris-town for Albany two days later. We were accompanied by several guards, but our progress home was without risk or hindrance, and we saw no signs of the troubles that were disturbing New Jersey. The closer we came to Albany, the more Mamma's health improved as well. I do not know whether this was from Lady Washington's elixir, or her anticipation at once again being in her own home, or simply the natural progress of her pregnancy; whatever the case, I was glad, and relieved that she was better. If it were not for the un-certainties of the war so close to us, the sunny June weather would have made our journey a pleasurable one.

The remainder of the month was far more eventful for our army, and therefore for Alexander. When people now think of a battle, they imagine a wide and airy field with tidy rows of combatants in gaudy uniforms following a well-ordered plan of attack and de-fense; much like a game of chess, with the generals on both sides moving their soldiers like pieces about the board.

Perhaps amongst the great powers of Europe, war is conducted with this kind of restraint and order. But in the war here in Amer-ica, battles were seldom so neat. In fact, to the British officers, the American way of fighting was dishonorable and disorganized, no matter that they soon adopted it themselves. Because General Washington never had the same sheer numbers of men and artillery that the British generals possessed, he often chose to engage the enemy in a manner drawn more from native warriors like the Dela-wares, the Shawnees, and the Iroquois. Soldiers fought amongst villages and forests, using whatever it was they found to their ad-vantage, or for their defense.

The British attack upon New Jersey that began in early June continued in this manner for several more weeks. I learned of it first from Papa, and then from Alexander, who could write to me only when he found a messenger to carry a letter through the lines to me. The so-called Battles of Connecticut Farms and of Spring-field were drawn-out affairs that savaged these towns. The local militia combined with the Continental troops to drive the enemy back to Elizabethtown, and finally again across the river to New York. It was considered a mighty victory for our side, and cheering to His Excellency, the soldiers themselves, and even Congress.

Yet while Alexander wrote in his most exultant fashion about these victories (and doubtless also wrote the same in His Excellency's official reports to Congress), it was the more sorrowful aspect of the fighting that lingered with me.

Many houses in the various villages were burned by the British as they retreated, leaving families homeless and bereft. I thought of how the same enemy had looted and burned my own family's house in Saratoga this way earlier in the war, and how they showed so little remorse over the destruction of private property.

But there were losses that were far more lasting than mere beams, clapboarding, and bricks. Over the course of the brief campaign, thirty-five soldiers were killed and one hundred thirty-nine wounded from the ranks of the Continental forces. According to Papa, these casualty figures were quite low, and a credit to the officers who'd taken such care of their men.

I doubted that the families of the soldiers killed or wounded would have agreed. Among those wounded was young Gabriel Ford, shot twice through the thigh. He was the eldest son of Mrs. Ford, whose house had been used by His Excellency as headquarters. I remembered him well, a cheerful youth of promise and a pillar to his widowed mother; he'd planned to attend the college at nearby Princeton in the fall, before he'd become so starry-eyed by the army that he'd volunteered for this campaign. My sympathy lay entirely with his poor mother, who had already lost her husband, and I cannot imagine the shock and sorrow she must have felt to see her beloved son brought home to her bloodied and bandaged.

At least Gabriel Ford was expected to make a full recovery from his wounds. Much more tragic was the tale of Mrs. Hannah Caldwell, the wife of the Reverend James Caldwell and one of our army's chaplains. During the Battle of Connecticut Farms, Mrs. Caldwell was trapped in her house with her young children and servants as the fighting raged around them. As she huddled with her son upon her lap, a British soldier fired at the window, and killed her where she sat. As her weeping, terrified children cowered to one side, more soldiers forced their way into the house, carrying off the family's valuables and ripping the jewelry from Mrs. Caldwell's lifeless body.

Now I am certain that there are those (particularly those whose sympathies lie with the Tory cause) who will say that this heinous act was simply an unfortunate act of war and the cost of our country's rebellion. But the outrage of it affected me deeply, and I grieved both for Reverend Caldwell and his pitiful, motherless children.

I learned the details of Mrs. Caldwell's horrific murder (for so surely it must be considered) not from Alexander, but from my friend Kitty Livingston, whose family property in Elizabethtown also suffered much damage at the hands of the British troops. Alexander's account was far briefer, and I suspect this was because he wished to spare my tender sensibilities from the realities of the war.

But I also suspect that the particulars of Mrs. Caldwell's death must have affected him, too, and on a most intimate level. As a young boy, both Alexander and his mother had been taken deathly ill of an island fever, such as too often occurs in the Caribbean. His mother perished, while he survived, but he had never forgotten the shock and sorrow of waking to find his mother's lifeless body on the same bed beside him.

All was a solemn reminder of how tenuous our mortal lives can be, and how quickly gone from this earth. While Alexander himself regretted that he'd not seen more action during the campaign in New Jersey, I thanked God that he hadn't, and had instead emerged unharmed.

In fact despite the swift beginning to the summer campaign, it soon wizened away with little more real fighting. While the British continued to hold New York and most of the southern states, General Washington and the Continental troops remained idle, waiting for reinforcements. In early July, they arrived: a French fleet bearing nearly seven thousand troops from France, as promised and arranged by Lafayette. The French troops landed to the north, in Newport, Rhode Island, and were commanded by Marshal Jean-Baptiste Donatien de Vimeur, the Comte de Rochambeau. These Frenchmen were part of an alliance that more than doubled the size of our forces, and most people believed with giddy hope that they would be our salvation.

As can be imagined, Alexander's ease with the French language made him much in demand as General Washington decided how best to employ the French to break the stalemate with the British and secure victory. But while His Excellency was in favor of the French immediately attacking the British stronghold of New York, Rochambeau disagreed with this plan, and refused to leave Rhode Island. To do so, he argued, would expose the French ships to the larger British navy that still held most of the coast under blockade. Instead of attacking New York, the French encamped in the city of Providence, and prepared to remain there until a plan more agreeable to them was proposed.

Alexander's frustration was clear in his letters, and I'm sure he reflected the overall mood of the American officers and army. To have the key to victory standing idle in Rhode Island must have felt like the bitterest irony.

But Alexander's restlessness was not limited to the state of the war. His letters to me, while as loving as ever, also returned to his old fears of being too poor or too humble to marry me. He worried that he was unworthy of me, and painted wretched pictures of how miserable I'd be wed to him and living in some mean little cottage. He told me of dreams (that were better called nightmares) where I had wearied of him, and he would come across me asleep on some grassy hillside beside another gentleman. Even when he'd pay me some sweet compliment—as he did when he called me his pretty little nut-brown maid—there was an undercurrent of uneasiness to it, as if he feared that I'd prove faithless if I were tested like the nut-brown girl in the old ballad. He was acutely conscious, as was I, of the false perception that he was marrying me for my father's money, and he was resolved that we would live only on what he earned, without assistance from my parents.

I reassured him as best I could, but just as this had been a challenge for me when we'd been separated earlier in the year when I'd been in Philadelphia with my father, and Alexander in Perth Amboy, it continued to be so now. When we were together, I knew what words to use to reason with him and to calm his doubts, and which little caresses and endearments would act as balms to the wounds he insisted on inflicting upon himself.

But I seldom found a way to do this with pen and paper, and his own ease with words only made my lack the more noticeable. The difficulties of sending and receiving letters on account of the war made our correspondence even more labored. Letters were often delayed, with some overlapping and losing their meanings, or on occasion even misplaced entirely. The only consolation was his teasing promise to punish me for all my delinquencies in writing— a punishment which I knew from pleasurable experience would be meted out in kisses, and was so little real punishment that it nearly inspired me to cease writing altogether.

Still I persevered, because even a jumbled letter to Alexander was a way to express my love and regard and desire to him. Although we couldn't yet choose an exact date for our wedding—that would depend on when His Excellency could spare Alexander long enough to come to Albany—we knew it would be in December. We shared our impatience to be wed, and each summer day that slipped past was one less that we'd have to wait.

I'd ways enough to occupy myself. As usual our house was filled with the cheerful confusion of my five younger brothers and sisters as well as their various friends and pets, and as promised, Angelica arrived with her two dear little babies as well. With my mother often weary from her pregnancy, I took over many of the burdens of our household's management.

I prepared for my new life, too, as every good Dutch bride would. For the remainder of the war, Alexander and I would likely live not in a house of our own, but in quarters hired for the use of officers and their wives. Whatever I brought to my new household must be easily packed and conveyed, and ready to shift at a moment's notice. I proudly marked linens—sheets and pillow biers and towels and washing-cloths—with my new initials, and took a special delight in every tiny cross-stitched *EH* that I made in blue thread. My mother and I together assembled all the sundry pieces necessary to begin a household from candlesticks to iron pans and pots for the kitchen, soaps and kettles for the laundry, and coverlets and hangings for our bedroom.

Because of my future status as wife to the senior officer of His Excellency's staff, Mamma also insisted that I have new clothes, from stockings and fine linen shifts to silk gowns to wear for evening entertainments. Perhaps I should have relished such lavish expenditure on my behalf, but in truth it made me uncomfortable.

"Mamma, please, no more," I said as we paused outside yet another mantua-maker's shop. "I don't need anything else."

She frowned. "There's the question of a new winter cardinal," she said. "You wore your old cloak so often last winter in Morristown that it's grown quite shabby."

"But you and Papa have bought so much—"

"We wish you to begin your marriage with everything you need," Mamma said. "We would have done the same for Angelica if she'd chosen to inform us of her attachment to Mr. Carter before she married him."

The truth was that Angelica hadn't required any of this, having married an increasingly wealthy man who had bought her all this and a great deal more, but I wouldn't say that to Mamma.

"You know that Alexander worries that he is too poor to marry me," I said. "He's sure to see your gifts not as generosity, but that you doubt he is capable of supporting me."

"I've heard this fretting from you before, Eliza," Mamma said firmly, "and I've no wish to hear it again. Yes, you may be marrying a gentleman who is at present impoverished, but your father and I are confident that through his industry and resourcefulness, he will soon remedy that."

"I believe that, too," I said, not wanting her to think I lacked confidence in his abilities. "But it's the present that concerns him, not the future."

"It shouldn't," she said bluntly. "While you may become a poor man's wife temporarily, you remain at present a rich man's daughter, and I won't have your aunts and cousins believe we have slighted you when they arrive for the wedding."

Thus, I had no say in the matter, nor did Alexander. My mother was a difficult woman to cross, as I tried to explain to him as best I could. At least I'd other things to write in my letters to divert him more agreeably, things that even he could not complain of.

He had suggested that I employ my time in reading, something I hadn't previously been inclined overmuch to do. As I've noted before, I was not Angelica. But because it was his wish, I began—and finished!—several books he'd recommended that were in my father's library: works by James Boswell, Jonathan Swift, and Laurence Sterne, among others. It was not easy work for me, but Alexander praised me much for the accomplishment, and in later years, when we would have learned guests at our table, I was proud that I'd read books they mentioned, and could therefore share my own opinions.

But Alexander obliged my little requests as well. When I begged that I might have a miniature portrait of him to keep by me while we were apart, he didn't reply, and I'd guessed it was too costly for him. Soon after, however, a small package was delivered to me, and in it was a very fine likeness of Alexander in a rosy-red waistcoat and blue jacket, painted on ivory by the renowned Mr. Charles Willson Peale of Philadelphia. I was overjoyed by such a treasure, and quickly set to work embroidering a special mat to better display it to the world.

In return I sent a little song I'd composed to amuse him, filled with the love and sentiments that were writ upon my heart. To be sure, it was not so fine as the poem he'd made for me, but still it pleased him, which was all I ever wished to do.

Best of all, I hoped he'd be to be steal away from the present campaign for a day or two to visit Albany if his duties with the army brought him within a reasonable distance. His Excellency spoke of traveling to West Point, now under General Arnold's command, and that wasn't so very far from us up the Hudson.

In this fashion, it was easy to lose myself in thoughts of Alexander and our wedding. The war seemed far away from us in Albany, and in the summer of 1780, it was. But as summer began to fade into fall, the news that filled Alexander's letters took a much more somber, even ominous, tone.

First came word of the calamitous Battle of Camden in South Carolina, wherein General Gates (the same foolish general who had stolen credit for the long-ago victory at Saratoga from my father) was routed and humiliated by the enemy. His defeat was so thorough that there were fears that North Carolina and Virginia would be next to fall.

Any possibility of Alexander leaving the army to visit me was now gone for this campaign; it was clear the army, and the country, needed him far more than I. The chance of losing all America had become so real that Alexander even suggested in perfect seriousness that he and I might leave this country entirely for the Continent and live instead in the city of Geneva, in Switzerland—a prospect I found mightily distressing.

But the most disturbing news came in September. After meeting with the French in Hartford, His Excellency and a number of his officers arrived near West Point with the intention of inspecting the fortifications there. While nearby, however, a spy was intercepted with incriminating papers and maps proving that West Point's commander, General Benedict Arnold, had sold himself to the enemy. He'd purposefully let the fort's defenses fall into disrepair with the intention of making a capture easy for the British, and had been forwarding many of His Excellency's confidential letters and dispatches as well. This was a treasonous act of complete betrayal to the American cause, and to so many of his fellow officers (including as my own father) who had previously extended themselves on his behalf.

Alexander himself was the first to read the dispatches of the captured master spy who oversaw the maneuvers of countless smaller villains in thrall to the king. The melancholy task of relaying Arnold's betrayal to His Excellency also fell to Alexander, as did riding with his fellow aide James McHenry in furious pursuit after the fleeing Arnold, who managed to escape to a British ship waiting for him in the river. Mrs. Peggy Arnold, whom I had met earlier in Philadelphia, was seemingly left behind and abandoned with her child by her cowardly husband, and had been discovered in a raving fit of madness caused by her husband's wicked acts.

It took Alexander two letters to convey so much, written hours apart, and numbered (as was our habit) so I would know which to read first. As I read them, I couldn't keep back numerous gasps and exclamations at Arnold's perfidious disloyalty, and the grief that His Excellency must feel at his betrayal. Once again Alexander had been thrust into the very center of a perilous situation, and it was only by merest luck that the spy had been caught in time to keep His Excellency, his officers, and West Point itself from falling into the enemy's hands.

I thanked Almighty God for keeping Alexander safe, and preserving His Excellency and the others from harm. But what stunned me the most was that in this particular tale of Alexander's escapade, two of the major players in the drama were known personally to me.

The first, most obviously, was Peggy Arnold. I hadn't liked her when we'd met the single time in Philadelphia, but I still could pity how her traitorous husband had fled, leaving her and their child once again in a vulnerable position.

But the second was the captured spy himself, Major John André, a gentleman known well within my family, and especially to me.

"Read this," I said, thrusting Alexander's first letter into Angelica's hand. She had received a letter from her husband by the same rider who had brought me Alexander's, and we'd taken them outside to a bench in the garden to read in relative peace.

Angelica's brows rose with curiosity as she put aside her own letter to take mine.

"Are you certain you wish me to see your billet-doux from your beloved Hamilton?" she teased. "Once read, such things cannot be forgotten."

"There's nothing in it that you cannot read, though you may wish you hadn't," I said. "Major André has been taken up as a spy."

"What?" she exclaimed, now reading the letter with more interest. "I've heard rumors, of course, but I never thought he'd been engaged so deeply behind our lines. And with General Arnold! Oh, Eliza, this is very bad."

I nodded, my heart racing so fast that I felt ill. "You do remember when he stayed here, don't you?"

"How could I not?" she said, glancing up from the letter. "He was with us for nearly a month, and at Christmas, too, which made him feel much more like a guest than one more British prisoner hoping to be exchanged. Such an entertaining fellow he was, with so many talents! We were all sad to see him leave."

"Yes," I said softly, struggling to control my sentiments. "Yes, we were."

To describe John André as an "entertaining fellow" was to do him the gravest injustice. Born in London, he was the most perfectly accomplished gentleman I'd ever met, able to speak several languages, tell amusing stories, dance with grace, cut silhouettes, draw, and paint to a wonder, and sing and write verse. As if those accomplishments weren't sufficient, he was also tall, charming, and prodigiously handsome.

André was, in brief, exactly the sort of gentleman to turn the head of an impressionable girl of seventeen, which was what I had been in November of 1775. Seven years older than I and a lieutenant in the British Army, he had been among the prisoners taken by Continental general Richard Montgomery after the siege of Fort Saint-Jean in Quebec. My father has always observed the formal dignities of war: although André was a prisoner, he was foremost a gentleman and an officer, and although he was on his way to his eventual imprisonment in Pennsylvania, Papa made sure that he and several other British officers became our guests for the Christmas season.

Oh, I was smitten! Although he took care not to beguile my affections, he was so kind to me that I'd wept when he'd left. I'd not seen him since, but I always remembered him as a friend—a friend whose actions in war had now put him into the greatest risk possible.

"How terrible that he'll suffer because of Arnold," Angelica said. "I cannot imagine a greater tragedy."

All I could do was sigh and shake my head with sorrow. As our father's daughters, we both knew the sentence for spies was execution. If André were judged an unfortunate officer following British orders, then he would be shot as a gentleman. If it were determined he was an out-and-out spy, then he would be hung in disgrace like a common criminal.

"What has Alexander written in the second letter?" asked Angelica. "Are there more details of André's capture?"

I passed it to her. "It's mostly about how shocked Mrs. Arnold was by her husband's villainy. I suppose they must be two of a kind, for I found her a sly, conniving woman when we met in Philadelphia. Papa wished me to like her, but I could not."

"Men have always been fooled by her," Angelica declared vehemently. "I'm certain that all this thrashing about by her, pretending to be mad, was only a performance. Even your Hamilton clearly feels nothing but pity for the creature, and he like all worldly gentlemen should know better. What manner of lady languishes in her bed to receive officers?"

I lowered my chin with a mixture of disapproval and dismay. I'd observed myself the charm of Mrs. Arnold *en dishabille*, and I'd rather she weren't displaying herself similarly to Alexander. One of his most endearing qualities was his constant desire to assist the weak and powerless; he could be the kindest man! But the eagerness with which Peggy Arnold appeared to have accepted his offers of compassion irritated me, knowing how false her motives likely were. That Alexander should write to me that he longed to be her brother, the better to be her defender, and that he'd offered her every proof of friendship—that was, to me, taking gallantry a shade too far.

But I wasn't pleased, either, with my sister's breezy remark about Alexander. I couldn't deny that there had been other women (I shall not dignify them as ladies) in his life before me, or that he still would smile at a pretty face other than mine. It was simply part and parcel of who he was, and I accepted it, knowing his heart was truly devoted only to me. But that didn't mean I wished my own sister to speak as if he were still a wandering rogue about the camp, especially not after he and I had been apart for the entire summer.

"In fairness, Angelica, I do not believe Alexander can still be called a 'worldly gentleman,'" I said. "In the past, perhaps, but no longer."

But my sister only shrugged. "Hamilton is a *man*, Eliza, and not even marriage to your saintly person will change that," she said. "When a woman such as Mrs. Arnold throws out her best snares, men are as helpless as weakling rabbits."

"Mrs. Arnold should not have cast herself upon his good nature," I said, wishing I didn't sound quite so prim. "It's her fault, not Alexander's."

"Mrs. Arnold has done a good many things she shouldn't have." Angelica leaned forward in confidence, though there was no one else in the garden to overhear. "Gossip says that she and André have long been lovers, and that she married General Arnold only to serve him up more easily to the British. It appears she's played both men false, however, and now must lie and simper further to save her own plump neck from the rope."

Somehow that sordid scenario sounded much more like fact than gossip, and fit with other rumors I'd heard of the Arnolds whilst I was in Morristown. Poor John André, to be sacrificed on such a traitorous altar! I didn't give a fig if Peggy Arnold ended her short life on the gallows, but I resolved to do what I could to help save him.

"As adjutant general, André should be a prisoner of considerable value," I said, refolding the letters to read again later. "Perhaps the British would consider trading Arnold for him. Alexander is so skilled at negotiating prisoner exchanges that I'm sure he could arrange it."

I rose, determined to answer his two letters at once, but Angelica caught my hand.

"You're not going to write to Alexander about André, are you?" she asked, reading my intentions as clear as the day. "Because if you are, Eliza, it would be a most grievous mistake."

I didn't deny my intention. "I'm acting to preserve an old friend. There's no harm to that."

"There will be to Hamilton," she said firmly. "Consider his response when you plead for the life of another gentleman—an enemy!—whom you once considered yourself to love."

"I was too young then to know what real love could be," I said quickly. "He was a friend, nothing more. If I ask Alexander to act on André's behalf, it's because I have perfect faith that he can save another worthy gentleman's life."

"Eliza, please," Angelica warned. "André knew full well the risk he took by his actions, and the consequences, too. Hamilton won't be able to save him, because his fate will be decided in a trial by His Excellency and the other generals. It has nothing to do with your 'perfect faith' in his abilities, and meddling in army affairs will only bring you—"

"I know perfectly how to write to Alexander," I said tartly, "and I do not require your advice to do so."

With that I left her behind and returned to the house, and nothing further was said that day, or the next, about Major André between Angelica and me.

I would, however, have done much better to have heeded her sage advice, and not let myself be led by impulse and sentiment, and a measure of shameful petty jealousy. If Alexander hadn't been so quick to champion Mrs. Arnold, then I might not have done the same for Major André, and more, I wouldn't have praised his virtues, his talents, and his dignity to the degree I did.

But instead I wrote not one letter to Alexander, but two, begging him in the strongest possible language to save the British major. Both letters were carried away swiftly by the same messenger who'd brought Alexander's to me. I prayed they'd accomplish their mission, and I prayed for both the British major as well as my own lieutenant colonel.

The next week crept slowly along, and with each day I fretted and doubted myself, and what I'd written even more. Through my father's dispatches came word that André had been found guilty, and had been hung as a common spy on the second of October. As can be expected, I wept for him bitterly, but if I were honest, a few of those tears were for myself and the girl I'd been when I'd loved him.

Yet there was more to my sorrow, too. I grieved that we lived in a time where such choices were forced upon us, and tragedies like this were commonplace. If André and Arnold had succeeded in their plan regarding West Point, then not only would the fortress have been captured, but likely His Excellency and his staff with it. I could just as easily have been mourning Alexander's execution as André's, a possibility I couldn't bear to contemplate.

Soon after the first news came my reply from Alexander, and if I'd hoped for absolution for my letters, I found none in his words. His account of André's execution was brief, though he promised a longer description to follow. Nor was there any mention this time of Mrs. Arnold.

For that matter, there weren't any of his usual effusive and poetical compliments to me, either. I wasn't his sorceress, his jewel, his angel, his charmer, his dearest black-eyed girl. Instead his tone was subdued and melancholy, even forlorn, and filled with reflection and humility. The self-doubt fair broke my heart.

He'd tried to have the method of André's execution changed from being hanged to being shot, but with no success. He'd been compelled to refuse a proposal for an exchange of prisoners because André himself had not wanted it. He'd attempted everything he could in the situation, and failed.

He'd failed, and though he did not say it outright, he clearly believed he'd failed me. As Angelica had warned, my unreasonable confidence in his abilities had made my request impossible for him to achieve, and for a man who found failure unbearable, it was a crushing blow.

Worse yet, he'd realized my sentimental infatuation for André (though I'd only called him a friend), and his imagination had blown it into much more of a romance than it had been. He didn't reproach me as I deserved, which would have been much easier to bear. Instead he once again found only faults in himself, comparing his own talents and accomplishments, his lack of fortune, even his appearance, unfavorably to the dead English officer.

Each humble word cut me to the quick. I'd done this to him. I'd been selfish, unthinking, impetuous, and interfering, and I'd hurt him more deeply than I'd ever dreamed possible. I was the unworthy one, not he, and with his letters clutched tightly in my hands, I wept anew for the pain I'd never wanted to cause so good a man.

How I wished we could be together, and I could tell him to his face how wrong I'd been, and how sorry I was to have wounded him, and how very, very much I loved him. We'd been apart too long, Alexander and I, and the strain of the separation was wearing upon us both. Letters were no longer enough. I wanted to hold him close, and kiss him, and make everything right once again the way it should be.

It would be, too. We'd only a handful of weeks before our wedding now, and until then, I'd take extra care with every word I wrote to him. I was determined that we'd weather this storm. Our love was strong, and I never for a moment doubted its power, not then, nor ever after.

For he was my Alexander, my Hamilton, and I'd always, always be his Betsey.

CHAPTER 9

Albany, New York
December 1780

"You must be cold there by the window, Eliza," Mamma said. "You'll know well enough when they arrive. Be warm, and come closer to the fire."

I shook my head, pretending I was warmer than I was as I sat inside the recessed window seat. Even with a large fire in the family parlor's hearth, winter always crept into the room from the windows and the corners, and it was only truly warm within a few feet from the fire itself. I wore a quilted wool petticoat beneath a wool gown, thick stockings, mitts, and a shawl over my shoulders, yet still my fingertips were so chilled that I was having difficulty holding my needle.

"I'm perfectly at ease here, Mamma," I lied cheerfully. "The sunlight is agreeably bright for my sewing."

"What she cannot wait to see in the bright sunlight is her bridegroom," said my sister Peggy in an exaggerated voice, and without looking up from the letter she was writing at the table nearer to Mamma and the fire. "She wants to see her darling *Hamilton*."

"Hush, Peggy, that's enough," scolded Mamma. "We are all eager to greet Colonel Hamilton."

I bowed my head over the tiny bonnet I was stitching for my newest sibling, and pretended not to hear them. Because fresh snow had fallen two nights ago and the Albany road was still covered, Papa had sent his own sleigh to the inn where Alexander and

Mr. McHenry were to have stopped last night. Even Papa had been unable to keep from teasing me about Alexander's arrival, telling me that he'd purposefully sent the sleigh to make sure my bridegroom wouldn't escape before the wedding.

I'd only smiled then, much as I smiled now. My family could say whatever they wished. Nothing would stop Alexander from coming here, and nothing would stop me from being the first to greet him when he did.

Alexander had received his first army commission as a captain in March of 1776. Nearly five years had passed since then, and he'd not taken a single leave of absence from the army. He had labored without pause, and during the time spent as a member of His Excellency's Family, he had kept the general's long hours as well, rising before dawn and working late into the night.

Now, in the last week of December 1780, he was finally stepping away from the Family and the army, and I was the reason. No, I shouldn't say that: *we* were the reason, Alexander and I together, and our wedding that would bind us forever as one.

His Excellency had grudgingly granted Alexander six weeks' leave, and when he had ridden from headquarters at Tappan, New York, only one friend from the Family was permitted to accompany him: James McHenry, the general's secretary, and a surgeon besides. Foreign-born (from Ulster, in Ireland) like Alexander, Mr. McHenry served without rank as a volunteer, which was perhaps why he was spared for our wedding.

I glanced out the frost-edged window for the thousandth time. December days were short, and with the sun already dipping lower into the sky, I prayed they'd be here soon, and safely.

I leaned closer to the window, blowing a small cloud upon the pane, and with my finger traced two overlapping hearts. I smiled at my foolishness, and as I did, I caught sight of the chestnut team and the sleigh behind it, dark and sleek against the white snow.

I dropped my sewing and raced from the room and into the hall. I didn't wait for a servant, but swung open the heavy front door myself and stepped outside, forgetting the cold. The sleigh was slowly making its way up the hill to our house, the horses weary and laboring, but all I saw was Alexander, standing in the sleigh and waving his hat to me. I laughed with delight, and hurried down the front steps, my skirts bunched to one side so I wouldn't catch my heel in my hems and trip.

He didn't wait for the sleigh to stop before he'd clambered over the side and into the snowy drive, and I ran toward him and he ran toward me. He caught me in his arms and swung me off my feet, and then kissed me with all the hunger of a starving man. There's an old saying that absence is a general cure for love, but from that moment I knew being apart had only made us love each other more.

"My dearest Betsey," he said, still holding me tightly. "You can't know how much I've missed you."

"I can, because I missed you that much, too," I said breathlessly, and kissed him again.

He made a rumbling noise of contentment deep in his chest. "I cannot wait until you're mine, my love."

"Nor I." I'm sure my entire family was watching us from the windows, and reluctantly I disentangled myself from him, though I kept my hand in his. Poor Mr. McHenry had been left standing beside the sleigh, discreetly gazing out at the river and away from us, and I stepped forward to offer him my hand.

"Good day, sir," I said. "How glad you must be that your journey is done, and I thank you, too, for bringing Alexander to me."

"Thank you, Miss Schuyler," he said, bowing. He was a stocky man with a full, intelligent face and an agreeable manner that made him welcome in any company. "Truth be told, I do not believe I could have kept him away even if I wished it."

"No, you couldn't," Alexander agreed, and the two men laughed, making me suspect that there'd been much discussion between them on that very topic. "Come, McHenry, we must pay our respects to the general and his lady wife."

"I'm sure you both wish to warm yourselves, too," I said, turning to lead them up the steps.

But Alexander hung back, gazing up at the house's tall brick façade. It *was* an imposing house, and sizable, too: larger than any other in Albany, larger than most in New York and Philadelphia as well. I'd lived there all my life and thought of it as my home and nothing more, but I realized how different a prospect it must be for him.

"Do you recall the first time I was here?" he said. "The last time, too. I was exhausted and spent from riding from Valley Forge in five days, and then being compelled to attend General Gates, and coax him into sharing his troops with His Excellency."

"Is that where you were?" I asked curiously. "I recall that you were most secretive about your mission."

"An old secret that has lost all its power," he said. "But I was impressed that you didn't pry, the way most women would have. Reticence is a rare quality in any mortal, and yours left its impression upon me."

"I should hope I possessed more qualities than keeping silent," I said wryly, amused that that was what he'd remembered of our first conversation.

"You were only quiet when it was appropriate, as any good soldier's daughter knows to be," he said seriously, still looking up at the house. "As I recall, you spoke freely of things that mattered, and I liked that, too. I never thought then that I'd return here now, and in these circumstances."

His humor was difficult to read, but then I was accustomed to that with Alexander. I tucked my hand into the crook of his arm, leaning against him with reassuring fondness.

"You do realize that by marrying me, you're becoming one of us," I said. "You must consider us your family now, and this your home."

He smiled crookedly, but at the house, not at me. "It's been many years since I could call any one place home."

I wondered exactly how many years that had been; most likely at least a dozen, before his mother had died, though from what he'd told me they'd lived in such squalid circumstances as to hardly qualify as a home. I didn't want him to be making comparisons again between those circumstances and the ones in which I'd been raised, comparisons that achieved nothing but to darken his mood.

"Come," I said softly, leading him forward. "I'm sure my parents are waiting inside, and then you will meet all the rest of my family."

We were a considerable number to meet, even without Angelica and Mr. Carter and their children, who would join us at the end of the week. Alexander had already met my sister Peggy, a year younger than I, but this was the first time he'd encountered my brothers, John, who was fifteen, Philip, twelve, and Rensselaer, seven, and my youngest sister, Cornelia, who was only four. Yet he met them all with great aplomb and charm, including Cornelia, who was notoriously shy with strangers. Even Papa's dogs liked him. Best of all was seeing how warmly my parents greeted him, as if he truly were another son.

He and Mr. McHenry (whom Alexander declared I must call Mac) would sleep in my brothers' bedchamber, with my brothers giving up their beds to sleep on mattresses on the floor, as they often did for guests. This was no hardship for my brothers, who were excited at the prospect of sharing their room with heroic gentlemen from His Excellency's Family. I could only imagine—though I did not wish to know—what kinds of outlandish tales were told in that room in the evening, but the result was that my brothers considered Alexander the finest fellow they'd ever met.

Things continued well through supper with much merriment, or so I thought. But at the end of the meal, when Mamma and I and my younger siblings rose to leave the table and the wine to the men, Alexander declined.

"If you please, sir," he said to my father. His tone and expression was serious, even somber. "There are certain important affairs I wish to discuss with Eliza alone as soon as is possible."

At that everyone fell uncomfortably silent, including me. But Papa was quick to offer us the privacy of his library, and we retreated there.

"What has happened, Alexander?" I asked with concern as soon as the door was closed and we were alone together. "Have the British—"

"Not at all," he said quickly. "Or rather, when I left Tappan, all seemed quiet on the various fronts. Here, sit beside me, so we can speak properly."

I'd thought we could speak properly as we were, but I did as he bid, sitting in one of Papa's mahogany chairs while Alexander took the other. It was all too formal, and being in a room that was so much my father's domain did nothing to put me at ease. Because no one had expected the library to be put to use this evening, the fire had been hastily lit for us and gave off little heat, and the shutters were drawn over the windows. I'd always found Papa's leather-bound books in their tall cases and his looming secretary desk to be almost forbidding, and by the light of the single candlestick that we'd brought here with us, the entire room felt uncomfortably cold and gloomy.

"Something has happened," I said, my uncertainty growing. "Is it my letters regarding Major André? If it is, Alexander, then I—"

"No, Betsey," he said quickly, and took my hand. "Not at all. That particular tragedy has played itself out, and as we agreed in our letters, there's nothing more for either of us to say. We have heard, however, through our agents that Arnold's treachery has earned him a far smaller price than he anticipated. He'd expected a princely sum from the Crown in return for his duplicity, but it seems that since he failed to deliver West Point, his financial reward is much reduced. Nor have they given him the command he'd hoped for, either. His new masters know he has betrayal in his blood, and won't trust him not to do the same again. Such is the curse of a Judas, yes?"

"Nothing he suffers can be punishment enough," I said vehemently. "I can't consider what would have become of you if his plot had succeeded."

"Fortunately, he didn't succeed," he said. "Although you will be glad to learn that the pitiful Mrs. Arnold was granted safe passage to cross our lines, and she and her child have been restored to her husband."

I couldn't keep back a small sound of irritable disgust at the very thought of Mrs. Arnold.

"You do know by now that she played you all for fools, don't you?" I said. "I'd not be surprised if she was behind her husband's deceit from the beginning."

Alexander frowned. "I didn't realize you'd so strong an opinion of her."

"It couldn't be otherwise," I said. "At my father's request, I called upon Mrs. Arnold whilst I was in Philadelphia, and she impressed me then as a false, faithless woman. I didn't realize it at the time, but she also urged me to encourage you to follow the same course as her husband, and preserve yourself by leaving the American cause—which she predicted was doomed to fail—for the Crown."

His frown deepened. "You didn't tell me any of this."

"Because Papa said that my impressions were mistaken, and that I shouldn't trouble you with them." I sighed. "I think he was as cozened by Mrs. Arnold as the rest of you. At least no harm came to you from my silence, or I'd never have forgiven myself."

"You're a perceptive woman, Betsey," he said, clearly taking what I'd said seriously. "A wise wife shall be a wonderful thing. We must always be honest with each other, you and I."

"Always," I echoed with conviction of my own. I was proud of Alexander's honesty and noble spirit, especially in comparison with the duplicitous marriage of General and Mrs. Arnold.

He rose from the chair and took two steps away, his hands clasped tightly behind the back of his waist. While we'd been apart, it had been impossible to remember exactly how handsome he was, and the realization of his manly beauty struck me again with breathtaking force as I watched him pace. But pacing with Alexander was never a good sign, and I braced myself for whatever was coming.

"I fear I've another reason for requesting to speak with you in private," he said, bitterness in every crisp word. "I have once more been denied promotion. Both General Greene and Lafayette had advised His Excellency to promote me to adjutant general, and yet again he has seen fit to refuse."

"Oh, Alexander," I said sadly. Promotion meant much to him, and he'd hoped that at last the general would agree to part with him from his staff. "I am sorry."

His back still to me, he nodded, his only acknowledgment of my sympathy.

"But there are other paths than the army, my dear," he continued. "At Lafayette's urging, there will be a special envoy—and envoy extraordinaire it will be called—sent to Versailles in the new year, to assist with Mr. Franklin's duties at the French court. It's believed another voice is required to remind the French of their obligations toward us in regard to the war, and to urge them forward."

I listened, bewildered. I'd always believed his future lay with the army exclusively so long as the war was fought, and the law after that. I'd never before heard him take an interest in diplomacy. He swept his arms through the air, warming to his topic.

"You know I've been much involved in the plan to raise a loan with the French," he said, "a loan to cover our country's expenditures from the war. I am also not without friends in this. Lafayette, Laurens, and General Sullivan have all been vocal for my confirmation."

"Oh, yes, that would be an excellent opportunity for you," I said faintly. My first thought was that an envoy at Versailles would be safely removed from the dangers of battle. My second, however, was how far that envoy would also be removed from me. Yet for Alexander's sake, I would strive to be encouraging. "Who speaks the French language better than you?"

He smiled. "Would Paris agree with you, too, Betsey? How would you fare among the grand ladies of the French court?"

I gasped. It was Angelica, not I, who had always yearned to travel abroad and see more of the glittering world. Such adventures had never been dreams of mine.

"I would go with you anywhere, Alexander," I said breathlessly, swept along in his enthusiasm. "But to envision me at Versailles!"

"You'd show them the courage and mettle of our American ladies." He took me by the hand and from the chair, and led me through impromptu steps of a minuet there on my father's turkey carpet, humming along for accompaniment until I laughed aloud. I supposed this was to show the manner of society we'd encounter at Versailles, but to me it was another example of how bland my life had been this summer without him to leaven it.

He sat again, and this time pulled me across his lap, a favorite place of mine to be. It was also a convenient posture for kissing, and being kissed, and as we indulged in that pleasure, his arm curled neatly around my waist, I was thankful my father couldn't see what was occurring behind the door to his somber study.

"There is another post open as well," he said after a bit. "If you've no use for the ladies of Versailles, then we could venture to St. Petersburg."

"St. Petersburg?" I asked, even more shocked than before. "In Russia?"

He nodded, clearly delighting in how many times he could amaze me in a single conversation. It was, of course, easy enough. Beyond being on the other side of the world, I'd only the vaguest idea of where St. Petersburg lay in relation to Albany.

"Congress will shortly be appointing a minister to Russia," he said. "The post requires a mastery of French, for that's what they speak at their court. I'm told I've been nominated for that as well."

"I should prefer Versailles," I said. "At least I know France to be a Christian country, even if it's Papist."

"Oh, Russia is Christian, too, though not the variety with which you're acquainted." I couldn't tell if he was serious or not, but then his smile softened and his gaze filled with fondness, and being serious no longer mattered.

"I've said not a word of this to your father or anyone else, Eliza, besides those who have placed my nominations before Congress," he said. "You are first in my life now, and I wished you to hear of this first, too."

I nodded, pleased and touched by his confidence in me. "You can be sure that I will tell no one."

"Especially not Angelica," he said. "The last thing I want is for John Carter to go scuttling off to his French accounts with so much as a rumor of that loan."

I nodded again, my eyes wide. I'd never before been asked to keep momentous international secrets. My own dreams for our future had always been so modest, while in comparison his seemed to be growing grander, and grander still. He was only twenty-five, and these honors to which he aspired would have been heady accomplishments for a gentleman twice his age. I remembered how Kitty Livingston had warned me of Alexander's ambitions, and Angelica, too, and I could hear their voices in chorus cautioning me again.

Yet I'd always told myself that I'd wanted more than the stolid Dutch husband that had once seemed my lot. When I'd first been dazzled by Alexander, it was his intelligence, his talents, his passions, his daring, that had made me love him just as much as his kindness and devotion. If his ambition led him to Versailles or

Saint Petersburg or to the very moon and back, then I would be by his side.

"To be sure," he said, "neither possibility may come to anything, and instead I'll be begging you to find contentment in some little cottage beside the Hudson."

I smiled, for that was a possibility I could easily imagine. "So long as you are there, I'll be happy."

I looped my arms around his shoulders and kissed him again. In the distance I could hear Cornelia wailing, no doubt distraught that her nursery maid had come to take her to bed. It must be later than I'd realized.

"We should return to the others," I whispered. "I don't want Mamma to come looking for us."

"There's one more thing." He took a deep breath. "You know that I'd discovered an address for my father, and that I'd written to invite him to our wedding. I'd even offered to arrange passage for him on a neutral French vessel so he'll run no risk of being captured."

I nodded eagerly. "When shall we expect him?"

"I've had no replies to my letters," he said, his expression darkening. "I do not believe we should expect him at all."

"I'm sorry," I said, and I was. Alexander's last memories of his father were so old now that I wondered if he'd even recognize the man should their paths cross again. But to have his father not bother to reply to his letters was a sad, disheartening event.

He shifted his shoulders as if they carried the entire burden of his father's neglect.

"Even if he'd no interest in me, I thought at least he'd wish to meet you," he said. "He has no other daughter, you know."

"No, he doesn't," I said. "But soon you'll have me as your wife."

"Mind you, you'll have me as your husband, too," he said, and at last he smiled. "My own Betsey. What more could I ever want than marriage to you?"

I married Alexander Hamilton on December 14, 1780, in my parents' parlor, the same room where we'd first met three years before.

Unlike the modern taste for lavish weddings, ours was a simple ceremony at noon in our Dutch Reformed faith, without music, ostentation, or pretense. Alexander and I stood before our church's minister and exchanged our vows, with a crowd of my family in attendance as our witnesses. While it saddened me that Alexander had Mac McHenry as his only guest, I cheered myself to think how he could now count upon my family, with all my dozens of cousins, aunts, and uncles as his, too.

This parlor was always a cheerful place, with tall windows on two sides that always drew the sunlight. Because snow blanketed the lawns around the house, the reflected sun was especially bright, as if blessing our union with its brilliance.

After much deliberation, Alexander decided to wear his uniform in all its noble simplicity, and in honor of our shared sympathies for liberty. In his pocket he carried the wedding handkerchief I'd worked as a gift for him, the finest Irish linen with a pattern of pulled threads, and a gift that he treasured always as a memento of the day.

As the bride I was entitled to two shifts of wedding attire. For the ceremony and the wedding breakfast that followed, I wore an elegant Polonaise gown of white satin, trimmed with silver ribbons and edged with bands of dark fur, it being winter. I'd pink stockings with bright green satin shoes on my feet, and a pleated cap of such fine linen that it was no more than a hazy crown upon my dark hair, which I'd left unpowdered for the morning. Over my shoulders was a sheer linen kerchief that I'd embroidered myself for the occasion with a pattern of wreathes and swags, and in my pocket for luck was a handkerchief edged in fine Italian lace, a gift from Mamma. As ornament, I also wore a strand of coral beads given me as an infant by my grandparents, and in my ears were gold and coral earrings from Angelica and Mr. Carter.

But my most treasured jewel was the one I would wear forever, the gold wedding ring that Alexander slipped upon my finger to make me his wife: a cleverly devised gimmel ring of two thinly wrought bands, one engraved with his name and one with mine. Together the bands twisted and fit snugly against each other into a single, shining gold band, without beginning or end. To this day, I have not taken it from my finger since Alexander placed it there, nor will I ever do so, not in this life.

As the day stretched into evening, more guests appeared at our house for a larger celebration, with dancing in our center hall and a late supper with bottles of Madeira that had been smuggled through the British blockades. I changed into a deep blue satin gown, trimmed with painted bouquets of flowers and ribbons, and powdered my hair as white as the drifts outside.

Our stable yard was filled with the sleighs of those who'd come a distance to attend. Our guests included every prominent Dutch family in New York, plus others of distinction in the state who offered us their best wishes.

Flushed and fortified with Papa's Madeira, Mac McHenry stood on the landing of the stairs to make a grand toast, classically inspired, in honor of Alexander and me. This toast included a long poem whose bawdy passages made my older aunts blush, and me, too, as was likely intended, although Alexander declared it worthy of a true laureate. Either way, it was one more thing that made our wedding unlike any other. Despite the rigors of her pregnancy, Mamma had been determined that our wedding would be Albany's most notable of the Christmas season, and there was no doubt she'd succeeded. I heard the revelry lasted so far into the night that it was morning before the last guests left.

I say I heard, not having witnessed it myself. Around ten o'clock, Alexander and I withdrew from the celebrations. I'd begged my parents for us to be spared the traditional wedding night humiliations, wherein the bride and groom were taken upstairs, undressed, and put to bed by their drunken friends with every kind of lewd jest imaginable. Perhaps Mamma pitied me, or perhaps she pitied Alexander with only a single friend to escort him, but she finally agreed and made certain that Papa relented as well.

Instead we slipped away on our own and hurried upstairs before anyone could take notice. It had been a long, long day, filled with excitement and many emotions. I'd so anticipated the moment when Alexander and I would first be alone as husband and wife, but when at last we were standing in the bedchamber, I felt suddenly shy.

"You're quiet, Mrs. Hamilton," he said, his smile crooked, and I wondered if he, too, were feeling the weighty significance of his moment.

I smiled, and blushed. "Mrs. Hamilton," I repeated. "How fine that sounds!"

"It does indeed," he said. "I am honored to present to you my wife, Mrs. Elizabeth Hamilton."

I curtseyed to continue the game. "My husband, Colonel Hamilton."

He took my hand to lift me up, and held it, beginning to draw me gently closer. "You cannot know how happy I am tonight with you as my wife."

Yet I hung back. "I hope I'll always make you that happy," I said, my heart racing as I thought of how much more worldly and experienced he was than I. I didn't know why I felt so skittish. This was Alexander, the man I'd chosen for the rest of our lives. "I love you so much."

"And I love you, too, Betsey," he said, his gaze slipping lower over my body.

Self-consciously I thought of how my elegant wedding attire had suffered from the crush at the supper and from dancing. My kerchief was crumpled and flat, my dress spotted with spilled wine, and everything was dusted with the powder that scattered from my disheveled hair.

"I should call Rose to undress me," I said, but before I could, he placed his fingers over my lips.

"Shhhh," he said softly. "You don't need your maidservant. We don't need anyone else now but each other. I'll help you undress."

I smiled in spite of myself, picturing my stalwart solider husband as a dainty lady's maid. "You needn't do that."

"But I want to," he said. "I'm your husband now, and I want to do everything for you."

"I don't know why I'm being so foolish," I said, tears stinging my eyes.

"You're not foolish," he said. "You're perfection. Love me as I love you, Betsey. Trust me, and our joy will be boundless."

I nodded, for I already loved him beyond measure, and trusted him with my happiness and everything else. I took a deep breath and kissed him, and loved, and trusted.

And indeed, as he'd promised, that night our joy was boundless.

* * *

For the next day and night we kept to ourselves, and though the rest of the household continued around us, Mamma saw to it that no one troubled us, and that our meals were brought upstairs to us on a tray. Not only did we keep to our bedchamber, but we seldom ventured from the bed itself. Such is the happy pattern of the newly wed, and we were no different, discovering a hundred ways to beguile and please and make our love our own. We were wonderfully suited to each other, my new husband and I. I do not know if I believed Angelica's claim that our family was particularly amorous, or if I should grant all credit to Alexander, who would have been glad to receive it as his manly due. Regardless of the reason, our passions and our satisfaction were in perfect balance, and blissful joy was ours.

Finally, and reluctantly, we rejoined the others after two days apart, appearing at family breakfast together. Although I was flustered to see my parents again, knowing how much had changed about me since I'd seen them last, they kindly didn't tease me or Alexander, but treated us the same as they had before our marriage. That first awkwardness soon passed, and I settled into the happy state of being Mrs. Hamilton.

But the army was much less understanding of honeymoons, and even the three days of our wedding was an interminable time for Alexander to be away from his desk and correspondence. A considerable pile of reports, dispatches, and letters from headquarters had been delivered for him just in the few days we'd kept to ourselves. He set to work immediately, his focus as intent as if he weren't a newly minted bridegroom, and he continued to work that night long after I'd fallen asleep in the bed behind him.

Though I'd wished we'd had more time alone together, I could scarcely complain. His devotion to his responsibilities was a kind of loyalty, and one of the inviolable qualities that made him so honorable a gentleman, almost to a fault. I'd always known this of him, and I respected it.

I soon learned, however, that even the most conscientious of gentleman can be seduced into performing duties of a more intimate sort, and over the next weeks letters from His Excellency were made to wait their turn. Nor did Alexander object, and in fact he was every bit as eager as I to be distracted from his work. I have never seen him more relaxed, more happy, more filled with hope, which only increased my own contentment.

I was also pleased to see the ease with which we became part of my parents' large household in our new roles as husband and wife. Papa in particular was swiftly coming to regard Alexander as another son as well as a military colleague and fellow officer, and I was delighted to see that the friendship that had begun last winter in Morristown had only deepened with our marriage.

Even my younger brothers soon discovered that Alexander could be persuaded to join them out of doors for a mock battle with snowballs, at which he proved ruthlessly adept. I watched them, cheering and laughing, and thinking of how much younger my new husband looked when he played the games of the childhood he hadn't had. He didn't hold back with my brothers, either, hurling the packed snow as hard as he could, taking risks, and dodging their missiles with determined agility. His intensity gave me an uneasy glimpse of the kind of soldier he must be in a true battle, and I prayed with all my heart that he'd never see another real engagement with guns and artillery in place of snowballs.

But among my siblings, it was Angelica's opinion that mattered most to me, and she, too, continued to laud my new husband for his intellect, his charm, and his wit, and congratulated me for falling in love with so amiable a spouse. Little wonder that I basked in the glow of her approval. But how could Alexander and Angelica not become friends? Their banter at the supper table was more entertaining than the playhouse, and I could only sit by and listen in wonder to their conversations. When English seemed insufficient for a specific point, they lapsed into French, and Papa joined them, for he, too, spoke that language.

I thought of that still-open appointment as an envoy to the Court of Versailles, and how much Alexander deserved it. Surely there couldn't be another man in the entire country who could fill the position with more skill and delicacy, and while I knew it was unwise to ask the Heavens for temporal gains, I still resolved to say an extra prayer or two that he finally be rewarded.

It was difficult not to share the possibility of the French appointment with Angelica. She would surely share my hope that Alexander would receive it in honor of his merit, but she'd also consider the real possibility that we—Angelica, Mr. Carter, Alexander, and I—could one day meet in Paris. Mr. Carter had promised to take Angelica there (and to his home in London, too) once the war was over and American ships were safe from capture, and to imagine the four of us in Paris—Paris!—at the same time was a dream indeed.

But one late one evening, Angelica revealed an entirely different sort of dream to me involving Alexander.

"I've never met a gentleman who enchants me more than your Hamilton," she declared grandly as we made our way upstairs. Mamma had already retired and the men were still at the table downstairs, as men do. As it was, Angelica and I had stayed there longer than usual ourselves, and all I wished now was to sleep, not begin another long conversation with my sister.

"He is my constant love," I said, stifling a yawn. "I'm glad you two have become friends."

"Friends, oh, yes," she said, sweeping her arms through the air. She'd had her share of drink tonight, too; she and Mr. Carter did enjoy their wine. "What if I asked you to share your darling husband with me, Eliza?"

I laughed at her preposterous request. "That's Papa's Madeira talking, Angelica," I said, bemused. "What would Mr. Carter say if he heard you?"

"John is not your Hamilton," she said slyly, pausing on the landing to lean against the railing. "I heard you with your bridegroom last night, little sister. What a lover he must be."

"He's my husband, Angelica," I said, blushing furiously. In most cases, I valued my sister's opinions, but not when she was like this. "We're married."

Angelica waved her hand as if this didn't signify. "I think we should share him," she said. "He could be our Lord Turk, and please us both."

"Angelica, no," I said, ashamed for her.

"He'd agree," she insisted. "What man would refuse?"

"My husband would," I said. "Yours would, too."

She shook her head and wrinkled her nose. "I think we should ask Hamilton his opinion."

"And I think you should go to bed," I said, gently guiding her

back toward the stairs, "and forget you've ever breathed such rubbish."

Fortunately, she did forget, or leastways never mentioned it
again. I wouldn't have shared her foolishness now except that it
proves how thoroughly my new husband captivated my family,
enough to make my sister speak so.

But as enjoyable as these weeks of holiday and honeymoon had
been, they too swiftly came to an end, as all such diversions do. It
wasn't just knowing that in early January we would leave Albany to
return to the army. No, the true end of this blissful time was announced in a pair of letters from Philadelphia that arrived in quick
succession.

The first letter came from his dear friend John Laurens, who
sorrowfully revealed that not only had Alexander been denied the
envoy's post at Versailles, but that Congress had instead awarded it
to Laurens himself, even though he'd lobbied most vehemently for
his better-qualified friend. Not knowing John Laurens, I could only
secretly wonder how, in good conscience, he could accept the position if he truly believed Alexander to have been the better candidate. Alexander, however, didn't question his motives at all, and
thus I knew well enough to keep my opinion to myself. In the
meantime, he put all his hopes into the Russian position, telling me
over and over how well-suited he was for it, as if I'd any say in the
final decision. How I wished I'd had that ability to make him
happy!

Three days later a letter arrived from John Matthews, the con-
gressman who'd nominated Alexander for the Russian post. I was
in the hall when it was delivered, and with the letter in my hand, I
rushed to the stables where Alexander was discussing horses with
Papa. I handed it to him without a word, and at once he excused
himself from my father and took the letter out of doors to read. I
followed, prepared either to rejoice with him, or offer consolation
if the news was not what he'd wished.

It wasn't. I saw at once from how empty his face became. Because I knew him so well, I recognized this as his blackest despair,
and infinitely worse than any other man's wild ravings.

"Come," I said quietly, slipping my hand into the crook of his
arm. "Walk with me."

Mute with disappointment, he nodded, and stuffed the letter into his pocket. I led him into the snowy gardens, away from the house and the sympathy of others. His pride would not suffer that, not now. I knew he'd be better served by the bleak austerity of the winter landscape, by bare trees and gray skies that would reflect his humor. Narrow paths had been cleared through the gardens, with only snowy mounds on either side to show where there'd be bright flowers come spring. In silence we walked swiftly, my steps hurried to match his, to the orchards, around the kitchen gardens, and back to what would be roses.

"It has nothing to do with my merits," he said at last, so out of context that I knew he'd been working entire arguments in his head all the while we'd been walking. "My qualifications were more than enough to meet the requirements of the post."

"Very true," I agreed.

"Laurens says it's because I am so unknown to the gentlemen of Congress," he said bitterly, his words little clouds of disappointment in the cold air. "I'm certain he's right. I have no property, no fortune, to give me stature, nor have I a father or other family to support me in the circles who have the power of decision. Whatever my successes, they are empty accomplishments in such a world without the false buttressing of fame to support them."

"There will be other posts and other positions," I said, soothing. "You underestimate your true value."

"I don't doubt my value to the country," he said. "What I lack is the reputation that brings my name instantly to mind for appointments. I can hardly gain that reputation by writing letters and making tallies."

"Your work for His Excellency is important, Alexander," I said. "He trusts you like no other."

"He trusts me to write letters for him in French, a skill he clearly regards as without value, else he would have learned it himself," he said. "All others around me have prospered and moved forward, while I remain to be buried by the same tasks and tedium. But no more, Betsey. I am done, and I'm resolved there must be change."

Surprised, I stopped walking. "How are you done? You're not resigning your commission, are you?"

"No," he said, though the way he said it made me think he'd

considered it. "As you and I have planned, I'll be leaving for New Windsor on Thursday, and you shall follow me soon after. I've given my word to return, and so I must."

I nodded with a certain relief, for this was indeed what we'd planned. He would go ahead by horseback to New Windsor in southern New York, the site of this year's winter encampment, and I would follow by sleigh with a selection of our belongings.

But he wasn't done.

"I've given my word to return," he continued, "and so I must. But our marriage has changed me, Betsey. Having you as my wife has given me a fresh determination. I'm no longer content to sit idle and wait for others to determine my future."

"What shall you do instead?" I asked, hoping I kept the uneasiness from my voice.

His voice, however, was filled with confidence and daring.

"That shall be decided in time," he said, his eyes glowing with his fervor. "Every indication points to the war ending this year. Before it does, before it's too late, I must seize my opportunity on the field of glory."

"But if His Excellency —"

"His Excellency is my general, but he is neither my friend, nor my ally," he said with a coldness that shocked me. "I can no longer rely on His Excellency or any other man beyond myself. All I need is a field command, and this time I'll find a way to get that."

My fingers tightened into the rough wool of his coat. I couldn't hold him back, nor did I wish to. All I could do was pray he'd find wisdom to match his enthusiasm, and luck to support his ambition and preserve his life. Impulsively he bent to kiss me, and I tasted his determination hot as a fever.

The wonderfully irresponsible romance of our courtship and honeymoon had ended, that was clear. Marriage and being Mrs. Hamilton were going to be much more challenging, and difficult, too. If I prayed for wisdom for my husband, I prayed for strength for myself.

In the coming months, we'd need them both.

CHAPTER 10

New Windsor, New York
February 1781

The first lodging that Alexander and I shared together as husband and wife was also the smallest house in which I ever lived. New Windsor had been chosen as the site of this year's winter encampment for its location on the Hudson River near the fort at West Point and not far from the city of New York, strategic advantages to an army. The benefits to those of us who followed the army were not as evident, and the word I heard most often to describe it was *dreary*—which it was. Unlike Morristown, the site of last winter's encampment, New Windsor was scarcely more than a village, and as such lacked a sufficient number of agreeable houses for quartering officers. Even His Excellency was compelled to make his headquarters in William Ellison's uncomfortably small farmhouse, as far removed from Mrs. Ford's splendid house as could be.

Our house was in the village, and consisted of a single room that served as kitchen, parlor, and bedchamber combined, with a ladder to a loft above, where our servants slept. Off in one corner of this room was an old Dutch box, or cupboard bed, such as was used since the days when New York was New Amsterdam. This style of bed was unfamiliar to Alexander, and vastly entertaining, too. Each night we'd climb into this bed and close its doors after us to create a snug, dark little room of our own. The doors made it much warmer than an English bed with drafty curtains, and much more intimate, as Alexander soon came to realize, and relish. But then marriage agreed with us both so much that we found delight in everything we did, so long as it was together.

At the same time, I was surprised by how much I missed my family, especially my mother. I'd bid the most tearful farewell to her, for I wouldn't see her again before she was once more brought to childbed. Because of her age, I feared for her and for the coming baby, too. In the years of her marriage to Papa, she'd lost seven children as infants (including a pair of twins and a set of triplets), an ominous pattern that I secretly dreaded for myself. Mamma, however, had only smiled serenely at my concerns, and said whatever came to pass would be God's will, not mine, which made me pray even more fervently both for her safe deliverance and a child of my own.

It was perhaps for this reason that I was especially grateful for the presence in camp of Lady Washington. She had shown great kindness toward me last winter, and she continued her favor now to the extent that I felt genuine friendship between us. I spent most afternoons in her company, and together we poured tea and entertained senior officers, their wives, and His Excellency's other guests in the headquarters' parlor. To be sure, this was a role I'd been well prepared to play, given how many diverse guests my parents had welcomed to our house over the years, but I believe it pleased Lady Washington to have another lady beside her to help share her responsibilities and make her guests at ease.

It also pleased me to be near to Alexander during the day, with him at work beside His Excellency, and I in another room in the same house with Lady Washington. We seldom saw each other— Alexander's duties were so various and pressing that he'd no unoccupied time to spend with me—but simply knowing he was near was a sufficient comfort to me.

I only wished that Alexander could have said the same. After his recent disappointments in regard to promotions and opportunities, I'd been well aware of his unhappiness, particularly with His Excellency. This had only increased since he had returned to New Windsor.

For various reasons, all the other aides-de-camp had left the General's Family, and from a full staff of eleven aides, the number had now dwindled to one, and that one was Alexander. (Another aide-de-camp, Tench Tilghman, was still considered a member of the Family, but constant plagues of ill health often forced him to be absent.) The amount of work Alexander was expected to complete would have crushed a less conscientious man; in the first five weeks after his return, he told me wearily that he had drafted over fifty letters, many in French, for His Excellency, in addition to even more composed and sent over his own name as aide-de-camp.

For nearly five years, Alexander had been with His Excellency nearly every day and often into the night. I'd only known the general in passing, as the commander-in-chief, as one of my father's closest friends, and as the much-loved husband of Lady Washington. Like most citizens, I was in awe of him, for his imposing height and figure, for his confidence, reserve, and bravery. No one was more heroic and emblematic of our fledging country than His Excellency, especially while riding the white horse he always favored.

Soon after I had arrived and was sitting sewing with Lady Washington, I was witness to a feat of purest strength by the general. Several townswomen who earned money by laundering officers' linens were standing over their large oaken washtubs in the yard, not far from headquarters. Of a sudden, one of them began to point and shout with incoherent distress, and then ran into the parlor where Lady Washington and I were sitting at our sewing.

"My lady, oh, my lady!" she cried without bothering with any customary signs of greeting or respect. "Sparks from the chimney've lit the roof of the shed a-fire! All will be lost, my lady, all lost!"

We rushed from the door after her in fearful haste, and stared up at the roof of the shed, which adjoined the house. A recent spate of clear days had blown the roof clear of snow, and now flames licked across and through the dry shingles. Sentries were running to the well to pull buckets of water, but the fire had a fair start upon them, and it appeared that headquarters would be next to burn.

While the soldier and washing-women flustered about in panic, we heard a great clattering down the stairs inside, and His Excellency himself ran from the house. Instantly appraising the situation, he didn't issue orders, as I'd expected, but instead himself seized the largest oak tub of soapy wash water and carried it into the house and up the stairs, the soapy water splashing out on either side.

He threw open the window of his office (which overlooked the shed), climbed onto the roof with the tub, and emptied it onto the flames. Nor did he pause, but returned to the yard to seize another tub of water and repeat the process. He did this three times in rapid succession, down and up the stairs to the roof, until the flames were doused and all that remained were the charred shingles, and the last wisps of smoke curling into the winter sky.

Now, I cannot venture the exact weight of an oaken washtub filled with water, except to say that it is a heavy burden, and an awkward one to carry as well. At least two women, and often two men, are required simply to tip such a tub sideways to spill and empty it onto the ground. Yet His Excellency, who at forty-nine years was not a young man, carried these tubs in his arms with ease. Both his strength and his presence of mind impressed me, and so I described the event to Alexander (who had been elsewhere in the encampment when it occurred) that night. We'd fallen into the agreeable habit of retiring to bed as soon as we'd finished supper, lying cozily together in the warmth and dark to discuss the day.

Alexander, however, had a very different reaction to my description of His Excellency's heroics.

"There's no doubt that the general is strong as the proverbial ox," he admitted. "But you must believe that his temper is every bit as strong, perhaps more so."

"Truly?" I asked, more from curiosity than disbelief. Papa had never mentioned this side of the general, and in the few times when I had seen him in company with Lady Washington, he had shown only a gentle devotion reflective of the regard he held for his wife. "I have found him daunting, but more on account of who he is, rather than for his temper."

Alexander sighed, rolling over on his back. "All of us who have been employed closely with him have received his wrath at one time or another," he said. "It's all the more fearsome because it's so unexpected."

"He's never been angry with you, has he?"

"You cannot be serious, Betsey," he said. "I've borne the brunt of his anger more times than I can count, and his abuse has only grown worse over the years."

"I'd no notion," I marveled, propping myself on my elbow. "None at all."

"That's how it should be," he said, and sighed again. "The war itself provides conflict enough without admitting to the world that the general has his flaws and weaknesses. He needs to be perceived as invincible, above the pettiness of ordinary men. Everyone who has ever been part of his Family understands, and agrees. But trust me, dearest: to be the target of his harsh, intemperate anger is not pleasant."

I remembered this conversation several days later, when again I sat in the company of Lady Washington and several French officers. As I've noted, the house being used as headquarters was small and the staircase open, with voices from the office upstairs audible to us below in the parlor.

As we sat together, our polite discussion of the last snowstorm was suddenly interrupted by the sound of His Excellency's furious voice. His exact words were not discernable, but the harsh severity of his anger was, and the three French officers stared down at their tea with obvious embarrassment.

Swiftly Lady Washington rose, and without a break in her smiling conversation, she closed the door against the hall and her husband's temper. It was neatly done, and from her ease, was clearly something she'd done many times before. Her brisk efficiency also proved what Alexander had said, for no mention was made of the general's outburst, not then or at any other time. It was as if it never happened.

Yet the general was not alone in his growing frustrations. As the winter weeks stretched on, Alexander spoke more and more vehemently of his discontent, and what he felt was the disrespect being shown him. He had always considered himself a soldier who had been forced to become a clerk for the good of the service; at the time he'd first become an aide-de-camp, he'd believed the position would be temporary, and assist his rise through the ranks.

Instead he'd watched other officers receive the promotions and appointments that should have been his. Even worse, nearly three years had now passed since he'd seen any real action on a battle-field, save for the skirmishes last summer in New Jersey.

As much as I preferred he'd never again see battle or risk a vio-lent death again, I knew how much these slights rankled at his pride and ambition, and fanned the misguided belief that he was some-how failing me. The longer the drought without a field command continued, the more I feared the consequences.

In February, I learned exactly what those could be.

I was alone at home in our little house in the middle of the day, sitting at the small table beside the fire and writing a letter to Papa. I heard the door behind me unlatch and swing open, and I turned with a start.

"Alexander!" I exclaimed with surprise, at once rising from my chair to greet him. It was the sixteenth, only two days after we'd warmly celebrated Valentine's Day, and I thought at first that he'd come home now at this unusual hour for the rare pleasure of seeing me. But as soon as he took off his hat and I saw his stony expres-sion, I realized there was a more serious reason than Cupid.

"Something is amiss, isn't it?" I asked anxiously. "You're home so early. What has happened?"

Without removing his coat, he dropped heavily into the arm-chair across from mine, his legs sprawled before me and his hat still in his hand.

"The thing is done, Eliza," he said. "He provoked me, and left me no choice."

"Who provoked you, my love?" I asked, though I'd already a notion of who it might be. "What did you do?"

"The general," he said wearily. "I was going down the stairs in that infernal farmhouse as he was coming up. He said he wished to speak with me and I agreed, and continued on the errand I'd begun, delivering a letter below to Tilghman, and then paused to converse briefly with Lafayette on a matter of business."

He paused now, too, taking time to recall exactly what had tran-spired. "This took two minutes, perhaps five at most, yet when I climbed the stairs to join the general, I found him waiting for me on the landing. His face was livid, and he accused me of keeping him waiting a full ten minutes, and therefore offering him blatant disrespect."

"Oh, Alexander," I said, placing my hand over his. "What did you say in return?"

"I told him that I wasn't conscious of it," he said, "but that if he found it so necessary to tell me so, then we must part. He nodded as curtly as a man can, accepting my decision. He returned to the office, and I came . . . here."

I nodded, though I still wasn't entirely certain what had occurred.

"Do you mean that you parted, and went about your separate business," I said, "or that you parted from his employ?"

He looked down into his hat, as if the answer lay there. "It's my intention to leave the Family, yes. You know I've considered this for some time, and now that the general has made my position untenable, my decision is firm."

I'd known he was unhappy, but these events still came as a shock. "Does His Excellency accept your decision?"

"If he didn't when we parted, he does now," he said. "Soon afterwards he sent Tilghman to follow me and ask me to return to his office to discuss the matter further."

"What did His Excellency say?" I asked, dreading his inevitable reply. Oh, there were times when I wished I did not know my husband so well!

"He said nothing, for I did not go to him," Alexander said. "Through Tilghman, I said that I'd made my resolution in a manner not to be revoked. I told him that while I certainly wouldn't refuse the interview if he desired it, I believed the conversation would only produce explanations that neither of us would find agreeable."

"Oh, Alexander," I said again, sadly, and this time unable to keep back my dismay. "He wished for a reconciliation, yet you refused?"

"I did," he said. "I said I would much prefer to decline the conversation, and he respected my desire."

I sat back and sighed heavily. "What shall come next for us? You haven't another post, have you?"

"Not yet, no," he admitted. "But now that I have resigned, I'm sure something shall be made available to me. A position or a post where I can make a genuine contribution beyond mere scribbling."

It sounded uncomfortably as if he were convincing himself as much as me; he'd been desirous of a field post as long as we'd known each other.

"I suppose we can no longer remain in these lodgings," I said with regret. The little house had many flaws, but for these last weeks, it had been ours. "I will have Rose begin packing at once. I suppose we can return to Albany."

"Nothing will happen immediately," he said. "I have resigned, yes, but His Excellency still has not accepted it. I will also continue my duties until another aide-de-camp fluent in French can be found as my replacement. The general may not respect me as I wish, but I respect the requirements of his office and the nation too much to make an abrupt departure."

It seemed abrupt to me. "I want you to be happy, Alexander," I said. "But I rather wish your decision had not come from a sudden disagreement with His Excellency."

"But it didn't," he said. "This has been simmering for months now. The strong words today were but a catalyst. I was entirely respectful, Betsey. I promise you that. I didn't once raise my own voice, or let rash anger get the better of me, as it did the general."

"You must write to my father at once," I urged. "He deserves to learn of this breach with His Excellency first from you instead of someone else."

I knew Papa would not be pleased by this news. Although he had come to regard Alexander as another son, he'd been friends with His Excellency far longer, and I suspected together they would agree that my husband had behaved rashly and impetuously. I only hoped Papa would forgive him, and not fault him to the point of an open rift.

"I will," Alexander said. "But the first, the very first, I told was you. There can never be anything but perfect honesty between us. That is why I wish you to know that I've conducted this affair in the most honorable and just way possible."

I nodded, but said nothing more, at a loss. I treasured his honesty nearly as much as his love, but the truth as I saw it was that he should have accepted His Excellency's offer of reconciliation.

"You're worried," he said gently, turning his hand to link his fingers into mine. "I can see it in your eyes. But this break was long overdue. I expect I'll receive only congratulations from my friends for having taken it."

This was not the case, however, as Alexander learned over the next days and weeks. All of his closest friends had at one time or another been aides-de-camp—John Laurens, Mac McHenry, Tench Tilghman, and Richard Kidder Meade—and should have understood exactly what he'd endured and how he'd been limited. Yet every one of them advised him to make amends with His Excellency, and remain for the sake of the efficiency of the staff. Both Lafayette and my father pleaded with him to reconsider and remain as well.

Alexander held firm, and would not change his mind.

When Lady Washington sent me a message the following day, requesting that I call upon her, I went with considerable trepidation.

It felt odd to be returning to headquarters, knowing what had happened there just the day before, but Lady Washington welcomed me as warmly as ever. She closed the door so we wouldn't be disturbed, and poured us tea; even amidst the rough hospitality of a winter encampment, she believed in the niceties of porcelain teacups and a silver teapot brought from home. She spoke lightly of the weather, the ice upon the river, and the queen's stitch covers she was working on canvas, one by one, for the chairs in the dining room at Mount Vernon.

Then, as I sipped my tea, she finally addressed the subject most on my mind.

"Dear Mrs. Hamilton," she began. "I expect you are waiting for me to address the little tift between our husbands."

Although I said nothing, my expression must have betrayed me, for she laughed softly.

"Be easy, I beg you," she said. "I've no intention of scolding or meddling or whatever else you fear I might do. Yes, my husband was unhappy that yours has chosen to leave his Family, and especially by the manner in which the breach has occurred, but he has accepted it, and thus so have I."

I couldn't keep back a gusty sigh of relief. "Oh, thank you, madam."

She smiled, stirring her tea with a muted click of her spoon against her cup.

"There's no need for thanks," she said, holding the silver spoon up to drip into the cup. "It was perhaps inevitable, given that they are both gentlemen of strong convictions. Colonel Hamilton will be difficult to replace—I may even be called upon to copy letters!—and my husband will miss his industry and his talents, but I believe this rupture between them may prove to be for the best. While anger is seldom wise in any situation, in certain circumstances it can become a forge in which better things are created."

I nodded eagerly. "At first I feared my husband acted upon mere impulse and temper, but I've come to see that wasn't so."

"It's the temper of redheaded gentlemen," she said, commiserating. "The general and I have been wed for more than twenty years, yet that temper still will startle me, all the more because he is most usually a man of measured kindness and even temperament. The saving grace of such outbursts is that they subside as quickly as they appear."

I never thought of His Excellency as having red hair since he was always scrupulous about keeping it powdered in a military fashion. Alexander dressed his hair formally with powder, too, but of course it was my prerogative as his wife to see him in undress, when his hair shown bright.

"That is the way with Colonel Hamilton as well," I agreed. "At first, I, too, was dismayed. But the more he explained his decision to me, the more I realized that he had made the one that was right for him, and most in keeping with his own convictions."

"Our husbands must make decisions with consequences, decisions that must be thoughtful, thorough, and just, and we must be ready to support them in those decisions when others will not."

I nodded again. "None of Colonel Hamilton's friends have agreed with his decision," I said wistfully, "yet I've come to accept it as the best for him, and for us as well, and he has thanked me for it."

"That is exactly as it should be," she said with satisfaction, "and exactly as I'd hoped you would say it was. We wives of officers are different from other women, aren't we? We see the terrible burden this war places upon our husbands in the service of our country. All we can do is pray for their welfare, and comfort them as best we can."

Her voice was soft and gentle, yet filled with the wise counsel and strength I so needed that I couldn't keep from sharing my doubts.

"Oh, madam," I lamented. Tears stung my eyes, and I looked down at my lap to hide them. "I worry so much about where my husband shall go next! What he desires most is a field command, and even as I agree and tell him I wish it, too, I dread that he may come to grief on some distant battlefield. I cannot fathom my life without him, madam, and if I were to lose him . . ."

My words broke off, the possibility too unbearable to speak aloud.

She set her cup down on the table beside her and placed her hand over mine. Her palm was soft, and still warm from the tea.

"Of course you are afraid for him, my dear," she said quietly. "Do not believe for an instant that I don't share those same fears for the general. Life is a fragile gift, and no one sees that more clearly than a soldier's wife. But you cannot let that fear be your companion, or it will steal away every joy that makes your lives rich. You must trust in the love you share, and God in Heaven."

I fumbled for my handkerchief and tried to smile. "That is what Alexander—that is, Colonel Hamilton—says as well. He says I must trust him."

"Trust him, yes, but trust yourself as well," she said. "It's together that you will be strongest. No matter what your worries or fears, they shall always be much more bearable together."

I bowed my head and blotted my eyes, yet nodded. Mamma had given me similar advice before our wedding, and I'd said much the same to Alexander myself. Yet hearing the words from Lady Washington made me once again see the wisdom in this simple message and the truth to it as well. In the future, and in times that tested me most in our marriage, I'd remember it in her voice, soft but firm, and find guidance and solace in the memory.

Thus in the wake of the argument (or tift, as Lady Washington had called it; others called if a feud, a fight, a battle, a falling-out, but they were wrong, even to this day) between His Excellency and Alexander, I did my best to be strong for Alexander, and I know that he did the same for me.

So often when he'd erred before, it was his own doing, and he almost always recognized his misdeed soon afterward, causing him to tumble into a dark wallow of recrimination, guilt, and battered pride, which could only be ended with apologies all around.

In the past, yes, but not this time. I was exceptionally proud of my husband's demeanor and discretion throughout these difficult days, and the control he exerted over his own temper. As he'd promised, he did not desert his post as an aide at once, as a man driven by pure anger would have done, or announce his departure with vituperative fanfare to the greater world.

Instead he stayed until replacements could be found, so as not to distress either the general or the workings of the office, and was equally determined to continue as if nothing untoward had occurred. He continued to draft letters for His Excellency and write orders, dispatches, and addresses, exactly as he had done for the previous four years. Further, to preserve the peace of the office, he told only his closest friends of the short-lived quarrel. Many other officers with whom he had near-constant contact through letters and dispatches had no knowledge of the rift with the general until he had finally departed the staff.

There were those among our acquaintance who credited Alexander's new composure to his marriage to me. I suppose it was, but not in the unflattering way that teasing bachelors meant with their hen-pecking jests. Rather, the incident with His Excellency became something that drew Alexander and me closer together, and which we confronted as husband and wife, exactly as Lady Washington had advised. With me beside him, Alexander truly did seem to have more purpose now, and I—no, *we*—were the stronger for it.

In early March, Alexander left New Windsor with His Excellency to meet with the Comte de Rochambeau and the other French officers in Newport, in Rhode Island, and to review the French fleet anchored there. The conference had long been planned, and Alexander's presence was essential. Not only had he drawn up many of the plans for the next step in the war this summer involving the combined forces, but his skill as an interpreter was in constant demand, and he was much respected by the French officers.

Few beyond His Excellency himself knew that this would be the final time Alexander would be at the general's side as his senior aide-de-camp.

Although he retained his commission as a lieutenant colonel, he no longer had an appointment with the forces stationed in New Windsor, and likewise we no longer had reason to remain in residence there. Until he learned where he would next be posted, I packed our belongings and returned to my parents' house in Albany. Alexander would join us once he'd completed his responsibilities with the French in Newport. It was a long journey north, but the tedium was considerably lightened by the company that agreed to join me: my Aunt Gertrude and Uncle John, and Lady Washington herself.

But there was little doubt that we all were in sore need of a change of location from New Windsor, and we had a happy event as an excuse to travel. In February, Papa had written proudly to me to announce that my mother had been safely brought to bed of a little girl. This was my mother's fifteenth child, born soon after her own forty-seventh birthday, a remarkable feat for any woman. Mamma sounded well enough in her letters, and clearly doted on her newest (and likely last) child, named Catherine Van Rensselaer Schuyler after herself. I was eager to see my mother again, and to show her how well I was prospering as a wife.

I was also eager to meet my new little sister, and see which among us she favored. I'd been an older sister as long as I could remember, and perhaps because of that, I'd always adored babies and young children. To be mother to Alexander's children was a dream I cherished above all others, and I spent more time than was likely wise imagining these unknown little cherubs: would they have Alexander's golden red hair or my dark eyes, his strong nose or my dimpled chin?

Babies were much on my mind. Despite Angelica's assurances, Alexander and I had been married for four months now, and I'd yet to conceive. In Albany, my aunts pointedly surveyed my waistline and made impolite inquiries, and Mamma offered sympathy and assurances that my time would come soon enough, which was almost worse. There were no guarantees. I could consider my parents with their houseful of children, and then look to the general and Lady Washington, who'd not been blessed with a single one. When Angelica wrote that she was expecting her third child, my joy for her condition was tempered by an unseemly regret for my own. My distress and frustration grew as each month passed, and though Alexander, once again with me, tried to make light of it for my sake, I knew that he was every bit as disappointed as I.

He watched me whenever I held my little sister Catherine, her wobbly small head in a white-work bonnet against my shoulder and my fingers spread to support her narrow back as I cradled her against me. I'd be kissing her forehead and whispering nonsense into her tiny dark curls, and then I'd catch his gaze, and the tenderness and longing I saw in his eyes mirrored my own. It hurt, that much longing for something I might never have, and I had to look away before I wept, and shamed us both.

Although Alexander was no longer an aide-de-camp, he decided that it would be advantageous to remain near to headquarters as he sought his next position. The new lodgings he found for us were less than a mile across the Hudson River from New Windsor on a long finger of land called De Peyster's Point. By the end of April, we were once again living in a small Dutch house of brick and stone, though this one had a pretty view overlooking the river, with the hills turning green with the new spring. I expected that view would be much less cordial in the winter months, when the wind would blow off the river, but Alexander assured me with confidence that we would be gone to a more permanent home long before then. I was determined to share his confidence, and unpacked only the things we might use each day.

There was another feature of this house, however, that did not enchant me. Alexander proudly pointed to a boat tied to a makeshift mooring at the end of the path. The boat was included with the house, and further, the house's owner's thick-armed sons would be willing to row the boat across the river to New Windsor and back for a small remuneration; the father promised his sons could make the crossing in less than half an hour.

Now, I had been raised on this same Hudson River, albeit farther to the north where the channel was less imposing, but I still maintained a healthy respect for the hazards of small boats in open water. I wasn't pleased when Alexander announced that he would on occasion employ the boat to cross to New Windsor, and when he tried to sweeten the prospect by offering to take me as well, I swiftly declined. Like most men from the Caribbean, Alexander could swim. I, like every other lady of my acquaintance, could not, and the prospect of being dragged down to the river's bottom by the anchor of my water-logged quilted petticoats was one I chose to avoid.

Yet despite Alexander's restlessness and the uncertainty of his future (and my refusal to employ the boat), we were wonderfully content that spring. By most standards, we could still be considered newlyweds, and able to find true happiness with nothing more than each other's company.

Now freed from his aide's desk at headquarters, Alexander attacked his future with furious energy. He wrote letter after letter, no longer for His Excellency but on his own behalf, beseeching every man of rank or influence whom he knew (and a few whom he didn't) in hopes of securing the much-desired field appointment.

But he was also looking beyond the army. The cost of the long war and the parsimony of the individual states had finally made the Continental currency issued by Congress worthless, and the only money that meant anything was hard coins from other countries. To seek a solution to the crisis, Congress had at last decided to appoint a minister specifically to address the country's finance—a decision that Alexander thought was long overdue. In fact, Alexander had many more opinions and thoughts on financial affairs than I'd ever realized.

With our windows thrown open to the breezes off the water, our little brick lodgings became almost a schoolhouse for me as Alexander outlined his beliefs and the policies he'd implement if it were up to him. He'd seen the woes that the states caused to Congress and the army, and doubted the country could continue in such a scattered condition. Instead he believed the individual states must abandon much of their individual powers, and come together to create a single, stronger entity through a national government. He believed this government should have the power to levy taxes and tariffs, create laws, and raise an army if necessary, all to better serve its citizens. Most of all he believed the country needed a single treasury or bank to secure a national currency, and do away with the worthless paper money issued by each state.

These were such new ideas that I marveled. To hear Alexander speak this way gave me fresh appreciation of his innate brilliance, and the complicated workings of his elegant mind. He could speak by the hour, raking his fingers through his hair as he paced back and forth, and I listened, rapt.

I was a sounding board for him, and he claimed that explaining to me helped him to clarify these complicated theories and notions. I'd heard many well-educated gentlemen discuss similar subjects at my father's table; Alexander outspoke them all with a depth of knowledge and a neatness of speech so that I, as untutored as I was, could understand him with ease, and share his excitement.

While Alexander himself could have made an excellent superintendent of finance, even I had to concede that the post would never be given to him: a twenty-six-year-old gentleman without family or fortune whose sole business experience had been working as a merchant's clerk on Nevis. Instead Congress chose Robert Morris, a former fellow member, a signer of the Declaration of Independence, and most importantly, a gentleman-merchant said to be the wealthiest in Philadelphia. I remembered seeing his carriage drive past me when I'd visited that city, with his family's crest painted on the door and footmen in livery with silver lace, as if he were a great nobleman in London.

Looking to the future, Alexander resolved to make himself known to Mr. Morris with a detailed letter explaining the same philosophies that he'd been explaining to me. And what a letter it turned out to be: page after page after page, the written equivalent of his addresses to me. He wasn't simply describing the monetary problems that Congress faced at present, but suggesting an entirely new kind of financial model for government to follow the war.

When his ideas came too fast and he became unable to keep still from excitement, he'd thrust the pen toward me, and I continued to write what he dictated as he paced the room. In jest I said I'd become an "aide-de-Alexander," which made him laugh. He said he preferred to think of me his "amanuensis," a much more elegant and literary Latin term. Either way, I relished the role, and when Mr. Morris replied with appreciative praise, I rejoiced with Alexander not just as his wife, but as his partner—and his amanuensis.

But he was sharing his ideas more publicly, too, in a series of articles that were published in the *New-York Packet* that summer. He did not credit himself as the author (something few gentlemen did, and also unwise for his military aspirations). Instead he wrote under the initials *A. B.*, yet those in power recognized him as the author, and took note.

As spring shifted toward summer, however, Alexander's thoughts were more often again with the troops across the river. The encampment would soon break for summer. Although Alexander no longer knew every detail of the army's activities and plans from headquarters—the sole feature of being an aide-de-camp that he missed, and sorely, too—he remained sufficiently informed to learn that His Excellency was determined to break the stalemate in the war this summer.

The largest concentration of British troops remained in the city of New York, which they had occupied since 1777. From Alexander's final days in headquarters, he knew that His Excellency was planning to combine forces with General Rochambeau's French troops and attempt to wrest control of the city from General Clinton. More recently he'd heard the attack could take place as soon as July, and already the first of the Continental troops were beginning to shift to another camp to the south and on the eastern side of the river, near Dobb's Ferry and only twelve miles from the city itself.

On the days when Alexander didn't have himself rowed across the river, he climbed to the highest spot on our point, and peered across the river with his spyglass by the hour, watching for signs of moving troops. It all made my heart heavy with dread, knowing I'd have no choice soon but to let him go.

When he finally received encouragement from His Excellency regarding a field post, before the coming campaign, he decided it would be best to rejoin the encampment to be in readiness. For safety's sake, I would return to my parents in Albany, and he took me there himself, spending only a few more precious days with me and conferring with my father before he left in early July.

As can be imagined, our parting was sorrowful, but he promised he'd steal away to see me again before any attack took place. Still, I watched from the dock as the sloop on which he'd sailed caught the breeze, and headed down river. He stood on the deck, waving to me, while I waved my handkerchief back at him.

How many other women over time had done the same with their sweethearts and husbands? How many handkerchiefs beyond counting had fluttered in the breeze as the dear one had grown smaller and smaller in the distance, to finally vanish from view? And how many of those same handkerchiefs had then been used to blot the fresh tears of separation, sorrow, and aching loneliness?

Yet I'd learned several important things from that spring. First, that the love that Alexander and I felt for each other and our marriage with it only grew stronger with each moment we were together. Second, that my husband was the most intelligent and thoughtful man I'd ever known, and that as much as he might long for battle-field glory, he would likely have much more lasting importance in shaping our new government once the war was won. I feared for his life, yes; but I also realized now that for him to perish in battle would be a terrible loss not just for me, but for our country.

There was one more thing I learned that June, as the days grew longer and warmer and the trees began to leaf with new green: by all my cautious reckonings, I was at last pregnant with our first child.

CHAPTER 11

The Pastures, Albany, New York
August 1781

When Alexander and I parted in July, my greatest concern was for his welfare. He was once again in the army's camp, where he believed a field command was to be given him as part of the upcoming military plans. Though I knew he wished this above all things, I hoped that Fate (and His Excellency) had a less dangerous path planned for his life.

It did not help to hear my father agree in his brisk military way, predicting that the three armies—Continental, French, and British—would meet this summer in a battle so momentous that it would likely decide the entire outcome of the lengthy war. This did little to ease my concerns for Alexander's welfare, and I wrote him more letters than I ever had before, all describing in teary detail how very much I missed him and prayed for his safety. Before we'd been wed, I'd longed to conceive his son or daughter as a lasting proof of our devotion, but now that I truly was with child, I was terrified that our poor little innocent might be born without a father, and never know his love.

Nor did I find much comfort in my sister Angelica, who was also visiting The Pastures for the summer with her children. She was pregnant, too, but her husband was entirely safe in Boston, which made her advice to me ring hollow at best. Waxing dramatic as any actress on the stage, she likened Alexander to a warrior about to make the most gallant and noble sacrifices on the field of honor, and urged me to be a patriotic wife and feel the same. I suppose it amused her to sigh on about him as if he were the hero in a romantic poem instead of my flesh-and-blood husband; it only served to upset me, and one night at supper I'd finally cried at her to stop in a shameful outburst that sent me sobbing into my bed pillow while she begged my forgiveness.

I must hasten to note that this was unlike my usual temperament. I'd always considered myself by nature a practical lady, not given to tantrums and tears or impassioned scenes. All this changed once I was with child. While I wasn't ill the way many women were, most anything—a slice of bread toasted too dark, a mislaid stocking—could set me to weeping so piteously that I feared I'd lost my wits.

Mamma calmed me as best she could, and assured me that this would pass as my time progressed. But this coupled with my worry for Alexander made for a long and miserable summer, and I both dreaded and longed for the post messengers that brought his letters and news of the army's intentions. Yet as much as I fretted and worried for his safety over the course of that summer, I was the one, not he, who was first confronted by the hazards of war.

Most people now will remember the war for the great battles with uniformed regiments led by His Excellency and others of his generals. But for those of us who lived along the northern frontiers, the war was a series of smaller events, attacks and raids led by Tories and the Indians in their hire. Crops and barns were burned, livestock stolen, and houses looted, and in the most deadly raids entire families were slaughtered and their bodies mutilated on the same land they'd worked so hard to clear and make their own.

These raiders had grown bolder with the rumors that the war might be reaching its climax, and in the spring of 1781, they'd come sufficiently close to Albany that my father had been warned to be on his guard. While Papa might no longer hold an active commission, he was still regarded as an important gentleman in the country, much involved in gathering military information. He was also known to be a member of Congress and a close friend and advisor to General Washington, and because of that, Continental spies had uncovered a plot to kidnap him and make him a prisoner for ransom in Canada.

Our house stood on the outskirts of Albany, not in the wilderness, and Papa doubted the Tories would be so bold as to attack him here. Yet still he warned us all to take care when we walked out of doors, and to keep within sight of the house at all times. A guard of six men stood in constant vigilance over us, with three on watch and three at rest in their temporary quarters in our basement, and our servants were warned to be vigilant as well.

In preparation for a possible attack, my father and the guards left their weapons near the door in readiness. However, after Angelica caught her little son, Philip, showing too much interest in these weapons, she did what most wise mothers would, and removed the guns herself to the cellar, where they'd offer less temptation.

August was especially warm that summer. The air was heavy and thick, and the usual breezes from the river that cooled our house on the hill seemed to abandon us. My mother and sisters and I dressed as lightly as possible, leaving off our stays and extra petticoats when we were at home, and forsaking silk for airy linen. The high-pitched whirr of cicadas in the trees added to the drowsiness of these days, and often the evening ended in a thunderstorm that did nothing to cool us, but only increased the steamy heat.

On this particular evening, we had gathered after supper in the large center hall with the doors on either side thrown open to catch whatever breeze we could. Mamma and I were stitching clothing for my coming child, while Papa, Peggy, and Angelica were reading, our chairs drawn close to the front door to catch the last light of the day. Angelica's two children, Philip and Catherine, were engaged in some sort of game using the black-and-white patterned floor, and baby Catherine slept in her cradle in the family parlor nearby where it was quiet and she'd be undisturbed. Three of the guards were at rest downstairs, while the other three were in the shade in the garden, their guns on the lawn beside them.

Everything was as it should be, except that it wasn't. One of our servants came into the house and addressed Papa, and we heard the man say there was a stranger at the back garden gate who wished to see my father.

While this seemed harmless enough to the rest of us, to my father, this was a signal. At once he briskly ordered the windows and doors shuttered and barred. Servants rushed to obey, pulling the heavy shutters over the windows and sliding the iron bars in place across them, while Papa hurried us upstairs and into the bedchamber he shared with Mamma.

"Keep together, and remain here," he said. "Stay quiet, all of you."

He took a pistol from the top of a chest where it had been loaded in readiness, and fired it from the window, a signal to summon help. He tossed aside the pistol and grabbed a musket leaning in the corner, taking care to keep to one side of the window where he wouldn't be seen.

I'd a quick glimpse of men with pistols and rifles on the lawn, not in uniforms, but roughly dressed, and I gasped with fear. At least half of them were Mohawks, their faces fearsomely painted red and black and their long hair gathered atop their heads, armed with not only rifles, but tomahawks, too. There were so many of them that I guessed they must have overwhelmed the three guards outside, and I was thankful I could see no more. Clutching at my skirts, Angelica's son began to cry beside me.

"Quiet," Papa ordered sharply as he cocked the musket with an ominous click. I took the little boy into my arms, holding him tightly to quiet him as best I could. Angelica was cradling her daughter, rubbing her palm across the child's back to comfort her even as her own face was taut with fear and her eyes squeezed shut.

We heard the men's voices now, loud oaths and shouts and other blasphemy that was intended to frighten us more, and the crashing of shattered glass as they broke windows in the rooms below us. They were beating against the door, attempting to break it down with heavy, drumming thumps that echoed through the dark house.

Little Philip whimpered and curled against me, and I tightened my arms around him, as much to comfort myself as him. Silently I prayed for him, and for all of us, and especially for Alexander's child, innocent and unknowing in my belly.

Suddenly Mamma cried out, her hands pressed to her face in alarm.

"The baby!" she wailed. "Oh, Philip, I forgot Catherine!"

She started for the door, determined to fetch the baby we'd somehow all forgotten in her cradle in the parlor.

But Papa seized her arm and held her back. "You can't," he said tersely. "It's too dangerous."

"I'll go," said Peggy, and before anyone could stop her, she'd darted from the room, her steps a brisk counterpoint to the men pounding on the door.

Mamma clutched at my father for support as she sank to her knees, overcome by the thought of losing not just one daughter, but two.

Abruptly we heard the front door to the house give way, and the attackers surged into the hall, grunting and cheering at their success. There were sounds of cracking wood, of breaking glass and porcelain, as the men roamed through the lower rooms, intent on plundering our belongings. I was shaking now, imagining Peggy with the baby in their midst.

Suddenly one man's voice rose above the din. "Wench, wench!" he shouted roughly. "Where is your master, girl?"

"He's gone to alarm the town!" Peggy cried as she ran up the stairs. In the next moment she was again with us, handing Catherine to Mamma. Her eyes were wide with terror, her hair disheveled, and there was a large slash in her petticoat. I held my arm out to her, and she came, hugging me close.

"They're taking all the plate from the dining room, Eliza," she whispered, trembling. "One of them threw his hatchet at me when I was on the stairs, and it caught my skirts."

"But you saved Catherine," I whispered back, and beginning to rock her gently just as I was doing with little Philip. "Oh, Peggy, you were so brave!"

Thinking quickly, Papa again leaned from the window.

"Come along, men, come along!" he shouted as if addressing a great party of men. "Surround the house, and seize these villains before they can escape!"

It seemed too obvious a ploy to work, but then, Papa was a general, and I was not. As we huddled together upstairs, we heard the men call to one another and then running through the hall and down the steps.

For a long moment the house was strangely silent, making our own sad little noises of distress—the children snuffling and whimpering, my sisters and mother struggling to muffle their tears—all the more noticeable.

Standing to one side of the window, Papa let out a long sigh, and though he uncocked the musket, he still held it.

"They're gone, praise God," he said, still looking from the window. "Peggy, are you unharmed?"

She nodded, tears streaming down her face, as the realization of what she'd done was finally becoming clear to her.

"I do not know what possessed you to risk yourself like that," he said gruffly, "but I shall always be thankful you did. Here's the militia from town at last."

He set the musket down and helped my mother to an armchair in the corner, pausing to kiss the infant Catherine in her arms. Little Philip abandoned me for his mother, and Peggy, too, went to Mamma. With the Albany men in the yard, the servants were creeping out from wherever they'd hidden themselves, their voices raised with excitement as they described to one another what had occurred. Father called for Mamma's maid and she came swiftly up the stairs, puffing her cheeks as she fussed about Mamma and baby Catherine.

I stood alone, and took a deep breath, then another. It was strange that in these last weeks I'd cried at everything and nothing, but now, when there'd been real cause, my eyes were dry. My heart still raced too fast within my breast, but knowing what could have happened, yet hadn't, gave me an odd kind of peace.

Papa must have taken note.

"Eliza, come with me, if you please," he said. "We must make these people welcome, and determine what misfortune has been caused below."

I nodded, and followed him. I'd often acted in Mamma's stead, though never quite in these circumstances, and in a way it was a relief to be busy. I ordered candles to be lit against the gathering dusk, and sent out refreshment for the men who'd come to our rescue. I greeted and thanked those among them that I knew, and I then set the servants to tidying things as best they could. As Peggy had said, one of the men had thrown a hatchet at her, and a sizable raw gash in the stair rail proved how close she'd been to being struck. I was shocked to see how much damage had been caused to our house in so short a time, much of it serving no use but willful mischief and destruction. Porcelain vases had been smashed, curtains torn from the windows, and chairs upended and their cushions slashed.

But what had attracted the intruders the most had been my parents' silver. They'd forced open the door to the plate closet and carried off all the larger and most valuable pieces—platters, tankards, candlesticks, bowls, and other vessels—leaving the shelves shockingly bare. It wasn't just the cost of the pieces that had been stolen; some had been in our family for many years, and for that reason were irreplaceable.

Papa came to stand beside me, and he, too, stared at the empty shelves.

"They meant to kidnap me," he said, as matter-of-fact as can be. "I'd been warned, but I didn't believe Waltermeyer would be such a fool as to come here after me by day."

I glanced up at him with surprise. "You knew the leader?"

"John Waltermeyer," he said with unabashed disgust. "He was at their head, and as brazen a Tory as any in the region, with some manner of puffed-up commission from Clinton to make him feel like the man that he isn't. The rest were only his underlings, and mercenary cowards at that."

"Cowards indeed," I agreed soundly, even though I was glad they'd abandoned their mission. "Can't they be found and captured, if they're known to you?"

"We all have better things to do than chase after them," he said. "Most likely they are well on their way to Canada by now. What will gall your mother the most when she learns of it is that Waltermeyer has been in this house as our guest."

It galled me as well. My parents were renowned for hospitality, but it was shameful when a former guest turned generosity against them like this. Waltermeyer's goal might have been to kidnap my father, but he also would have known the arrangement of our house, and exactly where the plate was kept.

"It grieves me that they captured three of our guards as prisoners as well," he continued. "By all reports, Ward, Tubbs, and Corlies tried their best to acquit themselves, but since Angelica earlier saw fit to remove their weapons, they were unarmed, and defenseless. I'll see that they're ransomed as soon as possible, and rewarded for their trouble."

"Oh, no." The three were amiable, dedicated men, and it saddened me to think that Angelica's maternal concern had caused them to be captured. "What of the other guards?"

"Slight injuries, noting mortal," he said, taking one final look at the empty shelves. "They'll recover. It's the others that concern me more."

By candlelight, his face looked old and worn, the events of the day showing their effect, and I slipped my hand into the crook of his arm. While others often judged my father as aloof, even cold, I knew the kindness in his heart. This evening he'd seen his family cowering in fear, and suffered considerable losses to his personal property, and yet his greatest concern now was for the soldiers who'd been captured in his service.

"But they didn't take you, Papa," I said softly. Though I wouldn't say so to him, I was doubly glad the kidnapping had failed; given his age and infirmities I wasn't sure he would have survived a forced march to Canada. "If the plate was a kind of ransom in advance, then it was worth every last candlestick to have you safe."

He smiled wearily, and patted my hand. "Hamilton is fortunate to have you as his wife, Eliza," he said. "I fear you're the only one of my daughters with sufficient sense to be a soldier's wife."

I smiled, too, for this was the highest possible praise from him.

"He won't always be a soldier," I said. "Soon I hope to be a lawyer's wife instead."

"The world is filled with lawyers," he said dismissively. "For now he's a soldier and an officer, and an excellent one at that. The general is fortunate to have his services at this time."

Ordinarily I would have considered that another compliment from him on Alexander's behalf, but the conviction in his voice made me pause.

"What have you heard, Papa?" I asked. "I know that Alexander writes to you of military matters that he cannot share with me. What has he told you?"

If I'd any doubts before, they fled as soon as I saw my father frown and duck his chin.

"That's a question for your husband, Eliza," he said. "Not for me."

"Alexander isn't here for me to ask, Papa, and you are," I said. "Please, if you have fresh news of him that I do not, then—"

"No, Eliza," he said firmly. "Any news of that nature must come from Hamilton himself."

I knew better than to press for more, but I hadn't long to wait. Alexander's next letter shared the news that my father had already known. On the last day of July, he'd finally been given command of a New York light-infantry battalion. For his second in command, he'd been able to choose Major Nicholas Fish, an old friend from his days at King's College. Although for my sake he attempted to mute his excitement, I read it in every word he'd written, nor did his assurances that nothing might come of the army's preparations offer me any comfort whatsoever. He promised to try to visit Albany to see me one last time before the troops began to move in earnest.

Even as I realized how difficult that promise would be for him to keep, I clung to this most slender hope to see him once more before he plunged into the fray of bloodshed. But later in August came another letter that dashed that hope completely, and worse, added much more to my worries.

He could not come to Albany. He couldn't ask permission, nor did he wish to. The target of the campaign that had occupied so much thought and attention over the past months was not the city of New York, but Virginia. His battalion, and much of the rest of the army currently at Dobb's Ferry, would be leaving for there shortly.

There were also many words of love for me and our child, and unhappiness at how far apart we would be for these next months, and how he could scarce wait for us to be reunited later in the autumn. These were meant to succor me, and they did; no man has ever written a more beautifully loving letter than my dear husband.

But as precious as his protestations were to me, they still couldn't soften the hard reality of our situation. I was wise enough in military matters to understand that the light infantry were often in the very thick of any battle. No longer would he be to the rear of the fighting, as aides-de-camp usually were, but in the very heat of the conflict.

Moreover, this could well be the last letter he could send to me with any certainty. The fact that he also included information on his personal funds and instructions for how I might make drafts upon them if necessary only proved to me that he was not only acutely aware of the risks of the coming campaign, but preparing for the unthinkable possibility that he might not return. Further, he wished me to be aware of it as well.

In retrospect, I realize this letter was remarkably indiscreet of him to send me. The success of the campaign depended upon surprising the enemy, and if his letter to me had been intercepted, or otherwise fallen into the hands of the enemy, then His Excellency's entire plan would have been revealed.

But at the time when I first read his words, I saw only his innate honesty, and how, even in such a situation, he was unable to tell me anything but the truth, which rendered his words of love and devotion all the more precious to me. It was a small solace, there in the middle of so much distressing news, but it was all that I had.

I took the letter to my father in his library, and let him read it through as he sat at his desk.

He sighed, refolded it along the creases, and handed it back to me.

"You husband writes an excellent letter," he said. "He is perhaps a bit free with his knowledge of troop movements, but no harm has come from it, especially if it brings ease to you."

"I'm sure he has written more to you," I said. "If you know when his battalion has decamped, or where they are bound, or any other news, I wish you'd tell me."

He gave a small shake to his head. "I doubt that would be of interest to you. It's dry, dull stuff."

"Not if it includes Alexander," I insisted. "Please, Papa. Don't keep things from me."

"I don't wish to distress you, Eliza," he said gently. "Hamilton agrees with me, too. You're in a delicate condition, and I won't risk any upset that might bring harm to you or your child."

I looked down so he wouldn't see the frustration in my face and interpret it as distress. I know that my family wished me to be calm for my child's sake, but I'd never liked being coddled. I was stronger than that. I pressed Alexander's letter between my palms, as if to feel his presence through the words he'd written, and my wedding ring, still so new, gleamed in the sun against the white paper.

"What he has written here," I said slowly. "It sounds as if he believes he might not return."

Papa leaned back in his chair, the wooden legs creaking beneath him.

"A good husband must consider every eventuality," he said carefully. "That is why he has told you how to obtain funds, if you find yourself in need of it."

"He also says that you have offered him money as well," I said. "He is polite about it, yes, and thanks you for your kindness, but you know he is proud, and doesn't wish to be indebted to you."

He ran his thumb back and forth over the carved, curved arm of the chair, a sure sign of muted impatience.

"I understand his pride, Eliza," he said. "But I regard your husband as another son, just as you are my daughter, and if you are ever in want, I would want you to rely on me. As a soldier, Hamilton understands, and is perfectly aware of the dangers he will face. You should be as well."

"I am, Papa," I said. Nothing about this conversation was easy. "Long ago, when you and I had first arrived in Morristown, you told me that Alexander had survived through the war because he was lucky. You said some men simply were."

He nodded, his expression softening.

"I remember," he said. "I remember, because it was a surprise to me. When your Hamilton first came to Albany, I didn't expect he'd last the winter, let alone the war."

"Do you still believe what you said, Papa?" I asked, my voice taut with urgency. "About him being lucky?"

"Yes, he's a lucky man," he said at once, smiling. "He was lucky to win you for his wife, wasn't he?"

"Oh, Papa," I said. "That's not what I mean."

"I know what you meant," he said, turning serious again. "You want me to offer you some sort of surety, a guarantee, that your

Hamilton will not be killed or wounded, and that he will return to you unharmed in any way. And I won't do that, Eliza. I can't."

I bowed my head over the letter in my hand.

He reached out and rested his hand on my shoulder, the weight of it comforting, and linking us together as father and daughter.

"I recall something else from our journey to Morristown, Eliza," he said. "I recall that you told me you believed Colonel Hamilton had been spared from danger for the benefit of the country. You believed that he was meant to do great things, and that nothing would stop him until he'd done them."

"I did say that," I said, surprised that he'd remembered.

He narrowed his eyes, watching me closely. "Do you believe it still?"

"I do," I said softly. "Except that now I believe it even more."

"Then you have your answer, Eliza," he said. "You needn't ask me. You already know."

Despite my fears, that wasn't the last letter I received from Alexander that autumn. While I knew he wrote to me whenever he could, the letters were delivered to me willy-nilly, sometimes three or four together, followed by another that had been written a month previously, and then none for what seemed an eternity. There were still others that were altogether lost, and never arrived at all.

It was the same with my letters to him, and his customary (and untrue!) complaint that I didn't write to him with sufficient frequency must, for once, have seemed justified. He'd been horrified when I'd written to him of the attack upon our home and the attempt to kidnap my father. He now worried for my safety just as I worried for his, which made the erratic delivery even more of a trial to us both. But in the middle of a military campaign with the army on the march, that was to be expected, and I told myself not to be disappointed when no letter came for me, or when all he'd sent was a scribbled line or two to assure me he was well.

Short or long, Alexander's letters were my best comfort, especially at night. Before I said my prayers, I always read his last letter again, concentrating on the part where he'd written how much he loved me. Alone in our bed with no one else to overhear, I'd prop his miniature portrait against his pillow beside mine, and read the letter softly out loud, trying to imagine his voice speaking the words.

Alas, my voice was no more his than the painted smile of the miniature possessed his warmth and charm, and I'd sadly put the letter in the wooden box with all the others he'd written me. I'd say my prayers—and oh, such prayers I said for him!—douse the candle, and climb into bed.

Even when surrounded by my family during the day, I felt Alexander's absence as a constant, gnawing ache, and it only grew worse at night. The bed we'd shared seemed too large and lonely, and I'd always sleep to one side, as if expecting him to join me in the course of the night. It was then that I missed him most: the warmth of his body, the gentle rhythm of his breath as he slept, the scent of his skin on the sheets.

I'd lie on my back with my hands settled protectively over the rounding swell of my belly, over our child. Alexander hoped for a boy (though his reasoning for the preference—that a girl combining our best qualities would be too devastating to men—was so outlandish that I was convinced he'd love a daughter just as well) and most nights I was sure the child I carried was a son. By now the baby had quickened, and whenever I'd feel those first little kicks of new life within me, I'd wish that Alexander was here to feel them, too. My sister had been safely delivered of her child, another boy, which made me only long the more to meet my own baby.

I'd leave the bed curtains open so I could see the night sky and the moon through the window, and think of how that same moon was shining on Alexander. He wrote to me that he believed that not just the last battles but the war itself could be over before the end of the year, and he'd be back with me by Christmas, never to leave again.

And each clear night I'd watch the moon rise, and pray that he was right.

As I have mentioned here before, my parents' house drew many visitors and guests. Because of my father's continued importance in the affairs of both state and county, every stranger of means or ambition made sure to present himself to Papa with a letter of introduction. In turn my father would often oblige them as far as he could, and through his kindness arrange other meetings and advantages to help the newcomer find his place in Albany.

Since New York City continued to remain in the hands of the British, Albany's importance had only increased, and each week brought fresh visitors to our doorstep. Depending upon their importance, some would be invited into our parlor for tea, or perhaps to stay to dine, at Mamma's discretion, and my sisters and I were expected to play our parts in the family's hospitality, too. I enjoyed it, and I was also grateful for the diversion from my own worries.

One afternoon Mamma, Peggy, and I were pouring tea for several gentlemen in the parlor when Papa joined us. With him was a gentleman in a dark gray suit, similar to Alexander in age and stature. There the resemblance ended, however. While handsome enough, this gentleman was dark, with a saturnine face and restless eyes beneath heavy brows. He was also notable for not wearing a uniform, a rarity for any man of his age at that time. Yet when Papa brought him to me, I held out my hand and smiled in welcome.

"This is Lieutenant Colonel Burr, Eliza," Papa said as the gentleman bowed over my hand. "He has come to Albany from New Jersey intending to solicit license to practice the law in our courts. He tells me he is also a longstanding acquaintance of your husband's, having served with him under His Excellency."

"How do you do, Colonel Burr?" I said, more eagerly than I'd been first inclined. Despite having attended two winter encampments of the army, I'd still met few of Alexander's friends and acquaintances. "Forgive me, I did not realize you were an officer."

He nodded, gracefully accepting my apology. "I was forced to resign my commission on account of ill health, Mrs. Hamilton."

"He is too humble by half," my father said. "He was an excellent officer who discharged his duty with uncommon vigilance. Hamilton may not have told you, but long ago, in the early days of the war, Colonel Burr relieved Hamilton and his company when they were cut off at Fort Bunker Hill during the enemy's attack at Manhattan, and by doing so, likely preserved his life as well."

"Then I must offer you my heartfelt thanks, Colonel Burr," I said. Alexander had in fact never mentioned this incident, but then from respect for my tender feelings, he often spared me from past exploits where his life had been in danger. "You must indeed be friends."

"I was only following the general's orders, madam," he said with becoming modesty.

"He also served as an aide-de-camp with the general," Papa said. "Unlike Hamilton, however, he only lasted a fortnight in that service."

Colonel Burr smiled, and nodded to my father as Papa excused himself to speak to my mother.

"I fear I hadn't the perseverance that Colonel Hamilton demonstrated in the General's Family," the colonel said. "I much preferred to be in the field than bound to a desk."

My own smile faded a fraction at that, catching a hint of disparagement for Alexander, and I couldn't help but come to his defense.

"Perhaps you did not realize, Colonel Burr," I said briskly, "that my husband resigned his post with His Excellency, and is instead serving as a field officer in the present campaign, commanding two companies of light troops from the Connecticut Line."

If Colonel Burr felt chastised, he masked it well. "I had heard that, Mrs. Hamilton, yes," he said. "Colonel Hamilton is to be congratulated not only for his command, but for having such a devoted and loyal wife."

"I thank you on my husband's account, Colonel Burr," I said, mollified, even if his flattery was obvious. "Have you a wife yourself?"

He shook his head, and there was no mistaking the regret in his dark eyes.

"Not as yet, no," he said. "But there is an estimable lady whom I pray will one day be able to favor me in that way."

"I pray that she will, too," I said in a rush of sentiment; in the manner of those deeply in love, I was so joyful in my affections that I wished the rest of the world to feel the same. "Would you care for tea, Colonel?"

"Thank you, madam, but I fear I must decline on account of another engagement," he said, bowing. "But please offer my regards to Colonel Hamilton, and the hope that I might call upon him at a later date. Your servant, madam."

I nodded and murmured farewell, but Colonel Burr's last sentence lingered. He'd purposefully said that he'd *hope* to call on Alexander in the future, not that he *would*. Ordinarily I'd have given no thought to such a nicety of phrase, but now I feared it was laden with ominous foreboding.

Grim thoughts, grim thoughts, yet for the sake of my baby, I did my best to put them aside. I believed I'd done an acceptable job of it, too, smiling and pouring tea as if I hadn't a care, but it was clear my parents thought otherwise. Papa came over to me, bending over to me so no one else would hear.

"You needn't stay here any longer, daughter," he said gently. He took me by the arm and helped me to my feet. "Come, let us retreat to the library, and study today's progress on the map."

I nodded, happy to be relieved of my hospitable duties, and happier still to be going to the library with him. Since we'd first heard of the summer campaign, Papa had kept a large map of the American states spread out on a table in his library. Whenever he received fresh news of the army's travels—whether from dispatches, letters, or newspapers—he would call for me (and only me, since I was the one of my siblings with the most at stake) to join him.

Together we'd trace the army's progress, from this town to the next, across this river or around that bluff. From Alexander's letters, I knew the army's day began early—Alexander raised his company at three in the morning, to be able to begin by four—and lasted until dusk. Haste was of the essence in this campaign, and everyone knew it. Sometimes Papa calculated that the troops marched ten miles in a day, sometimes twenty, while other days were entirely consumed while the troops were ferried by battalion across a river.

They marched through the city of Philadelphia, which must have been an impressive column of Continental and French soldiers stretching over two miles in length through the streets. I eagerly read the descriptions in the Philadelphia newspapers that arrived for my father soon after the event, trying to picture everything for myself from my visit there. Apparently, the weather in the city was very dry and the streets so dusty that the marching soldiers soon became coated with a film of the stuff. Their consternation was reported in the papers, on account of them being unable to make the smart military appearance they wished before the ladies waving from the windows. I thought wryly of my husband, who always wished to be as fastidious as possible in his uniform and general dress: how he must have loathed that dust!

A week later, they'd boarded the French fleet at Head of Elk in Maryland. Under sail their journey became much quicker, thirty miles a day, thirty-five, even forty. By the end of September, they were in Virginia, sailing up the James River to disembark and make their camp in the state's capital of Williamsburg. By the first week of October, they were finally less than twenty miles from Yorktown, the site of what all hoped would be the final major confrontation of the war.

"General Washington has every advantage," Papa said with satisfaction as together we leaned over the map. "From all reports, Cornwallis has trapped himself by his location, and all we must do is lay a proper siege."

"A siege instead of a battle?" I asked anxiously. I'd heard all about sieges from Alexander, who'd been fascinated by them from a tactical and intellectual perspective. From his description, a siege sounded much less dangerous. Soldiers took cover in trenches and behind fortifications instead of standing neatly in rows waiting to be shot.

Papa, however, wasn't nearly as reassuring.

"Oh, a siege is simply a different kind of battle," he said. "Both sides attempt to outlast the other, while seeking to undermine and exploit the other's position. Long-range attacks can be conducted by artillery, especially shelling, but there may also be close fighting as well along the barricades, and—"

He broke off suddenly; I suppose he must have taken note of my stricken expression.

"But I don't expect this siege to be like that," he said too heartily to be true. "I expect it will last no more than a week at most. Having the French fleet as well as their troops has changed everything. For once, His Excellency has all the advantages in his possession."

I looked down at the place on the map where all this was to take place. It was evidently so small a town that it hadn't been printed on Papa's map. He'd written it in himself—YORKTOWN—in heavy inked letters symbolic of the town's new importance.

"When do you expect this siege to take place?" I asked.

"Very soon," Papa said, giving the location on the map an extra tap with his forefinger. "It may even be underway as we speak."

I hadn't had a letter from Alexander in nearly a fortnight. He could be swinging his sword or firing a musket at this very moment, or he could also be lying—

But no: I would not think of that.

I raised my chin with determination, even as I clasped my hands together to mask their trembling. "Alexander wrote that he expected the siege to be over swiftly, too, and that he planned to be here in Albany once again by Christmas."

"I believe that is entirely reasonable," Papa said, and nodded with satisfaction. "Pray for him, Eliza, as I know that you do. But also recall all the preparation and care that have gone into this final moment."

I nodded, remembering how His Excellency had been planning for this when Alexander had still been an aide-de-camp. All those letters and dispatches he'd written in French, all the hopes that had traveled to Versailles with Lafayette and John Laurens, every conference in Newport with the French generals, had aimed for this single confrontation with the British.

"If we succeed as I expect we will," Papa continued, surprising me with his emotion, "then at last this wretched war will end, and our country shall find peace. Think of that, Eliza. It's been more than six years since we first went to war, and now, if the Heavens favor us, your child will never know anything else but peace."

Peace . . .

It was the last word that drifted through my head as I fell asleep that night, peace that would bring Alexander back to me, and peace that would keep us together for always.

Yet I didn't dream of Alexander, or even our unborn child. Instead I dreamed of a long-past day when I'd been only thirteen, still a girl, when my family had spent the summers in our house in Saratoga, and I dreamed of an event that had actually occurred to me.

In this dream, our rambling, clapboarded house was untouched by the British who would later burn it to the ground, because then, in 1770, our family was still British, too. Everything was exactly as I remembered it, from the rustling maple trees that flanked the front door, to the blue-and-white pot that Mamma had filled with yellow wildflowers on the parlor's sill, to the old stone mill wheel that served as the house's front step.

But what mattered about his particular day was that Papa had chosen me–not Angelica, not Peggy–to accompany him to Fort Clinton, and be presented to the Chiefs of Six Nations. Mamma had not been happy about it, but Papa had insisted, claiming the chiefs would see my presence as a sign of good faith.

I was surprised, and excited. The people of the Six Nations were the Iroquois, the Indians who had once lived upon our land, and still ruled the rest of the wilderness. Every so often, their chiefs would gather to meet with the military leaders like Father. Indians were common enough in our lives, appearing at our house to trade game and other goods, but I'd never seen a chief. Chiefs were like generals, or governors; they were grand, rare, important men.

I'd dressed in my best white linen gown with a blue silk sash and a wide-brimmed straw hat, and soon I was sitting in the carriage beside Papa in his militia colonel's uniform. The morning sun glittered off the gold lace and polished buttons of his scarlet uniform coat and glinted across the hilt of his sword, and I'd thought proudly that my father was the most perfect military hero I'd ever seen.

The fort wasn't far from our house, and our drive was brief. Stout upright logs formed the stockade walls of the fort, with raised, square tower-houses on the corners for surveying the river and the forests. The gates opened for us, and as soon as we were within, I'd seen the Chiefs of Six Nations waiting for us on parade grounds.

They'd stood in a ring, solemn and daunting as they watched us approach. None of them smiled. Their faces were painted according to their nations, with feathers and beads woven into their dark hair, or some with half their hair shaven clear away. They wore garments made from deerskin and fur mixed with trade cloth in crimson and blue, and elaborate jewels and bracelets fashioned from silver or brass. They were regal and splendid and more than a little daunting to me, and I understood now why Father had cautioned me to show no outward fear, but to be brave and strong.

"Remove your hat, Eliza," Papa had said softly. "Your cap, too. It's their custom for women to have their heads uncovered."

I did as he bid, looping the ribbons of my hat around my wrist and tucking my linen cap into my pocket. Mother would have scolded me for being out of doors without either, but here with the chiefs it was expected. The same breeze that tossed the flag overhead now ruffled my dark hair, tugging wisps free from the hairpins that held the tight knot at the back of my hair. I let them go, and didn't try to smooth them back.

The chiefs stepped aside to let us walk among them. I was curious and frightened at the same time, yet I tried not to let any of it show. I would be brave; I would be strong. Even in my dream, I knew the importance of that.

Several of the chiefs addressed me and smiled. I comprehended none of their words, spoken in their tongues, but I sensed it was all well-meant, and with Father beside me I felt my fears slip away. One by one, the oldest and most revered of the chiefs placed their hands on my head, covering my hair with their open palms, as a Christian will do in blessing. Perhaps that was why I was no longer frightened; I felt the kindness in their gestures, no matter their language, and the good wishes that came with it.

Finally my father said something more in their language to take our leave, and we bowed and left the circle. I'd waited until we were alone in the carriage again to ask Papa what the chiefs had said.

"Why, they took you in as if you were their own child, Eliza," he explained, "and made you a daughter of the Six Nations, exactly as I'd hoped. They gave you a new a name that means 'One-of-Us.' I presented you to them in trust and good faith, and they returned the favor by embracing you into their family."

"They did?" I'd said, awestruck. "I'm an Indian now?"

"After a fashion," he said. "You'll always belong to us first, of course, but it's wise to have friends and allies wherever you may go. The chiefs want the same things that I do, as all men do in every country: peace and prosperity and security for their families and their people. They don't want war any more than an Englishman, or a Frenchman, or a German does. But peace is fragile, and this is the only sure way it can be kept, through trust and understanding and respect. Never forget that, Eliza. No matter what happens, never forget it."

I hadn't forgotten. How could I, when another war had begun again only a few years later? I'd never forget, no matter what I dreamed, and yet again I heard my father's voice speaking still of peace, again and again.

"Wake, Eliza, wake," he said, his hand upon my shoulder.

Groggy with sleep, I turned my face from the pillow and forced my eyes to open. Though my room was gray with coming dawn, he was holding a candlestick, the flickering light flaring across his face, and my mother's behind him. She was crying and pressing her handkerchief to her eyes, and that was enough to draw me sharply awake.

"What has happened?" I asked anxiously, my first thought for Alexander. "What is wrong?"

"Not a thing," Papa said, his smile so wide it must have hurt. "Cornwallis and his army have surrendered, and our army has won. Your husband is not only safe, but a hero, and will return to you soon. It's peace, Eliza. At last, it's peace."

CHAPTER 12

The Pastures, Albany, New York
February 1782

So much has been said and written about my husband's role in
the final battle at Yorktown that I could write a thousand more
pages here on that topic alone, and fail to include it all. At the time,
we did not learn of the battle or its outcome until two weeks after it
had occurred. Given that nearly six hundred miles lie between
Albany and Yorktown, this is not surprising, and in a way, I was
grateful to be unaware of the exact moment when Alexander had
put himself into the most peril.

In fact, I didn't learn how precipitously, even recklessly, he had
embraced direct engagement with the enemy until much later,
when he himself told me, and even then I doubt I heard all the details. I also suspected that there was a conspiracy within my family
to keep the most alarming facts of my husband's adventures from
me on account of my pregnancy. Alexander did write to me immediately after the siege was done, to alert me that he was unhurt. Yet
he did so in the most contrite way possible, informing me that he'd
acted so boldly for the sake of honor and duty that he'd risked my
happiness along with his life. Fortunately, by the time I received
this letter, Alexander himself was once again in Albany and in my
arms, and so the shock of it was much diminished.

And how very fast he flew to me, too!

He remained at Yorktown long enough to witness the British
surrender, but as soon as he could arrange leave with His Excel-

lency, he'd taken to the road. He was shameless in his desire to return to me, and did not care who knew it. He stopped for nothing, not even to tell Congress in Philadelphia of the victory and surrender, as he was supposed to have done. He rode hard and fast, so fast that he exhausted his horses near Red Bank in New Jersey, and was forced to obtain others for the last leg of his journey. He covered the entire distance in less than three weeks: an astonishing feat.

But I'd no knowledge of any of this, or what day to expect his return. All I knew was that he was coming, and that he'd promised to return before our anniversary in December. Papa had warned me not to set my heart on this day or that, because I'd only court disappointment. There was no predicting a journey of that many miles, often through rough terrain and uncertain weather. I tried not to pin my hopes on any one day, but each morning when I rose, I prayed that by nightfall he might once again be with me.

On the afternoon when he finally did appear, I wasn't on the step to greet him, or even watching at the window. I didn't hear his horse, or the joyful salutations from my brothers and father as he entered the door.

I heard none of it, because I regret to admit that I was asleep. I was by then seven months gone with child, and because I was ordinarily a small woman, I'd grown more unwieldy and uncomfortable with each passing week. I tired easily, and it had become my habit to retire to my bedchamber each day after dinner. I told my family that I required the time for reading and quiet reflection for the sake of my child, but the truth (which I expect was no secret to them) was that as soon as I lay my head on my pillow, I was fast asleep, and remained that way for an hour or more.

I didn't hear the sound of the chamber door opening, or Alexander's footsteps as he joined me, either. All I heard in my dreams was his voice.

"My angel," he said softly. "My own dear Betsey."

I sighed, and kept my eyes tightly shut, clinging to the fading dream as long as I could.

Then he kissed me, and I realized it was no dream. I gasped, and flung my arms around his shoulders, pulling him down so he might kiss me again. I was crying, too, tears of purest joy and relief that a moment I'd so long anticipated had finally come.

"I cannot believe you're finally here, my love," I said, awkwardly pushing myself up against the pillows. "My love, my love! Let me look at you."

"I'm likely a sorry sight," he said ruefully. He was: in fact his appearance shocked me. His hair was crushed flat from his hat, his uniform was flecked with the mud of the road, and he smelled like his horse. But those things could easily be corrected. What made me worry was how thin he'd become, his cheeks hollowed and his uniform loose where it shouldn't be, and how dark circles of exhaustion ringed his eyes. There were also dozens of new freckles across his nose and cheeks from so much time in the sun, freckles that made him look more boyish despite his obvious weariness.

"You're not well," I said, swinging my legs over the edge of the bed. "Don't pretend otherwise, either. We must send for a physician."

"Hush," he said, hungrily kissing me again. "It's my turn to gaze upon my beautiful Betsey, and our child."

He knelt beside the bed, his face level with my belly, and stared at my roundness with unabashed awe. "Our son has grown considerably since I left."

"So have I," I said. I took his hand and placed his palm on my belly, moving it gently back and forth. "There! Did you feel the kick?"

He grinned in wonder.

"I did," he said. "That's my son."

"It could be your daughter instead, you know," I cautioned. "There is no true way of knowing."

"It's my son," he said confidently. "I'm sure of it."

I smiled, so grateful to have him back. Besides, I'd long ago learned that when Alexander was this sure of something, he was usually right.

"My dearest Betsey," he continued softly. "This is why I came home to you. This is why I did what I did, for you, for our son, for . . . for . . ."

He swayed, and I grabbed his shoulders. He was too heavy for me to support, and as he toppled over on the floor from exhaustion, I slipped down with him. Frantically I shouted for help, then bent over him, holding him as tightly as I could.

It was hardly the homecoming I'd envisioned, but at last he was home and we were once again together, and because I couldn't see into the future, I believed with all my heart that we'd never be parted again.

The long march, the siege and battle, and then the ride to Albany had all taken their toll on Alexander's health. He'd never been hardy, relying more on will and spirit than a robust constitution to accomplish the prodigious amount that he did, but the exertions and hardships of the last months finally proved more than even he could bear.

The best physicians in Albany were summoned, and though I had dreaded that Alexander was taken with camp fever, a common malady that claimed as many soldiers as battle-wounds, to my relief the physicians declared he'd no grievous illness beyond exhaustion. The prescribed treatment was lengthy, but not complicated. Alexander was duly bled to relieve any unfortunate humors that might have lingered from his efforts on the battlefield. He was ordered to remain in his bed, and not to rise for the next six weeks, or risk further weakness. As a restorative, a compress of flannel dipped in hot wine was applied to the pit of his stomach three times during the day, and his diet was restricted to strengthening nourishment, including new-laid eggs lightly poached, rich chocolate, light roast meats, savory soups, and clear jellies. He was permitted cordials and brandy for fortification, but no ardent spirits. His company was limited to our immediate family, much to the disappointment of all those in Albany who wished to call to congratulate him as a newly minted hero, and hear him describe the victory himself.

So weak was his condition that for the first weeks he was completely agreeable to these restrictions, and slept more hours than he was awake: a complete change from my husband's normal habits. I seldom left his side, striving to make sure that whenever he did wake, mine was the first face he saw. I tended to him myself as best I could, and reluctantly relied on the servants when his care was beyond me. My sister Angelica, visiting with her family for the holidays, gave me respite as well, and pleased Alexander no end with her fussing and petting him in French.

Slowly he began to improve and regain his strength, and though he credited me, I believe it was his own indomitable will that carried him through. We were quite a pair, my husband and I: I was round as a pumpkin while he was thin as a rail, and we laughed together at what a ridiculous couple we must present.

Ridiculous, yes, but also most contented. We conversed by the hour, making up for the months when he'd been away. I sat in a chair beside the bed, and sewed while he told me of the campaign, of adventures during the long march and through the last encampment. He recounted stories he knew would entertain me: how the patriotic ladies in Philadelphia had put thirteen candles in their houses' windows when the army had marched past, and how he'd been the only officer who hadn't become seasick when they'd sailed down the chop of Chesapeake Bay to Annapolis.

I heard how he'd been reunited with his dearest friends from earlier in the war, John Laurens, the Marquis de Lafayette, and Nicholas Fish, and how they had triumphed together. I watched how, for the benefit of my younger brothers, he thrillingly re-created his men's attack and capture of Redoubt 10 (a British stronghold fiercely defended by about seventy enemy soldiers), using their old toy soldiers and with his knees beneath the coverlet to represent the redoubt.

The stories I had to share were far less exciting, mostly news and regards from friends like Kitty Livingston and Lady Washington. I was able to tell him, however, of meeting his old acquaintance Mr. Burr.

"Burr is in Albany?" he asked with surprise. He was propped against the pillows and comfortably clad in a shirt and flannel dressing gown. His hair was untied and tousled around his shoulders, his face had lost its hollowed look, and his coloring was much improved, though the scattering of new freckles—I called them his Virginia freckles—remained. In short, to me my husband was altogether handsome, perhaps the most handsome gentleman in all the state. If I hadn't been so close to my time and he still under doctor's orders to avoid excitement, I would have climbed into bed with him and loved him as a devoted wife should.

Instead I merely nodded and rethreaded my needle, trying to concentrate instead on Colonel Burr. "He is here to study the law, and hopes to obtain his license to practice. He called upon Papa with a letter of introduction from General McDougall."

"Burr to study the law," he said, musing. "Before the war, he'd determined upon theology to become a minister like his father, and his father's father before him. I could have guessed even then that he'd give that up in favor of more stimulating career. What else could it be besides the law?"

"Perhaps you two shall study together," I suggested. "He seemed an intelligent gentleman, and well-spoken."

"Oh, he is that," he said drily. "He's a well-bred, impatient rascal, accustomed to having his own way."

"He also confessed to having serious attentions toward a lady," I said. "I wondered if it was anyone I know here in Albany."

Alexander laughed. "Oh, my dearest innocent angel," he said. "You truly have not heard of this lady, not from Angelica or any of your other female spies? The scandal is widely known."

"No, I have not," I said, disappointed that my news was so behindhand. "Who is she, Alexander?"

"She is a lady from New Jersey named Mrs. Theodosia Prevost," he said. "She is said to be well-spoken, generous, and learned, with a gift for French, much like your sister herself. That's all to her praise, and not where the scandal lies, however. Rather, not only is she said to be a good decade older than Burr, but she is also married to a British officer."

"Oh, goodness," I said, genuinely startled, and reminded again of how much more worldly Alexander was than I. "That's very wicked of them. Not only because she is an—an adulteress, but also because her sympathies must be with the enemy. No wonder he did not last as an aide-de-camp in His Excellency's Family."

"You did hear Burr's particulars, didn't you?" he teased. "He wasn't conducting his little intrigue with the officer's wife whilst he was with the general, or yes, he would have received a goodly sermon from the great man on the honorable demeanor expected of the army's officers. But I suspect it was more that Burr hasn't the temperament for the general's foibles."

"Perhaps not," I agreed, remembering how Colonel Burr had admitted much the same thing himself.

"No, indeed," he said, yawning expansively. "But then, he may not have the temperament for mine, either."

From this I still wasn't sure whether he enjoyed the company of the scandalous Colonel Burr or not. Like many gentlemen, Alexander often seemed to reserve his best insults for his closest friends. But we spoke no more of Colonel Burr, not then or anytime soon after, and he and his intrigue were soon put from my mind.

We celebrated our first wedding anniversary quietly, followed by Christmas and Twelfth Night, leaving the revelry of the season to my younger siblings. As I grew larger and more uncomfortable, Alexander's health improved, and soon the only way to keep him in bed was to surround him with the books he requested from Papa's library.

His old energy was returning, and with it his intellectual fervor. While the British surrender at Yorktown had effectively ended the war, a final peace had not yet been negotiated, and British soldiers continued to occupy New York City and less populous regions in the southern states. To Alexander, this was a time even more dangerous to America than the depths of the war had been, and he railed against the weaknesses of Congress and the imperative need for change in the government before the country could survive on its own. I listened and asked questions, wrote letters and made notes for him since Mamma forbid open bottles of ink anywhere near beds. It was as if he and I were again back in the small house on De Peyster's Point, with him *thinking* at a furious pace.

But on one of those gray January afternoons when dusk falls too soon and candles must be lit by the middle of the afternoon, his mood turned as melancholy as the day. He was for once silent, lost in his own thoughts as he lay against the pillows, staring out the window at the snow-covered garden and gray sky above it.

"When I went over the top of the parapet, I believed I was a dead man," he said softly. I was startled, for this was the first time he'd mentioned Yorktown in many days, and never in this subdued fashion, either. He was still gazing toward the window, though at that moment I doubt he was aware of the landscape beyond the glass, or me beside him, either.

"It was my duty to go first, Betsey," he continued. "I'd sought this chance to lead my men into battle, and I'd welcomed it. You know I've never been a coward, not one time."

"Never," I murmured, agreeing but letting him continue.

"Yet when I should have thought only of victory and a glorious death, I thought of you." Restlessly he raked his fingers back through his hair. "Even as I jumped from the parapet with my sword drawn and in amongst the enemy's guns, I thought of you and our son, and how desperately I desired to see you both."

"That was love, Alexander," I said, putting aside my sewing to take his hand. "There's no dishonor or cowardice to that."

He shook his head. "Everyone believes I acted from purest honor, duty, and courage," he said, "but in my heart I was afraid, afraid that I'd never see you again, afraid that I'd never see our son, afraid that he'd grow and live without a father as I did. How could I lead other men into battle with that much fear in my head and my heart?"

"But you did lead them, my love," I insisted. "You fought for us and our future together. You did your best, because you had a reason for fighting. That doesn't make you any less of a soldier."

"But it does," he said sadly. "It did. Love has no place in battle. In the past, before I married you, I fought with abandon and real courage, ready to sacrifice everything for freedom. I could face the enemy's guns and death without flinching. Now I hesitate, and stop to consider the cost. And that hesitation means the very death of a good soldier."

"You didn't do that at Yorktown," I said. On the contrary: every report I'd read had declared his actions to have been daring to the very edge of reckless, and his boldness and bravery were constantly singled out for admiration. "You put your life in jeopardy for the sake of liberty and for your men, and the world now lauds you as a hero."

"Eight men were killed in my company, Betsey," he said. "I'm praised by my superiors for having lost only eight, but I knew them. Good men, men who'd marched with me all the way from New York. They died following my orders, and my lead. Why did they die instead of me?"

"Oh, my love," I said gently. "You can't torment yourself with questions like this that have no answers. You've said yourself that such losses are the fortunes of war, both cruel and capricious. What more could you have given for the cause?"

He didn't answer my questions, but instead answered one of his own.

"I am done as a soldier," he said with finality. "I've resolved to write to His Excellency and resign my commission. Instead I intend to devote myself once again to studying the law, a pursuit that, while requiring dedication, does not demand the single-minded tenacity of a soldier."

As can be imagined, my heart rejoiced at this declaration. To have Alexander step down from the army and its dangers and obligations would be as Heaven to me. But I was also aware that this declaration could well be no more than a passing thought on a gloomy day, a resolution made more from my husband's current debilitation, and easily overturned upon his recovery. I wanted him to be certain, without any regrets or looking back.

"You needn't decide yet," I said. "I don't wish you to berate yourself if there were to be another crisis and His Excellency were in need of your talents."

"If matters became that dire, then His Excellency would need more than I could provide," he said firmly. "No, Betsey, my decision is made. I've had my share of glory. I'm determined upon the law. But most of all, I vow to devote myself to you and our child."

What sweeter words could there be than those? Certainly, it seemed as if the Siege at Yorktown had quelled the hottest fire of his ambition. If this was to be the future of our family, then I could ask for nothing more.

With Alexander finally permitted to leave his bed for a few hours a day, we began to join the rest of the family downstairs in the parlor. He particularly enjoyed listening to me play our fortepiano, and so did our child, who seemed to dance within me in time with the music. Alexander claimed that he'd fallen in love with me as I'd sat at my instrument on his first visit to our house years before, and that he never ceased to take pleasure in my accomplishment.

I was thankful that he could remember me as I'd been then, slender and elegant in a silk gown with plumes in my hair, because now I was a rare sight indeed. I wore a quilted waistcoat instead of stays beneath one of Mamma's old calico bedgowns, the only thing that remained that could encompass my belly, with the strings on my petticoat barely tied at what once had been my waist. Because my ankles and feet were so swollen, I could bear only thick knitted stockings that drooped without garters (because I couldn't wear them, either) and a pair of ancient backless slippers. I had to sit so far back from the keys of the fortepiano that my hands were forced to stretch straight before me, and by the end of even the shortest piece I was huffing and puffing with exertion. Yet still Alexander called me the most beautiful woman in the world, and I loved him all the more for it.

One afternoon, on a whim, he asked me to teach him a few simple notes. Because of the circumstances of his childhood, he'd never had the leisure or opportunity to learn to play an instrument, and he much regretted it. I bade him sit beside me on the bench, and showed him a child's tune. He concentrated on the lesson with the same intensity that he showed toward everything else, and soon had the pattern of the song learned. My mother and sister applauded, and he bowed his head as grandly as any maestro from the Continent.

I played the harmony part at the other end of the keys to accompany him, and after the first time, I began playing faster to tease him. Laughing and accusing me of foul play, he raced to match my speed, keeping pace even as he struck far more wrong keys than right. Out of breath, I laughed beside him, then suddenly gasped, and clutched at my belly. I felt a rush of wet warmth escape me, and to my mortification saw the growing puddle on the floor beneath the bench.

"What is wrong, my angel?" asked Alexander with concern, his arm instantly around me. "Are you unwell?"

"She's perfectly well," Mamma said, hurrying to my side and helping me to my feet. "It's time she was finally brought to bed with your child."

As can be imagined having borne so many children herself, my mother was an expert on the process, and like any general of rank, she swiftly took control of my confinement. She permitted me to kiss Alexander one last time, and then I was led upstairs while

Alexander was turned over to my father's care, in the way that these things have always been done.

Throughout the rest of the day, through the night, and into the next morning I suffered through my travail. I was tended by the same Dutch midwives who had helped bring me into the world twenty-four years earlier, and all my mother's other children since then. Even with their gentle guidance, I foundered on the waves of pain, beyond anything I'd expected. Like all women bringing forth their first child, I'd nothing for comparison, and so was certain my pains were beyond any before endured.

Through it all, I feared most not for myself, but for our child. I remembered the times my mother had given birth to babes who hadn't survived, their tiny, still, blue-white bodies wrapped not in swaddling clothes, but in winding sheets for burial. I could not fathom how a healthy child could be born from so much anguish, no matter how the other women reassured me.

It was only when I was at last delivered of my child, shortly before noon, and heard its lusty cry, that I could rejoice.

"A boy, Mrs. Hamilton, a fine son," the oldest midwife declared proudly, as if it had been her doing.

"Please, I wish to see him," I begged weakly. "I want to see my son."

Someone put him within my reach on my belly, still sticky with the blood we shared, and I cradled him as best I could. From that first touch, my hands across his tiny, wriggling limbs, I knew such love as only mothers feel, and I wept from the power of it. For a moment he was taken and washed and wrapped while much the same was done to me, and then again we were reunited. He was put to my breast to suckle and I held him tight, and gazed down at him in adoration, marveling at his miniature perfection.

"My own dear wife," said Alexander, suddenly with me. He was unshaven and disheveled, and I guessed he hadn't slept last night, either. "A son, they say?"

"Your son," I whispered. "Our son."

He touched his fingertip to our baby's cheek, a feather-light caress of wonder.

"You cannot know how I have longed for this," he said. "All my life, it seems, this is what I've wanted."

I understood. We were a family now. I'd never felt so loved, nor loved so much.

Just as I had made certain that Alexander had kept to his bed to recover from his final campaign, so, too, did he insist that I do the same for the full month of my lying-in. He had my mother as his ally, who agreed that it was the one sure way to regain my health after an arduous delivery. Though it went against my nature to be so idle, I'd no choice but to obey them, and happily gave myself over to doing nothing except lavishing attention on my new little son.

We named him Philip, after my father, a choice that Alexander himself suggested first and I'd heartily agreed. It did lead to some confusion in our family, since Angelica's older son was also named after my father, but not so much that we changed our intentions.

From birth, our Philip was a handsome, lively child with an even temper. He'd inherited my dark hair and dimpled chin, but the general shape of his face and features belonged to Alexander, or at least as much as could be determined with an unformed infant. He also shared his father's inquisitiveness, and watched every aspect of his world with wide-eyed interest.

But the center of Philip's world was his father, and the other way around as well. Alexander adored his son; there was no other way to describe the degree of affection he showered on Philip. Even before his son's birth, Alexander had resolved to be the best father possible, to make right all the long-ago wrongs that his own negligent father had inflicted upon him. Where other fathers would be content to leave their offspring to the care of mothers and nursery maids, Alexander took every opportunity to hold his son on his knee, or carry him about in his arms. It was to me the most beautiful sight, and one I never tired of watching.

I was also sure that Philip would share his father's rare gift for elegant speech, for while Alexander held him as they both kept me company, he discussed his plans for his future, and ours together. He did in fact resign his commission from the army early in the year, much to my happiness. His plan to turn his energies to a profession in law seemed doubly fortuitous. Not only would the law be a good match for his talents and a lucrative path toward supporting our family, but the state's legislature also seemed to smile upon him: a newly passed law prohibited lawyers with Tory sympathies from practicing in any state courts. Lawyers who were veterans of the Continental Army would be considered unquestionably patriotic, and able to reap a windfall of cases.

At least he would have been able to do so if he'd already completed the required law studies and three-year apprenticeship before he could be examined for the bar. While the legislature had created a special dispensation for those gentlemen who'd had their legal studies interrupted by their war service, the closing date for this was late January, an unattainable goal even for Alexander. Along with many other aspiring lawyers, he argued for a six-month extension. Knowing his abilities, I wasn't surprised that it was granted to him, but I was interested to learn that only one other veteran who likewise received an extension was Colonel Burr.

There remained another obstacle that to most men would have been insurmountable, but was only a passing challenge to Alexander. He had never formally studied the law while a student at King's College before the war. But he had read voraciously on his own, and had learned more of British law than many other so-called scholars. Instead of relying on a lengthy apprenticeship with an established lawyer, he decided he could learn better and faster on his own. This was confidence, not arrogance, and I didn't doubt he'd do it.

Throughout the rest of the winter and into the spring, he toiled many hours each day, reading and taking notes. He was often awake, dressed, and at work before I awoke, and I always retired to bed before he was done, a pattern that continued throughout our marriage. There was no rich library in Albany such as he'd had at King's College; instead he relied upon the books in my father's collection, and those in the private law library of James Duane, a well-respected lawyer and jurist, and an old acquaintance of Alexander's from his early days in New York City.

Also making use of my father's books was Colonel Burr, pursuing the same profession as Alexander. Occasionally I would pass him in the hall, or he would dine with us by Papa's invitation, and he was always cordial enough, even charming, to me. But I could never entirely forget what Alexander had told me about his intrigue with Mrs. Provost, and it made me uncomfortable in his company. Mrs. Provost's husband had since died in the Caribbean, and she now was a widow. Colonel Burr was expected to marry her, which, I suppose, would make her position more honest, if not honorable. And once when the colonel saw Alexander with me and Philip, he'd smiled, and praised him for a superior child. That sweetened my impression of him considerably, as it would with any mother.

My sister Angelica, however, didn't trust him. "Have you noticed how little Colonel Burr speaks of himself?" she said after they'd met during one of her visits. "He smiles and asks many questions and practices his wit most admirably, but he never speaks anything of substance. It's remarkable, really."

I frowned, thinking. "He has always seemed to be pleasant company."

"Which is exactly what he wishes you to think," she said, nodding sagely. "I imagine he's the very devil with women. You can tell from his eyes. He'd flatter a woman to agreeable distraction, and then be under her petticoats before she realized it."

I laughed, for my sister was every bit as accomplished at flattering gentlemen to agreeable distraction, though of course without the same consequences. Lately, however, she'd other matters on her mind. During her visit, she had announced that her husband Mr. Carter was now to be called Mr. John Barker Church, his true name. Apparently the rumors that had always followed him about a fatal duel had been true, and he had in fact shot a Member of Parliament some years before, precipitating his hasty departure from London and the assumption of a false name once he'd reached our shores.

But now he'd learned that the man had only been wounded and had fully recovered, and any charges against Mr. Carter—that is, Mr. Church—were dropped, and thus he had decided to end his guise, especially with the war between our countries done. It was odd to hear my sister now addressed as Mrs. Church, but she seemed so blithely at ease with it that I suspected she'd known all along. As can be imagined, my father was thoroughly displeased by Mr. Church's duplicity and the reasons behind it, but to my surprise, my own ordinarily truth-loving husband didn't disapprove at all.

"Church did what was necessary," he said, unperturbed when I told him. "He preserved his honor by the duel, and his life by assuming another name. Besides, if he hadn't done either, he wouldn't have come to our country, and we'd all have been deprived of his excellent acquaintance."

"But a duel, Alexander," I persisted. Duels were not common in Albany. To me, they were against both the laws of man and God, and a tragic waste of life. My husband, however, did not agree, and in fact during the war he had acted as the second to his friend Colonel Laurens in a duel with General Charles Lee.

Even knowing this, I could not leave it alone. "To think that Angelica's husband would fire at a man in such a murderous fashion!"

"From what I have heard, it wasn't the first time, either," Alexander said, either not sensing my disapproval or choosing to overlook it. "Church doesn't take affronts kindly. You know that of him. He's also an excellent shot."

Seeing no future to this conversation, I only sighed with exasperation and turned my eyes toward the Heavens. Clearly this was no more than another example of the occasional blind foolishness of men, to be found even in my own dear husband.

Yet in all, it was a blissful time for Alexander and me. Although he continued his interest in the affairs of Congress and politics in general, he seemed to be far more focused on passing the bar, and together we'd often speak of a future that now appeared quite tangible. It rankled him that we were compelled to live with my parents, but the truth was that since he'd left the army, he had no income, and wouldn't until he could begin taking cases. I accepted my parents' hospitality as an interim solution and no more, but for Alexander it was a disagreeable humiliation.

"The British are expected to leave New York by the end of the year," he said one Sunday afternoon in May as we walked beneath the apple blossoms in our orchard. We'd left Philip asleep with my infant sister Catherine, the pair of them watched over by the nursery maid, and had stolen this time alone for ourselves.

"The instant the British ships sail away, Betsey," he continued, "we'll move to the city ourselves. The courts will be overflowing with new cases, and I'll have my choice of the plum ones. I mean to find you a house on Wall Street, the finest house that can be procured, because that's what my delightful wife deserves."

"I should think we might wish to wait a few months, until the city is once again put to rights," I said. "I've heard the war has ravaged the streets and houses no end."

"All the more reason we should move quickly, before rents have a chance to rise." He reached up to pluck a blossom from a hanging branch, and presented it gallantly to me. "The last time I was there, many of the houses were still of the old Dutch model, but I'd prefer a fine house of brick."

I twirled the blossom's stem between my fingers and smiled, pleased that he was thinking such domestic thoughts, if improbable ones. I was looking forward to living apart from my family and being mistress of my own establishment, but it needn't be a fine house of brick on Wall Street.

"You know I'll be content with less," I said, tucking the blossom into the front of my bodice between my breasts. "So long as I have you and Philip, I'll always be happy."

"You are the best of wives, my love," he said, taking off his hat to kiss me. He was smiling afterward, looking down into the crown of the hat in his hand, and I smiled, too, never suspecting what he'd say next.

"Robert Morris has asked me to become the continental tax-receiver for the state of New York," he said, tracing a finger along the inner band of his hat. "He asked me once before in May and I turned him down, but then last week he wrote again to state that if I could be persuaded to take the position, he'd see that I'd earn a quarter of one percent of all the monies owed. I accepted."

I stared at him with dismay. Mr. Morris was the Superintendent of Finance for Congress. I'd known Alexander had continued to correspond with him after he'd first written to him last year, but I hadn't realized it had progressed to this.

"You've agreed to be a tax-receiver, Alexander?" I asked carefully, wanting to be sure I'd understood. "Now, when you're studying so hard for the bar?"

"It brings an income," he said, finally raising his glance to meet mine. "I want you to have that fine house, Betsey, and I don't want you to have to wait for it, either."

"But not this way," I said. "I listen to you, Alexander, and I've heard you say how the states—even New York—do not wish to give any moneys to Congress, and how they hold funds back as long as they can. Taxes or customs, it makes no difference, does it? And with New York City still occupied by the enemy, there won't be any collecting to be done in those counties. I do not pretend to your skills in finance and mathematics, but I am certain that a quarter of one percent of nothing is still nothing, isn't it?"

His smile had turned lopsided, the way it did when he was hedging.

"That is unfortunately true, yes," he admitted. "But it's also the reason why I've agreed to assist Morris by approaching the state legislature in Poughkeepsie to explain why the enforcement of federal taxation is so necessary."

"But consider your law studies, and how you have only until July to make yourself ready for the exam!" I exclaimed, my unhappiness with his impracticality growing by the moment. "How can you prepare yourself to represent Mr. Morris, and go before the legislature, and then act as a tax collector for Congress, too?"

"This is important, Betsey," he said firmly. "I fought in the war for a new country. If men like me don't continue to fight in other ways to create a government that is worthy of our first and truest ideals, then the entire war will have been for nothing."

"All I care for is you," I said softly, almost pleading. I didn't wish to quarrel with him, but I could see nothing good coming from this. "I know you can do so much, my love, but there must be a limit, even for you. Recall how only a few months ago you were so weak and grievously ill that you were forced to take to your bed."

"I assure you that won't happen again," he said confidently, and smiled. "You see how thoroughly you've restored me. Besides, no one expects me to storm the legislature with a sword in one hand and a pistol in the other."

"Pray be serious, Alexander," I said, placing my palm on his arm in tender restraint. "If you work yourself to exhaustion, you'll achieve nothing."

"I am serious, Betsey," he said, finally settling his hat once again upon his head. "I've no intention of making myself ill. But when opportunities present themselves for the betterment of my family and for the country as well, I will not look away."

He leaned forward to kiss me again, but I was too agitated for affectionate display, and turned my face so his lips found only my cheek. I stepped back, and swiftly began to walk toward the house, pointedly not looking to see if he followed.

But he had, and in a few quick steps he was beside me again.

"Betsey, my angel," he said, coaxing. "My own sweet girl."

When I didn't stop, he caught my arm and drew me to him, turning me so I'd no choice but to meet his eye.

"Eliza, please," he said gently. "Please. From the moment I wed you, my dearest, every choice I've made has been with you and our future in mind. You must remember that. Everything I do is for you and Philip."

I searched his eyes, longing to believe that this, then, was the truth. From all he'd said and done since he'd resigned his commission last February, I'd thought that he would complete his studies and become an acclaimed and successful lawyer. I'd thought that we'd move from my parents' house into a home of our own, and that our lives together would begin in earnest. Most of all, because he'd told me so, again and again, I'd thought that Philip and I were enough to make him happy.

I'd never foreseen difficult government appointments that would be impossible to fulfill, or journeys to Poughkeepsie that could last for weeks at a time. I hadn't realized that he still wanted to be so much a part of the government in Philadelphia that he'd always claimed to despise, or that the beckoning of powerful men like Robert Morris would be so sweet to his ears.

I hadn't known, because he hadn't told me.

But Angelica had, long ago before Alexander and I were wed.

"Your Hamilton may not lie to you outright, Eliza, but I assure you that in the course of your marriage there will be omissions that he'll justify and half-truths that he'll dismiss. Some shall make you laugh and others, alas, may make you weep."

I could not laugh now, and I would not weep.

With the back of his fingers, he lightly stroked my cheek.

"I love you so much, Betsey," he said, and I vow there were tears in his eyes to match my own. "You must know that there has never been another husband who loved his wife as I do you."

I did know, for that was the one truth that I'd never question. With a shuddering sigh, I gave myself over to his embrace, and the love that would always be mine as his wife. If he did choose to do these things for me and for Philip, then I must trust him that it would be for the best for us all. I must not doubt, but love.

And for the first months of summer, it seemed my trust in him could not be better placed. He passed the bar exam in July, exactly six months after he'd requested his extension, and exactly as he'd promised me he would, too. He was now an attorney with a fine title to prove his considerable accomplishment, though he jested he'd only become licensed in the art of fleecing his neighbors and acquaintances. No matter: I was exceptionally proud of him, and prouder still when he qualified as a counselor a short time later.

But the appointment as the state's tax-receiver was every bit as difficult and frustrating as I'd feared it would be. Those who owed taxes had no impetus to pay them, while the law, such as it was, gave Alexander no way to compel them to comply. There was little remunerative return to him for all the effort he exerted in the position, and it seemed to me a sorry waste of his increasingly precious time.

Yet despite his complaints (and oh, yes, he did complain), the appointment gave him reason to appear before the state's legislature with the goal of promoting a more effective way to collect taxes. He'd promised Robert Morris to do this, which would have been reason enough for him to make the three-days' ride south to Poughkeepsie.

But he also had the encouragement of my own father, who was serving as a state senator. To my chagrin, Papa took Alexander under his wing, and showed him about to best advantage to the other members of the legislature. Ordinarily I would be pleased by Papa's open affection and regard for my husband, but because of it, they both decided to lengthen their stay for several weeks. I will admit that they accomplished much, including the passage of a resolution calling for a new, national convention to overhaul the Articles of Confederation under which Congress weakly governed.

This should have been a resolution dear to Alexander's heart, considering how often he declaimed about the country's govern-

ment, and likened it to every toothless and infirm beast he could
name. Instead, however, he'd found the entire process disillusion-
ing and discouragingly slow, and the members of the legislature a
dull-witted and selfish lot whose main concerns were not for their
constituents, but only for their own personal gain. He claimed he
wished nothing more to do with it or them, and instead preferred
to marvel over how much he thought Philip had grown in the time
he'd been away, and how skilled his son had become at sitting upright unassisted. Of course I agreed on every count; how could
I not?

But in August came news of the most sorrowful kind. I'd never
had the honor of meeting John Laurens, but I knew how much his
friendship meant to Alexander, and how, since Yorktown, they had
strived to keep it aglow through letters. But while Alexander had returned to me in Albany after the last campaign, Laurens had been
unable to leave behind the rigors and adventure of battle. Little ac-
tual fighting remained in any of the states, but Laurens had found it
in a small and meaningless battle near his home in South Carolina.
Leading a charge, he was shot from the saddle, and died soon after.
The British left South Carolina less than a week later.

Like so many of our age, he was one more young man of promise and ability who'd been claimed too young, at only twenty-seven,
and because Laurens had been so dear to Alexander, his death affected my husband deeply. He mourned not only the loss of his
friend, but also the conclusion of the time they'd shared as soldiers,
and his own youth with it. At twenty-six, Alexander himself was
hardly old, yet Laurens's death made him feel the gloom of his own
mortality. Only Philip's innocence and infant promise seemed to
comfort him, our son's cheerful gurgles easing his sorrow far more
than any adult words of condolence.

I felt certain now that he'd devote himself to building his practice, and that the house he'd continued to promise would soon be
ours. His associate Aaron Burr had also passed the bar, and the office he'd opened was prospering. But in October, amongst the
many letters that came daily to The Pastures was one that set Alexander on another course entirely.

He came to me while I was at my music in the parlor, the open
letter still in his hand. He was grinning, smiling more widely than

I'd seen since he'd heard of Laurens's death, and as I played the last lines of the little song I'd been practicing, he danced a small jig of joy that made me laugh.

"I'd guess that must be good news," I said, "to make you caper about so."

"Oh, only the best," he assured me, "and all the more for being so unexpected."

He took my hand and raised me from the bench, and made me dance a few more steps with him while he hummed the tune I'd been playing. He ended by giving me a loud, smacking kiss that made me laugh again, and swat at him for being foolish.

"Tell me, Alexander," I said. "Or am I to guess you've been offered a position as a dancing master?"

"I could do that, you know," he said, and winked. "But it's something far grander than that. You recall when I came home from Poughkeepsie, convinced the entire legislature was nothing but a barn of incompetent dolts and nodding old fools?"

"I do," I said. "You've made sure I wouldn't forget, too."

"You should forget it, because now I judge them to be only the wisest and most prudent of gentlemen," he said, holding the letter out for me to read. "Read this, Betsey. They have chosen me as a delegate to represent New York at the next Continental Congress. I leave for Philadelphia next week."

CHAPTER 13

Philadelphia, Pennsylvania
January 1783

Journeys made in the winter months are never easy. Ice, snow, and winds are only part of the trial. Even when shod with ice shoes, horses seem to go lame more often in the cold, and roads that are hard-rutted with ice can break wheels and axles of even the sturdiest conveyances. If there is sufficient snow, the best mode of travel is a sleigh, which cannot be excelled for smoothness and speed, but leaves much to be wanted in regard to comfort.

No matter how many coverlets and furs are provided across the sleigh's bench, the biting wind still manages to steal its way to any skin left uncovered, and the coals in the foot-warmer that felt so cozy when the day began lose their heat all too soon, and with it vanishes all feeling in the toes and feet. Swaddled like eggs for market against the cold, there is no opportunity for amusement whilst traveling by sleigh: blowing pages make reading impossible, and hands tucked in mittens or muffs can do no needlework. Even conversation can be difficult, with the wind tearing away each shouted word, and refreshment is best left for the next tavern.

For the sake of joining Alexander in Philadelphia, I made such a journey from Albany in January 1783. To every hardship I've listed, I added one more challenge of the most taxing, albeit charming, sort: at Alexander's request, I brought with me our son, Philip.

Philip was nearly a year in age, bright-eyed and lively, with thick dark hair and round, rosy cheeks. He was accomplished at sitting, crawling, and standing, and was laboring mightily at walking without the helpful yet meddlesome hands of a larger person for support. However, he had next to no interest in being wrapped in thick clothes and tucked beneath furs, and in being made to sit still in a sleigh for hours on edge.

I had a single servant—my ever-capable Rose—with me to help, but still we were forced to stop much more frequently than I ordinarily would have, making the trip stretch out over more days. I do believe we paused at every respectable tavern and inn between here and Albany in addition to the houses of friends and distant family, all for the sake of letting Philip weary himself in the hopes he'd sleep in my lap during the next leg of the journey.

As arranged, Alexander met us at a tavern in New Jersey, and as parents who have been separated and one left with a restless child, I'd never been so glad to see him. With less snow on the ground in New Jersey than there had been in New York, we switched from the sleigh to a hired carriage, and rode to Philadelphia together as a family, with Philip snug and content in his father's arms. I understood, for after two months apart, I was mightily content to be with his father as well.

Philadelphia was much as I recalled it from my visit with my father nearly three years before, save without the uncertainty. For a city that had been occupied by the enemy, it appeared to me to be remarkably unscathed. I do not know if it was on account of the Quakers, who were much in evidence, or some other civic force, but the city was also more tidily kept than most, with the steps before the houses well swept and the streets free of rubbish. With the war largely over, there also appeared to be more building, more new houses, more ships tied at the waterfront docks, and in general a greater show of wealth and prosperity. The women we passed on the streets were much more richly dressed than in Albany, with extravagant hats and muffs, and fur edging their cloaks as they strolled along the streets.

"I don't recall Philadelphia being such a place of fashion," I said as we passed a particularly stylish lady climbing into her carriage, her liveried servants waiting upon her as if she were a duchess. "I hope I'll not shame you too much as a country cousin."

"Not at all," Alexander declared with gratifying certainty. "You will always shine in any company, my dearest. I'll grant that there are handsome women in Philadelphia, but a great many of them are in keeping to merchants who lavish every folly upon them, like oriental pashas with their harem-favorites. I'd much rather my wife cloaked herself in virtue and honor."

"As I should, being the wife of an esteemed delegate from New York." I looked after the woman with the carriage with new interest. "That woman, then—was she a rich man's mistress?"

He shrugged expansively, his eyes twinkling. "I do not tell tales, Betsey, nor whisper idle gossip or tattered scandal."

"Then she *was*," I said, and laughed happily. I knew he was teasing me from fondness, and it made me realize all over again how sorely I'd missed him. He might be but a humble junior delegate from New York with his son curled asleep against his shoulder, but it was evident that he'd patronized the tailors and barbers here in Philadelphia: his suit was new, plainly cut but of a rich, plum-colored woolen, as was his dark blue greatcoat with cape collar and silver buttons, and his hair had obviously been dressed by a Frenchman familiar with combs and pomatum. Nor did he looked peaked or overworked, as I'd feared, but sleek and handsome, so handsome that I proudly tucked my hand a little more tightly into the crook of his arm.

"Humble we may be, sweet wife," he said, "but I promised you I'd squeeze a few coins from our purse for you to visit a mantua-maker here."

"You needn't do that," I said quickly, but he held up his hand to quiet me.

"I don't need to do it, no, but I'd like it if you'd please yourself," he said. "You've such a generous soul toward others, Betsey. Spend a bit on yourself while you're here."

I nodded, and smiled at his kind indulgence. I hadn't had anything new since we'd been wed, refusing every offer of assistance from my parents and from Angelica, too. I'd kept my promise to Alexander to be a frugal wife, but if he said we could afford it, then I'd believe him.

But when we finally arrived at a small brick house and climbed the stairs to our lodgings, I wondered that we could afford much of anything.

We'd only two small rooms for our use, rented from the widow who lived below. There was a parlor and a bedchamber, each with a single window that overlooked the noisy street. The furnishings were sparse and well-worn: a bedstead with a trundle beneath for Philip, a small table for washing below a tiny looking glass, and an earthenware chamber pot in the bedchamber; and a table (which from the number of papers and books upon it, was clearly being used by Alexander as a desk), a bench, two chairs, and a chest in the parlor. A pair of fly-specked prints showing Juno and Jupiter were pinned to the wall, and that was that.

Alexander must have realized my misgivings from my expression.

"Lodgings are very dear in this town," he said apologetically, taking Philip to the window to show him the street. "I'm fortunate to have found this, and our landlady Mrs. Williamson provides our dinner, too."

"It will serve us well enough," I said, trying to be cheerful. "What about Rose?"

He glanced back over his shoulder at Rose, standing uncertainly with two of my boxes from the carriage.

"There's a space for servants in the attic," he said. "That's where my man is staying. Or we can arrange a pallet for her here at night."

"I'd rather Rose stayed here with us," I said, not wanting to imagine the servants' quarters that accompanied lodgings such as these. The driver was bringing the rest of my trunks upstairs; I was grateful that I'd heeded Alexander's warning, and not brought much with me.

But clearly he'd other concerns, holding Philip out and away from his splendid new greatcoat.

"Rose," he said with a sniff. "I believe the young gentleman needs his clout changed."

It wasn't until much later, when he and I were in bed together, that we were finally able to talk with any frankness. After a long separation, most women would not consider politics to be romantically alluring conversation, but for Alexander and me it was, and always had been. It was all part of the warm familiarity of him beside me in our bed.

"Nothing is ever accomplished," Alexander said with unabashed disgust, propping his head on his elbow to gaze down at me while we conversed. "There are too many committees, too many debates, too many adjournments and postponements and delays. Nor do many of the appointed delegates feel any obligations whatsoever to appear, making quorums impossible. I've yet to meet three of our party from New York, who haven't deigned to show their faces in Philadelphia once this season."

"I'm sorry of that," I said, though sorrier still that he was so unhappy. "You'd had such expectations."

He'd postponed beginning his legal profession in earnest to serve as a delegate, and I'd hoped he would have found the sacrifice more rewarding. Yet I could have predicted it, too, though I'd never say so. I'd witnessed it before. Alexander's mind was so quick and his obsession with both details and efficiency so thorough that he should in theory be the ideal delegate, but at the same time those same qualities could make him an irritant to men less driven than he. No man likes to be bettered by another who is wiser and works harder, and is younger, too. It had been that way for Alexander when he'd been employed on the general's staff, and I wasn't surprised that it was happening again here.

"I'd expectations of actually accomplishing something worthwhile," he said, "and not being halted by lazy fools who think only of their own states instead of a more encompassing vision. It is the same as it was in Poughkeepsie, only here there is more at stake."

I nodded, for I'd learned much of this earlier from his letters. "I should think that they'd be more interested in settling the government now that the peace treaty has been signed."

"I fear it's exactly the opposite," he said, impatiently shoving his hair back from his face. "Now that we're no longer at war, most of the delegates—and most of whom were never soldiers—believe there isn't a need for a unified government, let alone a single country. Taxes and tariffs, the courts, the military, would all be better served by consolidation. Yet the only thing that concerns my fellow delegates is the wretched sovereignty of their individual states, smug and separate. They refuse to see the weakness that comes from thirteen individuals as opposed to the strength to be found in a single entity."

"Clearly they need you to enlighten them," I said. "If anyone can explain the need for unity, my love, it's you."

He rolled onto his back with an exasperated sigh, throwing his arms over his head across the pillow. "They try my patience sorely, Betsey, and remain willfully blind to the truth. They're as jealous and petty of their holdings as girls with beaux at their first ball."

"You exaggerate, my dear," I said mildly. I settled myself in comfort upon his chest with my hands pillowed on my folded arms. "These delegates are considerably more jealous and petty than any girls I've known."

"That is true," he admitted, idly twisting a lock of my hair around his fingers. "Girls at a ball show more direction and sense of purpose."

I smiled. "I'll not quarrel with that."

"No, you wouldn't," he said. "But then you, Betsey, are so much more eminently sensible than any mere delegate. In the army, no matter what our state, we learned to serve under one flag, one general. We fought together, and we were victorious. If only more of the delegates had served in the field, then perhaps we'd have more success than this pack of—"

"Shhh, not so loud," I cautioned as his voice became more impassioned, and I heard Philip stirring in the trundle. "Don't wake our son unless you want him here in our bed, too."

He grunted, drawing me closer and sliding his hand along my hip, which was answer enough.

"There is no godly reason why ending a war should be so much more difficult than agreeing to begin one," he continued, lowering his voice but keeping the same fire in his words. "Yet that is where we are. How can we dismiss an army that hasn't been paid in years? How can we send our officers home to their families without the pensions they were promised when their commissions were signed?"

"It's wrong, dearest, and shameful," I said with conviction equal to his. I could believe no less. I was both a soldier's daughter and a soldier's wife. What Congress—or rather, the states that were represented by Congress—was doing *was* shameful. Soldiers must be paid, and yet the states refused to give Congress the money to pay them, and worse, made them the scapegoats, too. "You're right to fight for this."

"It's the same as standing firm for the men in my battalion," he said. "They risked their lives, and they deserve to be paid."

I sighed, thinking. "Haven't you made any allies among the other delegates? There must be at least one other gentleman who thinks as you do."

"Mr. Morris, of course, as Superintendent of Finance, though he is lofty above me, and his opinions must be more measured," he said. "I also suspect several others among the delegates who are too cowardly to admit their sympathies. But there is one gentleman from Virginia, Mr. Madison, whom I've mentioned to you before. He's a learned, thoughtful fellow, and he studied with Burr at the College of New Jersey before the war. He has the sufficient rigor of intellect to foresee the necessity of unified, federal government, and when three officers from this year's winter camp came down from Newburgh with a petition of grievances, he and I met with them, and offered our assurances."

"Then I am glad you have made his acquaintance," I said. "Is his wife here in Philadelphia, too?"

"Oh, Madison isn't married," he said, and couldn't keep back a wry chuckle. "He's a prim old bachelor who'd have no more notion of what to do with a wife than she would know what to do with him."

His hand slid a little lower on my hip to remind me that, unlike Mr. Madison, he knew perfectly well what to do with his wife, and how to please her, too. I smiled, shifting closer to him. It was cold in this room, but warm beside him.

"Then you must tell me the other wives of delegates I should call upon," I said. "I'm here not only as your wife, but your partner in this. I'm eager to lobby on your behalf to these ladies, who will in turn speak to their husbands."

I meant it, too. All my life I'd watched my mother gently steer support toward my father's various causes, all over a cup of tea, a fine dinner, or a glass of Madeira wine, and Lady Washington was a consummate hostess on His Excellency's behalf as well. As humble as our lodgings might be, I was still eager to do the same here in Philadelphia for Alexander.

But instead of embracing my offer as I'd expected (for we'd discussed the possibilities many times before in Albany), he only smiled ruefully.

"I wish that you could, Betsey," he said. "But the sad truth is that few of the delegates have brought their wives with them."

I nodded, disappointed that I couldn't help more. "It's not to their credit, abandoning their wives like that."

"Most would say I'm the selfish one, having brought you and our boy all this distance for no reason beyond my own wish," he said softly, cupping my face against his palm. "Yet I couldn't help myself. I had to have you here. I've missed you more than I can ever say, my wife, my counsel, my friend, my angel, my dearest, dearest love."

"My dearest, dearest husband," I said, leaning forward to kiss him. "That is more than reason enough."

While I did not regret joining Alexander in Philadelphia—I never in our life together regretted being with him, only being apart—I will concede that it was not an easy time for either of us. Alexander's numerous responsibilities were taking their toll on his person and I worried again for his health; his hours were long and thankless, with seemingly insurmountable challenges.

Mine were of a more domestic nature. While there were some ladies in Philadelphia whom I'd recalled from my earlier visit with my father, many had retreated to their estates outside the city. We could not afford to keep a carriage, nor did I wish the expense of hiring one, and so I restricted my circle of acquaintance by the distance I could walk.

This was not such a grave hardship for me, realizing the circumstances, but poor little Philip had neither the understanding nor the patience to cope with his newly limited world. At The Pastures, he'd been accustomed to the constant amusement and attention of our large family and the spaciousness of our house and property. Now most days his company was limited to me and Rose, and his boundaries had shrunk to the two small rooms of our lodgings, and he was most vocal in his unhappiness.

Our only solace came at night—and sometimes very late it was, too—when Philip and I were rejoined by Alexander. Then, as a family and as husband and wife, we took comfort in one another, and the cares of the day faded away.

Nor was it an easy winter for our country. The unhappiness of the soldiers at what would be the final winter encampment at Newburgh continued to fester. The soldiers realized that there would likely be no further use for their services, and their sole concern was to be paid what was owed them. Discontent was being sowed freely among the ranks, and yet the states continued to deprive Congress of funds to pay the soldiers.

For his services during the war, Alexander himself was entitled to a handsome pension as an officer of five years' standing. Yet to make certain there were absolutely no hints of partiality or special treatment attached to his name as a member of Congress, at this time he renounced all claims to this pension, a noble and selfless act that astonished his peers.

But this wasn't his only action in regard to the army. Although Alexander had had no communication with His Excellency since resigning his commission a year earlier, he took it upon himself to write directly and confidentially to the general, explaining the dire situation from the view of Congress. While Alexander harbored hope that the general would himself pressure the states, instead in March His Excellency chose to address the rebellious troops directly, successfully counseling them toward peace rather than rebellion.

But relief was only temporary. In April, Congress ratified the provisional peace treaty with Great Britain, finally bringing our long war to a close; yet despite desperate measures and resolutions aimed at producing more revenue to pay the army before sending them home, Alexander feared there would simply not be enough.

I had planned to remain in Philadelphia with my husband until the first week of July, and leave with Philip for Albany before the city's heat became intolerable and the air unhealthy with the summer miasma from the docks. But by the middle of June, the political circumstances were growing so desperate and uncertain that Alexander decided it would be unwise for us to remain in the city, and he hired a carriage for us to depart the following Monday.

On the Thursday before we were to leave, news reached Congress that a group of disgruntled soldiers was marching toward the city from Lancaster. On behalf of Congress, Alexander asked Pennsylvania's Supreme Executive Council (such a grand name for such a cowardly group!) to call out the militia to defend Philadelphia. They refused, saying there was insufficient cause, but the next day there were rumors that the dissidents were on the very edges of the city.

The rumors also claimed that if the soldiers received no satisfaction from Congress, they were then prepared to attack and pay themselves from the Bank of North America. In a curious twist of coincidence, the bank's president and largest shareholder was Alexander's friend and supporter Robert Morris, and the second largest shareholder was my sister Angelica's husband, John Church.

"It's a good thing that you're leaving with Philip on Monday," Alexander said as we took breakfast together. "My heart will go with you, of course, but I want you and Philip removed from any possibility of danger."

"But what you, my love?" I asked, unable to keep the fear from my voice. "You have been so much at the front of this conflict that I worry you'll be made a target."

He shrugged, gulping the rest of his coffee before he rose to leave for the day.

"I'll be safe enough," he said. "I'm hardly worth their trouble."

I found it difficult to be reassured. If the city were too dangerous for me to remain, then how could it be safe for him? Still, the streets appeared to be at peace, and I wondered if the alarms had been exaggerated. I'd planned to call upon Mrs. Mary Morris, the wife of Alexander's supporter Robert Morris, to bid her farewell. She was a gracious lady who had shown me much kindness whilst I'd been in Philadelphia, and her own young children had become Philip's playmates. The Morris house was not far from our lodgings, and so with Rose to carry Philip (who was growing larger by the day, and had become a robust armful), we set out.

As we waited in the parlor for Mrs. Morris to join us, I reflected on how swiftly this war, wrought by men, had forced changes upon us women. The Morris house was sizable and elegant, as was to be expected, but it had not always belonged to them. One of the more recent residents had been the military governor, General Benedict Arnold, who had lived here when he'd wed Peggy; now he was a traitor who'd be hung without a trial if he ever dared return, and they lived as exiles in London. How could she have known when she lived here that her life would take such a twisted turn?

Even Mrs. Morris, who lived here now, had seen her family's fortunes tumbled by the war as well. According to Alexander, her husband had extended vast loans to the army that were likely never to be repaid, and he'd also lost over a hundred of his merchant and privateering ships to capture.

As I sat waiting with Philip on my lap, I thought of how fortunate Alexander and I had been. To be sure, we hadn't had a fortune to lose, nor would Alexander ever have been tempted to betray his beliefs and country, but I never forgot how he himself had survived battles that had claimed far too many other sweethearts, husbands, and fathers. I thought of it each night when I lay curled beside him, and I thanked God every day for his deliverance.

But that afternoon in her parlor Mrs. Morris and I spoke only of cheerful matters, of embroidery patterns and recipes and how fast our children were growing. By unspoken agreement we said nothing of the difficulties facing our husbands in Congress—difficulties that, alas, soon proved impossible to ignore.

She had just led me into her garden to show me the buds on her roses when we both paused at once, struck silent by the same unfamiliar sound in the distance.

"Whatever could that be?" she murmured, but we both knew what it was: a crowd of angry men, voices raised, the soldiers from Lancaster.

"I should take my leave," I said, thinking only of Alexander.

"Stay here until we learn more," she urged. "I'll send a servant to discover what is happening."

The news the servant brought back was not auspicious. Scores of soldiers and other men were gathered before the statehouse with Congress trapped inside. The malcontents did not appear to be threatening either the property or the delegates within, but taverns and tippling houses in the area were doing a brisk business, and the situation would likely worsen.

"You may remain with me as long as you please, Mrs. Hamilton," Mrs. Morris said. Her own anxiety underscored the generous invitation, making her voice taut. As the Superintendent of Finance, her husband was most likely inside the State House, too. "You'll be safe here."

"Thank you, but I must return to our lodgings," I said, thinking that there likely wasn't any place in Philadelphia that could be considered safe. "I wish to be where my husband expects me to be."

Mrs. Morris shook her head, her brows drawn tightly together and her hands tightly clasped with anxiety. "Then at least let me send you and your son in our chaise."

I thought of the Morrises' chaise, with the elegant Morris arms painted on the door in gold, and what a pretty target that might make to the mob of men who believed themselves to have been cheated by the government.

"Thank you, Mrs. Morris, but no," I said. "I'll leave as I came, by walking."

"Then at least permit me to send two of my servants to accompany you," urged Mrs. Morris. "I can't let you go otherwise, not in good conscience."

I agreed to that, and soon I was walking swiftly with Rose and Philip between two of the larger Morris servants. No one paid us any attention. The few people on the street were instead concentrating on the crowd gathered along Chestnut Street. While I knew my little party should have taken advantage of this and proceed directly to our lodging house, from concern for my husband's welfare I insisted we walk one street out of our way so that I, too, could have a glimpse of the disturbance.

I wished I hadn't.

I could see the tall brick tower of the statehouse framed between the buildings on the corners at the end of the street. Soldiers filled the front yard and spilled into the street, blocking any traffic that wished to pass, and more soldiers had surrounded the sides of the statehouse as well. Though I cannot say for certain, I would guess there were at least four hundred gathered there, a sea of churning anger and resentment. Many were still in uniform, their coats faded and their breeches patched, which was the condition of most of the Continental troops after so many years. All carried their muskets, too, the long bayonets shining like a field of dangerous silver blades. I didn't doubt that those muskets were loaded.

Soldiers in themselves did not frighten me. Because of my father, they'd always been part of my life. But soldiers who were angry, half drunk, armed, and without officers in control terrified me. The delegates inside had closed most of the windows against the crowd, and I was surprised the soldiers hadn't broken the panes. Perhaps they didn't feel the need to: the delegates were trapped inside with no means of escape, and I could not imagine how this could be resolved peaceably.

And somewhere in the middle was my husband, unarmed and without resources, yet both blessed and cursed with the constant, reckless desire to act the hero.

I stood and watched, my heart pounding with dread for Alexander's sake. I'd never felt so helpless. There truly was nothing I could do, yet still I stood rooted to the paving stones, unable to look away.

Behind me Philip whimpered and said my name. Automatically I turned to take him from Rose. Not only was Philip fretful, but fear radiated from the three servants, too. They hadn't the right to tell me that we should leave, and that we didn't belong here. That was my responsibility, as were they. All I could do now for Alexander was pray that he'd find the wisdom he'd need. Without a word, I turned, and led the way back to our lodgings.

I sat by the window, waiting for Alexander, and I waited long after the sun had set and the moon had risen, and both Philip and Rose had gone to sleep. Though I didn't wish to admit it to myself, I was listening as much as waiting. We were only a short distance from the statehouse, and if any real violence had been done, I would have been able to hear the gunshots.

At last I saw the shadow of Alexander's slight figure in the street, and heard his footsteps come wearily up the stairs. I embraced him at once and held him close, grateful beyond words that he'd safely returned.

"You're leaving tomorrow morning, as soon as the sun rises," he said. His shoulders sagged with fatigue and his clothes were rumpled, but he was otherwise unharmed. "I had to pay the rogue at the stable double to drive on Sunday, but I don't want you here another day."

"But what of you, my love?" I asked, helping him shrug free of his coat. "You can't tell me you're safe, because I know you weren't today. I passed the statehouse this afternoon after I'd called upon Mrs. Morris. I saw the soldiers gathered there, and—"

"They're mutineers," he said grimly. "Call them what they are. They've turned their back on their duty and their officers. They have reason, yes, but not this way."

"I don't care what they're called," I said. "You could have been killed, and you know it."

He shook his head, but didn't disagree. "They let us pass unharmed today, but I wouldn't vouch for tomorrow."

"Then what will you do, Alexander?" I asked, pouring him a glass of wine. "You can't stay here."

"The delegates met tonight at Boudinot's house," he said, "and agreed that if Pennsylvania again refuses to call up their militia for our protection, then we'll convene instead in New Jersey, in Princeton. I doubt the state will do what it should, and I'll likely be trudging in your footsteps by evening tomorrow."

He emptied the glass and stared into it, his thoughts elsewhere. I'd often seen him discouraged here in Philadelphia, and frustrated, too, but this was the first time I'd seen him resigned.

"There needs to be change, Betsey," he said, "but no one here is ready for it. Until the states realize that Congress needs power, real power, to accomplish what it must for the good of the country as a whole, then there is little point to being here. I'll remain a delegate long enough to sign the final peace treaty, but no longer."

"You'll return to Albany?" I asked, daring to hope.

"Before the summer is done," he said. "Then at last, my own dear Betsey, you and I shall go to New York."

My journey back to The Pastures with Philip and Rose was without event. By the time I reached Albany, there were already letters from Alexander waiting for me. The Pennsylvania militia had in fact been called out soon after I'd left the city, and the mutiny had dissipated without any further trouble. Alexander and Robert Morris contrived to have the soldiers paid, through bills personally guaranteed by Mr. Morris. But Congress had still determined to shift to New Jersey, and was meeting now in crowded quarters in Princeton. Nothing had changed beyond their location, however, and Alexander reiterated his plan to quit Congress and once again join me.

But there was little peace to be found at The Pastures, either. While Philip and I were warmly welcomed back home, both Mamma and Papa were grim and unhappy, and with good reason, too.

Only days before, my younger sister Peggy had stunned everyone by eloping. Unlike Angelica, who had also eloped, there could be no objections to Peggy's new husband's family. They were Dutch descendants like us, and distant cousins of my mother's family as well. But while Stephen Van Rensselaer was his late father's eldest son and in line to become the tenth patroon of Rensselaerwyck, he was also scarcely nineteen, a recent graduate of Harvard College.

My sister Peggy was twenty-five. While no one was so impolite as to say that Peggy was too old for Stephen, there was considerable talk about how Stephen was too young to marry in general. Although legally of age to choose a wife, he wouldn't inherit his estate (his father having died when he was a young child) until he was twenty-one. When he and Peggy had first shown interest in each other, older members of both families had cautioned against the match, but Peggy had always been impulsive by nature, and apparently Stephen was as well. Knowing Peggy, I was surprised, but not shocked, and I prayed they'd be happy together. My poor mother, however, was still reeling.

"I am at a loss," Mamma said to me once we were alone. I'd scarcely been home an hour when she'd taken me into her bedchamber and shut the door, specifically to speak of the elopement. "It was disgraceful enough that Angelica chose to ignore our wishes and blessings for the sake of Mr. Church, but to have Peggy do so, too—why, it has quite broken your poor father's heart."

I guessed it had likely made our family the talk of Albany and our vast extended family as well. To have one daughter elope was scandalous enough, but now to have had a second one forgo the ritual of a Schuyler wedding in the parlor was almost an insult to my parents, and one not quickly forgiven. It had taken months before Angelica was again welcome at The Pastures, and even longer for her husband, and I wondered if Peggy and Stephen would face the same fate.

"You father had made his opinions on the match very clear to them both," Mamma continued, clearly wounded. "Yet your sister disobeyed him."

"Oh, Mamma," I said, sitting beside her on the bed to take her hand. "Perhaps Peggy didn't understand."

"She understood," she said emphatically, "and Stephen did as well. Now, I'll grant that there are some gentlemen of Stephen's age who have already attained the thoughtful maturity of their station, but he remains in the first flower of impetuous youth, full of impulse and passion. He's hardly the steadying force your sister needs. He can't be. Two peas in a foolish pod, that's what they are, and all I can do now is pray that they won't repent of what they've done."

"Perhaps they'll surprise us all, Mamma," I said, striving to play the peacemaker for Peggy's sake. I recalled how I'd been so eager to wed Alexander that I, too, had proposed an elopement, only to be dissuaded by Alexander's wisdom. Now I was glad we'd shared our joy with my family, but I still could feel empathy for Peggy and Stephen. "I hope they do, if they loved each other that much."

My mother's deep sigh showed exactly what value she placed on that love—no matter that she'd risked a great deal for love herself.

"Your sister climbed from her bedchamber window to meet him," she said forlornly. "It's all Angelica's fault, of course, for having eloped with Mr. Church. Once Peggy saw what Angelica had done, her heart was set on following. But climbing from the window like a thief in the night!"

I could all too easily picture Peggy clambering down a rope with her petticoats flying above her garters, just as I could imagine Stephen persuading her that it was the proper thing to do. My mother was right: they were two peas in a foolish pod.

Mamma pulled a handkerchief from her pocket and blotted the corners of her eyes.

"Nothing is as it should be any longer, Eliza," she said softly, her voice breaking. "If it were not for you and Hamilton, I should be in the blackest despair over my daughters. First Peggy, and now this sad news regarding Angelica. I do not know how I shall bear it."

"What news of Angelica?" I asked swiftly, a score of unfortunate possibilities springing to mind. My older sister could be equally as impulsive as Peggy, but in less predictable ways. She was also with child again, and I prayed she hadn't come to grief.

"You must not have received her letters," Mamma said, pressing her handkerchief to her cheeks again as fresh tears spilled forth. "Now that the war is done, John has decided to sail to France for the sake of settling his accounts, and take her and the children to live in Paris. To *Paris*, Eliza!"

I gasped, stunned. In a way, it made perfect sense: Mr. Church had come to New York in 1775 to escape his past and to make his fortune in the war, and he'd always intended to return to either London or the Continent, whichever proved more welcoming. He'd no reason to remain now that hostilities from which he'd so profited had ended. For her part, Angelica longed for what she perceived as the irresistible allure of the Old World, and Mr. Church's promises to take her there had been much of his allure as a suitor. Nor could I question his desire to settle his final accounts from his wartime trading; Angelica had hinted to me that he'd still substantial funds outstanding from having supplied the French army in America.

Yet there was so much more to such a voyage. Crossing the ocean was always hazardous, and even the most experienced of shipmasters couldn't guarantee a safe passage. I was loath to think of Angelica and her children in peril from storms or pirates, and then to imagine them living so far from us, in another country entirely. Once they sailed, I might not see any of them for years, or perhaps ever again in this life. She'd three little ones now, Philip, Kitty, and John, and the fourth to come at the end of the year. Before long her older children would entirely forget their aunt Eliza, and the one yet born would have no knowledge of me at all. I'd let myself believe we would all live near one another in New York, as Angelica and I had once dreamed, but now—now that dream was done.

Mr. Church was eager to sail no later than the end of July, before hurricane season made crossings more dangerous. For one brief, final visit, Angelica came with her children to The Pastures. Because I'd no notion of when we'd meet again, I spent as much time with them all as I could, making sure that my Philip, too, was often with his cousins. On the evening before they were to leave us, I took one final long walk with Angelica, our arms linked.

"I don't wish you to be so sorrowful, Eliza," she said. Thanks to her husband's burgeoning wealth, she already looked as if she'd embraced the sophisticated airs of Paris; she wore a pair of sizable purple amethyst drop earrings and a necklace to match, the gold settings glittering in the fading sun. "I've wished all my life to visit Paris."

"I know you have," I said, unable to do as she'd bid and keep the sadness from my voice. "I'm happy for your sake, Angelica, but I still will miss you. To have an entire ocean between us!"

"We'll write often," she promised. "Hamilton has already sworn to write me with all the news that you forget."

"He will, too," I said. He and Angelica were avid correspondents, writing often to discuss books and treatises they'd both read as well as the family news I often forgot. Although Alexander assured me my letters were far more dear to him, I didn't doubt that hers were the more interesting. "His letters are so much better than mine."

She smiled, and to my amusement, she didn't disagree. Instead she linked her fingers into mine, and leaned her head against my shoulder.

"I shall miss you, too, Eliza," she said. "You, and your little Philip, and our dear Hamilton, but most of all you. No woman has ever been blessed with a better sister."

"Nor I," I said softly. "You must make certain that Mr. Church doesn't keep you abroad forever, but brings you back home to us in good time."

"He won't keep us in Paris forever, no," she said, a hint of melancholy in her voice now, too. "But he does wish to reside in London, at least while our children are young. I'd hoped that over time he'd come to view New York as his home, too, but he still longs for England."

I nodded, understanding. Even a woman as independent as Angelica must bow to her husband when it came to where they'd make their home.

"But perhaps we needn't be kept apart for long," she said, willing herself to be more cheerful. "Perhaps rather than me imploring

John to return to New York, you should have your Hamilton bring you to Paris. Imagine us together as fine ladies of fashion!"

"I can imagine you that way, Angelica, strolling through the golden halls of Versailles in full hoops and with jewels around your throat," I teased, unable to picture myself ever in such a role. "I'll be perfectly content as Mrs. Hamilton of New York."

"You may be content with such a mundane life, but Hamilton won't be," she said. "He'll never be satisfied with being a mere attorney. I'll expect him to have replaced Clinton as governor of New York by the time we return."

I laughed at that. "He swears he's had his fill of politics, and that all his dreams have been dashed," I said. "The past year in Philadelphia with Congress has soured him on it, and now he vows to dedicate himself entirely to practicing law."

She glanced at me slyly. "Do you truly believe that, Eliza? In your heart, and with your head? That your brilliant, mercurial husband will so meekly bow his neck to the yoke of the law?"

I looked away from her, out to where the sun was setting over the hills. She knew me so well, my sister, and she knew my husband, too. Even as I longed for Alexander to be happy with the profession he'd chosen, I'd wondered if such contentment was possible for him. I didn't need my sister to remind me of his ambitions and dreams for the new government. But then Angelica had also always been drawn to the most public aspects of my husband's character—the parts that were indeed brilliant and mercurial—and ignored the side of him that was kind and generous and endlessly devoted to Philip and me.

"Alexander will follow the path that he chooses for himself," I said carefully, a truth we could both agree upon. "For now, I believe that path leads to a law office on Manhattan Island."

"Perhaps it does, perhaps it doesn't," my sister mused. "We shall all see in time, won't we?"

It was nearly dark now, with the servants lighting the first lanterns near the stables, and reluctantly we turned back. The shadow of The Pastures loomed before us, a reassuring block of warm brick and memories sharp against the twilight sky. It remained the only lasting home that either of us had known so far, and there was good reason why we always returned here, even now as we were about to say good-bye.

Our farewell had begun in earnest.

"Mamma says she'd always believed that her daughters would live within a day's ride of The Pastures," I said softly, "and that none of us would ever dare go any farther."

"She has Peggy and Stephen at Rensselaerwyck," Angelica said. "That's not far. Now that they're married, they'll never leave the manor, unless Peggy chooses to climb from the window again."

"Don't say that to Mamma," I warned, but still I laughed with her.

"She and Papa will have you and Hamilton in New York," Angelica said. "True, it's not Albany, but it's not so very far away, either."

"But you shall be in Paris," I said wistfully. "Oh, Angelica, sometimes I feel that all I ever do is say good-bye to those I love most, over and over and over again."

She didn't answer, and in that moment I realized she felt the same as I. The men we loved would determine our destinies along with their own, no matter how we might wish otherwise.

We walked the rest of the way arm in arm, our heads bowed, in sisterly agreement. We said nothing more, nor did we need to.

CHAPTER 14

New York City, New York
June 1784

Alexander prided himself on being a gentleman of his word, and as soon as he was done with Congress, he made arrangements for us to move from Albany to New York City. The last of the British troops sailed from the harbor on November 25, 1783, and the wagons with our belongings had rumbled up before our new home soon after, during the first week of December.

Alexander had even kept his long-ago promise to me of a house on Wall Street. Ours was number fifty-seven, an agreeable brick house of three stories with a small balcony, and far more pleasant and commodious than any other place we'd yet lived. Beside it was number fifty-six, which Alexander used as his office. Wall Street was wide and comparatively untouched by the war, unlike so much of the rest of the city. We weren't quite at the most fashionable end of the street (where Colonel and Mrs. Burr lived), but the other houses, offices, and shops around us were all well kept and neat. There were even a few buildings that retained the stepped roofs preferred by the Dutch, a familiar sight to me from Albany, and one that made me smile as if seeing old friends.

So handsome was our new house, in fact, that when we first arrived I suspected its rent was more than Alexander could comfortably afford. He had just completed a year earning very little as a delegate to Congress, and a year before that in recovering from the war and in studying for the bar, as well as his negligible position of tax-receiver. To be sure, his prospects were excellent. Because by law no lawyers with Tory sympathies were now permitted to practice their profession, there were fewer than fifty attorneys in the entirety of the state. Any lawyer with ability, education, and a modicum of luck was bound to prosper, and Alexander possessed all of those qualities in abundance, plus an invaluable reputation as a patriotic hero from the war.

But prospects did not pay the grocer or the butcher, nor satisfy the hairdresser who came each morning to tend to Alexander's hair, nor even the laundrywomen who washed our stockings and linens. Like most wives, I was not privy to the details of my husband's financial affairs, but I suspected our humble resources were stretched as far as they could be and perhaps beyond. Finally one morning while he was dressing for court I dared to ask if this were the case, and whether I should be making any extra economies in our household.

"My dearest wife," he said, clearly startled I'd broach such a subject, and a bit wounded that I had as well. "How has this concern arisen? Have you wanted for anything? Have I not provided for you and our son as I should?"

"No, no, Alexander, not at all," I said quickly. "But if there is a need to be frugal whilst we establish ourselves here in this place, I shall happily oblige."

"There is no need for any obliging, Betsey." He smiled as he finished buttoning his waistcoat, and came to kiss me. "I don't want you worrying about such trivialities, especially not now."

He rested his palm gently on my growing belly. I was expecting our second child at the end of the summer, and we both hoped that this time we'd be blessed with a girl, a sister for our son. Philip was now two, a chattering, toddling fellow who was more his own little man every day, and as dear as he was, I was anticipating the sweetness of another new babe.

"You must follow your sister's orders," he continued, "and think only the most beautiful of thoughts to ensure a handsome daughter."

I laughed softly, and placed my hand over his. Angelica had given birth to a daughter in December in Paris, and named her Elizabeth in my honor. Even before then, Alexander and I had decided that if our next child were a girl, she would be called Angelica.

"No more worrying, Betsey," he continued with mock severity. "Not about money, or anything else."

He kissed me again, which was often his way of ending our conversations, and a delightful way it was, too. It wasn't until much later, when it no longer mattered, that I learned I'd been entitled to my worries. Alexander was too proud to borrow money from my father, but he hadn't the same scruples about small loans here and there from more solvent friends. Yet he was adept at juggling, and he always paid back what he'd borrowed. During those early years in New York, I was never the wiser. I trusted him, and I obeyed my sister, and did my best to think only the most beautiful of thoughts.

But New York City in 1784 was not a place for beauty of any kind. If the war had barely touched Philadelphia, it had ravaged and ravished poor New York. The city as it stood now bore little resemblance to the handsome place I'd remembered visiting when I was a girl. Several hard-fought battles, a number of calamitous fires, and eight years of occupation by the British army had left much of the city in ruins.

Without timber, laborers, or inclination, nothing had been rebuilt, and looting and other thievery was so commonplace so as to go largely noticed. It wasn't just the enemy that had caused this mischief, either. Hundreds of Tory sympathizers had crowded into the city for refuge, and many had lived in makeshift tents and lean-tos among the broken foundations of once-splendid homes, churches, and public buildings. Standing water that collected in the hollowed remains of cellars turned foul, and empty merchant docks along the waterfront rotted from disuse. Every tree, fence, and garden bench had been claimed for firewood, and the entire city had a scraped, flat look because of it.

Now with the peace in place, the Tories who could had fled to Canada, to Britain, or to the Caribbean, and their absence left more holes in the city's fabric. They'd taken more than simply their families: with them had gone their wealth, their knowledge, their professions. Overnight the city's population had shrunk to a fraction of its former size.

But if many left, many others were returning. Some, like us, had come for the opportunity presented by a city in need of rebuilding. Many more were patriots who had been forced to leave because of the British population. Now faced with the shattered remnants of their businesses and homes, they came together into a vengeful crowd of discontent, greed, and resentment, determined to attack any of their neighbors reputed to harbor Tory sympathies.

The persecution was blatant, and shameless. I witnessed the effects myself. I often passed a small shop in the next street that specialized in writing paper and pens. The shop was owned by an older man who'd come to New York decades ago from Liverpool, and his wife, who had been born here. Alas, there were rumors that they'd survived the occupation only because they'd been protected by the army as Tories. One morning as I walked by, the shop was empty, the front window smashed, the door torn from its hinges. In the street before the shop were the blackened remnants of a fire, charred fragments of wooden boxes and furnishings and curling bits of singed paper like drifting leaves. I paused to look with concern, and asked another passerby what malady had happened to the poor proprietor.

"The old rascal got what he deserved last night," he said bluntly, smirking. "Him and his wife, too. We've no use here for Tories who think they're better'n the rest of us."

I never learned what became of the shopkeeper or his wife, and never saw them again, either.

By March, matters had only grown worse. The legislature passed the Trespass Act, stating that good patriots had the right to sue any Tories responsible for damages to homes and properties left behind during the war. The Sons of Liberty, who had done so much to spur along the Revolution, re-emerged in a nefarious new form, and took the hatred another step further. Instead of espousing liberty and freedom as they once had, they promoted the persecution of Tories and Loyalists, and called for anyone who'd held Tory beliefs to be forced to leave the state by the first of May.

It was impossible to avoid the ugly uneasiness gathering the city. Alexander, of course, did not avoid it, but instead jumped directly into the middle of the conflict. He began writing essays for the newspapers again, this time under the Roman name of Phocion, and pleading for tolerance.

The pleas went unheard, as everyone except my husband had expected. But despite the pseudonym, everyone also knew that

Alexander was Phocion, and he was accused of being a traitor, a sympathizer, a secret Tory in the pay of the British government—all harsh words for a man who'd served the cause of freedom so well.

But while I was indignant upon Alexander's behalf, he was not. The criticisms only spurred him to work harder.

While his first cases in the city had been to settle the usual misunderstandings between businesses and bickering amongst families, he soon plunged into cases that defended the rights of Tories who'd remained, cases too prickly and unpopular for most other lawyers. As with all the cases he accepted (and unlike most other lawyers), he only took on those in which he believed the plaintiff was in the right; he cared far less about their ability to pay his fees, which meant that he wasn't above accepting a pipe of wine or a side of beef in lieu of payment. For Alexander, it was the principle that mattered most, not the fee, and by the summer, those principles loomed large indeed to him.

His most prominent case of this nature was presented in late June, and pitted a wealthy patriot widow, Mrs. Rutgers, who had owned a brewery ruined in the war, against Mr. Waddington, a Loyalist, who repaired the ruin at his own cost under martial orders of the occupying army, and made the brewery once again profitable. Now Mrs. Rutgers was suing Mr. Waddington for the astronomical sum of eight thousand pounds, claiming that this was the rent owed her for the use of her property.

The fact that Alexander had accepted a case against a woman plaintiff showed me how important a case he considered it to be. He tended to be as gallant in his practice as he was in life, and often took cases for the sake of assisting a woman in difficulty, especially widows and spinsters who had no natural male champions.

As always, Alexander explained this all to me as a way for solidifying his own thoughts and arguments. As always, I listened, this time over a long supper.

We'd a small enclosed yard behind our house, and the two of us often dined there now that the spring had given way to warmer summer evenings. Like every other house in New York, our trees had been sacrificed to the war, and though I'd planted new saplings in the spring, for shade we relied upon a wide swath of striped canvas that we'd had strung from one wall to the next overhead: our

Turkish tent, as Alexander cheerfully called it. In that spirit I'd put cushions on a bench beside the table, and when we'd no guests, we sat cozily side by side rather than with the table between us. We were informally dressed, too, I in a printed calico dressing gown and he in a chintz banyan, and both of us ready to discuss his most important case thus far.

For reasons of sentiment, it was clear to me that the plaintiff, the widowed patriot Mrs. Rutgers, would be favored to prevail, and that this would be a difficult case for any attorney to win. I didn't state this opinion at first, however. Though I might never have formally studied the law, I had learned a few things about how best to present my opinions to my husband.

"How proud I am of you, dearest," I began, smiling. "To take a case that every other lawyer in the city has avoided as being too prickly and difficult, and to champion poor beleaguered Mr. Waddington, too."

He frowned a bit, and I realized perhaps I'd been a shade too effusive.

"It won't be the swiftest case on the docket to be decided, no," he said slowly, appraising me. "But then you knew that, Betsey, didn't you?"

I concentrated on refilling his glass with more wine. "You have always been a gentleman remarkable for your charity and kindness, Alexander, especially where your defendants are concerned."

He made a small disgruntled sound in his throat. "There's more at stake than mere kindness, my dear."

"Kindness is never 'mere,' Alexander," I said. "Especially given the grievous manner in which many of New York's residents are being treated."

"Very well, then," he said, raising the glass toward me in a salute before he drank. "There is more than charity at stake. A victorious country is judged by how it treats those whom it has vanquished. The treaty of peace that Congress signed stated that no former Loyalists were to suffer any further losses, not to their persons, liberty, or property."

So this was how he'd begin, and a good beginning it was, too. "That's all true," I said.

"It is indeed," he said firmly. "The sympathies of Britain and

France, too, lie with the exiled Tories who have come to rest in their midst, telling their pitiful tales and making us out to be the ogres. If we wish to garner any respect in the greater world, we can't behave like those ogres, which is exactly what is happening here in New York."

I sighed, remembering the burned-out shop of the poor paper seller. "We do have our share of ogres, particularly in the legislature."

"Particularly in the Governor's House," he said with open disgust, and I realized from the tone of his voice that he was slipping from his prepared thoughts into personal opinion. "Clinton is a ringleader more than a governor. He ignores the peace treaty as if it holds no sway over New York. He panders to the lowest sort of ignorant rabble, and incites them to believe they are entitled to far more than they are. If he so much as glances at a prosperous gentleman and whispers 'Tory,' then that is permission enough for his followers to hector and destroy that gentleman and steal his goods and lands, without risk of repercussion."

I nodded, for it was no secret that Alexander did not like (nor was in turn liked by) the present governor of New York, George Clinton. My father didn't like him, either. In another time, they might all have been friends, or leastways amiable acquaintances, since they'd much in common. Clinton had served in the army and the militia, he was a friend of General Washington and an ardent patriot who'd signed the Declaration of Independence, and from his own pocket he'd supplied the Continental Army with supplies, much as had Robert Morris and my father.

But Clinton's concept of patriotism included a deep and irrational hatred of Tories as a whole, as if every one of them, young or old, men or women, held the same beliefs and the same degree of evil. He dangerously condoned arrests, whipping, and even tarring and feathering of Tories. With his encouragement, the New York legislature had passed stringent laws to punish these people, and had encouraged the seizure of Tory-owned properties and goods as a way to fill the state's coffers, and thereby reduce taxes. As can be imagined, Clinton was very popular for these policies, particularly among the farmers to the north of the state, and he had been reelected repeatedly because of them.

They also made the governor a very anathema to Alexander.

"I know you understand, Betsey, for we've spoken of this many times before," he said. His voice was growing louder with urgency, his hand tapping restlessly on the tablecloth, and I was sure that if we hadn't been sitting behind the table together, he would have already been on his feet and pacing.

Gently I covered his tapping hand with my own, hoping to calm him. "We have indeed spoken of this many times, my dear. Recall that I'm Mrs. Phocion as well as Mrs. Hamilton."

Yet his fervor was so great, it was as if I hadn't spoken at all.

"The people came together as a single country to fight the war," he said. "But now that it's over, Clinton's petty vengeance and punitive extortions only serve to divide the citizenry into suspicious factions and mob rule. We can't have that, Betsey. We can't have that at all."

"Will that be your argument in defense of Mr. Waddington?" I asked mildly. "That mob rule is not acceptable?"

He scowled and paused, then smiled as he realized what I was doing.

"I believe you know otherwise, Betsey," he said. "My argument will be that Clinton's Trespass Act illegally violates the treaty of peace ratified by Congress, and that Mrs. Rutgers has no grounds for her case."

"Exactly so," I said, and smiled in return, and in triumph, too. "You're not only remarkable for your kindness, Mr. Hamilton, but you can be quite clever, too."

"As are you, my dearest wife," he said, leaning forward to kiss me. "As are you."

In the following weeks, the case of *Rutgers vs. Waddington* was much celebrated. Alexander's defense was lauded for its coherence, its brilliance, and its fairness, and everyone who was in the room to hear him was impressed by his sheer gift for legal argument and logic. Chief Justice James Duane (the same gentleman who'd given Alexander the freedom of his law library whilst he'd been preparing for the bar) handed down a split verdict as his final ruling. Mrs. Rutgers was entitled to rent from Mr. Waddington, but only for the time before the British occupied the city. The two sides agreed to the sum of eight hundred pounds, a tenth of what Mrs. Rutgers had originally sought, but more than she might now expect to receive.

But what pleased Alexander the most, however, was what Chief Justice Duane wrote in his ruling: that no state could change or abridge a federal treaty. New York could no longer set itself above Congress, or create new laws that ran counter to the treaty of peace. Governor Clinton and the legislature were being forcibly brought to heel. This was exactly what Alexander had been saying for nearly as long as I'd known him, and to his mind, it was the best vindication in the world. He was still crowing by the time he came home, and it had been a long time since I'd seen him so pleased by the results of his toil.

After this, I doubt there was anyone in the city of New York who did not know Alexander Hamilton. Of course, some knew it in praise, while others could only speak it in derision or scorn, or denounce him for aiding his onetime enemies. Governor Clinton was said to be especially displeased, spitting every kind of foul slander and epithet from Poughkeepsie toward New York. My husband didn't care; I believe he gloried in it.

In fact, he'd crowed so much that my secret fear was that he'd once again discover a taste for politics. But this time, my fears were unfounded. When one of the newspapers put forth his name as a possible candidate for the legislature, he quickly made sure it was withdrawn. I was overjoyed, and delighted that he concentrated instead on his now-flourishing practice.

Cases came his way from similarly distressed Tories at a rapid rate, so many that he took on more clerks and law students to assist him, and his office hummed with activity as these newcomers attempted to match my husband's furious pace of work. It wasn't simply his legal work that occupied him. He also took on several other responsibilities that would have been all-consuming for a lesser gentleman, but for Alexander were simply more facets to his complicated life.

He continued to dabble in writing essays, and published again as Phocion. Always aware of the importance of education (for education had been key to his own self-betterment), he first helped create and then served upon the Board of Regents, supervising all matters pertaining to teaching and education within the state. He also was a trustee of the university he'd attended when he first came to New York, now renamed Columbia College, and likewise assisted the institution in their recovery from the war. He had agreed to serve as the business agent for Angelica's husband whilst they were abroad, no easy task given the purposeful complexity of Mr. Church's affairs.

Perhaps most notably, he was deeply involved in the founding of the first bank in the city, the Bank of New York on Pearl Street. For guidance he turned to his old ally Robert Morris, who had helped found the first bank in the country in Philadelphia, the Bank of North America, and to Mr. Church, who was one of the Philadelphia bank's primary investors. Following their advice, Alexander then drew together the first supporters and investors from amongst New York's most influential gentlemen, and wrote the new bank's charter as well. For Alexander, the Bank of New York wasn't simply another business venture, but a way to put many of his long-standing theories on finance to work. He also saw the bank as a way to bring more capital into New York to help rebuild the still-struggling city after the war.

As busy as he was, he still found time to devote to Philip, whom he considered the most perfect child in all Creation, and to me. While I might have wished to have more time with Alexander to myself, I understood how important—no, how essential—it was for his happiness to be of as much use as possible.

And we *were* happy those first early years in New York. Alexander would make lighthearted jests about his "lucrative practice," as if such a thing were ripe for ridicule. The truth was that he was successful, and though neither of us were spendthrifts, we could now indulge in things that made our lives more agreeable. Gradually the rooms in our house acquired handsome furnishings, paintings, and looking glasses. We often had friends and acquaintances to dine, and dine well. The wedding gifts—the porcelain plates and teacups, the silver candlesticks and platters—that we'd received years before finally were unpacked and put to use. We kept a smart gig and horses for traveling about town and making calls. Alexander patronized both a French tailor and a French hairdresser, and the rituals of both, conducted in the French language, pleased him no end.

Another change in our household since coming to New York was the employment of servants. This had been a determined decision on which Alexander and I had firmly agreed, but not an uncomplicated one.

At The Pastures, nearly all of the servants, in the fields, the stables, and the house, were Negros owned by my father. Since girlhood, I had accepted this as children do, but as I'd grown older it had never made me easy of conscience. I read of slavery in the Bible, but as a Christian woman the notion of owning another person as property was troubling, and difficult for my conscience to accept. Though my parents were benevolent owners, I'd still witnessed the heartbreaking agony of families being separated and children sold to different owners. Even Papa was not above this, for the slaves he used at his Saratoga mills were so skilled at their trade that he had, on occasion, sold one or two men to other landowners at a profit whilst retaining their wives.

For Alexander, experience had made slavery even more of an anathema to him. His earliest employment in the Caribbean had involved him directly in the odious trade of slavery, with all its humiliation, pain, and misery. After the war, he'd found it impossible to reconcile the freedom promised by the Declaration of Independence and the enslavement that continued for so many of the population. He became one of the earliest members of the New York Society for Promoting the Manumission of Slaves, and unlike many of the other members (who still retained their own slaves, even while calling for an end to the practice), our household practiced what he espoused.

When Alexander and I had first been wed, Mamma had continued to make a loan to us of Rose, who had attended me for many years. When we had set up our housekeeping in New York, Mamma had again offered us the use of Rose, but I'd told Mamma that I wished Rose to be given her freedom first, so that I might pay her honorable wages. Mamma had been shocked, and refused outright, claiming that Rose was much too valuable. As much as this saddened me—for I remained very fond of Rose—I'd held firm, and left her behind at The Pastures.

Instead I'd hired two young women as maidservants in Albany who'd been eager to come to New York: Greetje, who also looked after Philip, and Johanna, who could also help me dress for evening. Later in the year, we also took on a cook, Mrs. Parker, who, though younger than I, was skilled in every manner of cookery both plain and fancy. She'd been widowed during the war, and had found it difficult supporting herself and her children. I considered myself fortunate to have found her, and being a mother myself, happily gave her leave to have her young daughters in the kitchen with her whilst she worked.

But the most noteworthy addition to our family came in September, with the birth of our first daughter, Angelica. Unlike Philip, whose arrival had been preceded by my constant fear for Alexander's safety, Angelica was born during a more peaceful time in my life, and perhaps because of that, my travail was far easier. Alexander still fretted over me as my time had approached, and at his insistence I was attended by the esteemed Dr. Samuel Bard, General Washington's personal physician. I missed the familiar, womanly comfort of the midwives in Albany and even more I missed having my mother at my side, too. Still, perhaps because of the more learned skills of the male physicians who delivered the rest of my children, all my babies survived not only their infancies, but their childhoods as well, a blessing few mothers can claim.

"I did predict a daughter," Alexander said, cradling our tiny new girl in his arms as soon as he was admitted again into my presence. "Though I'd no notion she'd be as beautiful as this."

I smiled wearily, delighting in the sight of them together. Thanks to Philip, my husband had become very adept at holding babies, a skill most men never did acquire, nor wished to. But Alexander loved his children the same way he did most everything, with fierce concentration and all his heart besides. To watch him with our daughter lying in the crook of his arm, her long linen gown trailing over his sleeve and his face bent low over hers, was to me the sweetest sight imaginable.

"I believe she already has your dimpled chin," he said. "A winsome feature for a girl."

"Philip has it, too," I said. "It's a Van Rensselaer chin, from my mother."

"It's a Hamilton chin now," he said proudly, slowly walking back and forth. He was not only confident holding babies, but he'd the knack for calming them, too, by making them feel protected and secure. He'd once told me he'd no memory of ever feeling safe as a young child, which had touched me no end. I suppose it also explained how he knew instinctively what a baby most longed for.

"Philip won't be happy," he continued. "He did have his heart set upon a brother."

"He'll change his mind in time," I said. "My brothers always did."

"As they should have." He smiled warmly at me, then looked back down at the baby. "Perhaps our girl will be a bluestocking like her aunt Angelica, and surround herself with books."

"If she does, she'll be as much like you as my sister." Alexander continued to read voraciously, but I wondered if Angelica still found the time with four children of her own. "She'll certainly have enough books to choose from."

My eyes begin to drift shut. Now that the first excitement of greeting our daughter had passed and all was well with her, exhaustion was sweeping over me. I was tired, and I was sore, too, as could only be expected.

"How selfish of me to keep you awake, my dearest," whispered Alexander, so contritely that I forced my eyes open once again to gaze at him.

I was thankful that I did. Our daughter was asleep in his arms, and he was smiling at me, his handsome face so full of love that it was more than enough to bring the sting of tears.

"If our Angelica possesses even half of your grace, wisdom, and beauty, my angel," he said softly, "then she will be a most fortunate woman."

"She'll be who she's fated to be," I said wistfully, and touched our daughter's cheek with my fingertip. "I only wish Angelica were here now to see her."

In truth, I wished my sister were here for me, the way she'd been when Philip had been born. Over a year had passed since she and her family had sailed away to Paris, and I still missed her dreadfully.

"I wish she were here, too," Alexander said. "Perhaps Church will relent and bring her back to New York in time for Twelfth Night."

But while I knew that Alexander had written to both Angelica and her husband, urging them to return (as had I) for our daughter's birth, Mr. Church did not share the same impetus to return to America. There was always one more bit of business that detained him in Paris, or one more event at the French court that he considered important to attend.

The fall changed to winter, and winter into spring and summer. Our daughter cut her first teeth, and soon could not only sit on her own, but had learned to pull herself upright with the help of any nearby chairs or table legs, or, more often, her brother, Philip. After his initial disappointment at Angelica's birth, Philip had embraced his role as her brother, and though they were not so far apart in age, he was without doubt her protector and her idol. Already Philip showed a generosity of spirit that was rare in three-year-old boys, yet reminded me of his father, and the gentleness he displayed toward his infant sister was a special joy to me.

There was one more event that solidified our household, and pleased me greatly, too. By early 1785, we had lived more than two years at our house on Wall Street, and I thought of it as our home. We lived there at the mercy of a lease, however, an arrangement that was what we could afford in those first years. Having never lived in a property that had been truly his, the fact that we rented made Alexander uneasy, and he longed for the security of ownership and the respectability that came with it.

He was on occasion called to courts out of the city and farther to the north. From one of these distant locations, I received a hastily written note from him in March. The subject was one of great importance to us, and of great urgency, too. Our house was being offered for sale, for the substantial sum of £2100. The owner wished to sell promptly, and given both the house and the pleasant neighborhood in which it was situated, he would likely receive many offers. As the present tenants, we were being offered the first opportunity to purchase the house, but likewise, we couldn't wait until Alexander returned to town to make our offer. Instead, he left it to me to attend the seller's agent as soon as I could, and agree to a purchase that was acceptable to all parties.

The owner's agent in New York was another attorney well known to both of us: Colonel Aaron Burr. We had, of course, known Colonel Burr since our early days in Albany, and because he and Alexander were often in court together, and because we'd many acquaintances in common, we frequently saw the Burrs at suppers, assemblies, and other social engagements. The colonel was in attendance far more often than his wife, who suffered so greatly from a recurring ailment as to be nearly an invalid, poor lady.

But this was to be a business call, not a social one. I dressed in a sober habit of blue worsted with silver buttons and a black silk hat with a curving black plume, and though Colonel Burr's office was not far away, at the end of Wall Street near City Hall, I had myself driven to make a good show.

Most importantly, I had directions from Alexander to take the greatest care whilst speaking with Colonel Burr. I was well aware that the colonel and Alexander were together considered the most skilled and successful of the younger lawyers in New York, and to say that they were rivals was not so far from the truth. Because Alexander had taken time away from his office to serve in the legislature and in Congress, Colonel Burr had risen more quickly, but most in the city believed my husband to be the more gifted in the courtroom.

To Colonel Burr's credit, he did not keep me waiting.

"Mrs. Hamilton, good day," the colonel said, rising from his desk as soon as I was ushered into his office. As was his custom, he was dressed in gray so dark as to be black, in keeping with his dark brows and eyes. Some people said he did this purposefully to distance himself from my husband, who did like to wear strong colors to favor his fair complexion.

"Good day to you, Colonel," I said, holding out my hand to him. "How does your wife?"

His smile of greeting turned solemn. "She is not as well as either of us could hope," he said. "I pray that the warmer months will prove kinder to her. I will convey your regards to her."

"Please do," I said, taking the chair beside his desk. "And how does Miss Burr?"

"Ah, my sweet Theodosia," he said, his smile warm with paternal pride. It was no secret that his daughter was the joy of his life, all the more so after his poor wife had struggled to bear him any further children who'd survived.

"My daughter does very well, thank you," he continued, sitting across from me. "She thrives. She blossoms. I trust that in time she and Miss Hamilton shall become the most genial and devoted of acquaintances."

"I pray that in time they shall," I agreed. Mrs. Burr and I had in fact already introduced our daughters to each other, although Theodosia, being nearly two years of age, had shown little interest in Angelica at six months, as was expected. "At present I don't believe that Miss Burr has much regard for my daughter's conversation."

The colonel laughed softly, the way he always laughed, as if he were slightly embarrassed to be caught doing something so frivolous. It was another way in which he differed from my husband: the colonel was reticent to the point of being guarded, while Alexander could be ebullient almost to a fault.

"I regret that patience is not one of Theodosia's virtues at this time," he said. "In that I fear that she takes after me."

"Then while Miss Burr may be forgiven on account of her age," I said, "I will not try your patience any further. My husband received your message concerning the sale of our house. While he is unavoidably detained by a case in Chester, he has asked me to act in his stead, and offer for the property."

He turned his head slightly, though I couldn't tell if he were amused, or appraising me. "He must trust you, Mrs. Hamilton."

"He does, Colonel Burr," I said as evenly as I could. "We understand the house is offered for sale at £2100."

He nodded, and I continued.

"Then we agree to the purchase at that price," I said. "However, my husband would prefer to pay half the sum as soon as can be arranged, with the other half to follow within a year."

Colonel Burr frowned, and tented his fingertips together while he considered. "I do not believe my client can agree to those terms."

I raised my chin, praying I didn't betray my anxiety.

"Very well, then," I said. "Would the owner consider receiving the full amount at the end of ninety days?"

Colonel Burr sighed with a show of regret. "I fear I'm not permitted by the owner to accept anything less than the full amount immediately."

I nodded, a quick little jerk of my chin. I couldn't disappoint Alexander, not when our home was at stake, and I prayed I was hiding my anxiety.

"Is there another arrangement that would make our offer acceptable, Colonel Burr?" I knew we couldn't offer more money, because we likely didn't have it. Alexander wouldn't have told me to stagger the payments otherwise. But he hadn't told me what to do next, or what else to offer, or not. Whatever else was said now would be my own words.

The colonel nodded, as if deep in thought, though I suspected he already knew what he'd say.

"There is a possibility, Mrs. Hamilton, yes," he said delicately. "I believe the owner would accept the additional ninety days if General Schuyler would agree to act as a surety for the debt."

Sharply I drew in my breath, and stared down at my lap, not wanting him to see my uncertainty. I'd no doubt that my father would agree, for he'd offered this and more many times before. I also knew that he wouldn't be called to make good the debt, because Alexander would never allow it to happen. The surety would only be for ninety days, only three months, and the house—our home—would in fact belong to us for good, and Alexander would at last be the property owner he'd so longed to be.

The decision was hardly as simple as it seemed, however. Alexander's pride had always kept him from borrowing from my father. He'd be bound to balk at it doubly now because his rival Colonel Burr would know he'd been unable to provide for his family without assistance.

But I didn't want to disappoint Alexander, and I didn't want Colonel Burr to believe he'd somehow won, and most of all, I didn't want to lose our home.

"I am sorry to have caused you such obvious confusion, Mrs. Hamilton," the colonel said, his voice rich as velvet. "I'll understand if this is too difficult a decision for you to make without your husband to—"

"But I have decided, Colonel Burr," I said, resolved. "We will agree to the purchase at ninety days, with my father as surety."

Although my heart raced as I accepted the agreement, I managed to smile serenely for the sake of the colonel, as if there'd never been a doubt. But as soon as I returned home, I immediately wrote to both Alexander and to my father, explaining what I'd done, and then prayed feverishly that I'd made the right choice.

Alexander returned home within two days, sooner than he'd expected, and because he'd been traveling, my letter with my carefully worded explanation had missed him. I had no choice but to explain again in person, standing with him in his library before he'd even shed his coat or boots, and with the door shut against any interruptions from the servants or the children.

He listened to each word, his expression not changing as I spoke. Finally, he nodded, but still said nothing.

"I'm sure Colonel Burr didn't believe we could reach an agreement," I said finally. "He seemed almost disappointed that we did."

"That's usual for him," Alexander said, and sighed. "Are you happy with this purchase, Betsey?"

"I am," I said quickly, my words rushing out in an anxious torrent. "I know the sale wasn't done the way you would have wished, but it shall always be ours now, and no one will be able to make us move from it against our will. You earned it for me and the children, and I'm proud of you that you did. My father's surety is incidental. It's our house now, yes, but it's also our home. Ours together, Alexander. So yes, I am happy."

He nodded, and at last, he smiled. "My dear, wise angel," he said. "Then I am happy, too."

Finally, in July of 1785, my sister and her family returned to New York. To my sorrow, and to Alexander's as well, Mr. Church insisted that the visit be unbearably brief; I believe they spent longer aboard the ships that brought them and then carried them away than they did on our shores. We had them in New York with us for a handful of days, and then Angelica and I and our children traveled to Albany to visit our parents. Returning to New York, Alexander would then accompany the Churches to Philadelphia to settle more of Mr. Church's business, and finally they would sail from that port no later than early August. It was a harried, hectic pace, not one I'd wish for myself, nor did it please my sister, though she remained too politic to say so aloud in her husband's hearing.

Although Alexander and I had invited the Churches to stay with us in New York, Mr. Church had preferred lodgings. In truth, they were probably too many for our house to accommodate—Angelica and Mr. Church, their four children, a governess, and five servants—and I knew how Mr. Church did like his privacy.

At least he agreed to let me give a supper in their honor. We invited their friends from New York and from the war, and a few more of our own as well, to make a large and merry company. Such a sizable gathering taxed my little household, but I borrowed a few other servants and a few more chairs, contrived appropriately fancy dishes for the table, and spent indulgently on the wines.

As was always the case with Angelica, I felt as if a brilliant, fiery star had once again come streaking into my world. After two years in Paris with Parisian mantua-makers and milliners at her disposal and an indulgent, wealthy husband to pay her bills, she'd become even more beautiful, more fashionable, more elegant.

She swept into our house dressed in a gown of rustling purple silk taffeta, edged with pale green pleated trim, and her extravagantly full skirts flicked around her as she walked. Her hair was frizzled into a huge puff around her face with long beribboned curls down the back, and dusted with the palest of lavender powder. In her ears, she wore enormous gold hoops with pearl drops, and around her throat was a necklace of more pearls mingled with garnets.

She had the seat of honor beside Alexander, with Mr. Church sitting beside me. Angelica swiftly put my husband (and every other gentleman) under her spell, regaling us all with titillating gossip of the French court as the pearl earrings bobbed against her cheeks. She'd also become good friends with the prominent Americans in Paris, including Benjamin Franklin, the first American envoy, as well as the second, Thomas Jefferson, and had amusing tales of them, too. Of course Alexander relished every word, encouraging her by speaking French and applauding her wit.

If Angelica had been born to other parents, I believe she could have earned her living on the stage, because she possessed a rare ability to make everyone in the room watch her, and be entertained by her wit, extravagance, and beauty. As had so often been the case in our lives, I could only sit in near-silent awe of her, and marvel that I'd such a glorious lady for a sister.

It wasn't until she and I and our children were once again at The Pastures that I'd opportunity to converse with her more intimately. With the children left in the house with servants, we went walking together in the gardens early one morning, when the day was still cool and the dew glittered on the grass and dampened the hems of our linen petticoats. Here Angelica was simply my sister, without the constant desire to be the cynosure of society.

"I'm with child again," she said when we were far enough from the house to be outside of anyone's hearing. She said it as an unremarkable announcement, a matter of fact, with neither joy nor sadness in it. "That's part of the reason John wishes to return to England so soon, that the child be born there."

"Is he pleased?" I asked tentatively. Alexander had greeted both my pregnancies with great pleasure, but Mr. Church was much more reserved by nature, and besides, Angelica had already given him two boys and two girls.

"He will be if it's another boy," she said, looking straight ahead. "He prefers the boys. He sees them as having more use in life, and more purpose."

I thought at once of my own little Angelica, and how Alexander adored her like a miniature goddess. How sad that Mr. Church didn't feel the same devotion for his daughters!

"Perhaps you can return here next summer, and stay longer," I said. "Consider how much our children would enjoy it."

But she only shook her head, twisting a loose strand of hair back beneath the brim of her straw hat.

"I've not told this yet to Mamma or Papa," she said, "and I'm not sure I will, for it will only hurt them. I don't know when, if ever, we shall return here. John desires us to live entirely in England. He has already purchased a home for us in Mayfair, in London, and is seeking a second house in the country so that he might stand as a member to Parliament."

"Oh, Angelica," I said softly, trying to think only of her, and not of how I was in essence losing my older sister. "Perhaps in time he will relent."

"Once John determines his mind, he never alters from it," she said. "But I shall adapt. I did in Paris, and I'll do so again in London. You'd be thoroughly amused, Eliza, to see the ease with which your New York–bred sister can conquer society abroad."

But she didn't sound amused herself. "All those parties," I said, "and the clever gentlemen who follow you about—you made it sound so diverting."

"What else would you have me say, Eliza?" she said with an unhappy shrug. "When I first met John, this was the life I told him I wanted. He hasn't forgotten, and he's given me everything I wished. But now—now I would trade it all for my summers back here in Albany."

"I'd like that, too," I said wistfully, but she only shrugged again, this time as if to shrug aside my sympathy.

"But you, Eliza—how you bask in the warmth of your husband's love," she said, deliberately moving the conversation from her life to mine. "I vow your Hamilton grows more sleek and handsome by the year. Life in New York must agree with you both admirably."

"It does," I said, and with a certain pride, too. "Alexander is content with the challenges of his profession, and he's devoted to our children. Once you warned me of his ambitions, but after the frustrations of Congress, he seems to be cured of public life except for observation at a distance."

"That's a credit to you, Eliza," she said. "To see you together, there's no doubt that he loves you even more today than when you were wed."

I blushed with pleasure at this truth. Children and marriage had ripened our love, and I considered myself the most blessed of wives to have Alexander as my husband.

"Yes, Hamilton loves you well," she continued, "and after witnessing his regard for you myself, I hesitate to speak further. But for your own good, you should know what is being whispered."

My blush deepened, but not with pleasure. "There is nothing to whisper, Angelica. Alexander possesses much charm, and unlike many other gentlemen, he is perfectly at ease in the company of ladies. I would much rather have a husband who retains the air of a young gallant, than one who has become a dour curmudgeon before his time."

Yes, I meant Mr. Church, which was most unkind of me to say, but Angelica took no notice.

"Perhaps I have been too long in Paris," she began, "where even shopkeepers keep mistresses, and a faithful husband is the rarest of all creatures. When Hamilton is spoken of—as he often is—it is largely to praise his intelligence and his wisdom. Yet there is also quieter talk of how he is perhaps too fond of the company of ladies, his manner a shade too flirtatious, even lickerish, for a gentleman of his stature and accomplishment."

I stopped, too shocked to walk farther. "My husband has many enemies, Angelica," I said, my voice shaking, "and there are those who will say and write any kind of slander to harm him. But that my own sister would dare repeat these calumnies to me—"

She turned to face me, her expression solemn. "It's better that you hear it from me than from another, isn't it?"

"Not when it's lies!"

"Even the worst lies often have a breath of truth to them," she said. "What you dismiss as gallantry might be perceived as more by others. I consider him as another brother, and yet think of how openly he flirts even with me."

I didn't want to consider it, any more than I wanted this to be one of my final conversations with my sister before she sailed.

"Alexander means nothing by it, Angelica, I am sure," I insisted. "How could he, sitting at the same table as Mr. Church and me?"

"My dearest Eliza," she said gently. "I don't wish the rumors to be so. I love both you and Hamilton too well for that. Tell me the tales aren't true, that you've never had reason to doubt him, and I'll believe you."

"None of it is true, Angelica," I said vehemently. "Alexander is my husband before God, and the father of my children. I love him and I trust him and I honor him, and I will not hear anyone, not even you, say otherwise."

"Then you won't hear further upon the subject from me," she said, looking down and away from me. "Forgive me, Eliza, if what I've said has hurt you, for that was never my wish. But be aware, as every wife should be. Hamilton is a charming, handsome gentleman, and the more successful he becomes, the more other women will take notice. Be aware, my dear. Just . . . be aware."

CHAPTER 15

New York City, New York
February 1786

I sat closely beside Alexander in the gig as he drove, a blanket over our laps and my hands deep inside my muff. As was usual along the city streets, our progress was slow on account of the wagons, horses, cattle, and people that all crowded along the thoroughfares at a much slower pace than Alexander wished. We likely would have traveled just as fast if we'd walked, but Alexander wouldn't hear of it, insisting that I should be coddled. I was six months pregnant with another child, and although this would be our third, my husband still treated me with the same care, tenderness, and a bit of wondering awe that he'd shown me before Philip was born.

I glanced at him now as he concentrated on driving. I'd always loved his face in profile, the strong, sharp lines of his nose and chin balanced by the seductively sweet curve of his mouth. He was twenty-nine now, and although he lamented that his youth was done, to me he'd only grown more handsome with time. I wasn't alone in this conviction, either. Even now, I saw how other women we passed on the street would pause to gaze upon my husband in admiration, and I was thoroughly proud to call him mine.

This wasn't new, of course. He'd always been the kind of handsome gentleman who drew female eyes to him. But as much as I was loath to admit it, I was more conscious of this kind of admiration after Angelica had remarked upon it last summer. She'd cautioned me to be more aware and I had, though by doing so I'd felt low and mean, as if I were distrusting Alexander, or worse, countering my marriage vows.

My only solace had been that, to my eyes, Angelica's worries had been exaggerated. Perhaps she truly had been too long in Paris, observing French manners. Oh, there were plenty of New York women—and not a few ladies—who openly flattered and flirted with him, even in my presence. In turn he was polite and solicitous, and charming because to be so was in his very nature, but I never once witnessed him encouraging any of them, or stepping across the line of genteel gallantry. Further, every day he reminded me again of his love for me in a hundred small ways, so many that I was sure I was the only one with a claim to his heart. Wasn't this third child, conceived of love and ardor, proof enough?

"Here we are, Betsey," he said, interrupting my pleasant thoughts, and reminding me of the errand upon which we were engaged.

Being married to Alexander meant my life took many curious turns, but I had never before entered the city's gaol, nor, as a lady, had I ever intended to. The gaol was in fact our destination this morning, a grimly forbidding building that was more a fortress of brick with few windows, and those crossed with iron bars against escape.

I held closely to my husband's arm as he helped me from the gig, and together we climbed the stone steps that led inside. Beneath my heavy cloak, I was dressed more for an afternoon call than for visiting a gaol, but Alexander had assured me that my attire was exactly right: a cream-colored silk Italian gown with a pink silk sash and an embroidered gauze kerchief. I'd had my hair fashionably curled and frizzed in a style that Angelica likened to that worn by the Queen of France, and my head was fully powdered even at this early hour. I'd balked at wearing jewels to a gaol, even though Alexander encouraged me to do so, and in their stead I wore a slender black ribbon tied loosely around my throat as my only ornament.

"I don't want you to be frightened, dearest," Alexander said as we waited in the gaoler's parlor. "Recall that Mr. Earl is a debtor, not a common criminal."

"I'll admit to being uncertain, Alexander, but not frightened," I said, "But even you must grant that this is most unusual."

"It is," he admitted. "But it's a small act of great generosity that will help Mr. Earl resolve his present difficult plight."

"I don't deny the benefit to Mr. Earl," I said, "and after having gone first, I'll happily sing his praises to the other ladies in town, as you suggest. It's just that I've never sat for my likeness before."

This was true. Despite my parents' wealth and position, they hadn't placed importance upon portraits or paintings in general, especially when artists were so rare and charged a premium for their service. Mamma and Papa themselves had only sat for a single portrait apiece, and those many years before.

But this *was* an unusual circumstance. Although an accomplished painter who had been trained by masters in London, Mr. Earl was sadly given to drink, and had fallen into such debt that he had been committed to gaol until he could meet the demands of his creditors. Through Alexander's efforts, and assistance from the Society for the Relief of Distressed Debtors, Mr. Earl had been provided with paints and canvases with the hope that he could earn his way to freedom through portraits. Mine would be the first.

It was typical of the many charities my husband did for others. He recalled from his own miserable childhood the rare beneficences that others had shown toward him, and as a result he never turned away anyone in true need. Yet he also always acted quietly, without fanfare, and from pure kindness and self-satisfaction.

"I assure you that sitting for a painter is not a painful experience," Alexander said, teasing me solemnly. "Besides, I've always wanted a portrait of you, just as you so fervently demanded one of me. Ah, here we are."

The head gaoler himself ushered us back to a tiny closet of a room that had been converted into a makeshift studio. Mr. Earl greeted us shyly, ducking his head as he bowed; he had the woebegone look of a man down on his luck, from the droop of his shoulders to how the latchets of his shoes were tied with scraps of string instead of the fancy buckles that he'd likely been forced to sell against his debts.

He scarcely spoke, but bade me sit in the single armchair, turning me slightly. I was aware of the thickness of my waist on account of my pregnancy, and he thoughtfully suggested I rest my hand on the chair to take attention away from my belly. Then he went to stand behind the canvas on his easel to begin his work, and soon the only sound was the muted *shush* of his brushes moving across the canvas.

Alexander stood behind him in respectful silence, watching the painting take shape. He'd been right: posing wasn't difficult.

"Is it like me, Alexander?" I asked anxiously when Mr. Earl paused to mix fresh paints.

"Yes," he said with satisfaction. "Though it's barely begun, I can already see that Mr. Earl's genius will capture your beauty and your spirit, too."

For the next fortnight I visited Mr. Earl for additional sittings. In an odd way, I enjoyed the time to sit alone with my own thoughts, away from the demands of our household and children. I do not know if, as Alexander claimed, the finished portrait captured my beauty or spirit, but I was pleased by the contentment in my face, a contentment that I'd felt at the time of the painting.

My only quibble was minor. Mr. Earl painted a narrow black ribbon or cuff at my wrist that wasn't on my gown. I thought it had the look of mourning, and found it particularly unsettling, and perhaps unlucky, given my pregnancy. When I asked him why, he said that it was his way of making my hands seem paler and more graceful, and that he did the same for most every lady's portrait. I couldn't quarrel without wounding him, and so let the black cuff, however peculiar, remain, and I praised his skill to all my acquaintance so he received more commissions to pay his debts.

What mattered far more to me was how pleased Alexander was with the portrait. He had it hung in the front parlor, and went so far as to invite friends to the house to admire it, and drink a bumper to its beauty, which embarrassed me even as I recognized it was my husband's way of paying tribute to me as well.

"You can't deny it's a splendid portrait," he said, standing before it. Our guests had gone, and we two lingered alone before we'd douse the candles and retreat to bed. "Though not as handsome as the original, it will keep me company when you and the children visit your parents."

"She's a good deal more quiet than I, too," I said wryly. "The painted me won't chide you for not wearing a quilted waistcoat when it's cold, or tell you that if you keep working so late, you'll make yourself ill."

"I said that the portrait will keep me company, not that it will be a perfect substitute." He wrapped his arms loosely around my shoulders, holding me close to his chest as we both gazed up at the portrait. "I like having you look after me. I know how much I miss you when we're apart."

"I miss you, too," I said softly. "You should have had Mr. Earl make you a miniature portrait. This one would be a little large to carry with you when you must travel for trials."

"Not just trials," he began, then paused, his arms tightening a fraction around me.

Even before he spoke again, I understood what that slight hesitation meant, and my heart sank.

"I can't stand by any longer, Betsey," he said softly, and I realized that from how we were standing, with my back against his chest, he didn't have to look me in the eye. "The Confederation of states is foundering, and our esteemed Governor Clinton is one of the leaders determined to make the country sink for his own gain."

"You're going to stand for the Assembly again, aren't you?" I asked, unable to keep the sadness from my voice. "Did my father put you up to it?"

"Yes," he said. "But while your father has told me how much my voice has been missed, this is my decision, not his."

I'd wanted to believe that he'd been content with the law. I'd told myself that the joys of our little family were sufficient to keep him from the drama of public office. I'd believed it, and yet deep down I hadn't. He burned with ideas and energy. From the first time I'd met him, I'd the distinct sense that he'd be destined for great things, and it had been much of his early appeal to me. It still was.

I turned in his arms to face him, awkward with my belly between us. "Will you be here when the baby comes?"

He nodded. "I'll make certain of that, my angel."

"Thank you," I said softly. I looked down so he wouldn't see the tears that were likely in my eyes, and rested my palms on his chest, the way I always had. Not so long ago, my hands had rested upon the rough wool of a soldier, and now he wore the rich superfine of a successful gentleman. He was my strength, my pillar, yet once again I must share him with a score of angry gentlemen far from home. But because he wished it, and because he might do those great things for the country his children would inherit, I'd no choice but to let him go back to Poughkeepsie.

I blinked back the tears, and forced myself to smile. "When does the next session begin?"

As everyone expected, Alexander was elected again in April to represent the City and the County of New York in the State Assembly. The following month, our second son was born, with a shock of black hair and a lusty voice that would rattle us all awake throughout the night. We named him Alexander, after his father, who kept his promise and was home the night of the birth.

Home then, but not for long. Not only was he now often gone to Poughkeepsie for the meetings of the State Assembly, but he was also appointed by that body as a commissioner to represent New York to a small conference on the state of national commerce, which required much preparation.

With him away so often, I closed up our New York house and retreated with our children to The Pastures, where the air was healthier for them. My sister Peggy also came often from Rensselaerwyck bringing her young son and daughter, too, so that the infant cousins could be together.

Peggy and I both wished that Angelica could be there with us as well, particularly this summer. The child my older sister had been carrying the previous summer had been born, a third son named Richard Hamilton Church, soon after they'd arrived again at their home in Paris. I'd rejoiced at her safe delivery, but Angelica's own joy was obviously mitigated by the baby's frailty. Unlike his siblings, he was never strong, and despite all the best efforts of the physicians in Paris and then London, he had finally given up his innocent soul to Heaven after only a few short months of mortal life. Sharing her sorrow for the nephew I'd never had the chance to meet made me appreciate my own little ones even more, and thank God for their sturdy health.

Angelica was distraught with grief, as can be imagined, and Peggy and I both longed to be able to comfort her in person, and not just by letter. Privately I suspected that if Mr. Church had not been so insistent upon hauling my sister back and forth across the ocean whilst she was in a delicate condition, then the son she'd carried might have been of a stronger constitution and survived; of course, I would never be so cruel as to share that opinion with my poor sister, who in her grief already blamed herself too much. But Mr. Church had no plans to return to America that year, and so poor Angelica suffered without our consolation.

I returned to New York City in September, in time to help prepare Alexander for traveling to his commerce conference in Annapolis. I worried over his decision to ride by himself on horseback to Maryland. He had attempted to maintain as much of his legal work in New York even as he served in the Assembly, and he worked prodigiously long hours. He'd never seem to require as much sleep as most men, but even he had his limits, and over the summer he'd developed a raspy cough that had not gone away. Given the state of his health, I'd preferred he travel by coach or sea instead, but he'd insisted that the ride through the autumn countryside would do him good. He was right, too. He remained an excellent horseman, and being out of doors and away from his office proved the proper prescription, for he claimed by the time he arrived in Annapolis, he felt thoroughly restored.

I suspect, however, it was more the company he found in Annapolis than the journey that restored him. The conference consisted of only a dozen gentlemen, but among them was James Madison, the small, scholarly representative from Virginia whom he'd met during the Continental Congress, and who shared many of his views. In fact, from Alexander's telling when he returned to New York City in October, the entire conference soon set aside the question of interstate commerce—its reason for convening—and instead devoted its conversation and energy to proposing another, much more important convention to revise the old Confederation to favor a stronger federal government. By the time they all returned to their home states, they took with them a resolution for a Constitutional Convention to be held in Philadelphia.

Alexander himself arrived home late one night toward the end of September, after the children and servants were abed and I myself was already undressed and ready for my prayers. I was surprised but delighted to see him after he'd been away, and happily greeted him in the hall wearing only a dressing gown over my nightshift, my feet in slippers and my hair plaited for bed.

"You should've stopped at an inn along the way," I chided after he'd kissed me. "It's not safe for you to ride so far alone at night."

"The harvest moon lit my way," he said grandly, still holding me close. "Besides, I wanted to come home to you."

"I'm grateful that you did, dearest." I smiled, and kissed him again. He smelled of leather and horse and sweat, the wonderful scent of his homecomings, and reluctantly I slipped free. "I'll wager you didn't stop to eat, either. Come to the kitchen, and I'll make you dinner."

"You know me so well, Betsey," he said, reaching out to tug playfully on my braid as he followed me into the kitchen. Not wanting to wake the servants, I made him dinner myself from what was on hand, and I sat with him in the kitchen by a single candlestick while he ate. It was like the old days when we'd first wed, especially when he began to tell me of the Convention, of what had been accomplished and what hadn't. After his first glass of wine, he retrieved his saddlebag from the hall and handed me a copy of the Convention's resolution.

"You wrote this, Alexander, didn't you?" I'd only to skim the first paragraphs to recognize his words and style.

He shrugged with a carelessness that didn't fool me for a moment. "I wrote the first draft," he said. "Others had suggestions."

Looking over the edge of the paper, I raised my brows, waiting for further explanation.

"The Virginians found my initial efforts too impassioned," he finally admitted. "Madison begged me to be more moderate, or else lose his state's support."

"I can only imagine," I murmured. I could, too. I'd been listening to Alexander at his most unguarded for years. The subject of the resolution was so dear to his heart that it was easy enough for me to guess the dramatic and—to most men—terrifyingly extreme suggestions that he'd put forth in that first draft.

He reached across the table and covered my hand with his. "I wouldn't have had to edit it to such a degree if you'd read it first."

"Perhaps," I said, even though he was likely right. I didn't read everything he wrote before he shared it with others—and in fact, since I'd become so occupied with raising our children, I'd sadly read less and less—yet I appreciated that he, too, was remembering fondly to earlier days in our marriage, and the furious compositions on finance that he'd addressed to Robert Morris.

I set the paper down on the table, smoothing it thoughtfully with my palm. "When would this Constitutional Convention take place?"

"First the states must agree to it," he said. "Then each state must choose its delegates, and finally a date can be chosen. So the answer, I suppose, is as soon as possible, which won't be very soon at all. I should hope we'll gather early in the new year."

" 'We'?" I repeated. "You are certain you'll be a delegate?"

He smiled with assurance. "Not even Clinton would dare block me from it now."

I smiled, too, but sighed as well, for I suspected that matters would not be so simply resolved. "I should congratulate you, then," I said. "This is exactly what you've wanted, isn't it?"

"It's a beginning," he said. "There's no time to be lost. We must move forward and we must make changes, substantial changes, else the country will collapse."

As tired as he must be, his enthusiasm was giving fresh energy to his voice. I listened, and I nodded, impressed with all the great plans he had for this new country of ours.

But I also thought of the more cautious gentlemen like James Madison, and wondered if Alexander would need to be more circumspect in order to gain allies. Sometimes with him, confidence could be like strong drink, and go directly to his head so thoroughly that he'd forget tact and reason.

"One step at a time, Alexander," I cautioned. "Pray take only one step at a time, and don't tread upon anyone else who wanders into your path."

He grinned, bowed his head, and touched his fingers to his forehead in a wryly subservient gesture of acknowledgment. I smiled in return, for it was amusingly done, even as I knew he would not heed my advice. I wasn't sure he could have done so, even if he'd wished it. He'd never grasped, or perhaps had chosen not to, that reserve was not the same as duplicity. He'd always valued honesty above all other virtues, but there were times where a little less of it might have stood him in better stead in the political arenas.

As the year ended and another began, it was clear that his concerns for the country were well-founded. Individual states levied taxes however they chose, and like niggling misers, refused to send their fair share (or, in some cases, any share) to the federal government for the good of the whole country. As a result, there was no money to address the enormous debt that remained from the war, and the loans granted by other countries went unpaid. To make matters worse, each state continued to print its own worthless paper currency, making debts impossible to settle and merchants unwilling and unable to extend further credit for goods.

I saw the evidence of this myself. A simple visit to a draper's shop for a length of linen for a child's shirt could become a mathematical adventure. Should I pay in dollars, or shillings and pence, French guineas or Prussian thalers? All of those coins and bills were common currency in our city, and I'd seen them come into our house, too, by way of my husband's fees. But which would give more value as a housewife at market? Which would garner more respect from a shopkeeper, and offer the most advantageous rate of exchange?

Yet it wasn't only the merchants who felt the pinch. Farmers and other small landowners were unable to pay the ever-increasing taxes, and being faced with foreclosure and ruin. Near the end of 1786, a large group of these impoverished farmers from western Massachusetts took matters into their own hands, and began shutting down courts and threatening officials.

Well-organized and armed under the leadership of a onetime militia captain named Daniel Shays, the men soon became emboldened to attack armories and raid private shops, and threatened worse. The mob of angry men grew as it surged east toward Boston, an open rebellion if not out-and-out civil war.

To me, this grim news was especially frightening. Most of the rebels had been soldiers during the war, men who had never been justly paid for their service, and they had much in common with the disgruntled soldiers who had threatened Congress (and my husband) in Philadelphia three years before.

As a veteran himself, Alexander sympathized with the rebels

even as he railed on to me about how such martial demonstrations needed to be swiftly suppressed before they threatened the nation as a whole. One of his less popular beliefs was a need for a national standing army to address conflicts like this, and I believe that if it had been up to him, he would have sent a full national army to Massachusetts to put down the rebellion. In public, however, he was more measured, and pointed to the disturbances as more proof of the need for a stronger national financial system.

By the time Alexander returned to the state legislature in January, the Massachusetts rebellion had been quelled by local militia and the leaders captured, but the warning it had raised was still much in people's minds. Or at least it was everywhere except in the small and narrow minds of Governor Clinton and his followers. Even the fact that this session of the legislature met in New York City, in the Old Royal Exchange, did not sway the governor from his insistence that the Confederation of states was perfectly adequate, and worse, that the suggested changes were to be despised, even feared.

While other states swiftly approved the proposal for a new Constitutional Convention and chose their delegates, Governor Clinton made sure that New York dragged its feet. Alexander fought heroically, in sessions and debates and with individual assemblymen, too, and each late night when he came home and our children were abed, I'd listen as he recounted every denial and scornful aside with me, and planned his next move.

One day he gave a speech defending a congressional proposal for an import tax that he knew would be defeated, and yet I heard from my father, in attendance as a state senator, that Alexander still spoke with passion and dedication for nearly ninety minutes, and nearly collapsed from exertion when he was done. The measure was promptly defeated, as he'd expected, but defiant and determined, he insisted that we go to the playhouse that same evening, if only to prove his resilience to the Clintonians.

To hear Alexander tell it (and I did, many times), Governor Clinton's pettiness knew no bounds. When at last the New York delegates were chosen to attend the Constitutional Convention, Alexander was chosen—for not even the governor could overlook a gentleman who'd helped institute the Convention—but the two other gentlemen were firm followers of Governor Clinton, and guaranteed to vote together and against Alexander.

Still, when he left for Philadelphia on a warm, drizzling morning in the middle of May, his mood was buoyant and optimistic. His old mentor General Washington had agreed to serve as the Convention's president. Under the general's firm leadership, Alexander hoped the delegates would not be content with a few mends and darns to the old Confederation, but would instead, like master tailors, begin anew with a fresh bolt of cloth, cutting to measure to suit the needs of the country.

I do not know exactly what occurred during that long summer in Philadelphia, or what was said behind the shuttered blinds and closed doors of the statehouse. Nor do I know what my impassioned husband discussed with the other delegates whilst dining at their lodgings in the Indian Queen Tavern. Because of the delicate nature of the Convention's discussions, all delegates had been sworn to complete secrecy, and none could have taken this oath more seriously than Alexander. He would not break his oath, even for me.

But I'd other, more sorrowful matters to occupy myself as well. My younger sister Peggy and her young husband had two charming children, a three-year-old daughter named Catherine after our mother, and a one-year-old son named Stephanus, to honor his grandfather. Our children had played together during our visits to The Pastures, and my daughter Angelica was particularly fond of her little cousin Catherine, singing her songs in her warbling voice as Catherine clapped with delight.

Yet in the space of a single terrible week that summer, my poor sister lost both her babies to scarlet fever, as first Catherine, and then tiny Stephanus, sickened and died. I rushed to Peggy as soon as I heard the grim news, taking care to leave my own children safely behind in New York. Although I didn't arrive until after the burials, I still was able to offer what comfort I could to Peggy. Swathed in black, my usually lighthearted sister was distraught with grief, her face so swollen from crying that I scarcely recognized her.

Hand in hand, she led me at once to the now-empty nursery at Rensselaerwyck, where we were surrounded by her children's toys and belongings, as poignant as any ghosts. With the house in deep mourning, the curtains were drawn and the air in the room was heavy and still, gloomed further with shadows and loss. Here my sister and I sat together on a bench where only a fortnight before she'd played with her sweet darlings. My poor, dear Peggy was mute with grieving, and could do nothing but weep the heaviest tears of a despairing mother as I held her close and wept too over her unimaginable loss. It was all I could do, and all that could be done, beyond praying for the little souls now free of their suffering.

Peggy's sorrow remained with me on my journey back home to New York, and I wept anew as I held my own children close, determined to cherish them even more. What sadder reminder was there of how fragile life could be for those who were most dear to us?

Although the Constitutional Convention lasted well into August, Alexander didn't remain in Philadelphia the entire time. He frequently came home to New York City and to me and the children, and to attend to his practice. This wasn't unusual among the delegates, most of whom returned home at some point or departed for good to tend to their affairs. But where nearly all the other delegates were gentlemen with property and incomes, our little family depended on what Alexander himself earned from the law. I did my part as the frugal housewife, closely watching our expenditures. I welcomed the gifts of cheeses, flour, and fruits that my parents sent down from their farms down the river to us, and I anticipated the day when my husband would be able to devote all his energies to his practice.

I also interpreted his trips home as signs that the Convention had not gone as he'd wished, and though I couldn't know the reasons why, I tried to cheer him as best I could. Our children did that as well, lightening his humor with their chatter and play. He wasn't a somber, distant father, but threw himself into their games with cheerful abandon. With them he could be entirely his own man, with no worries of how he'd be judged, and he loved them all the more for it.

On his last visit, however, our house was quiet, and our family subdued. Living in such a sizable city, I took every safeguard I could to preserve our children's health. This included inoculations against the smallpox. Dr. Bard followed the latest practices of the day by inoculating our children before their second birthdays. The procedure itself was simple enough: a small nick in the skin of the left arm to introduce the infectious matter was all that was required.

But young children did not understand either the procedure, or the fever that came a week later, or the jalap purges that followed, and the necessity to lie abed quietly. Alexander, who at fifteen months was the perfect age for the procedure, had developed the proper desired fever and only a handful of pustules, but he was so fretful and unhappy that I'd taken him from his bed and into the parlor. I opened the windows to admit the evening's cooler breezes, and then sat on the sofa with my feverish child in my arms. Gently I rocked back and forth to ease him, and when that didn't help, I put him to my breast for comfort.

That was how Alexander found us, sitting by the light of a single candlestick.

"How is my Alex faring?" he asked softly with concern. Gently he brushed aside his little son's dark curls, damp with fever, and cupped his palm over the child's forehead. He was half-asleep, poor baby, his eyes nearly closed.

"Better, I think," I said. "I didn't want him to wake Philip or Angelica."

"No," he said, bending to kiss me over our son's head before he, too, sat on the sofa. "He's still very warm. I know it's all part of the inoculation, but I don't like fevers, especially not in the children."

I didn't like them, either, but having been born in the Caribbean, my husband had a special dread of feverish ailments. A fever had killed his mother, and he'd nearly died himself more than once.

"Alex will be fine now," I said. "Dr. Bard says so."

"Then I suppose we must trust," Alexander said, though his expression betrayed far more worry. "I thought you'd written me that he'd been weaned."

"Almost," I admitted, protectively holding the child a little closer to my breast. Alex *was* old for suckling now, and in truth I was more reluctant to end it than was he. "Most times he'd rather drink from a cup now. But tonight he wanted the comfort, and I couldn't deny him."

Alexander nodded, agreeing, or at least leaving the decision to me. Of course, there was more that neither of us was saying, but we each understood. As soon as I'd weaned both Philip and Angelica, I'd become pregnant again almost at once with our next child. I believed in my heart that children were God's blessing on a marriage, and Alexander and I had always wanted a large family. The children we had were impossibly dear to us, but the thought of adding yet another while our lives—and the country—were so unsettled was a sobering one.

"Poor little man," Alexander said, watching his son. "I hope he's better before I must leave on Thursday."

"Is it possible for you to stay another day or two?" I asked with more hope in my voice than I probably should have ventured.

"No, I must return," he said, and the deep sigh that followed spoke volumes.

"Is it as bad as that?" I asked carefully.

"Has the Convention proceded as I'd hoped? No." He shrugged, and shook his head with resignation. "I've been called a monarchist and a traitor, and I've had my opinions twisted about and thrown back at me. The Constitution that is being wrought is not what it could have been, and yet, I will support it, for the good of the country."

I didn't need to ask more. In the last months, he'd once again turned to writing letters to the New York newspapers attacking how Governor Clinton sought to block the new Constitution, and his supporters had been quick to attack Alexander, focusing not on his political beliefs, but with personal slanders and name-calling. It had been very public, shameful, and ugly, and had wounded Alexander—who remained acutely aware of his parentage and past— more deeply than I'd expected. If the Convention had had any of the same elements, then I understood why he wasn't eager to return, and why our family was his sanctuary.

"Before I leave, I've something else to ask of you, my love," Alexander said. "Do you recall Colonel Antill?"

"I recall attending his poor wife's funeral with you several years

ago," I said. It had been a heartrending sight that would always remain with me: the grieving widower and their six young children,
one a mere babe in arms, sobbing and lost, as they stood over the
yawning grave of their wife and mother. Alexander had served
alongside Colonel Antill in the war, and had attended King's College with him, too, and when in desperation the colonel had appealed to my husband for assistance, Alexander had of course
given it to him. "Is he faring any better with his law practice since
then?"

"He's taken to farming now," Alexander said, "and done as
poorly at that as he did with the law, and appears to be a man broken in spirit and body. He has come to me to beg an extraordinary
favor. He wants us to take his youngest daughter Fanny into our
care."

I remembered that tiny, wide-eyed baby who'd never known her
mother. I thought of how desperate Colonel Antill must be to ask
such a thing. In that instant I forgot all my uncertainties about
adding another child to our family, and the next day, Fanny came to
live with us, as completely and as loved as if she'd been another
daughter of our own blood.

As imperfect as Alexander judged the new Constitution to be
and as painful as the process had been, he was still among the
thirty-nine delegates who signed the document in September 1787.
His was also the only signature to represent New York, the other
two delegates having left early in protest, and in union with Governor Clinton.

I rejoiced to have my husband home once again, and the
children—our three plus Fanny Antill—couldn't have been happier to have their father back. I waited until we were alone in our
bed with the curtains drawn tight, to tell him my own news.

"I'm with child again," I said softly as I lay beside him, his arm
curled around my waist.

He rolled over to face me, propping his head on his arm.

"A springtime baby," I added.

He smiled slowly, letting the happiness spread across his face,
and gently placed his hand over my belly.

I smiled, too, and with relief as well. "You are pleased?"

"I am as pleased as a husband could be, my love," he said, and drew me close to kiss.

It was a blissful homecoming, but by the next morning, the loving husband had vanished, and he was as grim-faced and determined as if once again going to battle.

In a way, that was exactly what lay ahead. The Constitution still had to be approved and ratified by a majority of nine states. The debates and approvals would be made directly by citizens in state conventions, not by the various states' legislatures and their politicians.

The arguments raged in every state and likely every tavern, too, with some men seeing the proposed new government as absolutely essential, while others deplored it as an abomination based so closely upon British models as to be a return to the same tyranny of colonial times. As can be imagined, New York was one of the most contentious states, with Alexander as the voice for the Federalists (as supporters of the Constitution had become known) and Governor Clinton as the leader of the Anti-Federalists. The passions of both groups ran high, and debates of the state convention were angry and heated, and filled with ungentlemanly invectives.

But in the fall of 1787, Alexander turned to his favorite weapon, the written word. He imagined a series of essays in the form of letters, to be published in the three largest New York newspapers for all to read.

On account of his public services and his law practice, however, he was prodigiously busy, and no matter how much coffee he drank, even he required a modicum of sleep. He wasn't able to find time to compose his thoughts with clarity until October, when together we sailed north by way of a sloop on the Hudson to Albany. He was presenting a case before the state court there, and I accompanied him so that I might see my parents.

Because of the uncertainty of the winds and currents, such a journey upriver was more like a short voyage, and could take as long as a week. But on board the sloop Alexander had no distractions, nor could further work be brought to his attention. In this relative peace, he could write as intensely as he pleased on his battered portable desk, the hinged mahogany box that accompanied him everywhere. In this fashion, his thoughts were interrupted only when he invited me to join him on the deck to discuss some particularly thorny question while he paced back and forth, dodging sailors and other passengers and ignoring the changing colors of autumn on either bank of the river.

The epistolary essays as he conceived them were intended not only to persuade, but to explain the need for the new Constitution with clear examples of how the old Confederation had failed, and of how the new plan would correct these errors and weaknesses in the future. He enlisted his fellow delegates John Jay and James Madison to write essays as well, with each gentleman concentrating on topics of his own expertise. The essays were addressed to the citizens of the state of New York, and to protect the authors' identities, they would be published under the name of Publius, in honor of Publius Valerius, one of the founders of the ancient Roman republic.

The first of the essays was published at the end of October, and the last in August 1788. There were eighty-five in all; Mr. Jay wrote five, Mr. Madison twenty-nine, and Alexander fifty-one. Together they were known as *The Federalist*.

I will not attempt to paraphrase *The Federalist* here, for I would surely fail. But I recommend the essays (which were compiled almost immediately and published as a book) to anyone who wishes not only to understand the tenets of our government, but also to glimpse my husband's true and lasting brilliance. They are remarkable documents on their own, but to me, who witnessed their furious creation as he toiled at his desk late in the night and early in the morning, they were nothing short of a miracle. He was, I think, more proud of this written accomplishment than any other, and I was in turn proud of him.

Even Alexander will admit, however, that the essays might not have had the effect on the citizens that he'd hoped. More important in swaying voters were the dramatic arguments he delivered in person to the convention in Poughkeepsie. Yet while Governor Clinton's influence still held firm, and while New York was one of the last states to finally ratify the Constitution—and by the most slender of margins, too—in the end it finally did so. The Anti-Federalist factions in the north of the state blamed Alexander, and likely cursed him as well.

But in New York City, the stronghold of the Federalists, my husband was a veritable hero. When news of the impending ratification reached the city, the celebration among the people was even more glorious than when the last British ship had sailed from the harbor three years before.

Alas, my husband was still in Poughkeepsie and could not witness it for himself, for surely he would have been endlessly gratified to see such heartfelt appreciation for all his labors. I was shortly to travel north with our children to Albany and The Pastures for the summer, but fortuitously we were still in the city for the celebrations.

A parade was planned down Broadway, and with my five little ones (including Fanny Antill and my own newest son, James Alexander, born in April) in tow, I went to a friend's house on that street to watch the festivities from her open windows. The day was overcast with a light drizzle early in the day, but nothing could dampen the high spirits of those who marched and the cheering crowds that gathered to watch.

I heard that more than five thousand men participated in the parade, a sizable group for a city of thirty thousand souls. There were brigades representing every kind of tradesman, shopkeeper, artisan, and merchant, all carrying emblems of their employment to show their support for the new Constitution. A military-style band played stirring music, with thumping drums and squealing fifes that thrilled Philip and Angelica, but frightened the younger children. Colorful displays were mounted upon flat wagons and drawn through the streets to represent more trades. Marchers tried to outdo one another in their gaudy costumes, and every horse in the parade was likewise decked with ribbons and cockades. One banner even featured a portrait of my beloved husband, surrounded by a wreath of laurels.

But the most spectacular display came near the end. Drawn by ten dray horses came a miniature frigate nearly thirty feet in length, her masts towering as high as the rooftops, and canvas waves to support her as she sailed down Broadway. Painted in gold across the stern was this brave vessel's name: the Federal Ship *Hamilton*. As the ship slowed to a stop before Bayard's Tavern, not far from where we were watching, it changed pilots to demonstrate the shift from the Articles of Confederation to the new Constitution, while guns fired in noisy celebration.

Explaining how all this was in honor of their father, I bade the children to clap and cheer, not that they required my encouragement; the painted ship was a sight they would all long remember. It was all a splendid, heartening show, so grand that tears stung my eyes to see my husband so venerated.

My only regret was that Alexander was not with us. Not only would he have delighted in the spectacle, but the glorious memory of the parade and the enthusiastic support it represented would have brought him much consolation through the darker days ahead.

CHAPTER 16

New York City, New York
March 1789

"There," said Alexander, pointing out across the Battery and out toward the open sea. "The largest ship, bearing down upon us. That's hers."

Beside him, I stared out onto the horizon, striving to see which particular ship he meant among the many sails that dotted the waters around New York. The midday sun was bright and I squinted a bit, even with my face shielded by the sweeping brim of my hat and a green silk parasol as well, and the breeze from the sea was brisk and salty in my face. Yet I would never complain, but be grateful instead. With every little gust, these same breezes were carrying one of the dearest people in Creation closer to me: my sister Angelica.

"You know there could still be hours before your sister will be able to disembark," Alexander cautioned. "I don't even know if the pilot has gone aboard yet to bring them into the harbor. As much as Angelica might desire it, even she cannot come skipping across the water to us."

"I wish she could," I declared.

Alexander smiled, doubtless imagining my sister doing exactly that, her petticoats daintily lifted above the waves.

We hadn't seen my sister in nearly four years, and while I'd missed her beyond words, I think Alexander had missed her nearly as much. Ever since Mr. Church had at last agreed to spare her for a visit with us, her family in America, both Alexander and I had been in a fever of anticipation. Each night I'd added extra prayers for her safe journey, while Alexander had checked daily with the ship's owner for any news of her progress across the Atlantic.

Now with equal reluctance we decided to retreat to a nearby coffeehouse for refreshment, and to wait until the ship was closer. Neither of us suggested returning home until we had Angelica with us.

My sister was arriving at the perfect time, too, for New York was an exciting place to be in 1789. After putting aside the old Articles of Confederation under which the country had been run since the war (and which to me had seemed to have taken a trudging eternity to accomplish) the business of forming a new kind of government felt as if it were racing along at a breakneck pace, with some fresh occurrence happening most every day.

The newly elected Congress, consisting of both a Senate and a House of Representatives, had met for the first time in March, in Federal Hall. General Washington had been easily elected as the country's first president, and was even now making his way to New York from his country seat at Mount Vernon to be sworn into office in an elaborate ceremony. There would, of course, be balls. In anticipation of these events, visitors streamed into the city from every part of our country, and from the countries of Europe, too, and I never knew when I'd be introduced to a lady from Georgia in a milliner's shop, or be seated next to a Prussian nobleman at a supper.

But as far as I was concerned, the best part of having New York City as the country's new capital was that there was no further need for my husband to travel in the service of his country. He had resigned his place in the state Assembly, and had every expectation of a position in the new federal government here in New York once President Washington was inaugurated.

In the time since we'd first moved to Wall Street, I do not believe that Alexander and I had passed an entire month together without him having to make a journey away from home for one purpose or another. Now he slept in his own bed beside me every night, and we both were much the happier for it. The last time I'd seen Alexander this exhilarated had been before he'd departed for

Yorktown, and the final battle of the war, though how relieved I was to think that there'd be no such further bloodshed and mayhem in his life.

We waited not two hours for Angelica's ship, but nearly four, yet those long hours were swiftly forgotten when I was at last able to embrace my dearest sister. We both wept with joy, and she clung to me laughing because her legs were so unsteady on land after the long voyage. Then it was Alexander's turn, and fresh joy and tears and laughter combined. I kept touching her arm, her shoulder, her hair, reassuring myself that she was truly with me. Even after weeks aboard ship, she was beautifully and expensively dressed, with an enormous plumed hat that must have been anchored with countless pins to keep from blowing away with the harbor's breeze. But I thought with concern that she looked tired, doubtless from traveling, and older, too. I reminded myself that she'd lost a child; that would be reason enough to have caused the new web of fine lines about her eyes.

Because she had traveled with only her lady's maid, we insisted that she stay with us. I feared our house might seem unbearably humble after Down Place, their estate near Windsor, as well as their sizable house in London, but she declared our home to be delightful and snug, and made herself instantly at ease. Of her niece and nephews, only Philip remembered her, yet she quickly won over the others, including Fanny, with dolls and toys from the best shops in London. For Philip, she'd brought a set of specially painted lead soldiers.

"Do you see his blue and buff uniform?" she asked, leaning close to Philip as she stood one of the soldiers on her open palm. "He's dressed in the same uniform as your father and his men wore at Yorktown."

Philip's eyes shone bright with awe, and so did Alexander's, too, and I knew our son would not be the only one playing with the soldiers.

But my sister had brought gifts for us as well, a set of French histories, luxuriously bound in gold-trim leather for Alexander, and a gold necklace set with honey-colored citrines for me. I gasped when I opened the case, and glanced swiftly at Alexander.

He had always declined my father's generosity, and I worried that Angelica's costly offerings would vex him as well. But I suppose because they'd come from Angelica, he only nodded, and urged me to put the necklace around my throat now. I did, with Angelica fastening the clasp for me.

"Most handsome, Betsey," Alexander said while my sister beamed. "You must wear that to the ball."

"Oh, yes, Eliza, you must," exclaimed Angelica. "The color favors your coloring to perfection."

I smiled, and touched my fingers lightly to the necklace. In truth the necklace was much more to my sister's taste than my own, and the large stones were weighty and chill against my skin. I would rather have worn the strand of garnet beads (much like those worn by Lady Washington) that Alexander had given me to the ball as I'd planned, but now, to please them both, I knew I'd no choice but to wear my sister's gift.

Later, when the children were finally asleep, the three of us settled into the parlor, and of course the talk turned at once to politics. Falling back into the patterns of our girlhood, I preferred most often to listen while my sister conversed with my husband, and content myself with stitching a new dress for my daughter while their quick, clever words darted back and forth around me.

"There was never any doubt that His Excellency would become president, was there?" Angelica asked. After dinner she had changed into a loose-fitting sultana of shimmering pale blue silk, and now she sat comfortably curled on the sofa with her feet tucked beneath her. "But Mr. Adams as vice president! How being second—even second to His Excellency—must gall that insufferable man."

"If Adams believed he'd win the presidency, then he was likely the only one in the country who did," Alexander said. He, too, had changed into more comfortable dress as he often did in the evenings, replacing his coat and waistcoat with a banyan over his shirt and breeches, and his favorite and thoroughly disreputable slippers on his feet. "I suppose you must have crossed paths, if not swords, with Adams in London to have conceived such an ill opinion of him."

Angelica sighed dramatically. "Mr. Church and I knew him in

Boston, and we knew him in Paris, and then there he appeared again in London, and now you tell me I must know him here in New York. Will the man give me no peace?"

I glanced up from my needle. "Mr. Adams may well say the same of you, Angelica."

At once Angelica puffed out her cheeks and squeezed her brows together, the very picture of Mr. Adams.

"Preserve me!" she said in a querulous voice. "It's that odious creature Mrs. Church, traipsing after me clear across the ocean and back!"

We all laughed, for it could well be true. The dour and fussy John Adams was perhaps the one American abroad who'd find nothing to recommend in my endlessly agreeable sister.

"I cannot have you ridiculing the man in my hearing, Angelica," Alexander protested, even as he still was laughing. "He seems a good enough man, and I must find a way to work beside him."

"You will, my dear," I said, soothing. "Mr. Adams is another attorney, and you attorneys always manage to find a way to cooperate with one another."

"You won't win him through his wife, Hamilton, the way you usually do," my sister warned. "Have you met the lady? She is shrewd, in the way of Boston ladies. She will be suspicious of you on pure principle, and refuse to be charmed."

"Is that a wager, *ma chère soeur*?" Alexander said, addressing her fondly in French. "That I cannot charm Mrs. Adams?"

"No, it is not a wager," Angelica said sternly. "To offer such a wager would be no better than picking your pocket. Mrs. Adams shall judge you to be a coxcomb, Hamilton, and compared to her husband, she'll be correct."

Alexander feigned incredulity, even as he laughed. "A *coxcomb*?" he repeated. "That's a bit strong."

"It's the truth," insisted my sister, and I couldn't disagree. With his French tailor and his love of bright silks, my handsome husband always stood out amongst a crowd of more soberly dressed gentlemen, particularly the ones like Mr. Adams and Mr. Madison who dressed all in black like stout crows. Still, I could sense my sister preparing to skewer poor Mr. and Mrs. Adams further, and thought it best to divert her.

"Tell us more of Mr. Church, Angelica," I said. "Is it true that he intends to stand for Parliament?"

"Oh, my, yes," she replied, but without much of a show of enthusiasm. "That is why he purchased the property at Wendover, so he could pretend a connection to the borough. To serve his nation in Parliament has always been his greatest desire, you know."

"If he'd remained in this country," Alexander said, "he could have served in our Congress, and we'd all have been grateful for his wisdom, too."

For a moment I was sure I glimpsed sadness in her eyes, but she rallied again to sound gay. I recalled our conversation years before at The Pastures, of how we'd both wed not only our husbands, but our husbands' aspirations and fortunes as well.

"Parliament is his greatest desire," she repeated, as if striving to convince herself. "Such company we keep in London and at Down Place because of it, too. Consider this, Eliza, if you will: your dearest sister, a humble daughter of liberty, has entertained His Royal Highness the Prince of Wales in her drawing room."

"Prince or not, I'm sure he's become one more conquest for you," said Alexander. "I'm sure your powers are every bit as potent in London as they are in New York."

"You are too generous, Hamilton, too generous by half," she said, smiling winsomely. "But what of your own ambitions? Papa wrote me that your efforts to unseat the vile Clinton failed to proceed as you'd hoped."

Instantly Alexander's expression clouded, and I dreaded what he'd say. As involved as he was in the new federal government, he'd been unable to keep himself away from the election for the governor of New York, and his deep dislike of Governor Clinton had instead induced him to promote another candidate, Judge Robert Yates. Alexander had recruited his city friends to join the fray, including fellow lawyer Aaron Burr, who, though an Anti-Federalist, was a good friend to Judge Yates. Alexander had also indulged in his now-customary attacks on Clinton's record and motives through letters in the newspaper, a tactic which I pleaded with him not to choose.

I was sadly right, too, for the replies from the Clintonian factions came swiftly as more scurrilous personal attacks on my husband's character, honor, and parentage. Alexander's love of truth and his tendency to speak his thoughts on impulse made it easy for his foes to predict how best to wound him. There was even an accusation that he'd broken his vows to me, a slander that shocked and—I shall admit it—hurt me, too, even though I knew it to be false.

"Yates lost," he said bluntly. "Clinton won. I suspect betrayals in certain quarters."

"Please, Alexander," I cautioned, knowing too well what was about to follow, but he plunged ahead.

"You recall Colonel Burr, Angelica, do you not?"

My sister's brows rose with interest. "A handsome fellow, with black hair and brows. I recall him being at The Pastures to make use of Papa's books."

"After the election, Clinton offered Burr the position of state's attorney general." He paused, the kind of lingering, dramatic pause he'd perfected in the courtroom, but seldom used at home. "Burr accepted."

"Did you wish the position for yourself, then?" Angelica asked curiously.

"Not at all," he said with ripe indignation. "Nor would I ever deign to accept so much as a dry crumb offered by Clinton. But the fact remains, however, that Burr did, and turned his back on his friend Yates, and ignored his promise to me to combat Clinton. He demonstrated no loyalty to his friend, no conviction in his own proclaimed beliefs."

As was so often the case with my husband, that brief summation only hinted at his true feelings. For all his many virtues, and as a man who lived so much in the public eye, Alexander could on occassion be too quick to see slights or insults. In this case, he'd been stung by what he perceived as Colonel Burr's betrayal to the Federalist cause, and from the moment he'd learned the other attorney had accepted the position as state attorney general, what had been a congenial rivalry between Alexander and the colonel degenerated into an active suspicion and dislike that served neither gentlemen well.

"Perhaps Colonel Burr did not behave as a gentleman of honor should," Angelica admitted, running her fingers absently along the lace edging on her cuff. "But if you truly wished to have defeated

Governor Clinton, Hamilton, you should have run for the office yourself."

I gasped with dismay. For some months now, Alexander had been serving as a trusted advisor to the incoming President Washington with the expectation that he would receive an appointment in the new government, and in the meantime he'd been continuing his law practice as well. The very last thing he needed to be considering was running for governor. The governorship of New York after George Clinton finally left it would be one of the most difficult and thankless offices imaginable. I would sooner want my beloved husband to thrust his uncovered hand into a writhing nest of vipers than to become governor, but Angelica had always encouraged Alexander's ambitions, often with more enthusiasm than practical sense.

Fortunately, he only smiled. "You overestimate my popularity, *ma chère*."

"I do not," she replied staunchly, leaning toward him in her eagerness. "When the Constitution was confirmed last summer, Eliza wrote to me that the people were dancing in the streets to the tune of your name, and that there were even some who wished to change the name of the city to Hamiltoniana."

His smile widened, and I admired once again how adept my sister was at flattering gentlemen without them realizing it.

"That was here in the city," he said. "Unfortunately, there is the rest of the state to consider as well. Citizens to the north do not find me to be nearly as palatable."

Angelica nodded sagely, as if this were the wisest of conclusions, rather than simply common sense to anyone familiar with New York.

"Then you must forget them, and their petty concerns," she said. "You are meant for grander things. What a pity you are not to be the vice president in Mr. Adams's place. What marvelous things you and the president could accomplish together!"

I expected him to demur again, as he had in regard to the governorship. To my surprise, he didn't, I suppose because he liked Angelica too well to rebuff her. But he did glance briefly at me, as if to reassure me first that he'd no plans to usurp Mr. Adams.

"We could," he said, smiling. "For now I will be content to serve wherever His Excellency believes I'll be of the greatest use."

But my sister wouldn't accept this as an answer.

"Do not put me off with empty platitudes, *mon cher frère*," she persisted. "What true statesmen doesn't wish to climb to the loftiest heights of his country's Olympus?"

"In time, Angelica, all in good time," he said with good-humored patience. "New York is not Delphi, and there are no oracles here for predicting my future. Or perhaps there are in London?"

"Mr. Church shall win his borough, if that is what you mean," she said, managing to sound both blithe and bitter, an unhappy combination. "The British elections are so terribly corrupt that so long as enough money is passed about, he is guaranteed his precious seat in Parliament. It's not as it is here, not at all. Nothing is."

Abruptly she looked down at her lap and her shoulders sagged as she buried her face in her hands. Hastily I put aside my sewing and went to sit beside her on the sofa, my arm around her shoulders.

"You've had a long day," I said gently, "and a longer voyage. I cannot conceive of how weary you must be, and yet here Alexander and I have been prattling on and keeping you awake."

She raised her face and shook her head, as if to shake off the excuses I'd offered her. I'd expected her to be crying, but her eyes were dry, her mouth a tight line of self-control.

Alexander rose, and yawned. "I, for one, am thoroughly spent," he announced. "Angelica, Betsey and I are delighted to have you safely with us."

"Thank you, Hamilton," she said, standing as well in a rustle of silk. "Your kindness—yours and Eliza's—is more welcome than I can ever say."

He stepped forward to bid her good night, and she kissed him lightly on each cheek, in the French manner she'd acquired whilst living in Paris. He bowed, and then left us alone together as he went to check the locks and doors one last time before bed.

"Shall I call for your maid to help you undress?" I asked as I linked my arm through Angelica's. "Or shall we pretend we're girls again, making do for each other?"

I was glad to see that made her smile. "Dear Eliza," she said. "I should like that above all things."

Since her maid had already helped her from her traveling clothes and she now wore only her nightshift beneath the sultana, there wasn't much left for me to do but brush out her hair. When we'd been girls, she, Peggy, and I had taken turns each night brushing and plaiting one another's hair, a constant, calming ritual before prayers and bed that had always ended our days.

Now Angelica sat before me once again in a straight-backed chair, her hands folded quietly in her lap as I began to pull the pins that held the stiff, arranged curls in place. One by one I dropped them into the dish on the nearby table until her hair was free and loose. At last I began to draw the brush through her heavy hair, a deep brown like my own. It took long strokes to brush out the stickiness of the salt spray from the sea as well as the fashionable powder that her maid had dusted on this morning.

She sighed with contentment and let her head drop back as her neck relaxed with each pull of the brush. I was surprised to see gray scattered through her dark hair; she was only thirty-three, a year older than I.

"You don't have to tell me tonight if you don't wish to," I asked. "But if there is anything that either Alexander or I can do to help you, then—"

"There isn't," she said quietly, her voice leaden with melancholy. "These last years I have done my best to make England my home for the sake of John and our children, but it's a dreary place, filled with cold and chilly people, and—and it is not here."

There was nothing I could say to that. "I'm glad Mr. Church permitted you to come visit now."

"I begged," she said flatly. "I told him Mamma and Papa were unwell, and I was needed here."

"They aren't well," I said. "Papa's legs have become so bad that on his worst days he's nearly a cripple, and cannot climb the stairs without assistance, while Mamma is troubled by her lungs. You didn't lie."

"I would have done so if I'd needed to." She sighed deeply. "If it were not for my children, I do not think I would return to England at all, but remain here forever."

A dreadful thought rose unbidden. "Is that why you didn't bring the children with you? Because Mr. Church wants to make certain you'd return to him?"

She sighed again, more restlessly this time, and her folded hands twisted together into a tight knot in her lap.

"He wanted them to be safe," she said. "A long voyage is taxing on a child's constitution. Besides, Philip and Kitty are both at school now, and John and Elizabeth have their tutor and governess. I could hardly interrupt their education."

I scarcely bit back my words as I put aside the hairbrush and began to braid her hair in a single thick plait. I'd always thought Mr. Church a taciturn gentleman, but never a cruel one. Yet to deny Angelica the pleasure of bringing their children to visit their Schuyler grandparents seemed cruel indeed.

"It will all be well enough, Eliza," my sister said, as if she'd read my thoughts. "John will see that our children are well looked after. He's an excellent father that way, and a good husband, too. He loves them—and me—dearly, you know. But when I see your Hamilton, how handsome and clever and kind he is, and how happy you make each other, and how he looks at you, and you look at him . . . but no, I will not be sentimental, or maudlin. While I am here in New York, I am resolved to be content, and find pleasure in every moment, and most especially in my time with you and Hamilton."

Alexander was still awake and reading when I later joined him in bed.

"You were gone much longer than I expected," he said, closing his book to watch me. "Is your sister that unhappy?"

"She is," I said as I undressed myself, not bothering to call my maid. "She misses her children, and in her way I believe she misses Mr. Church as well. You've read her letters. Even with all her fine talk of Prince This and Lord That, she dislikes London and misses America, and wants nothing more than to live here instead."

"*Ma pauvre soeur,*" he said. "I am sorry that she didn't bring at least one of her children with her. Your parents will be disappointed she didn't."

"Mr. Church wouldn't permit it," I said, unable to keep the indignation from my voice. "She hinted that he was keeping them in England almost as hostages, to make certain she returned."

Alexander frowned. "I find that difficult to believe of him."

"You wouldn't say so if you'd seen Angelica's face," I said, sitting on the edge of the bed as I braided my own hair for the night. "I know he is the father of those children, but she is their mother, and she should be permitted to bring her children to see her family."

"Did you say that to her, Betsey?"

"No," I said, though now I wished I had. "I wanted to, but I feared it would only make her more unhappy in her situation."

"Every law in both Britain and America would claim that Church is completely within his rights," he said. "As the head of his family, it is the father who is entitled to make whatever decision he deems best for the welfare of his children."

I paused my braiding to look at him. "Even if that is completely counter to the mother's wishes?"

"The law doesn't see it that way." He tapped his fingers lightly on the cover of the book in his hand. "You'd trust me to decide the best for our children, wouldn't you?"

"Of course I would," I said. "I do. But you are not Mr. Church."

He smiled. "Nor are you Angelica."

I wished he wouldn't smile, not about this. "But according to the law, then, the only right a mother has to her child is to give it life. That isn't fair, Alexander."

"Perhaps it's not," he said patiently, "but it is the law, and I'm afraid it's your misfortune to be married to a lawyer who will tell you so, even if it pertains to a woman I regard as my sister as well as yours."

No argument with the law was ever tolerated in our house, nor, if I were honest, anywhere else. The laws weren't fair to Angelica or any other mother like her, but it could not be helped, no matter how much I wished otherwise.

I knelt beside the bed and put aside my frustration before I said my evening prayers, making sure to include an extra plea for Angelica's happiness and Mr. Church's understanding. As always, I wished that Alexander would join me, but he claimed that Sunday service was sufficient for him, and instead returned to his book until I was done.

When at last I climbed into bed beside my husband, he was

yawning as he reached out to snuff the candlestick on the table beside the bed.

He put his arm over my waist, and I moved closer to him. "You know I would never do what Angelica has done."

He grunted drowsily, clearly wishing our conversation was over so he could sleep. "In what sense, angel?"

"I would never board a ship and sail so far and be away from you and our children for months and months," I said, lowering my voice to a whisper. "I couldn't. I love you too much to be apart for so long like that."

"I know you wouldn't," he said softly. "But that's the difference between you two, isn't it? I may love Angelica as a sister, but I love you as my dearest wife."

I smiled and he kissed me in the dark, and then, finally, we slept.

On April 30, 1789, General Washington swore the most solemn of oaths to become President Washington, the first for our country. He took the oath standing on the balcony of Federal Hall, now the home of Congress, and in plain view of the thousands of people who thronged the streets nearby. Not wishing to be crushed in the crowds, Alexander, Angelica, and I instead stood on our own little balcony, and peered down Wall Street to make out what we could of the momentous event.

The new president had consulted Alexander as one of his most trusted advisors on the details of the ceremony, and so my husband could describe what we weren't able to see. The swearing of the oath was as simply done as possible, without crowns, trains, scepters, or any other of the empty trappings of royalty. Instead our new leader was clearly regarded by all as first gentleman of the country, a man of unimpeachable honor and courage chosen for his merits rather than his bloodlines. The new president even wore a plain suit of clothes for his inauguration, fashioned from cloth of American manufacture and without so much as a hint of regal ermine.

Who could not be an avid patriot on such a day? From our little balcony, we cheered as lustily as we could, and afterward together drank a toast to our new president, and to the success and prosperity of our brave new country.

Inspired perhaps by the general excitement and celebration that vibrated through New York, Angelica was able to keep true to her word to put aside her unhappiness. Although we spoke often of her children and her husband, she showed no more of the misery that she'd revealed on the first night. I didn't doubt that it remained buried deep within her breast, and it saddened me that she'd become so adept at hiding her true thoughts and sorrows, especially from those who loved her most. Still, I reveled in her company, and while her family doubtless missed her presence in London, mine in New York were delighted to have her in their midst.

It seemed as if there were some new entertainment—a ball, a supper, a patriotic play—every night in honor of the president, but the greatest of them all was the Inauguration Ball, given during the first week of May at the Assembly Rooms on Broadway, not far from our house. Like every other lady who'd been invited, I'd a new gown for the ball, and at Alexander's insistence, it was the most expensive I'd had since we'd been married. Cut from pale blue silk that shimmered by candlelight, the gown followed the newest fashion, and was so light and airy that it floated like a silken cloud around me as I walked or danced. With the gown I wore a sheer embroidered kerchief crossed over my breast and a darker blue sash at my waist, white plumes in my hair, and the gold necklace that Angelica had given me.

As had always been the case, my sister outshone me in a brilliant red dress edged with a Roman pattern of gold embroidery with a patriotic sash of red-, blue-, and white-striped silk, and the largest pearls New York had ever seen around her throat. She wore no kerchief, instead presenting her bosom framed by a daringly low neckline edged with a stiffened lace collar.

Pinned on her bodice was a brooch with a miniature portrait of Mr. Church, framed in diamond brilliants. As she explained to anyone who'd listen, she'd promised him to wear it to the ball so he could attend in painted spirit, if not in person. It was a wise thing to do, too, for there were many people acquainted with Mr. Church who wondered why she was in this country whilst he remained in England, and would be quick to taint her visit alone with slanderous speculation.

But the most stylish member of our trio was my handsome husband. If my gown had been costly, I wouldn't have been surprised if his French tailor's bill was even greater. His coat was green-striped silk, cut away at the waist in the newest style, and worn over a heavily embroidered waistcoat and close-fitting black silk breeches. He'd both the confidence and the bearing to wear such fashionable attire with elegance, and he was without doubt the most dashing gentleman in the room. I didn't doubt that he set numerous female hearts fluttering, and I was glad that the only one that mattered to him was my own.

The company at the ball was the most notable and brilliant ever assembled in our country. In addition to the president and vice president, those in attendance included the cabinet officers, most of the members of Congress, the French and Spanish ministers, and various military and civic officers, as well as the wives and daughters of these gentlemen. The ladies wore jewels and plumes in their hair, and the military gentlemen were in full dress, their chests glittering with medals and ribbons.

As souvenirs, every lady was given an ivory fan, made in Paris, that opened to reveal a likeness of Washington in profile. Every gentleman received a commemoratory sash, skillfully painted with an American eagle and embroidered with a constellation of stars spelling out the new president's initials.

The guests that we were most eager to see, however, were my sister Peggy and her husband, Stephen Van Rensselaer, down from Albany for the festivities. The grief over the deaths of their first two children had been somewhat softened by the birth of another son, Stephen, the year before, and I was glad to see that he'd helped restore much of my younger sister's former high spirits. The reunion of Peggy and Angelica was filled with tears that were both happy and sad, shared by me as well. We three sisters had been so inseparable as girls, yet husbands and circumstances had parted us for too many years.

To my considerable honor, I danced with President Washington. He recalled me warmly from the days of Morristown and New Windsor as a young acquaintance of Lady Washington's, as well as being Alexander's wife and my father's daughter. In truth, to say I danced with the new president is not quite accurate; President Washington never actually danced, but chose instead to walk through the steps of a dance. He was said to do this to preserve the dignity and gravity of his station, but I'd always suspected it was more that, being so large a man, he wasn't comfortable attempting the hops and runs required by most dances.

By contrast, my husband was never one of those gloomy men who clung to the walls at a ball, but enjoyed dancing and the gallantry that accompanied it. While I danced with numerous gentlemen, Alexander took particular care to dance often with Angelica, so that she, too, was never without a partner. They made a splendid couple, enough that others paused to watch them dance, and I enjoyed seeing my dear husband and sister so happy in each other's company.

As the evening progressed, and the celebratory wine flowed, our spirits rose, too. At one point after Angelica had completed a particularly lively jig with my husband, one of her garters came untied, and dropped to the floor beneath her skirts. Alexander noticed the fallen ribbon, and retrieved it for her.

Now, at that time, a woman's garter was regarded as an essential but intimate part of her dress, often imprinted with the shape and size of the fair limb that it embraced. As a result, garters often became tokens between lovers, and the fact that Alexander now dangled my sister's garter before her like an impudent silken worm was exactly the kind of bawdy silliness that often appeared in comic plays from London.

"I believe this is yours, *ma chère soeur?*" he said archly, holding it out to her.

She snatched the garter from him, laughing. "Even such gallant gestures, sir," she teased archly, "do not make you a Knight of the Garter."

Alexander bowed grandly before her, and, laughing all the while, Angelica tapped her palm lightly on each of his shoulders in turn as if conferring an imaginary knighthood.

But Peggy always liked to have the last word, and she did so now.

"Don't encourage him, Angelica, or he'll only expect more," she said. "Especially since the title he most desires is Gentleman of the Bedchamber."

"Peggy!" I exclaimed, startled and a little shocked by her boldness, even as I laughed with the others. It was all wine-fed foolish banter and nothing more, nor did I take any real offense from it, either. But as Peggy often did, she'd pushed the jest too far, and it was left to her husband to make some bland comment about the music to ease the awkwardness of the moment.

As I said, the entire business was done in less than a moment, and I'd forgotten all about it by the time we left for home.

But to my mortification, others were not so forgetful, nor so forgiving.

Alexander had been as good as promised a post in the cabinet in relation to finance, a deep secret that everyone in New York seemed to know, but the appointment could not be made until Congress had determined exactly how the government would function in regard to financial affairs.

In the meantime, he had involved himself in the belated selection of New York's first senators to Congress. My father was an undisputed choice for one of the seats, but Alexander had also begun promoting a good friend of his, Rufus King, over Governor Clinton's preferred candidate, Robert Livingston. That, combined with rumors of the coming appointment, meant that once again, my husband's name—or rather, a cryptic version of it with some letters replaced with asterisks that fooled no one—and reputation were publicly ridiculed in letters printed in the newspapers.

One morning Angelica and I were taking tea in our small back garden whilst my youngest son, James, was napping inside. I had my sewing, and my sister had one of the morning newspapers spread on the table to read. Always an avid reader, she devoured the New York papers with the same ferocity that Alexander did, and as we sat together, she'd read aloud items she judged to be of particular amusement or interest.

"These letters are every bit as loathsome as the ones in the London papers," she mused as she skimmed over the page. "So much venom and bile! Haven't these men anything better to do with their days than squander them composing vitriol for print above a false name?"

"I wish you'd tell that to Alexander," I said. "It's one thing to write useful essays for publication such as *The Federalist*, but too often he cannot resist wallowing into dreadful skirmishes and name-calling with Governor Clinton's followers."

She didn't answer, and I glanced up from my sewing to see her focused intently on what she was reading, her fingers pressed to her lips and her brows drawn together.

"What is it?" I asked uneasily. "What are you reading?"

She sat back in her chair, her hands spread over the paper as if covering the words could make them disappear. "Some dreadful individual who signs himself only as R. S. is accusing Hamilton of being an—an adulterer."

"Not again," I murmured unhappily, steeling myself. "Read me the pertinent part."

She took a deep breath, and read swiftly. " 'There is also a certain puffed-up Attorney of this town who would force his advices upon the State-House, even as he flaunts the Laws of good Christians & keeps a HAREM of sisters for his pleasure.' "

"Oh, Angelica," I said, appalled. Although the letter did not address my husband by name, everyone who read it in New York would know it meant Alexander, Angelica, and me, and perhaps even Peggy as well. "I'm sorry."

"No, it is I who must apologize," Angelica said. "You know I have the greatest of affections for your Hamilton, but like a sister for a brother and no more. It is so hateful for anyone to imply otherwise."

Her face was flushed with agitation, and she paused to compose herself before continuing.

"I shall arrange lodgings for myself at once," she said, "and leave this house before—"

"Hush, Angelica, I beg you," I said, as upset as she. I hated to think of how someone who'd observed the affection we shared among us had chosen to misinterpret our devotion so grossly, and twist it into something it wasn't. "You will stay nowhere but here. These falsehoods have nothing to do with you. They're only the inventions of evil men bent on spreading rumor and scandal to injure Alexander's good name."

"But surely Hamilton will see it," she protested. "This is entirely mortifying."

I sighed, dreading his reaction. "He is in court today, and may not see it," I said. "I'll speak to him when he arrives home. I'm sure he will agree that the last thing we should do is lend credence to these lies by having you move to other lodgings."

He came home promptly that evening and in a cheerful mood because his case had been ruled in his plaintiff's favor. After he'd greeted the children, I followed him into his library, and closed the door after me.

"We must talk," I said softly, not wishing to be overheard. "There is a letter in today's—"

"About the 'harem of sisters'?" he asked, shrugging out of his coat. "I saw it. I'd hoped that you wouldn't."

He seemed surprisingly even-tempered, which made me wary. "Angelica saw it first."

He winced. "I am doubly sorry for her sake as well as yours."

"I told her that we must ignore it," I said swiftly, praying that this time he'd listen. "I told her that to dignify such outrageous lies with a reply would only give them fresh life. You agree, don't you, Alexander?"

He sighed, and dropped heavily into his armchair.

"You know I don't like to let affronts like this go unnoticed," he said. "To permit a liar go free only encourages him to lie again. But when I showed it to Troup—"

"You showed this to Mr. Troup?" I asked, aghast. Robert Troup was another attorney, but more importantly, he was Alexander's oldest friend in New York. The two had shared rooms as students at King's College and had fought in the New York militia together in the earliest days of the war.

"I did," he said. "He pointed out several things that in the heat of the moment I had overlooked. The blaggard who wrote this stopped short of naming me, or even using a discernable cipher in his slander, so no offense was directly offered. Further, Troup said— and wisely, too—that since you and Angelica are included by innu-endo, I would do better to take no notice, or risk having you made targets of future attacks. For the sake of you two ladies, I must agree."

I sighed with relief so audible that he smiled. "Mr. Troup is a wise man."

"Wiser than I?" He patted his knee, and I perched upon his thigh with his arm around my waist, as if we were again courting sweethearts.

"Not at all," I said, circling my arms around his shoulders as I kissed him fondly. "But I agree that we will hold our heads high and ignore this. The next item I wish to read of you in the newspapers should be an announcement of your appointment to the cabinet."

The summer passed swiftly. Angelica was still with us, and together we found much that was entertaining in the new capital. Lady Washington had arrived to take her place as the president's wife, and Angelica and I became regular attendees of her weekly receptions at the presidential residence on Cherry Street. Although Lady Washington confided to me that she found the receptions tedious and tiring, no one who attended saw anything but the first lady of our land, as gracious as her husband was noble.

Visitors from every state crowded into these receptions, and the ladies vied with one another to be the richest in their dress. The fashion was for tall plumes worn in the hair—a fashion that Angelica whispered was required at Queen Charlotte's receptions in the royal palace in London—but that unpatriotic fact did not deter the younger ladies from striving to outdo one another with the nodding height of their plumage, every bit as silly as the birds who'd worn the same feathers first. One of these vain young ladies had the misfortune to step too closely to the candles in the chandelier overhead, unwittingly setting her headdress aflame. Only the quick action of a young gentleman preserved the lady, if not her plumes, and his fire-fighting skills made him the toast of the evening.

There were also the usual plays, dinners, and entertainments, and because my father was one of the newly elected senators, he brought my mother down from Albany to New York, and we saw them often as well. The greatest single event of the summer, however, was a splendid and moving celebration of the Fourth of July that featured many of the officers who had once served in the army under President Washington, now united as members of the Society of the Cincinnati. My husband was one of the youngest of the company, but so many others of these brave men whom I'd recalled from the war were already becoming bowed and faded with age; the sight of them gathered together touched me deeply, and made me think melancholy thoughts of the too-swift passage of time.

In our house, Angelica made herself a favorite aunt with my children, and she was never too occupied, nor too well dressed, to take one into her lap. I suspect she lavished upon them the attention that would have gone to her own children, had they been with her; mother's love is boundless that way. She and Philip, now eight, became especially close, and I only regretted that Angelica's own son Philip could not have been here as well.

Alas, that first scandalous gossip which had arisen in the spring regarding Angelica and Alexander still simmered through the city, a whisper here, a snigger there, a snide remark from ladies in a shop that I was meant to overhear. The talk distressed me, for it not only belittled my husband and my sister, but also insulted our marriage, and my constant fear was that some malicious boy at school would repeat the tales to Philip. Through it I prayed for strength and held my head high, and tried to employ the genteel serenity of Lady Washington, who had endured her share of wicked gossip in her time, as my model.

Finally, in early September, President Washington signed the bill that created the country's first Treasury Department, and a week after that Alexander was confirmed as its first secretary. It was a momentous job, the most important and difficult of all the cabinet positions, and the one with the most responsibility. Yet as young as my husband was for the post—he was only thirty-four—there was clearly no other gentleman in the entire country more perfectly suited for it. Angelica had wished us to give a celebration in his honor, but he'd no time for it, and the day after his appointment he was already at work at his desk in his new offices. I could not have been more proud of him, or of having such a husband.

But like every summer before and since, this one finally came to an end, too. The leaves fell from the trees and the winds that whipped up Wall Street from the harbor were cold with the approaching winter. It was then that Angelica came to me with a new-arrived letter from her husband in one hand, and her handkerchief in another.

"John wishes me to return at once," she said, tears streaming freely down her cheeks. "He says I have been away too long, and that our children are unwell from missing me. Oh, my poor babies!"

I'd known this day would come, that she couldn't remain with us forever, but still the impending separation devastated both Angelica and me, and Alexander as well. She arranged her passage for five days later, days that passed far too swiftly. The morning she left I was too distraught to accompany her to the dock, and our farewells at the house were awash with tears.

It fell to my husband and our oldest son to see her to the London packet. Alexander confessed that he and Philip had wept, too, as they'd stood on the Battery and watched Angelica sail from our lives, and why shouldn't they? Only God in His grace knew when we would all be reunited, or even if we were destined to meet again in this life.

While my family felt Angelica's departure sorely, to me it became a kind of grief that I could not overcome. It didn't help that Alexander's new responsibilities claimed nearly every second of his time. He often left the house without taking breakfast and did not return until late into the night, after the children were asleep. When he did arrive at home, his mind was so exhausted by numbers and decisions that he would undress and retire directly to bed, and at once fall into a deep sleep beside me. He'd nothing left for our usual conversations, nor for the affections of husband and wife.

This was to be expected, of course, given the magnitude and the importance of what he was doing for the country. I would have been the most selfish of wives to have complained.

Yet the depth of my own sorrow frightened me. I felt lost and adrift in a way I couldn't explain, not even to Alexander, or perhaps especially not to him. When I'd first fallen in love with him, I'd been in awe of his many dreams, and I'd been every bit as sure as he himself that he'd been born to achieve great things. But now that he was doing exactly that, I felt as if I'd somehow been left behind. Ever since Angelica had left, I'd felt unable to keep step with the frantic pace my husband had set for us, and worse, I began to doubt myself, and wonder if I truly possessed the strength and spirit to be his wife. Was it any wonder that I was unhappy? I'd always considered myself to be a cheerful soul, able to find joy in the most ordinary things, but this misery gripped me in its talons and would not let me go.

My parents took notice, and with growing concern Papa spoke directly to Alexander. When he gently suggested that I might wish to return to The Pastures with my mother for a few weeks, I burst into tears. I didn't want to leave him. But he insisted and finally I went, taking the younger boys and my daughter with me.

As much as I'd loved the excitement of New York City during the first year of the new government, once I was away from it I realized how the smoke and racketing of city life, the hectic pace and frantic gaiety, had all worn at me. Instead of drawing strength from Angelica, this year I'd struggled to keep pace with her, and overlooked how she'd always enjoyed society far more than I. That, too, had taken its toll upon me.

In Albany, I bundled myself in a heavy cloak and walked alone by the hour, sometimes praying aloud like some ancient pilgrim as I trudged across the snowy fields. I let the cold, clear air heal me, and I found my solace and my strength in the familiar hills and rivers of my girlhood. Most of all, I remembered who I was, and only then did the darkness and the doubts begin to slip away from my soul. I thought of how much Alexander loved me, and I him. I laughed with my children, and I played songs on my old fortepiano so they could dance around me.

I was restored. It was time to return to the city, and most of all, to my beloved Alexander.

CHAPTER 17

New York City, New York
March 1790

Even if I were to fill every one of these pages with nothing but my husband's accomplishments as secretary of treasury, I would still fall far short of listing them all. So many were launched in that first year of the new government, too.

As soon as his position was confirmed, Alexander hired a staff of nearly forty men, and instilled in them a scrupulous devotion to their combined task. He set up the department's systems of bookkeeping, accounting, and auditing. He created a customs service to bring immediate income to the government's coffers, and when it became apparent that many of the collectors of these taxes were not entirely honest in regard to reporting smugglers—long a tolerated practice—he suggested a system of guard boats to patrol the country's coastline. He advised the president on everything from finances to protocol. Because there was as yet no secretary of state, he unofficially met with a British diplomat to begin establishing an economic rapport between his country and ours.

But most of all in those first months, Alexander labored on Congress's first request, his *Report on Public Credit*. In brief, its purpose was to outline exactly how bad the country's situation was as to debt, and what steps were best taken to relieve it, and make America trusted, even by the great countries of Europe.

By the time I returned from Albany, Alexander was already

deep into writing this, and unlike his other work at the Treasury Department, it was being written at home, alone in his library.

Now I understood why he'd written to me so plaintively of how much he'd missed me when I'd been away. He wasn't accustomed to being a solitary writer. From the beginning of our marriage, I had been his sounding board, the definitive test of his writing. Pacing back and forth, he could formulate his ideas aloud to me before he wrote them down. Unlike most men, he did much of his composition beforehand, in his head or whilst speaking, and by the time his words were committed to ink and paper, his ideas were fully formed and reasoned.

From the first day I returned, I joined him in his small study in the back of the house, curled in the armchair near the fire with my sewing. After nearly ten years of listening to my husband's financial opinions and theories, I was likely as knowledgeable as the gentlemen who sat in Congress, and perhaps more so than some of the more obstinate ones. These conversations between Alexander and me had become a vitally important part of our marriage, another kind of partnership, and I realized their absence had contributed to my unhappiness last autumn.

By the time the report was done and printed into a pamphlet, it was fifty-one pages and tens of thousands of words in length. The night before it was to be read aloud to the House of Representatives, Alexander could not sleep, tossing so restlessly beside me that I could not sleep, either, which was perhaps his intention all along.

"They will find a thousand things to fault, Betsey," he said with gloomy resignation once he realized I was awake. "I know it. Half of them won't have the patience to comprehend my arguments, and the others have already made up their minds before they've heard a word."

"Your arguments are logical and concise," I said, "and your solutions are wise and necessary, as any man of intelligence will understand."

"But that's the true problem, isn't it?" he said irritably. "Much of Congress appears to consist of half-wits and pea-brains, unable to figure their own reckonings in a tavern, let alone a nation's budget."

"I know few gentlemen are as clever as you," I said, resting my palm on his chest, "but if you wish them to accept your recommendations, a little humility would not be amiss."

"A mountain of humility wouldn't help," he said, and groaned. "It will be like the old Congress all over again. They won't approve it because they've already decided they won't, from sheer perversity."

"Do not be so pessimistic, Alexander," I urged gently. "Congress nominated you to find a solution, and you have. They will criticize, and they will debate. That's why they're here. But your solution will be a weighty meal for them to swallow whole. Let them take small bites, and decide that way if it's to their taste."

He groaned again. "So long as they don't vomit the entire meal back upon my shoes."

"Even if they do, you must vow not to take offense." Lightly I tapped his chest, a kind of wifely remonstration. "Try not to take their criticisms to heart, Alexander. It is the report they will be attacking, not you."

He didn't answer, but rolled to his side to face me, shoving his hair back from his face.

"You will come tomorrow, when the report is read aloud?" he asked, betraying his anxiety. "You'll be there in the galleries?"

"You know I shall," I promised. Women were permitted to sit in the galleries of Federal Hall to observe Congress. I hadn't attended before, but I'd heard from other ladies that depending on the day and the debate, Congress could be as dull as yesterday's dishwater with senators asleep in their chairs, or as raucous as a bare-knuckles fight between sailors, with shouting and disorder. I prayed that the reception to Alexander's labors would fall somewhere between the two, and for him, I'd climb to the gallery to watch.

"I cannot stay the entire day on account of the children," I continued, "but I'll be there when it begins."

"I'll find you." He smiled, and lightly touched his fingers to my cheek. "And make certain you pray for me, my love. Given how surly the men from Virginia and the Carolinas have already been toward me, a bit of divine support would be most welcome."

I did pray for him—though I did not go so far as to wish ill upon the senators from Virginia and the Carolinas—and the next day I made my way up the narrow stairs to the gallery. I sat with several other ladies, wives of congressmen whom I'd met at Lady Washington's receptions, and just as a small flock of hens will draw together against a hazard, we formed a sufficient bastion of respectability to keep away the coarser men who'd also come upstairs to watch.

Because as secretary Alexander was a member of the executive branch of the government, he was not permitted to present his paper directly to the House, although he was seated to one side. He must have been watching the gallery, for as soon as I was settled, he looked directly toward me, and smiled.

I think that must have been the only time he smiled in Federal Hall that day, or many after that. I remained through the lengthy reading, and returned at my husband's request to hear the debates that began a week later. From them, one fact became abundantly clear: that while my husband had been occupied with the herculean task of devising this financial plan, he had also made a good many enemies.

I had suspected as much. Alexander could be charming and engaging one moment, and then with a blunt, unthinking word or two, permanently destroy all the previous good will. Honesty was both his blessing and his curse.

But to listen to endless attacks not only upon my husband's plans, but his allegiances to the country, and even his patriotism—he was several times accused of being an English sympathizer!—was more than anyone, especially he, could swallow with grace. It was difficult enough for me, sitting straight-backed in the gallery while those around me turned to look at me, eager to see how I'd respond. I didn't give them either the satisfaction or the tattle, but it wasn't easy.

Some of my husband's attackers were to be expected, men whose states had always aligned against the Federalists, but there were others who shocked me with their vehemence, the first of these being James Madison from Virginia. I'd always considered Mr. Madison, one of Alexander's fellow authors of *The Federalist*, to be among his staunchest allies, until he, too, attacked the report, calling it a betrayal of the ideals of the Revolution, and a great deal more besides. Agreeing with Mr. Madison was the other senator from Virginia, Colonel James Monroe.

The new senator was already known in New York society, for several years before he'd married a lady from our city, Miss Elizabeth Kortright. Tall and reserved in his speech, Colonel Monroe seemed content to let Mr. Madison make the most salient arguments, and then he would agree. Unfortunately, this meant that the colonel, too, like Mr. Madison, publicly agreed to disagree with my husband and scorn his report, much to Alexander's dismay.

Yet as wounded as Alexander was by the debates, he somehow managed to hold himself back from the fray, and let his supporters defend the report. For my part, I ceased attending the debates after the first three days.

"I know you wished me to go so that I might tell you what is said, Alexander," I said warmly when I told him my decision. "But as your loyal wife, I cannot sit there any longer and listen to those *simpletons* attack your beautiful report. I suppose that makes me a poor sort of Christian, unable to turn the other cheek, but I simply cannot bear it any longer."

He laughed, and somehow found the forbearance not to toss my own cautionary words to him back at me.

"My poor put-upon Betsey," he teased. "I warned you how vexing our country's congressmen can be."

But on the first of April, he wasn't laughing, and neither was I.

He came home earlier than I expected. I was sitting in the parlor on the sofa with a children's primer in my hand, and pressed close beside me was our daughter, Angelica. Now six, she already knew her alphabet, and was beginning to pick out short words, especially when helped by a picture beside them.

I looked up expectantly when I heard his voice and step in the hall, ready to praise our daughter's cleverness to him. One look at his face, however, and I knew that some trouble had just occurred.

But Angelica saw no such warning and immediately flew to her father, holding her arms up to him as she always did. He plucked her up, swinging her high to make her squeal, then set her carefully back down.

"There you are, little miss," he said, kissing her lightly on the forehead. "Off you go, for I must speak to Mamma alone."

Still she hesitated, not wanting to give up her father's company quite so fast.

"Please, Angelica," I said firmly. "Find Johanna in the kitchen, and tell her I said you may have a biscuit."

That made her leave, and Alexander shut the door after her. "I'm glad you weren't at Federal Hall this morning."

"Then pray sit and tell me why," I said, hearing the tension in his voice that was never a good sign. I patted the sofa's cushion in encouragement, but he ignored me, and instead began pacing back and forth before me, his hands clenched tightly together behind his back.

"A self-righteous representative from South Carolina named Ædanus Burke, and a man I scarcely know, decided the debate was the proper time to declare me a liar," he said, giving each word a sharpened edge. "He was called to order by another from his state, yet still he persisted, and repeated the charge more loudly, so all would hear it."

"Why on earth would he do such a thing?" I asked, shocked.

"He has taken offense from the eulogy that I offered for General Greene last Fourth of July," he said. "You heard it, Betsey. Do you recall any untruths?"

"Not at all," I said. "I remember it as a beautiful tribute to the general's memory."

"Exactly!" he exclaimed, flinging his hands out for emphasis. "But Burke now claims that by praising a northern general, I somehow insulted the militiamen of South Carolina and questioned their bravery. *That* is his empty reasoning for calling me a liar, Betsey, and such an insult to my honor is not to be borne."

"If you can't recall the slander, then I doubt anyone else will, either," I said quickly. "Please don't take it to the papers, Alexander, I beg you. If you draw attention to his foolish words, then you'll only make more people aware of them."

"I've no intention of making this public," he said. "This is between Burke and me, and will be settled between us as well. I will explain to him the consequences of his words, and what will occur if he does not offer an apology."

"What consequences?" I demanded, although I could already guess. "Alexander, please. What consequences?"

But he turned on his heel without answering, and no matter how much I pleaded with him that evening, he refused to explain further. As he bid me good-bye the next morning, he was much more agreeable, and with relief I guessed a night's sleep had brought him peace.

I'd guessed wrongly.

"I've written a short letter of explanation to Burke," he said pleasantly over our midday dinner. "If he fails to reply in an acceptable manner, then he now knows what conduct I shall expect from him, and an interview will be unavoidable."

I set my teacup down on its saucer with a clatter. Even I knew what gentlemen meant when they spoke of "an interview."

"You cannot be serious, Alexander," I said with disbelief. "You would challenge Mr. Burke to a duel over *this*? You would risk your life and the happiness of your family for *this*?"

My husband's smile was maddening. "It will not come to that if he does what he should, and apologizes."

But Mr. Burke didn't do what he should. Instead he wrote to my husband reiterating what he'd said before, but even more forcefully—a letter that Alexander showed me only because I demanded to see it.

I couldn't stand by any longer. I went immediately to my father's house to ask him to intervene.

"He cannot do this, Papa," I said with despair. "He won't listen to me. To fight a duel, to risk his life for something as *foolish* as this!"

My father lowered his chin and looked very grave.

"It's a serious insult, Eliza, and a clear insult to Hamilton's honor," he said. "Because Burke spoke as part of the debate, it's also now included in the public record."

"But if it isn't true, why does it matter?" I cried with mingled frustration and fear. "Mr. Burke is the liar, not Alexander, yet now he would risk not only his life, but the happiness and security of his family. He speaks of defending his honor, but who will defend our poor children if they are left fatherless? Oh, Papa, I cannot lose him!"

"Pray don't distress yourself, Eliza," Father said, patting my arm. "I'll speak to him."

The next evening, a group of grim-faced congressmen including my father and several of Alexander's closest friends called at our house, and closeted themselves with my husband in our parlor for a good hour. I do not know what was said, or whether they called upon Mr. Burke as well, for this was all kept from me, being a mere woman. The following day, however, Alexander received another letter from Mr. Burke. The letter conceded that he'd misheard Alexander's speech, that the so-called lie had been only words taken out of their original context, and that the entire affair was no more than a misunderstanding.

Suddenly agreeable and full of good fellowship, Alexander wrote back to accept the apology. Just like that, the whole affair was done.

"You see, Betsey, no harm was done to anyone," Alexander said to me that night, his reassurance tainted by a certain unbecoming smugness. "Burke admitted his error, his accusation was withdrawn, and my honor preserved."

"No harm, no, if you discount the fearful anxiety you caused me," I said, unwilling to be so easily mollified. "What if you'd been killed, shot dead for no reason?"

"But I wasn't," he said, trying to pull me into his arms.

"But you *could* have been," I insisted, pushing back. "Please, Alexander, for my sake and for the sake of our children, promise me that you'll never again let yourself be drawn into such insanity."

"My own dear Betsey," he said, his voice low and seductive, and this time I let him pull me close. "You must know I'd never willingly leave you, or our children."

In that moment, my steely resolve abandoned me, and I thought only of how much I'd miss him, his love, and strength if he were gone. I held him close, burrowing my face against his shoulder so I wouldn't weep.

It wasn't until the following morning that I realized how, lawyer that he was, he hadn't promised me a thing.

In addition to warmer days and sunny skies, spring brought an intriguing new gentleman to New York to join the president's cabinet as the secretary of state. A Virginian planter by birth, Thomas Jefferson was, by reputation, no stranger to me. My sister had known him well in Paris, where he'd served as the American minister to France, and to hear her lavish praises upon him, I suspected he'd been another of her conquests, or perhaps she'd been his. Doubtless not wishing to shock her provincial younger sister, as she often playfully called me, she'd never confessed to having followed the regrettable fashion of Parisian ladies and taken a lover—but if she had, I do believe Mr. Jefferson might have been her choice.

Alexander was eager to make Mr. Jefferson's acquaintance and to see what measure of gentleman he would prove to be, and so soon after he'd settled himself in his lodgings in New York, we entertained him at a supper at our house. I enjoyed giving dinners and suppers like this, one of the opportunities I had to meet the gentlemen who so filled my husband's days and conversations.

From Angelica's description, I'd expected Mr. Jefferson to be a true patrician, but my first impression was of an overgrown, gangling youth, his face spotted overall with freckles. He wore an embroidered coat of brilliant blue silk and red smallclothes, certainly the attire of a stylish French gentleman, yet he had none of a gentleman's presence or bearing. Unlike my husband, who had retained his strict military bearing, Mr. Jefferson moved as loosely as one of my children's toy puppets with string for joints, and even at table he sat lazily unbalanced with one arm flung over the back of a chair.

Still, he was a most agreeable guest and made good company at our table, and like Alexander and Angelica, clearly delighted in books and learning, sprinkling phrases in French and Latin through his speech, though he offered surprisingly few opinions of his own. Angelica had warned me that he was very particular in his food and wines, having developed exceptionally refined tastes whilst in Paris, but he was cordial enough with our more humble New York fare. He was in fact so personable that I marveled that he was reputed to be good friends with his fellow Virginians Mr. Madison and Colonel Monroe, neither of whom made amiable society. Most of all, however, I was relieved to see that Mr. Jefferson and Alexander appeared to enjoy each other's company, a fortunate convenience considering how often they'd be expected to work side by side in the government.

They soon had their opportunity. One of the most contested elements to Alexander's proposed funding bill was the assumption by the federal government of the various war debts incurred by the individual states. State taxes would therefore be lessened, but the federal government could now levy federal taxes to raise funds for the betterment of the entire country. Consolidating the thirteen debts into one seemed a logical action, but the representatives of states with lesser debt howled at what they perceived as a gross inequality. They failed to see the overall good to be gained for the country as a whole, and instead thought only of how they did not wish to be forced to pay another state's debt.

Despite Alexander's fierce lobbying for assumption, it was voted down by the House in April. In early June, the rest of the funding bill was passed, and the issue of assumption was presumed by all to be as good as dead and buried. Except, of course, by my husband, who continued to see it as an essential key to federal finances and to binding the states irrevocably together as a union, and was determined not to let it fade away.

But there was also another, equally heated question facing the congressmen: that of the location of a new capital city. No one denied that a permanent capital needed to be established and built to serve the country's needs—and likewise an interim capital decided while the permanent one was constructed—but again the northern representatives favored a site more convenient to them, in either New York or Philadelphia, while the men from the south endorsed a more centrally located placement along the Potomac River.

There was far more at stake than mere convenience, however. The winning site would be poised to become one of the great cities of the world, another London, Paris, or Rome. The value of property surrounding the new capital could soar overnight. There would be a boon in all the building trades to create the new buildings of government as well as housing for new citizens. Most of all, those who lived closed to the new capital would surely be the ones most likely to be heard by Congress, and their desires addressed more swiftly than citizens who lived at a distance.

Considering itself the front-runner, New York City had already spent substantial amounts to make the old statehouse into Federal Hall, improve other public buildings and streets, and had begun work on a new president's residence. Those in favor of the Potomac location argued that it represented an opportunity to build from scratch, without any existing impediments. It had become a rancorous stalemate, with neither side wishing to concede to the other.

As can be imagined, Alexander was in favor of New York City as the permanent capital. So was I: not only because my husband wished it, but because our home and friends were already located there, and it was also a convenient location for me to visit my family up the river at The Pastures. I'd no desire to pack up my household and children to remove south to a rented house in Philadelphia, or worse, even farther away to the shores of Virginia.

There was also another pressing reason for us to remain in New York City. I wasn't sure we could afford to live in the larger and more expensive city of Philadelphia. As soon as Alexander had accepted his appointment as secretary, he'd given over his entire law practice to his old friend Mr. Troup, not wanting there to be any hint of a conflict between his new position and his old profession.

This was admirable and honorable, yes, but it placed our little household in the same predicament that we'd before encountered when Alexander had served in the Congress of the Confederation, and later in the Constitutional Convention. We simply hadn't the funds to afford it. As perhaps the most prominent attorney in the state, Alexander had earned an excellent living, and we'd all grown accustomed to the little luxuries that his toil had made possible: the fine wines, his tailor and my mantua-maker, the small but growing collection of French and Italian prints on the walls of our parlor, the schools for our children, and the elegant furnishings in our house.

As secretary of finance, however, Alexander's income had plummeted to a mere $3,500 a year. For President Washington and the other members of his cabinet, all of whom were wealthy, older gentlemen with plantations, land, and investments that earned them substantial incomes, their government salary was inconsequential, but for us, it was all we had, and with a houseful of young children to support as well.

Yet Alexander still wished us to live with the same outward grandeur as the others, and though I felt I constantly scrambled to balance our expenses as best I could, he assured me over and over that we would be fine, and that any setbacks we suffered would be temporary. Because he claimed it was essential to his position in the cabinet, we continued to dress fashionably, attend the theater and the assembly, and entertain our friends and his associates with costly dinners and wines at our house. It remained our secret irony that the secretary of finance teetered on the edge of insolvency, but that was the uncomfortable truth of our situation, and the possibility of moving to Philadelphia kept me awake at night wondering how we'd possibly manage.

But whilst this brave new government prided itself on being a true republic, we all were learning that some things must still be accomplished in the older style of politics, with private meetings between prominent statesmen held late at night behind closed doors. One warm night late in June, I was awakened by Alexander entering our darkened bedchamber, attempting to be silent but making a poor show of it.

"What time is it, my love?" I asked sleepily, pushing myself upright against the pillows.

"Half past midnight," he said, his figure shadowy in the dark room. "But such things we've accomplished tonight, Betsey!"

"Then light a candle and tell me," I said, instantly awake, "and stop fumbling about in the dark like a clumsy thief."

"I didn't wish to wake you," he said contritely, striking a flint for a spark to light one of the candlesticks. He was still fully dressed for evening in the clothes he'd worn to dine at Mr. Jefferson's lodgings in Maiden Lane, and from the slight slur and giddiness to his voice I suspected the company—all male, and all involved in the government—had drunk a good deal of wine to ease their discussion.

"So what exactly did you accomplish tonight while good Christians were asleep?" I asked, looping my arms around my bent knees as he shed his coat and his waistcoat. "Who was in the company?"

"Jefferson, of course," he said, dropping into a chair to unbuckle his shoes and pull them off. "And Madison. Those are the ones who mattered. But listen to what we agreed, Betsey. You know how Madison and his followers refused to support assumption."

"I couldn't live in this city and not know that," I said. "But the question is done, isn't it?"

He grinned, tugging at the knot in his neck cloth to work it free. "It's done, my love, but not in the manner you're thinking. Madison has finally agreed to sway his block of nay-saying representatives to vote for a new bill with assumption at its heart. It is a wonderful compromise, Betsey. A lovely, beautiful compromise!"

He might have been half in his cups, but I was not. "Beautiful or otherwise, Alexander, a compromise implies that if Mr. Madison agreed to change his mind in this, then you must have offered something to him in turn, too."

"It does," he admitted, pulling the tails of his shirt free from his breeches before he drew it over his head in a billowing cloud of wrinkled linen. "But the sacrifice will be well worth it in the end."

"It had better be," I said. "You'll have to tell the rest of the world in the morning. You might as well tell me now."

"Yes," he said, rubbing beneath each of his arms with the bundled shirt. "In return for Madison's votes, I agreed to urge that the permanent capital shall be built on the Potomac, and the temporary one shall be Philadelphia."

"Oh, Alexander, you *didn't*!" I cried, shocked beyond measure. "You abandoned New York? You, who consider yourself a New Yorker, tossed this city's future prospects away for the sake of a bill that has already been defeated once?"

He nodded, still holding that wretched shirt in his hands.

"There are times, Betsey," he began, "when personal preference must be put aside for the good of the nation, and—"

"No," I said flatly as the magnitude of what he'd done swept over me. "This isn't a preference, Alexander. This is our home, or it was, and now I do not know how we shall be able to hold our heads up when we walk down the street."

But my thoughts were nothing compared to what my father said when he heard the news. He came directly to speak with Alexander, who, fortunately for him, was not at home, leaving me alone to receive the full brunt of Papa's ire.

"I know he is your husband, Eliza," he thundered, standing in the front hall with the door to the street still wide open behind him and my footman cowering beside it. "Until this day I have also regarded him as another son, but this—this makes me question every favorable thought that I have had of the man."

He struck his walking stick sharply on the floor with every word, no doubt imagining he was doing the same to my husband.

"Papa, please," I began, trying to take him by the arm. "It's not wise for you to upset yourself in this way."

He shook me off. "Don't coddle me, Eliza," he ordered. "You know as well as I that what your Hamilton has done to New York is nothing short of a complete betrayal to those who have supported him from the moment he washed up on the shores of our harbor."

He was far from alone in his opinion. When the House approved the Residence Act in July, officially naming both Philadelphia as the current capital and the Potomac site as the future one, New Yorkers united in their anger, and their anguish, and Alexander's part in it brought comments wherever we went. Of course, I defended him as best I could; as unhappy as I'd been (and still was) with his decision, he was my husband. And, to be honest, to those in Philadelphia and the southern states, his part in the decision was lauded.

But what was perhaps most surprising of the whole affair was Mr. Jefferson's part in it. Before the act had even been signed, he began to tell about town a curious version of that infamous dinner.

First of all, he painted a picture of having discovered Alexander walking in a disheveled and witless state in the street—which anyone who knew my fastidious husband realized would never be the case—babbling that he would soon be forced to resign. Then, Mr. Jefferson, having invited him to dine from purest pity and inviting Mr. Madison besides, next portrayed Alexander as scheming and duplicitous as he arranged the compromise. In his telling, Mr. Jefferson made himself out to be a complete innocent, a polite host without any notion of the political wickedness that he claimed rose up over his dining table.

His tale was utterly self-serving and entirely false, save for the fact that the three men had dined together at his lodgings. It changed my initial good opinion of Mr. Jefferson for the worse, as it did for Alexander, too. Behind a pleasant façade of agreeable manners and taste, the secretary of state had revealed himself to be a conniving man, not to be trusted, as well as a man jealous of my husband's greater power, accomplishment, and good favor with the president.

Despite the ultimate success of the Residence Act and the acceptance of assumption, Alexander now had not a new friend in the cabinet, but an envious rival. And although I hadn't the grasp of history that my husband possessed, even I knew that without caution and care, a rival could all too easily turn to an enemy.

Congress met for the last time in Federal Hall in New York City in August 1790, and even before then, Alexander had already leased new offices for his department in Philadelphia, and made arrangements for his staff to remove there as well. Although the Residence Act did not require the government to relocate to Philadelphia until December, he saw no reason to linger, and before long he had his department running at its usual energetic yet efficient pace that matched his own.

To avoid the unhealthy heat of late summer, I closed up our house on Wall Street and retreated with our children to Albany while Alexander arranged his new offices and lived in temporary lodgings in an inn. As can be imagined with the entire capital removing to Philadelphia, houses for rent were at a premium, and Alexander was unable to find one suitable for us and for our means until October, when at last we joined him there.

"Will it suit?" he asked after we'd walked through the still-empty rooms of the new house. The children had already run ahead out into the walled backyard, and Alexander and I stood together in the front hall, the first time we'd been alone since I'd arrived with the children earlier in the day.

"I know it's not our old house," he continued, "but will it do well enough for now?"

"It will suit us admirably," I said firmly, wanting to reassure him. The house wasn't perfect: there were sooty places above the fireplaces that made me suspect the chimneys might smoke, the stairs were steep, and the windows were smaller and the rooms darker than I liked. But on the whole, the square brick house was sturdy and solid and large enough for our five children and servants, and a good cleaning from the attic to the cellar would cure a great many of its ills. "The best part is that we'll be here together."

He smiled with relief. He glanced past me and through the open back door to see where the children were, then circled his arms around my waist and kissed me: not the dutiful kiss with which he'd greeted me when our coach had arrived, but a lasting lover's kiss to remind me of how much he'd missed me. Left breathless, I smiled up at him, and slipped my hands familiarly inside his coat and around his waist, the way I always did.

"You were away too long," he whispered. "I was a lonely man without you."

I chuckled softly, and wondered how I'd forgotten exactly how fine a man he was. He did look tired, though, with new lines of overwork around his eyes and a leanness to his waist that he could ill afford. But just as I'd soon refurbish the house to my liking, I intended to look after my husband as well, to compensate for all the late nights at his desk and too many meals that he'd eaten in a tavern while we'd been apart.

"You won't be lonely now," I teased, glancing back at the children. "I've brought you plenty of company."

"They've all grown since I've seen you last," he said wistfully, following my glance. "Philip in particular. He'll be taller than I before long."

I smiled with pride. Philip was almost nine now, so handsome a boy with his father's strong jaw and my dark hair and eyes that strangers paused to remark upon him. He might well have inherited his grandfather's height—he likely would be taller than Alexander before he was done growing—but there was already no doubt that he'd a good share of his father's brilliance, and excelled at his lessons.

"Philip couldn't have grown that much," I said. "Not since July."

"Still, we must think of sending him to a proper boys' school soon," Alexander said. "One that will prepare him for college."

"He's only eight," I protested, unwilling yet to see my firstborn sent away to board. "There's time enough."

"There's never enough time for everything," he said almost mournfully, and looked back to me. "Consider how I've become old and weary—"

"Thirty-five is scarcely old!"

"There are days when I feel as ancient as Methuselah himself," he said. "But you, however, never change, but remain the same black-eyed girl who scolded me and stole my heart."

"And you're the same undersized, earnest aide-de-camp who stole mine, too," I said softly, swaying closer to him. "At least in all the ways that matter most."

Behind us came the clatter of children's footsteps on the bare floorboards.

"Oh, no, Fanny," said Angelica with open disgust. "We can't go in here, because Mamma and Papa are *kissing*."

We laughed, and stepped apart, though Alexander continued to keep his hand at my waist as if fearing to let me go.

"I told you, Betsey, there's never enough time for everything," he said ruefully. "Never enough time at all."

CHAPTER 18

Philadelphia, Pennsylvania
January 1791

One of the advantages of the house on Third Street was its close proximity to Alexander's offices at the Treasury. It was but a short walk for him from one to the other, and as a result I could often coax him to put aside his labors, however briefly, and come home to dine with us at midday. But the nearness of the office also meant that the siren song of his work was even more difficult to resist.

I know there are many who believe my husband was driven by ambition, greed, and a lust for power, but I believe that the strongest attraction for him was the desire to create and build, and to integrate immense projects and ideas so that they prospered for the good of the whole. That was the real satisfaction for him, solving the puzzle of the government's creation, and there were days and long nights where he could no more resist solving one more problem or writing one more plan than a hardened drunkard could resist that next drink.

While I had dared to hope otherwise, the capital's move to Philadelphia made no alteration in Alexander's zeal for his office. If anything, after his initial successes in his first year, his determination seemed only to increase. He continued to develop a coastal guard to protect the revenue that came from import customs, and a post office to increase communications between the states. He proposed an excise tax on all distilled liquor (whiskey being the most popular in America at that time), instead of a tax on individuals or property that might excite memories of the loathsome British taxes of the 1760s.

But the project that most occupied him was a plan for a Bank of the United States to secure and stabilize the national economy. To his satisfaction, the bill proposing the bank's establishment found little resistance or debate in Congress, and passed easily through the Senate. Mr. Madison, now firmly an opponent of Alexander's, attempted to block the bill on grounds that it favored the north with it merchants and manufacturers over the south—his south—that relied upon slave-run plantations as well as smaller farmers. Finally the bill was passed by the Senate, and it remained only for President Washington to sign into law, a near certainty given that the president, too, realized its necessity.

But when Alexander came home in the middle of a January afternoon—never a fortuitous sign—I knew from the grimness of his expression that matters must not be going as he'd expected.

"Come walk with me, Betsey," he said with no further greeting, and I hurried to get my cloak and fur muff and told the servants to mind the children. Most often when he'd a difficult problem, he paced his library, but if the problem were more sizable, he required the length of a city street, and chose to walk outdoors. For the most challenging problems, he'd ask me to join him. It had been a long time since we'd walked together like this, and I'd no idea what to expect.

I learned before we'd taken ten steps beyond our front door.

"Jefferson is trying to convince the president to veto the banking bill," he said, his voice surprisingly even.

For once I was the indignant one.

"The dog!" I exclaimed, so loudly that he shushed me. The day was cold and gray, a weakling sort of afternoon, with dirty patches of snow still gathered in the streets, and few other people abroad, let alone in hearing. Still, he was wise to be cautious.

"I am sorry, Alexander," I said, lowering my voice. "But for Mr. Jefferson to wait until now to attempt to undermine you!"

"It's completely in Jefferson's character to do so," he said. "The man keeps his thoughts to himself behind a pretense of not caring, waits, and then strikes at the last moment."

"The *dog*," I repeated vehemently, a slight against canines, I know, but I couldn't help myself. "That great, lying, spotted *dog*."

At least that made my husband smile. "He is at that."

"Do you know his argument?" I asked. "On what grounds does he protest?"

"It's the usual one with the Virginians, although carried further," he said, beginning to walk more quickly. "He believes I am a despot in the making, traitorously in sympathy with the British, and with designs on creating an American aristocracy."

I shook my head in furious denial. "Why must they always say that of you?"

"Because a despot is an easy villain, one his Virginian voters will understand," he said. "But he also claims that the banks of Europe are the seat of all decadence and corruption, and that a single American bank would only destroy the values for which the Revolution was fought."

I gasped with righteousness, a little puff of outrage in the winter air. "How dare he say that, considering that he's an infamous coward who never once has worn a uniform to defend his country?" I demanded. "When it's common knowledge that he ran and hid in the woods rather than face Cornwallis's men?"

Alexander grunted, all the acknowledgment he'd make. We both knew I wasn't exaggerating; the charges of craven cowardice against Mr. Jefferson were entirely true. Even tiny little Mr. Madison had served in his militia, while Mr. Jefferson had spent most of the war lolling in Paris amidst the luxury he so deplored for everyone else.

"It's all part of his ideal America," Alexander said. "A simple country of self-reliant farmers in the wilderness, without banks or government."

"And nary a rainy day or failed crop, either," I said with disgust. "How easy it is for him to preach simplicity whilst he surrounds himself with rich food, French porcelain, and furnishings covered in silk velvet, and easier still to urge self-reliance when he embraces the evil of slavery, and orders his Africans about to do his every bidding."

"Oh, Betsey, my Betsey," he said fondly. "If only all the entire cabinet and Congress were as vehement in supporting the president as you are."

"I'm serious, Alexander," I said, looking up at him from inside the hood of my cloak. "He has no sense of the modern world. He believes America should be like those fanciful printed linens the French so love, sweet-faced shepherds and shepherdesses frolicking amongst the greenery. I'm *entirely* serious."

"I know you are, dearest, and I love you all the more for it," he said. "And I will be serious, too. The president has come to me for more reasons why he should sign the bill, and not heed the Virginians. I have only a few days to write my reply."

"But you already know what you'll say," I said, a little breathless from keeping pace with him.

"For the most part, yes," he said. "I've a few more arguments to work out."

I nodded, understanding, and saying no more. If he wished my opinion, he'd ask it, but for now the act of walking would serve him better. He took my nearest hand from my muff and tucked it into the crook of his arm, clearly in need of that small, silent comfort. I soon found the air to be too cold, however, and instead moved my hand from his arm to the pocket of his coat for warmth. He smiled, and patted my hand through the wool, and we walked that way, side by side and in step, the hem of my petticoat brushing over the toes of his boots.

As we walked, my thoughts were more ordinary: how best to remake over an old jacket of Philip's to fit James; remembering that Angelica's music-master was coming for her lesson tomorrow, not Thursday; and whether I'd have time this afternoon to bake a pie for supper with the last of the Albany apples stored in the cellar.

But mostly I enjoyed the time with my husband, however silent he might be, and the peace to be found from walking through the city. Although I considered myself a staunch daughter of New York, I will admit that Philadelphia had much to recommend it as a capital. Unlike New York, with its maze of crooked streets crowded into the narrow tip of its island, Philadelphia had been arranged from its inception into a tidy grid of streets named after trees from east to west, and numbers from north to south, making it convenient for both residents and visitors.

In the seven years since Alexander, Philip, and I had first lived here, the city had changed and prospered, with every last reminder of the war wiped away. But then, I thought wryly, the same could be said of Alexander and me, too, couldn't it?

When we finally returned to our house, Alexander went immediately (and silently) to his library and began writing his defense. He had promised it to the president on Wednesday morning, and late Tuesday evening he summoned me again to help him take down his draft and write out a fair copy. We toiled together through most of the night, but when the sun rose, he had his defense ready to present, all forty neatly written pages of it in my sloping hand.

The president read it, accepted all my husband's arguments, and signed the bill into law. Alexander had once again achieved another goal, and the country would have its first national bank.

And the rift between Alexander and Mr. Jefferson widened, and grew deeper still.

But while my husband had won, in March my father lost in a most shocking way. Running for reelection for his seat in the Senate, he was upset by a man who possessed none of my father's wisdom, his loyalty, or most of all, his honor.

Alexander was furious, and convinced that the usurper had been supported by Governor Clinton as another way to attack my husband through his family. This alliance became even more disturbing when Alexander learned that both Mr. Jefferson and Colonel Monroe had made a special journey to New York to meet with the new senator, and, it was rumored, to plot together the downfall of the secretary of the treasury.

The man who defeated my father and became the new senator from New York was Aaron Burr.

While Philadelphia was an agreeable city three seasons of the year, it became intolerable in the summer. Though often extreme, the heat alone was not the reason that most everyone who could afford another residence in the country fled the city in the months of July through September. The summer brought fevers, and Philadelphia in particular had become notorious for some of the worst outbreaks of yellow fever in the country, killing people old and young by the dozens.

From the beginning of our tenure there, Alexander and I had decided that while he must remain for work, I would leave with the children during the most dangerous season, and take them to The Pastures. Not only would they be safer there in the country air, but it was also an unspoken way for us to economize. Alexander still refused any financial help from my father, but he wasn't above letting my parents feed his family while they visited, a not inconsiderable expense.

This year, too, I felt it imperative that I visit my father, who was chagrined and in low spirits from having lost his seat in the Senate. I had grown accustomed to having him nearby whenever Congress had been in session, first in New York and then in Philadelphia, and I sorely missed his presence.

Though I was loath to admit it, I was also anticipating a sojourn in the country for myself. Though my duties as the wife of the secretary of the treasury were not nearly so onerous as my husband's, I was expected to entertain not only his various friends within Congress, but also general supporters of the president. The creation of the first bank and the flurry of financial confusion that followed meant that Alexander needed every ally that could be mustered, and I'd been willing to do my part.

To be sure, I enjoyed helping him in this way, but I won't deny that it wasn't inconsiderable work, not the least of which was keeping a pleasant smile for all who entered our house. Lady Washington had taught me well. The wives of statesmen must mingle and charm, and through their conversations more statesmanship is accomplished than perhaps their husbands realize.

It was a curious coincidence—or perhaps not, given their unpleasant personalities—that neither Mr. Jefferson, a widower, nor Mr. Madison, a confirmed bachelor, had a wife in the city to represent their interests. At least Mr. Adams, another who considered my husband objectionable, had brought his wife to Philadelphia, and while I found Mrs. Adams daunting, we were more agreeable to each other than our husbands ever were, which I hope in turn eased the business between the gentlemen. (And yes, I heard from others that Mrs. Adams did in fact believe my Alexander to be a coxcomb and worse, exactly as my sister had predicted; although Mrs. Adams herself had the good grace not to say it to my face.)

But though I wasn't as exhausted as Lady Washington—who so loathed her official responsibilities that she referred to herself as the "first prisoner of the state" rather than first lady—this degree of social gaiety was undeniably tiring, and I welcomed the excuse to put it aside for the summer. I was determined not to slip into the same private misery that had plagued me before, and returning to The Pastures with my children seemed the best way to do so.

I also wondered privately if the hectic pace of our lives was responsible for my not conceiving another child. I had been breeding regularly since Philip was born, but now James Alexander was three, and there'd been no sign of another babe to follow him. I was only thirty-four. If it were God's will that we would be blessed with four children and no more, then I would be content, but I often caught myself thinking of a new baby, and prayed my days of childbearing weren't quite done yet. I also wished that Alexander could join us in Albany, for he, too, was in sore need of a respite, and I hated to picture him alone as any other bachelor for the summer in our large, echoing house.

One evening in late June, shortly before I was to leave for The Pastures, we'd one last gathering of our closest friends. As one of the ladies played for us, a maidservant came to where Alexander and I were sitting, and whispered that a woman had asked for Colonel Hamilton, and was even now waiting in the front hall. Because she'd offered no card, I was skeptical, thinking her to be some manner of trades-woman. When the maid continued, however, saying the woman was weeping and in distress, my reserve melted, and I thought only of going to assist the poor creature. But as I rose, my dear husband, ever thoughtful, said that I shouldn't trouble myself, but instead remain with our guests. Since the woman had requested him by name, he would see her, and return as quickly as he could.

He left, and was gone perhaps a quarter of an hour. Later, after our guests had departed, he told me the woman's sad history.

"The poor woman was beside herself," he said. "Her husband has abandoned her for another, and left her quite destitute and friendless here in Philadelphia."

"How dreadful!" I said, commiserating. "How wicked and thoughtless a man he must be!"

"Indeed," said Alexander. "What manner of man would treat his wife so? Being originally from New York herself, she appealed to me in desperation, and quite threw herself upon my charity with the hope that I might assist her return to that city, and her friends there."

"I trust that you offered to arrange passage for her." Because my husband was known for his charity, he was often approached like this, but as a lawyer, he was also wise enough to separate those in true need from others who wished only his money. "She shouldn't be forced to linger here any longer than is necessary."

"I did make that offer, yes," he said. "We agreed to meet again once she had consulted her friends."

"Then you did your best to relieve her suffering," I said with approval. "What a pitiful story! I hope that this is not the last we hear of her. A city like Philadelphia can be a dangerous place for a desperate woman."

"She's a pretty young thing, too," he said. "I advised her to take care and to trust no one, from fear she'll come to harm. Her name was Mrs. Reynolds, in the event she should ever call here again while I am out."

I nodded. At the time, I took no notice of the fact that Mrs. Reynolds being a young, pretty woman in distress might have increased Alexander's desire to assist her. I'd seen it before, and I'd likely see it again, for his gallantry where women were concerned hadn't diminished over time. I'd always found his gallantry endearing, for as his wife, I received the lion's share of it myself. I was proud of how my husband still treated me as an ardent lover would, and I couldn't think of another woman of my age and acquaintance who could say the same.

Soon afterwards I left by coach with my brood of five children. Alexander rode with us as far as Elizabethtown, bidding us the most sorrowful of farewells from there. Yet the carefree sojourn that I'd expected to find in Albany was not to be. Our youngest son, little James, began to feel unwell just beyond New York City, and by the time we reached The Pastures, he was feverish and dull-eyed and listless, lying curled against me on the seat of the coach.

We sent at once for Dr. Stringer, our family's physician in Albany, with my fear rising by the moment for my little one's life. I recalled all too well the tragedy that had struck my sister Peggy's family. But to my relief, Dr. Stringer immediately eliminated both yellow and scarlet fevers as the cause of the indisposition, but beyond that he could not determine the exact nature of the fever.

I worried that the other children would become ill, too, with all of us having traveled together in close company, and poor little James was isolated in my room with only me to tend him. I carefully followed all of Dr. Stringer's remedies, from keeping James snug in a flannel waistcoat and dosing him regularly with barley water and rhubarb elixir, yet still he did not improve.

Of course, I'd written to Alexander immediately to let him know of James's illness, and he'd written directly, his fear for our son as desperate as my own. Of all our children, James was the only one to favor Alexander's coloring, with the same rosy cheeks, blue-green eyes, and red-gold curls, and perhaps because of that he'd a special place in my husband's heart.

If he'd not been so embroiled in the business of the new bank, I'm sure my husband would have come to James's bedside himself. As it was, he wrote every day begging for fresh news of his darling boy. As a young man, he'd considered for a time studying medicine, and still from interest read widely in medical journals. From these, he'd several suggestions for treating the fever that I shared with Dr. Stringer, and when James failed to improve, we did turn to Jesuits' bark, as Alexander had recommended.

Still my little one grew no better, though likewise he grew no worse, but as his mother I would have traded my own health to have his restored. I sat with him by the hour, bathing his small body with cool water and singing softly to quiet his restlessness. He was constantly in my prayers, and I worried guiltily that by longing for another baby, I'd somehow caused my little James's illness.

Finally, in late August, the fever began to subside, and my poor little boy began to be more himself. His illness had taken much from me, however, and when Alexander urged me to remain with my parents longer than I'd originally planned, I reluctantly agreed, lingering in Albany until the first week of September.

Besides, Alexander had another surprise waiting for me. He'd decided we required a larger house, and had found another, grander home for us in the same neighborhood in which we lived now. While we were away, he was having all the rooms painted, and further, having a stable sufficiently large for a carriage and six horses built on the property. I supposed he judged us now grand enough to keep a carriage, though given our finances, I did wonder how it was possible.

In addition, in November we took our son Philip, now ten, to board and study with the Reverend William Frazer, the Episcopal rector of St. Michael's Church in Trenton, in New Jersey. Reverend Frazer had an excellent reputation for preparing young gentlemen for admission to college, and from the beginning he and Philip had a mutual regard conducive to our son's swift progress. We left him with a sizable stock of books and sheaves of paper for compositions, a sufficiency of new clothes (he outgrew things so quickly!), and a basket filled with the small lemon cakes that I knew he'd always loved so well—everything he'd need to prosper in his studies.

All this I knew, and applauded. Yet as Alexander and I said our final farewells to Philip in the small rectory parlor, I still couldn't keep from reaching to smooth our son's errant dark curls, and smooth his collar, and then draw him close to hold one more, one last time. He stood stiff and awkward in my embrace, wanting to be manly, and yet at the very last he'd flung his arms around me and hugged me tight with the same fierce abandon he always had.

"I cannot believe we've left our boy behind, Alexander," I said, still twisting to look back at the rectory as our carriage drove away. "My own sweet Philip!"

"We haven't left him, Betsey," said Alexander, his own voice tinged with melancholy, too. "He's left us. It's the way of the world, you know."

"I do know," I said, blowing my nose yet again. "But he was our first. I still recall him as a tiny, helpless infant, born so soon after Yorktown."

"And now he's an independent young fellow, eager to begin his life without us trailing after him," he said softly. "At his age I'd all the responsibilities of a grown man, but this seems to have happened in the blink of an eye."

I placed my hand over his, thinking exactly the same. While I'd been tending to James in Albany, Alexander himself had been unwell, though he hadn't confessed it to me because he hadn't wanted me to worry. I was worrying now, however. He'd an old ailment of the kidneys, born from his days sleeping out of doors in the cold as a soldier, that often plagued him in the fall. It wasn't so bad that he'd paused in his work; instead in fact he'd lately burdened himself further, to the point that I wondered if at last he'd accepted more responsibilities than he could reasonably answer.

Although he still stood straight as a ramrod, lean and handsome and younger in appearance then most men his age, I also thought he seemed more preoccupied, more closeted away in his own thoughts. In the past, he'd always shared his worries with me, but now I felt there were things he was holding back, things he wasn't confiding as he once would have done, and it saddened me.

Thus one year ended, and another began. I'd always liked the New Year. When I'd been a girl, there had been a large party at The Pastures and all of us children had been permitted to stay downstairs until midnight. Then, as the tall clock in the parlor chimed twelve times, we had all trooped outside, where Papa and the other men at the party had shouted and fired their guns to chase away the old year and salute the new one. It had been wildly exciting, hopping up and down to keep warm on a cold, star-filled night as the gunshots had rung out over the snowy fields.

Although this year we weren't in Albany for the holiday season, I still clung to that notion of the new year bringing a new beginning. Yet although Alexander and I celebrated in Philadelphia with our family and friends and drank merry toasts to President Washington to welcome in 1792, the new year soon shed any semblance of hope or good cheer.

In fact, just as I look back and recall the first two years of President Washington's first term as a time of optimism and accomplishment, of great things said and achieved for the betterment of our country, I remember the last two years of that same term as a dreary muddle of recrimination, backbiting, and public name-calling.

And despite how I wished it were otherwise, my husband was in the very thick of it.

This is not to say that he and his department did not continue to be the most productive member of the entire government. The measures that he'd set in motion in the first two years—from the cutters that now guarded our coasts, to the new coinage, to the system of a national bank—all had proved so successful that the country as a whole was running more efficiently and more prosperously than anyone had expected. Alexander continued to implement and refine what he'd already created as well as expand his interests to include the development of textile mills in New Jersey and other manufactories with the hope of one day rivaling England.

But the rivalry between Alexander and Mr. Jefferson had sunk to bitter hatred. It was not simply that they disagreed on nearly everything, which they did. It was that each had come to believe the other stood for ideas and theories that would destroy the country. As a Federalist, Alexander could not tolerate anything that Mr. Jefferson, a Democratic-Republican, stood for. Each judged the other to be a dangerous zealot, aspiring to seize control of the country. Each believed the other already had too much power, and too many followers who accepted and trusted the false doctrine. And each believed the other influenced the president to an excessive degree.

Nor were their quarrels confined to the offices of state. Far from it. To hear Alexander tell it, Mr. Jefferson dared to begin his scathing attacks against Alexander even when they were in cabinet sessions led by President Washington. I was appalled to learn that matters became so ill-humored between them that the president himself had been forced to order them to stop their argument, as if they were a pair of squabbling children instead of two grown, intelligent men holding distinguished government positions.

"To force the president to intervene between you two is dreadful, Alexander," I said, thoroughly shocked when he told me of their latest confrontation one evening as we sat together in the parlor. "You should at least show him the respect due to him as your former general. There was a time when you would have quaked if he'd so much as glanced at you with disapproval, and now you openly defy his wishes in his presence."

"It's not my doing, Betsey," he said, surprised and a bit wounded that I hadn't taken his side. "If Jefferson weren't so determined to utter his nonsense without provocation, then I wouldn't need to defend myself."

"There shouldn't be any need for either provoking or defending," I said, feeling as if I truly were addressing four-year-old James instead of my husband. "Not in a cabinet meeting. Even if Mr. Jefferson says something untoward, can't you ignore him, and concentrate on the general discussion instead?"

He sighed, as much as saying that I didn't understand, and looked back down at the book he'd been reading.

Perhaps I should have let him have his peace, and not persisted. But each time I saw President Washington in company, I was startled by how much he'd aged in these past two years. Gone was the towering, intimidating commander I remembered from Morristown. He was sixty now, but appeared far older, and visibly frail. Whilst in office, he had suffered several serious illnesses that would likely have killed a weaker man. His face was pale and blotchy and his eyes sunken and guarded, and the false teeth that we all knew he wore forced him to perpetually clench his jaw to keep them in place. Lady Washington had told me that all her husband wished to do was retire to Mount Vernon and never give another thought to politics, and whenever I heard Alexander describe these pugnacious cabinet meetings, I understood why.

I put aside my handwork, and came to sit close beside my husband.

"Please listen to me, my dearest," I said softly, touching his cheek to distract him from his book. "I know it's your nature to defend yourself and your honor, but you will be the greater gentleman if you can even once take no notice of Mr. Jefferson's barbs. I'm sure the president will be most grateful if you do."

He glanced up at me, and sighed heavily.

"For me, then," I said, playing my last card. "For my peace, and for the sake our next child."

Shamelessly I placed my hand on the small swell of my belly. To our great delight, I was finally with child again, and I didn't doubt that all the antagonism toward Mr. Jefferson that Alexander brought with him could well have ill effects on the baby.

At once he took my hand, and kissed it.

"My own girl," he said contritely. "You are right, of course, in your infinite wisdom. The general does deserve better, as do you. Because you have asked, I shall make every effort to control the warmth of my temper."

I smiled, and silently prayed that he would at least try.

But if he did, his resolution did not last. Less than a week later, he couldn't wait to tell me how at the latest cabinet meeting he'd completely confounded Mr. Jefferson by speaking for nearly an hour without stopping, which must have been a trial to everyone else in the meeting, too. It seemed as if now the entire government was aware of the acrimony between the two men. The other wives of congressmen freely offered their commiseration to me, and hostesses became leery of inviting both us and Mr. Jefferson to the same suppers, fearing an out-and-out battle royal in their dining rooms.

The only joyful event that came of that summer was the arrival of our fourth son in August. The birth was an easy one for me, and likewise the baby himself proved of an easy, mild disposition, disproving all my fears to the contrary. We named him John Church Hamilton, after Angelica's husband, and she and Mr. Church returned the favor by calling their own new son, born soon after ours, Alexander Hamilton Church.

By the end of the year, the results of the second presidential election were confirmed, and once again General Washington was elected president, with Mr. Adams from Massachusetts again his vice president. Although this was good news in general for Alexander, the Federalists had lost seats in Congress, and the Democratic-Republicans who'd replaced them were eager for a fight, and alas, eager to see my husband deposed.

Rumors that Alexander had inappropriately used foreign loans to pay national debt became so common that the House asked Alexander to present a full accounting, with detailed reports of all the Treasury Department's accounts. Of course, the rumors were unfounded, and fed by Mr. Jefferson, but still Alexander was forced to answer them. He did, in vast detail, and proved his innocence.

Still determined to see my husband discredited and his career destroyed, Mr. Jefferson encouraged his minions in Congress to file resolutions censuring his behavior, and requesting that the president remove him from the cabinet. These, too, were soundly voted down by Congress, and my Alexander's reputation was vindicated and restored to its usual shining brilliance.

But the vitriol soon spilled over once again into the newspapers, where it became appallingly public. While Mr. Jefferson often had others write on his behalf—including his fellow Virginians, James Monroe and James Madison—Alexander was his own best defender, and took an almost unseemly pleasure in doing so. His work appeared so often on the pages of the Federalist-inclined *Gazette of the United States* that he might as well have been an editor himself, countering every word the Democratic-Republicans printed in Mr. Jefferson's newspaper of choice, the *National Gazette*.

On the printed page, Alexander was in his very element, dashing off letter after letter over various names borrowed from the ancients. Whenever he worked late in his study, I came to know from how fast his pen was scratching across the paper when he was writing an ordinary letter, and when he was composing yet another screed against the Democratic-Republicans.

I thought wistfully back to the days of *The Federalist*, when he'd used his argumentative powers toward a productive purpose, days that now seemed so long ago. At least his only weapons were a quill and ink, and he and Mr. Jefferson had never launched into the dangerous, posturing talk of duels of honor.

The news from France of the deposition of their king added another fresh layer to the quarrel. While most Americans applauded the French for pursuing their own liberty and freedom from royalty much as we had done, Mr. Jefferson was avid in his admiration, believing that America should throw all its support behind the new French government. And as usual, Alexander preached caution, especially once war was declared between Great Britain and France, and fortunately, President Washington agreed with him. The American states were finally finding their own footing, and the last thing anyone wished was for us to be drawn into a ruinous war between France and Britain—anyone, that is, except Mr. Jefferson.

Yet as contentious as the politics in our government had become, all of it paled beside the calamity that struck Philadelphia in the late summer of 1793.

Instead of having me travel to The Pastures with the children for the warmer months, Alexander had taken a summer residence for us a short drive from the city. Called Fair Hill, it became our pleasant retreat, and I was especially happy that Alexander could relax here with me and the children, and have some respite from his near-constant labors as well as from Mr. Jefferson.

We were especially grateful for Fair Hill as the summer's heat worsened. After a spring filled with rain, the summer proved dry and wickedly hot, and even the children were content to lie idle in the shade during the worst heat of the day. The weather was so taxing that Alexander brought back stories from the city of dozens of poor people dying from the heat, especially those who lived in the crowded lodgings near the docks or toiled in the hot sun for their livings.

But soon the news he brought to us grew much more serious. The people had died not from the heat, but from yellow fever, and soon it wasn't only poor people who were taken ill. Alexander described scenes that were all too familiar to him from his childhood: of carts that passed each morning to collect the bodies of the dead, of warning placards tacked to the door of every house where someone had sickened, of a desolate city of deserted streets and empty shops.

He'd heard that people were dying at the rate of twenty a day, and I begged him not to return to town, but to stay with us where he'd be safe. When clerks in his office began to fall ill at their desks, he finally relented, and remained with us at Fair Hill. I thanked God for His Mercy, relieved that my little family was safe together.

But on the second night I was awakened to the sound of Alexander retching in the chamber pot. I found him sprawled on the floor, too weak to climb back into bed, and with the chamber pot half-filled with noxious vomit beside him.

"Here, my dear," I said, crouching down beside him. "Let me help you back to bed."

He shook his head. "Have the children taken at once away from here, and next door," he ordered, his voice a rough rasp. Even by the moonlight I could see his face was sheened with sweat and his nightshirt clung damply to his body. "Don't touch them or kiss them yourself. Then send for Dr. Stevens."

"Not Dr. Rush?" I asked anxiously. Dr. Benjamin Rush was the most respected physician in the city, and the one fearlessly treating the most patients with the fever.

"Dr. Stevens," he insisted, and then bent to vomit again.

Terrified, I summoned servants at once to do as he'd bid, carefully issuing my orders at a distance from them. I could hear my poor children awakened from their sleep, weeping at the sad news and crying for me. I held firm and kept away from them, as Alexander had told me to do, even as it broke my heart. Then I rushed back to Alexander, staying with him as we waited for the doctor.

I'd mercifully never encountered yellow fever, but I'd heard enough not only to be able to recognize the signs in my poor husband, but also to know how the odds for his survival were not in his favor. Even Dr. Rush, who employed the most modern and aggressive treatments of bleeding and purges through enemas, had had limited success bringing patients through the fever.

"I wish you'd let me summon Dr. Rush," I said softly as I sat beside him, changing the cool, damp cloth I'd placed on his forehead. Daylight was slowly beginning to show through the curtains, and though Alexander had ceased vomiting, he was sweating profusely, his breathing shallow.

"I trust Stevens more," he said without opening his eyes. "We knew each other as boys on St. Croix."

"You did?" I asked, surprised. Dr. Stevens was new to Philadelphia, having recently married a woman from the city, and though Alexander had mentioned him, I hadn't realized their acquaintance was so old.

"He'll have more experience with yellow fever than Rush," he said raggedly. "Besides, Rush is one of Jefferson's followers, and he'll kill me if given the chance."

"Oh, hush, Alexander, not now," I said, appalled that he'd mention politics now.

"I was teasing you, my love." He smiled, a ghastly grin, and opened his eyes, squinting painfully at the light from the windows. I gasped; I couldn't help it. The whites of his eyes were bright red, made all the more shocking in contrast with his pale irises.

"Am I that horrid to gaze upon, Betsey?" he asked, and though I knew he was teasing me still, I fought back my tears. I couldn't lose him; I couldn't.

"You will recover, Alexander," I ordered fiercely. "You will *not* die."

He smiled again, his eyes drifting shut. "I won't," he said faintly. "Not to oblige Jefferson."

By the time Dr. Stevens arrived, I couldn't tell if my husband were unconscious, or sleeping. The doctor immediately began his treatment: a cold bath, Peruvian bark, and brandy with burned cinnamon, and a dose of laudanum at nightfall. There were no traditional purges, no blood-letting, which made me uneasy, but if Alexander trusted this physician, then I must as well.

"How do you fare yourself, Mrs. Hamilton?" he asked me as soon as Alexander was back in his bed. He stared at me closely, doubtless looking for signs of the disease. "In nearly all cases of a husband taken ill, his wife is sure to follow."

I swore that I felt perfectly well, and determined to nurse my husband myself. That afternoon, I stood at the open window, and waved and called across the yard to our children to reassure them, and tell them their papa and I loved them. In this same way, I arranged for friends to remove our children from the area entirely, and find sanctuary at The Pastures. But three days later, I was dizzy with a grievous headache, and before long I, too, began retching.

When Dr. Stevens came to call upon Alexander, he could now count me as his patient as well. I'd never been so ill, passing in and out of consciousness and suffering from outrageous fever-dreams and deliria. But Alexander's faith in his old friend was well placed. My husband recovered first, in a mere five days, and I soon after.

After several more days to restore our strength, our one goal was to travel to Albany to retrieve our children, and reassure ourselves that they'd escaped the fever. But our journey north proved a difficult and taxing one. The entire coast was terrified of the epidemic, and so many people had fled Philadelphia only to subsequently die that no taverns would admit Alexander and me once they learned who we were, fearing that we'd carry the contagion.

We weren't the only ones, either. Refugees from Philadelphia crowded the roads, stopping to sleep beneath trees and in open fields because they'd nowhere else to go, only to be chased away from those modest shelters by farmers who were likewise frightened of the fever. The entries to New York City were blocked to us as well, and even the ferries denied us passage. It didn't matter that Alexander was the secretary of the treasury, or that we carried letters from Dr. Stevens swearing that we'd been cured. We were pariahs, and no one wanted anything to do with us, our servants, our carriage, or even our luggage.

Even at Albany, within sight of our destination, we were forbidden by an edict from the mayor of Albany from crossing the river. I wept to think my babies were so close and yet denied to me, and forlornly I paced back and forth along the river's edge as I longed for some way across. It took all of my father's persuasive skills before we were finally permitted to cross, and at last be reunited with our children. Mercifully, not a one of them had contracted the disease, and our reunion was sweet indeed.

We returned to Philadelphia slowly. Although Alexander appeared fully restored to health, he found his mind had been left uncertain by the fever, and occasionally confused. Dr. Stevens assured him that this was not a lasting consequence and would pass, but it was reason enough for him to take his time before returning to his duties.

But as grim as the year had been, it did close with fortuitous news. Declaring himself sick of Philadelphia politics and their shameless corruption (of course meaning Alexander), Thomas Jefferson resigned from his post as secretary of state, and retreated to his home at Monticello.

CHAPTER 19

Philadelphia, Pennsylvania
May 1794

"Perhaps you should play your piece one more time, Angelica," I said, standing in the doorway to the parlor to listen as my daughter practiced. "You'll want to be prepared if you're going to play for our guests tonight."

"Yes, Mamma," she said without turning back to look at me. She consciously straightened her back and took a deep breath, the way her music-master had taught her, and then began the song yet again. "I promise it will be *perfect.*"

Angelica was only nine, yet she so loved music and playing that I never had to urge her to practice. To be sure, the new piano— now the centerpiece of our parlor—would inspire anyone. Alexander had charged my sister Angelica to find the best possible instrument in London for a young lady, and she'd happily obliged, sending an elegant rosewood instrument inlaid with scrolling vines that was as lovely in appearance as it was sweet in sound. All of our children, including Fanny Antill, had been given music lessons, but only Angelica had true talent. She'd always been a quiet child, small and dainty, and in our house filled with noisy boys, she'd found both her voice and her retreat in music.

I smiled as I listened, touched by her solemn determination, and remembering how as a girl, I, too, had wanted my pieces to be perfect before I performed for my parents' guests. Angelica was already dressed for our gathering in a white muslin dress with short puffed sleeves, and the ends of her pink silk sash trailed down over the piano bench. Her dark hair was knotted high on her head, although little wisps had already begun to escape as she played.

I turned as Alexander came down the stairs, and I pressed my finger over my lips so he wouldn't interrupt Angelica's playing. He smiled, and joined me to listen, and when our daughter finished, he applauded loudly. She turned and smiled shyly, blushing with pleasure.

"*Bien fait, ma chère fille,*" he said. "*Bien fait en effet.*"

"Thank you, Papa," she said, sliding from the bench to join us. "I wanted to learn another but—"

"*En français, Angelique, en français,*" he said mildly, smiling as he corrected her. "*C'est la règle pour ce soir, oui?*"

She smiled, and curtseyed prettily. "*Oui, Papa.*"

I smiled, too, for though I'd never learned to speak French properly myself, I'd heard enough from Alexander over the years to understand much of it. He'd reminded Angelica (who, like our older sons, was learning the language at their father's insistence) that tonight she was to speak only French as best she could. This was no mere display of genteel accomplishment, but a special consideration to our guests, one that I wished I could do as well.

I was certain our guests would appreciate it. Philadelphia had become a haven for French persons fleeing the Revolution in Paris— *émigrés*, they were called—and we were entertaining a dozen of them at our home tonight, as we tried to do at least once a week.

Like all good Federalists, Alexander and I had no sympathy for the barbaric Jacobins who were destroying France in the name of revolution, or the rule of the vengeful, violent mob with its guillotine. I couldn't begin to imagine the horrors that many of these *émigrés* must have witnessed. Some had belonged to the highest ranks of French society and were known to my sister Angelica and Mr. Church from their time in Paris, and they sent these poor souls to us in Philadelphia, knowing that my husband not only could help ease their arrival, but also spoke their language.

In their haste to escape, many of the *émigrés* had been forced to leave their belongings behind, and they arrived on our shores nearly destitute. Once-grand ladies who had attended the martyred French queen now stitched men's shirts, and former noblemen were reduced to teaching American children how to dance. To me the saddest were the new widows with children, often sent away as a last gesture of love by fathers who were later executed on the guillotine before the howling mob. The plight of these ladies grieved both Alexander and me deeply, and while I collected clothing and food, he contributed with his usual generosity to their welfare.

There was no such sympathy to be found among the Democratic-Republicans. Alexander had predicted that although Mr. Jefferson had left his post and the capital, he would still exert considerable influence on his party, and that prediction was completely accurate. From distant Monticello, he let it be known that he found no fault with the bloody reign of Madame Guillotine, and in fact encouraged it as a necessary purge of corruption. He dismissed the memory of how our own revolution would not have succeeded without the assistance of the old regime of King Louis or from nobleman like the Marquis de Lafayette, and instead pressed to make alliances with the bloodthirsty Jacobins.

As was usual with Mr. Jefferson, such blunt and wrongful thinking could only put America herself in peril. When the excesses of revolution forced Great Britain into a war with France, President Washington was wisely adamant that our country remain neutral, and refused to let us be drawn into favoring one side only to anger the other. Our country was still too fragile and without either a standing army or a navy to engage in a war. As Alexander urged, too, peace was the only course that made sense. To this end, the president had sent John Jay as an envoy to Britain, and James Madison as ambassador to France.

Briefly Alexander himself had been considered for the post in London, a possibility that had excited me no end. Angelica and I had often dreamed of such a reunion, imagining us together with our families in cosmopolitan London. I hadn't seen my sister in nearly five years. Her letters made little secret of how being the wife of a member of Parliament held no pleasure for her and how much she envied me being wed to the chancellor of the exchequer (playfully using the English term for Alexander's position), and we both longed for the day when our husbands' lives might bring us back together. Alas for our giddy dreams: the president finally decided that my husband was too important to him and to the government here in Philadelphia, and could not be spared to go abroad.

Most likely he couldn't. As disappointed as I was (and my sister was devastated), my husband's talents were so varied, and spread so thin over so many different areas within the government, that his absence could well have been detrimental to the running of the entire machine of state. The Democratic-Republicans complained incessantly of how Alexander wielded too much control and made too many decisions for any single man, but I doubted they'd any true notion of exactly how many demands were placed upon his capable shoulders every day.

And yet he wouldn't have wished it otherwise. Not only had he become indispensable to the president, but through his ability and relentlessly hard work, he had made himself the second most powerful man in the country.

I couldn't miss the strain of this enormous responsibility. There were new lines carved deep around his eyes, and his hair was beginning to thin and creep higher on his forehead. He worked too late, took too little exercise, and seldom slept enough. While he'd always been a devoted father, he constantly regretted not being able to spend more time with his children and with me, and that, too, only added more pressure to his burden.

The summer of 1794 brought all this to a head, and tested us both in ways that we hadn't anticipated. The excise tax on distilled spirits (commonly called the Whiskey Tax) that Alexander had initiated in 1791 had never been popular, particularly along the western frontier. The odious beliefs of Mr. Jefferson and other Democratic-Republicans were widely accepted among the farmers and other rough men who chose to live far from the eastern cities. Their dislike for the tax and their loathing of government in general had been fueled by tales of the Jacobins in France, until in the spring, it had boiled over into open rebellion.

Some of the government's tax collectors were tarred and feathered. Others were threatened, their homes burned and their personal property destroyed. That old symbol of rebellion, the Liberty Pole, sprang up in small towns and settlements, and the Republican societies that had begun as a dozen disgruntled men now numbered in the thousands. There were even rumors that the western rebels had ordered a guillotine from France, and were intending to use it.

Mindful of the events in France, Alexander believed that a strong show of force was imperative to put down the rebellion, and urged the president toward this path. If the government appeared resolute, he argued, then most likely the rebellion would melt away without any real resistance. Yet because the army had been dissolved at the end of the revolution, the federal government had only local militia at its disposal. President Washington was reluctant to call them out, knowing this would be unpopular in every quarter; there was also the very real chance that the militia might instead choose to side with the rebels.

As if this grim news were not difficult enough for my husband, our youngest son, Johnny, not even two, had developed a mysterious and worrisome ailment. At first I'd thought it only a cold or chill of the kind so common in young children, but day by day he worsened, with a low fever and a persistent cough, and as his appetite faded, he began to lose flesh. What frightened me most was how he didn't cry, the way most babies did, but instead lay too quiet and still. Dr. Stevens had no answers, and neither did any of the other physicians we consulted. Every remedy was tried to no avail, and though no one would say it aloud, I feared that my baby was simply fading away.

I had his cot moved into our bedchamber to watch over him, his raspy breathing and rough little coughs waking me throughout the night. But on this night when I woke, the room was terrifyingly quiet. With sick dread, I turned swiftly toward his cot and reached for him.

The cot was empty and the sheets cold, and I gasped with uncertainty. Only then did I realize that Alexander's side of the bed was empty, too, and that our bedchamber door stood open, and when I looked into the hall, I saw a sliver of light coming from beneath the door of his library. I wrapped a shawl around my shoulders, and opened the library door as quietly as I could.

By the light of a single candlestick, my husband was sitting at his desk with the usual piles of papers and letters before him. His hair was a tangle and his feet were bare, and wrapped in a blanket and resting against his shoulder was Johnny, his eyes half-closed in drowsy near-sleep, his breathing still raspy. They must have been there for a long while, for the baby's half-parted lips had made a large blotch of dampness on the shoulder of his father's silk dressing gown.

"How is he?" I asked softly, closing the door so we wouldn't wake the other children.

"The same," Alexander said, blunt and sad at the same time. "At least he's sleeping now."

"Not quite, but almost." I sat on the edge of the second chair, anxiously watching Johnny. "I'm sorry he woke you."

"I was awake already," he said, glancing down at the papers. "This business to the west, Betsey—I cannot keep my thoughts from what is happening in France, and what could happen here. When a rabble is allowed to defy and trample laws that were passed for the common good, then what meaning can those laws have? What manner of society will be left without order, without reason or respect?"

I was so accustomed to his usual brisk and energetic way of addressing challenges that his pessimism now unsettled me. Perhaps we'd listened too much to the harrowing stories of the *émigrés*, or perhaps we both realized that in this monstrous society he described, he would be one of the rabble's first targets.

"I don't believe that you and President Washington will let it come to that," I said, striving to convince myself as much as him. "This isn't France."

He continued to look down at the papers, his fingers tracing gentle circles between Johnny's shoulder blades.

"We're preparing for war," he said quietly. "It's not widely known, of course, but at the president's orders, we are placing requisitions for everything our soldiers will need."

I was acutely aware of Johnny's breathing in the silence between us. The president and his cabinet had just sent envoys to Europe to keep peace, while all the time they'd been planning a war at home.

"When?" I asked finally.

"That will depend on the rebels, Betsey," he said. "If they choose to abide by the laws and disperse, then there will be no need for a military endeavor. If they don't, then I would imagine a campaign will begin in late summer, to conclude before winter."

"The season for war," I said, remembering. "At least this time you will be here, and safe from danger."

Finally he looked up at me, and I knew even before he spoke.

"The president will once again assume his role as commander-in-chief to ensure our success," he said. "He will lead the troops, and I will accompany him."

I held his gaze, and I didn't look away. I wanted him to see how much his decision was hurting me. Because it *was* his decision: not the president's, not Congress's. There was no urgent need for the secretary of the treasury to be part of a military expedition. Not even General Knox, the secretary of war, was going. Yet because my husband wanted to be there at the president's side and likewise wanted the excitement (I cannot call it anything else) of riding out into the country before a shining show of guns and men, he would willingly put himself in harm's way, before men who hated him and wished him harm. If he went riding off on this fool's errand of a war, it was because he wanted to go, and he would choose that instead of me and his children.

"I'm pregnant, Alexander," I said, the words sounding harsh and flat even to my own ears.

He flinched as if I'd struck him. "Are you certain?"

I nodded. It was a fair question to ask—my courses were never regular, and I'd only just weaned Johnny three months earlier—but the inherent doubt to it wounded me.

He nodded, recovering as he considered the news. No matter the circumstances, my husband was seldom at a loss for words.

"That's splendid news, Betsey," he said. "Most excellent. Truly, I am the most fortunate of husbands."

I tried to smile, and tried harder not to cry. I knew this was the sixth time I'd made such an announcement to him, but oh, how perfunctory and formal his response had been!

"I would have told you before," I said, my voice breaking. "If it weren't for Johnny . . ."

"Oh, my love, please don't cry," he said softly. "I'll be back before the baby's born. I'll be here with you. You have my word."

My anger crumbled. I could never remain angry at him for long, not when he spoke to me like that. I went to him then, circling my arms around him and our baby both, and finally, I let my tears flow: for him, for us, and for the entire foolish, foolish world.

Soon after, at the doctors' insistence, I took Johnny with me to Albany. It was not just that they hoped the more salubrious air of the country would help my little boy; the doctors and my husband feared for my health as well. Even as I knew this was wise counsel, I hated leaving Alexander and our other children behind. Our two oldest sons, Philip and Alexander, were away in Trenton studying with Reverend Frazer, and Angelica, Fanny, and James would remain in Philadelphia with their father and the servants. My leaving was especially difficult on Angelica, who with a child's intuition may have understood the gravity of my situation as well as her little brother's.

This pregnancy was different from my previous ones. I was often ill and plagued by headaches, and weary to the point of exhaustion. As much as I hated to leave Alexander and my older children behind in Philadelphia, even I was forced to admit it was for the best, and by the time I reached The Pastures, I was so unwell that I needed to be helped from the carriage.

Both Johnny and I were given over to Dr. Stringer's care. I was put to bed, and permitted to do nothing for myself, while Johnny was given yet another regimen that included limewater and laudanum. It fell to my mother instead of me to take my son outside each day for the fresh air that the doctors had prescribed, and I watched them together in the gardens each morning from my window. Alexander wrote to me almost daily, letters full of worry and concern and love for both me and Johnny.

But just as he'd done years ago whilst in the army, he carefully omitted from his letters all but the briefest mentions of the plans to confront the rebellion, not wanting to distress me or my unborn child. And just as before, I pressed my father for the details my husband wouldn't give me. The rebels were variously estimated at six, seven, eight thousand men, all armed. To face them, militia forces were being summoned from as far away as Virginia. By most reports, the expedition would set out in September.

Slowly, slowly Johnny began to improve, growing stronger and more alert each day, and by early August I could finally write to Alexander that our prayers had been answered, and that Dr. Stringer considered him out of danger. I felt better, too, and well enough to travel. Although my parents and Dr. Stringer urged me to be cautious, I was determined to return to Philadelphia before Alexander left. But I soon discovered I was not nearly as recovered as I'd thought, and for the sake of my unborn child I was forced to rest for some time with friends in New York City before I finally returned home in October. By then, Alexander had left.

I was convinced my beloved husband would be killed by the rebels, and I had terrible nightmares of his head on a pike, as if he'd been murdered by Jacobins. I wrote him frantic, desperate letters, and no matter how he tried to reassure me and tell me of their success in quelling the rebels, I still feared for him.

One night in late November, I woke in great pain. I summoned Dr. Stringer to my side, but his best efforts were to no avail, and I miscarried our child.

Alexander came home on the first of December, riding with an escort ahead of the army. I hadn't been expecting him, and was sitting in bed, writing letters, when I heard his voice in the hall below and his step on the stair. I swiftly set aside my pen and writing desk, intending to meet him, but I'd only gotten so far as to be sitting on the edge of the bed when he rushed into the room.

I'd written to him of how I'd lost our baby, and I saw at once from his expression that he'd received the unfortunate news. He didn't embrace me at once, as I'd expected, but hung a few steps back.

"My dearest wife," he said, his voice filled with sorrow. "I never meant to do this to you. Everything that has happened is my fault. If I hadn't gone away . . ."

His words drifted off, and he held his arms outstretched in grief and appeal, and then let them drop to his sides. He hadn't paused to change his clothes, and I thought of how many times he'd been away and returned to me like this, his cheeks ruddy from riding in the cold, his jaw bristling with last night's beard, and his clothes dusty from the road.

Yet this time was different. I still ached too much with loss. I'd no spirit left within me for rejoicing or celebration, and though I'd thought my weeping was done, at the sight of him fresh tears welled up from deep within me.

"Betsey," he said. "I cannot undo what has been done, but as soon as I received your letter, I knew at once what I must do. I have resolved to go to the president directly from here and resign from the cabinet. I intend to return to the law, and devote myself to you and our children."

I caught my breath, shocked, for I realized what a monumental sacrifice this would be. For the last seven years that he had been the secretary of the treasury, he had defined the post, and he had in turn let it define him so closely that I wasn't sure he could tell any longer where the secretary left off and the man—my husband—began. I would never have dared ask him to resign, nor would I even have thought to do so. This grandly generous decision that he was making had to be his, not mine, for I didn't want to be blamed if he later thought better of it.

"You would do that, Alexander?" I asked slowly. "You would make so large a sacrifice for me?"

"I would," he said. "I will. I have given more than I should to the government, and it's time for me to step back and instead tend to those whom I love most of all."

I wanted so much to believe him, and I tucked my hands around my body, hugging myself.

"Once you resign, it will be done," I warned. "You won't be able to return."

He nodded decisively, without hesitation. He was standing before the window and the pale winter sunlight washed over his shoulders, and I realized there were tears in his eyes as well.

He took a single step toward me. "My dearest wife," he said. "I love you more now than I ever have."

At last I silently held my arms open to him, and he came to me, and together we grieved for what we'd lost, and hoped for what was still to come.

To my joy, Alexander did exactly what he'd pledged, and resigned that afternoon, effective when the new congressional session began in January. No one in Philadelphia had expected it, the least of all President Washington. The president tried to persuade him to stay for the last year of his own term, but Alexander held firm.

I still marveled that he did, for in many ways he had been at the height of his powers in Philadelphia. The rebellion had been quelled in the best way possible, with measured authority and a minimal loss of life. Everything that he had created or put into effect during his tenure was running effectively, and the country was at ease and at peace.

Needless to say, the Democratic-Republicans believed otherwise, harping on the perceived indignities of the Whiskey Rebellion and other old slanders dredged from the past. As Alexander's last proposals were combined into a bill before Congress, Senator Aaron Burr tried to introduce a number of Democratic-Republican-approved amendments to the bill, amendments that Alexander thought undermined his proposals for no reason except to be contrary. Fortunately, the bill passed without the amendments, and at last Alexander was free.

We turned the key to the door of the Third Street house for the last time in February 1795. I'll admit that while I was thankful to be done with the politics of government, I'd also made many friends in the city, and I was sorry to be leaving them behind. I'd borne one child while I was here, and lost another, and yet overall, Alexander and I had been happy. But I was eager to return to New York City, the city that still felt most like our home.

We spent the rest of the winter and the spring at The Pastures, the first break that Alexander had permitted himself from work in years. He did little but read, ride, and a little writing, and played a great deal with the children, which they adored. As a boy in the Caribbean, he'd never ridden a sled, and he took to it now with ferocious delight, racing down the long hill before our house with the boys. He took turns taking our younger sons, James and John, down the hill with him, tucking them securely between his knees while they shrieked with delight, and I watched with the trepidation that all mothers do. Each night before supper, I played my old pianoforte in the parlor, and Alexander and our daughter, Angelica, would sing ballads together, their voices in the most pleasing harmony imaginable.

The best part of the day for me was the end, when he and I would retire to bed together, without any talk of politics crowded in between us. By the end of the first fortnight, he was smiling and laughing again as he hadn't in years; by the end of a month, he looked like a new man.

And yet as idyllic as this all might seem, the reality of our lives was never far away. He insisted on reading the New York newspapers that my father had brought up the river each day, and after supper they often shared their outrage at this or that, while Mamma and I had no choice but to listen.

One evening as we all sat together in the front parlor, however, I learned far more than I'd expected. One of the more outrageous New York Democratic-Republicans (and a friend of Mr. Burr as well), Commodore James Nicholson, had accused Alexander of having profited so handsomely from his position in the Treasury and from British bribes that he could retire with ease, having an account with over one hundred thousand pounds sterling in a London bank.

"I cannot believe that even Nicholson would present such a statement," Papa said indignantly. He sat in his customary chair close to the fire, where the heat of the coals might warm his knees. "The man is a rascal, Hamilton, but for him to imply that you have accepted so much as a single penny, let alone a sum of that amount, is preposterous and supremely insulting."

I sighed, only half listening as I darned one of the boys' stockings. Seated across from me, my mother knitted a new scarf for James, who'd become her unabashed favorite from the time he'd spent here with her when he'd been so ill. She and I had already tried to steer the conversation away from politics to the snowman the children had built in the yard earlier in the day, but Alexander and Papa had been unable to resist returning to their favorite topic once again, and now Mamma and I were resigned to another evening of listening to it.

"Clearly, Nicholson has no knowledge of my private affairs, or my banking accounts, either," Alexander said, standing before him with one arm resting against the mantel. "If he did, he'd realize how laughable such a charge is. I have left office far more poor than when I assumed it. Why, my entire fortune in the world cannot be above five hundred dollars."

My father laughed, considering this an exaggeration for effect, but Alexander sounded to be in earnest. I looked up sharply from my work, unsure of what exactly he was claiming.

"I am perfectly serious, sir," he continued, addressing Papa. "I own neither house nor property, and there has never been enough to spare for investments. Beyond our household furnishing and the clothes that Eliza and I possess, we are as good as paupers. We're charming and amiable paupers, to be sure, but paupers nonetheless."

"Please, Alexander," I said uneasily. "Do not make jests like that."

He smiled, and indeed he was both charming and amiable.

"It's not a jest, dearest," he said. "Surely you were aware of that."

"How could I be aware when this is the first you have said of it to me?" I didn't dare look at either of my parents.

"You knew the meagerness of my salary," he said. "Living to the expectations of the office on what I was paid would have been impossible, and it has exhausted all my resources."

I flushed. He wasn't faulting me—to his credit, he never did that—but he was making it sound as if our apparent poverty had been unavoidable. I thought of all the times I'd tried to be cautious in our spending, and how he in turn had assured me that it wasn't necessary. I thought of the large house and stable on Third Street and the carriage and horses that we'd kept, the boarding school for the older boys and the various private teachers of French, music, dance, and needlework for the girls, the costly clothes—oh, the clothes!—that we'd both bought for the entertainments and ceremonies of life in the capital. And because of it all, it now appeared we had nothing.

"You're not serious, Hamilton," my father said, clearly uncomfortable with what he'd just heard. "You can't be."

"I am," Alexander said, and when he answered, he looked to me, not Papa. "I gave away these last years of my life to the country, and now I must make good on it. I calculate it shall take me five or six years of steady work to clear my debts and be ahead. But for the sake of Eliza and the children, it will be done."

"Hah." My father looked down at the table, lost for words. "That's not what I ever expected to hear from you, Hamilton."

It wasn't what I'd expected, either, even when I pressed my husband later when we were alone together in our bedchamber.

"I have always been an honest man, Betsey," he said, jabbing the poker at the coals in our fireplace for more warmth, "and I've been honest now. At present we are in debt, but in time, we won't be."

"You were hardly honest when I asked you before," I said, standing beside him as he fussed with the fire. "I've seen our household account books and reckonings. Our rents and tradespersons' bills are always paid, and we've been able to give to those less fortunate as well. Has it all been done with borrowed funds? Are you in danger of landing in the gaol for debt?"

"Oh, not at all," he said, too blithely for my tastes. "I have been compelled to borrow sums from close friends familiar with our circumstances. They understand that they will be repaid in time."

"Which friends?" I asked, though I could guess. He'd many wealthy acquaintances in New York, men who'd worked and invested and prospered along with the city since the war while Alexander had chosen to work for the government. The irony of his position was that the man who had single-handedly created the financial system of the country and the first national bank with it had been left unable to balance his own accounts.

He set the poker back into its stand. "Our most generous friend has been John Church."

I pressed my hand to my mouth. Yet I wasn't really shocked: there was already considerable trust between Alexander and Mr. Church, who was likely the wealthiest gentleman of our acquaintance. Even as I wondered if Angelica knew of such a loan, I suspected that she might have been behind it. At least I could be a bit more at ease with the debt, confident that they would never demand repayment from Alexander in court.

"Still and all, Alexander," I said. "If we are paupers, as you say, then we must economize, and spend less."

"I'm confident that we shall manage, my love," he said, taking me by the hand. "It's simply my responsibility to earn more, and now that I'm again a private citizen, I intend to do so. I don't want you ever to worry on account of funds or anything else, and I'm determined to see that you don't."

But I soon learned that I'd every reason to worry. Because we hadn't yet found a house to rent in New York (I now suspected because we could not yet afford one), the children and I remained for the summer in Albany with my parents, while Alexander leased a small space for himself for lodgings and for an office. Upon his return to the city, he'd almost instantly again become the top attorney in the state with more clients than he could reasonably handle, and I believed he'd be so busy that he'd little time for politics.

I was mistaken. Despite filling his days with legal work and court appearances, he now found time to write and publish even more letters and essays for publication defending the Federalists and attacking the Democratic-Republicans.

The most contentious topic in this last year of President Washington's second term was the treaty that John Jay, a Federalist, had negotiated with Great Britain. According to Alexander, the purpose of the treaty was simple enough: to keep America from becoming entangled in the current war between Britain and France, to outline a trade agreement between America and Britain, and to resolve several remaining issues that persisted from the peace that had ended the Revolution. The points of the treaty all seemed both simple and necessary, and it had the full backing of President Washington, who hoped it would soon be approved by Congress.

But the Democratic-Republicans had attacked the treaty on every point, claiming that it conceded too much to Britain and earned nothing for America. Further, as dictated by Mr. Jefferson from his lofty Olympus at Monticello, the Democratic-Republicans believed that America should ally itself with France in the war, and pursue the madness of fighting Britain.

This time the Republican supporters weren't far away on the frontier, but in the cities as well, and their members gathered in the streets to spew their false, destructive rhetoric and burn copies of the treaty. In Congress, Mr. Madison echoed Mr. Jefferson's whispering voice, his attacks spreading beyond the treaty to the Constitution itself. Even worse, he and other Democratic-Republicans began to attack that most venerable of gentlemen, President Washington himself, saying he was so far in his dotage that he'd been ripe for manipulation by my conniving husband. They accused both the president and Alexander of being monarchists, which could not have been further from the truth.

It was a gauntlet that Alexander found impossible to ignore. Not only did he leap to the treaty's defense in a series of published essays under the name Camillus, yet another ancient Roman general, but he also wrote a second series of letters as Philo Camillus, praising the work of the first series.

But far worse than any letters were the reports I heard through others that he'd impulsively attended a Democratic-Republican meeting in Wall Street not far from where our first house had stood. He'd attempted to address them, and been struck in the forehead with a thrown rock. Shouting and streaming blood, he'd first dared challenge Commodore Nicholson (the very man who'd accused him of having a secret bank account) to a duel, and then done the same with yet another Democratic-Republican, Maturin Livingstone.

Fortunately, both quarrels were resolved by their seconds before I ever learned of it. But I could scarcely believe that he'd behave so rashly, so foolishly, and so dangerously, after he'd promised me otherwise. How far removed this sordid scene along Broadway was from the parade of only a handful of years before, when crowds had cheered the float of the Federal Ship *Hamilton*!

When next my husband came to Albany, I saw him riding slowly up the hill, and hurried to meet him outdoors before anyone else.

"Now, this is a fine surprise," he said as he climbed stiffly down from the saddle. "Good day to you, my love."

I kissed him in greeting. "You're here earlier than we expected."

"For a change, the roads were good," he said as one of my father's servants came running from the stable to lead the horse away. Before Alexander handed him the reins, he reached deep into his saddlebag and withdrew a smaller cloth bag.

"For you," he said wryly. "Other men might bring their wives jewels or gold, but I know what pleases my Betsey more."

The bag was heavy and lumpy in my hands, and I guessed its contents before I'd even opened it.

"Lemons," I said with happy satisfaction. "You remembered."

"I did," he said. "Those just came into port yesterday. Now you've no excuse not to bake me my favorite lemon cake."

He took off his hat and wiped his sleeve across his forehead, and as he bared his forehead, I recalled why I'd hurried out here to speak with him.

"I know what happened here," I said, reaching up to touch the healing cut, surrounded by a yellowing bruise, that crowned his right temple. "I heard that when you tried to address the crowd, they threw stones at you. You're fortunate you weren't killed."

He jerked his head back from my hand. "Who told you of that?"

"I read it in the newspapers," I said, cradling the bag of lemons against my hip as if it were a clumsy, weighty baby. "Word also came back to Papa that on the same night you demanded satisfaction from two other men. Thank God in Heaven that your seconds talked you from such a rash course."

"There was no real danger," he said. "Livingstone and Nicholson each knew they were in the wrong, and offered their apologies. Shall we go inside? I've candy for the children."

"In a moment," I said, placing my hand on his sleeve to hold him back to me. "I wish to speak with you first, Alexander. You're not some wild young buck, and you cannot keep behaving as if you are. You're forty years old, with a law practice, a wife, and six children dependent upon you, and you cannot keep putting your life so foolishly in jeopardy like this."

He sighed, and sat heavily on the stone steps of the house, resting his arms on his bent knees. I sat beside him, the bag of lemons beside me. I tucked my skirts around my ankles to keep them from catching the breeze, and waited for his answer. I was willing to wait all day if I had to.

"It made sense at the time," he said at last. "A great deal of sense. If the crowds had come to hear the Democratic-Republicans' lies regarding the Jay Treaty, then they also deserved to hear the correct views. I gave them that opportunity."

"But clearly, they didn't want to listen to it," I said, raising my gaze to dwell upon his battered forehead. "It's one thing to present your views through the newspapers. It's another entirely to put yourself in the path of dangerous men who'd like nothing better than to wound or even murder you."

He grunted, no real answer, and so I continued.

"Your sons are old enough to watch what you do, Alexander," I said softly, placing my hand on top of his. "Do you wish them to learn from you in this? Do you wish them to resort to fisticuffs in a dark street with anyone who holds a different opinion, or demand satisfaction for every slight and grievance?"

"No," he admitted. "But when I see how these infernal Democratic-Republicans have no regard for Jay's Treaty, but worship the Jacobins as if they were gods, ready to tear down everything that's been so carefully built for their benefit—I can't stand by and do nothing, Betsey."

"I'm not asking you to be idle," I said. "I'm only asking that you demonstrate some of your considerable wisdom before you act. You've risked your life often enough for this country, and if you don't take care, sooner or later your luck will abandon you. And I love you too much to see that."

"You are right, dearest, you are right," he said ruefully. "For your sake, I must be more rational, more thoughtful. As soon as the treaty is passed, I promise I'll step back from politics entirely. You have my word."

He raised my hand and kissed it by way of a pledge, and I smiled in return. But I'd heard this promise too many times by now. It was not that he willfully broke his word to me, but more that his very nature found such promises impossible to keep.

Yet because my love for him continued to burn brightly—and in fact I felt as if I grew even more devoted to him with each passing year—I did not quarrel with this latest promise, or question it aloud. Instead I simply agreed, and prayed that perhaps this time he might find the strength to keep it.

Soon after this, I joined Alexander in New York. Our new home was at 26 Broadway, and like most of the houses in the neighborhood, it was three stories tall and fashioned of brick, with an enclosed yard and small garden in the rear, and of a size for our large family. The house was not only pleasantly situated within the city, but also conveniently close to Alexander's office. I considered this house as more our home, and less a setting for entertainments, than the second house in Philadelphia had been. To be sure, we continued to offer a hospitable table to our friends, but now that Alexander was no longer secretary, gone, too, were the lavish entertainments for mere political acquaintances and dignitaries. I did not miss them. I preferred a less formal supper or dinner, one that relied more for its success upon the food and conversation than wine, spectacle, and an extravagant display of silver. It was also a wise transition, given the new economies I'd put into place for the household (which, fortunately, Alexander hadn't yet recognized for what they were).

Most importantly, in the new house we were once again united as a family. While Alexander enjoyed our time in Albany, he always seemed to draw his energy and fiercest intensity from the city around him, and I hoped our presence would prove a sobering influence.

It did, to the extent that Alexander didn't engage in any further brawling in the streets, or issue challenges for duels. He did, however, throw himself into the presidential election for a leader to replace President Washington. Like every good New York Federalist, his primary goal was to confound Thomas Jefferson and keep him from the presidency. But he'd never particularly cared for John Adams, either, the current vice president, who was the Federalists' leading candidate. To him, Mr. Adams was high-strung and often irrational, and perhaps most damning to Alexander, he had no military experience, somehow avoiding the army during the Revolution, which meant he was without any of the qualities that had made President Washington so unrivaled as a leader.

Instead Alexander attempted to promote a more moderate gentleman from South Carolina named Thomas Pinckney for president, hoping that Mr. Adams would again be elected to the lesser position. Despite his best efforts, Mr. Adams was elected president, and the odious Mr. Jefferson vice president. When Mr. Adams learned that Alexander had lobbied against him, the disaffection between them grew into open scorn and contempt.

This election had irrevocably changed the government. Instead of the friendship, respect, and regard that Alexander had always enjoyed with President Washington, he now was confronted by two men who actively despised him. If ever there were a time for him to turn his back completely on politics, this was it.

But Alexander had two final services to perform for President Washington before he left office, and both depended on me as well.

The first involved one more French *émigré,* escaped from the horrors of the Terror in Paris to wash up upon our welcoming shore. Georges Washington Gilbert de Lafayette was no ordinary refugee, however. He was the fifteen-year-old son of the Marquis de Lafayette, one of my husband's closest friends and fellow officers from the Revolution. President Washington had regarded the marquis almost as a son, and in gratitude the marquis had named his only son after the then-General Washington.

But the Jacobins had treated the elder Lafayette most barbarously. Not only had he been separated from his family and imprisoned, but his wife and their two young daughters were imprisoned as well, while his grandmother, mother, and sister had all become victims of the guillotine. Only his son had escaped capture with his tutor, Monsieur Frestrel, and had made their way to Philadelphia. At first General and Lady Washington had welcomed the pair to the President's Residence, but their presence created a diplomatic quandary. The boy was a refugee, and if he was given sanctuary in an official residence, he could single-handedly corrupt America's careful neutrality. When the president asked if we, as private citizens, might shelter him instead, Alexander agreed in an instant. There was always room for another, or two, in our house.

As could only be expected, Georges was shy, thin, and melancholy, and for the first weeks in our house, he followed me about like a lost puppy. Georges's English was better than my French, though I soon found the best way to communicate with him was through apples, gingerbread, and slices of pie with cheese, the common language of all boys. Although he and our son Philip were close in age, they could not have been more different in temperament. Yet when Philip came home from boarding for the holidays, Philip and Georges became fast friends. For Alexander, who justly feared for the marquis's life, the friendship between their sons had an almost noble and poignant symmetry that, out of the boys' sight, made him weep.

The second, and final, service that Alexander performed for the president proved to be perhaps the most enduring of their long time together. The president wished to deliver a farewell address to all citizens. The address would be published so that it could reach as many citizens as possible. Its message would reflect not only the president's Federalist beliefs, but also his trust in the Constitution. The president wanted it to serve as a call for citizens to put aside their divisive quarreling, and come together in a single, strong, unified country—the country he had always envisioned, and the country he had served not just as president, but also as commander-in-chief during the Revolution.

The president had always realized he'd no natural gift for composition, and required the assistance of another to give shape to his ideas. When he'd considered not running for a second term in 1791, he'd shared his notes with Mr. Madison, then in the president's favor as a fellow Virginian, and he'd written a first draft that had subsequently been put aside. Now, however, the president naturally turned to Alexander to write this important document, giving him not only his own notes, but also the old draft penned by Mr. Madison.

Because it was important that the country believe the address was the president's own words, Alexander took great care to compose it in secret in the evenings, away from the constant bustle of clerks, clients, messengers, and students that filled his law office. Instead he wrote the address entirely at his desk at home, and he was adamant that I sit beside him.

Writing at home also meant he could be informally dressed, as was often his custom for serious writing, in an old silk dressing gown over his nightshirt. It was early August when he began, and the windows to his library were thrown open to let in any cooler air that might come our way. Through a trick of the evening breeze, we could smell the saltiness of the harbor in the air that ruffled up from the water along Wall Street, and hear the bells on the ships tied up at the docks. Beside the open window, fireflies brushed against the wide green leaves of the mulberry bush, bright dots of light in the night.

"I have to consider that many people will have the address read to them, much like a sermon," he explained, tapping the end of his pen against the edge of the desk. "The words must sound as well upon the ear when spoken aloud as when read."

I nodded, curling my bare feet beneath me in the chair. I'd

brought a stocking to knit while he wrote, mindless handwork that wouldn't take from my concentration or require light, for the two brass candlesticks on his desk were for him, not me.

"Commence when ready, Colonel Hamilton," I teased, lowering my voice to make it sound masculine and military. Even though writing the address was a serious matter, sitting here with him reminded me of all the other papers and essays and reports he had composed with me over time, especially when we'd first been wed.

He smiled warmly at me, likely thinking back to that time, too. "I don't believe a lieutenant is necessary tonight," he said. "Rather you must be to me what Molière's old nurse was to him."

I nodded eagerly, for he'd explained this story to me so many times that it had become part of his writing ritual, too. Apparently, the French playwright Molière had read his work out loud to his old nursemaid, relying on her ear to tell him if the words sang as they should or not.

"*Mais oui,*" I said, two of the few French words I knew, and he chuckled. He held up the small sheaf of papers that was Mr. Madison's draft.

"We won't be requiring these," he said, pointedly putting them aside on a nearby chair. "I fear Madison's words are much like him. Stolid and heavy, yet without much substance."

"You don't need them," I said confidently. "You've plenty of words of your own."

"That I do," he said, dipping his pen into the inkwell, and I realized his thoughts were already gathering. For a long moment, he held the pen poised over the paper, and then began to write, saying the words out loud for me to hear as my needles clicked away their stitches.

"*Friends and fellow citizens,*" he began. "*The period for a new election of a president*—no, *of a citizen*—*to administer the executive government of America*—"

"Perhaps it should be the 'United States' instead of America," I suggested. "If he wishes to urge the country toward unity, then it cannot be stated often enough."

He nodded without looking away from the paper before him. "*The executive government of the United States . . .*"

It took us several long nights before he had the words to his sat-isfaction, and as we often did, I wrote out the final copy for him to take to the president for his approval. In the end, it was thirty-two pages long, and for Alexander it had become something of a labor of love and regard, the last he'd do for his president and his gen-eral. No one was aware that he'd done it, exactly as was proper.

The farewell address was printed first in Philadelphia on Sep-tember 19, 1796, and reappeared in numerous cities throughout the country afterward. It was almost universally hailed and applauded, and treasured for containing the final public words of a great gen-tleman. Only the Democratic-Republicans dared mock it, and by so doing, only made mockeries of themselves. The address was so pop-ular that enterprising printers made it available in pamphlet form, selling briskly for many years afterward, its wisdom never fading.

Not long after it first appeared, Alexander and I were on our way home from a pleasing autumn walk along the Battery when an old soldier approached us. Bent and scarred, yet still wearing the tattered remnants of his blue uniform coat from twenty years be-fore, he'd a bundle of the pamphlets to sell from a haversack over his shoulder.

"His Excellency's final address to th' nation, sir," he said, wav-ing a copy in Alexander's face. "Help a poor old soldier, sir, an' read the words of th' greatest general in th' world."

Alexander bought a copy, generously giving the man four times what he'd asked.

"Another for the collection," he said as he handed it to me. "Poor old fellow! He's no idea that he just sold me my own work."

Once again he glanced back over his shoulder to the old soldier, his gaze lingering with a melancholy air. It wasn't until later, when I thought about it again, that I realized when my husband had pitied the "poor old fellow," he'd really been speaking of himself.

CHAPTER 20

New York, New York
May 1797

"Will you not play, Eliza?" my sister Angelica asked as she joined me where I stood beside the card table. "You needn't worry if you don't know the rules. Loo is a wickedly simple game, and I'm sure you'd have it after a hand or two."

"Thank you, no," I murmured. "I'd rather watch."

The play itself might be simple, but to me what was truly terrifying was the speed with which the players, women and men, won and lost large sums, and without showing any reaction, either. Mr. Church himself was dealing the cards, his fingers quick to dispense pasteboard and luck, good and bad. He'd only grown heavier whilst he'd been in London, his face rounder and his chin swelling grandly over his tightly wrapped neck cloth. Following the new fashions, he'd ceased to powder his hair, and instead wore it cropped, shiny, and very black against his face.

"Then I shall watch with you," Angelica said, looping her arm through mine. "Anything to be in your company once again."

I smiled, just as I'd been smiling ever since Angelica, Mr. Church, and their five children had returned to New York two weeks ago. I still didn't know what had brought them back: whether Angelica had finally worn her husband down with her constant pleas to return to America, or if Mr. Church himself had at last soured on his heady life in London.

No matter. Alexander and I could not be happier to have them back with us, and it was clear that the rest of New York society agreed with us. Mr. Church had had Alexander purchase the grandest house available for them so that once he and Angelica had arrived, they could be immediately at home, and immediately giving parties like this one.

Overnight the Churches had become the wealthiest family in New York City, and they lived on a scale of ostentation that had never been seen here before. Their house was filled with carved and gilded furnishings, paintings and sculptures, silver and porcelain, and because Mr. Church liked to play and wager, they'd also brought with them the accoutrements of a private gaming house. It was all very fast and very extravagant, and fashionable New Yorkers flocked to parties like this one.

Her diamond earrings swinging, Angelica leaned forward to kiss the top of her husband's head. "For luck, darling."

He grunted in acknowledgment, and didn't look up from his cards. I know my sister loved her husband, but I couldn't help but think I'd made much the better choice in mine, even if mine was poor and hers was rich.

The crowded room seemed suddenly warm to me, and I opened my ivory fan.

"I believe I'd actually prefer to go to the other room and sit for a bit, Angelica, if you do not mind," I said. "I'm feeling a bit tired."

Angelica's merriment immediately changed to concern. "Are you unwell? Should I find Hamilton?"

"No, no, I'm perfectly well," I protested as she guided me to a silk-covered settee. "Only tired."

I was halfway through my seventh pregnancy, the first since I'd miscarried three years before, and because of that misadventure Angelica in particular was treating me as if I were made of glass.

"You look so beautiful tonight, Eliza, that I forget that you're *enciente*," she said, using the French word that made my condition sound so much more elegant than it was. "That gown is perfection."

I smiled wryly. There was much less distinction (though much the same cost) in gowns now, with nearly every woman in the room in white cotton muslin, short sleeves, and a high waist, and I was no exception.

"If it makes you overlook how sizable I've become," I said, "then I must be sure to thank those dressmakers in Paris and London for contriving a new fashion that conveniently hides the waist."

"You're not the first to make that observation." Angelica lowered her chin and raised her brows, the way she did when ready to relay an especially delicious morsel of scandal. "Of course, you are respectably wed and so there's no doubt that your child is your divine Hamilton's, but Mr. Church vows that the fashion was first designed to accommodate all the London ladies with lovers who need to hide their little inconveniences."

" 'Little inconveniences'!" I repeated, stunned she'd use that expression, and instinctively I rested a protective hand across my belly. I do not know which shocked me more: that my worldly sister could speak so blithely of innocent babies, or the wanton ladies who'd conceived them outside of marriage.

"Ah, you know how blunt Mr. Church can be," she said, unperturbed. "In truth he used a much more direct word."

"I pray he doesn't use it in Alexander's hearing," I said uneasily. "One of the papers in Philadelphia claimed that Mr. Adams himself has taken to calling my husband 'that Creole bastard,' and I'm terrified that Alexander will go demand satisfaction from the president on account of it."

"Oh, dear," Angelica said. "Although no one would fault him if he did. And consider the service he'd do for the country, ridding us all of that fussy little bag of noxious wind!"

"Don't even make jests like that, I beg you," I said. I was serious, too. Soon after Mr. Adams had been elected, Alexander had written him a long letter of congratulation, and included a compendium of suggestions and proposals for managing his new responsibilities as president and negotiating the government. It was all sound advice drawn from my husband's long experience at President Washington's side, and presented in the most respectful fashion possible. President Washington would have considered it both generous and useful, as any wise man would.

But Mr. Adams wasn't wise. He was, as Angelica had said, a fussy little bag of noxious wind. Instead of finding my husband's memorandum useful, he declared it to be insulting, and wondered aloud whether the man who'd written such a piece of rubbish had lost his wits. As can be imagined, this ingratitude had not sat well with Alexander, who'd every right to feel insulted by the ill usage. It had taken considerable persuading on my part to convince him not to take offense.

"The best I can say of Mr. Adams is that he has no use for the capital, and keeps to Massachusetts instead," I said, fluttering my fan before my face. "The more distance there is between him and Alexander, the better."

Angelica shook her head. "What manner of president avoids his own capital?" she said. "And what a slovenly display that makes to the rest of the world! There should be parties every night, musicales, balls, and all with the most brilliant company that can possibly be assembled."

Of course, my sister had just described this very party of her own, and certainly the capital—which I heard had become a sad and empty place—would benefit from having her in charge of official entertainments. I thought of Mrs. Adams with her sharp tongue, proudly plain and old-fashioned, and then Angelica as she sat beside me, dressed in a provocatively sheer white dress with a diamond necklace and earrings, and towering white plumes in her artfully curled hair.

"At least Mr. Jefferson as vice president remains in Philadelphia," she continued. "He can be depended upon to offer a certain level of elegance and civility to the capital city."

"Not now," I said. My sister continued to retain a favorable impression of Mr. Jefferson that was entirely at odds with my own, although I prayed that with time she'd come to see the man for the false, conniving rogue that he was. "I've heard that Mr. Jefferson has so completely assumed the guise—and surely it is a guise—of the plain and honest Democratic-Republican that he wears only rough homespun and answers his door himself, his hair unpowdered and unkempt."

Angelica's eyes widened. "That does not sound at all like the gentleman I knew in Paris!"

"I have it on the best authority." I nodded sagely, making little jerks with my fan for emphasis. "I know you believe that the politics in London are especially uncivil, but you'll soon see that the style here in America is every bit as ferocious, and marked with backbiting, lies, deceit, and ill will. I cannot tell you how relieved I am to have Alexander removed from it."

The sorrowful truth was he'd not so much withdrawn from politics, as politics had removed from him. Although Alexander had resigned from his post in the cabinet, he had harbored hopes that he would continue as a kind of advisor to the new government, as he'd done during the final year of General Washington's term. He hadn't confessed as much to me, but I recognized the signs, and I would have been surprised had it been otherwise. The arrangement would have made perfect sense, too. President Adams had decided to keep the cabinet members chosen by President Washington, and those men were not only staunch Federalists, but Alexander's friends. My husband had had every right to expect them to reach out to him for help addressing difficult problems, for the good of the country as well as the Federalist cause.

But so great was President Adams's dislike and distrust of my husband that he wanted nothing to do with him. Further, he seldom consulted his own cabinet, either, effectively excluding them from his circle of counselors, too. Every attempt my husband made to contribute was sharply rebuffed, or even ignored outright. After being involved and consulted on every major decision for so many years, my poor husband had overnight become an outcast.

His pride was badly wounded, as anyone's would be, and he couldn't help but feel unappreciated and unloved. He tried to look for other diversions. He concentrated on his legal work. He doted on our children. We spent considerable time in the company of the Churches. Because Mr. Church had lost his much-desired seat in Parliament shortly before returning to America, and he and Alexander commiserated on the gross unfairness of their mutual governments, and the idiocy of those now in power.

It was about this time that I arrived home one afternoon to find a foreign gentleman, colorfully dressed, just departing our house. This in itself was not unusual, for New York was a cosmopolitan city, and many visitors from abroad came to call upon my distinguished husband. But this one was in turn distinguished himself, or at least he'd made himself out to be so to my husband.

"Do you know who that man was, my dear?" Alexander asked,

his excitement clear. "None other than the great Roman-born sculptor Giuseppe Ceracchi, a master-carver in marble. He has just undertaken an important work capturing the likenesses of the greatest men of our time, to be on public display in a gallery, and has begged my indulgence to be among them."

"As you should be," I said, pleased for his sake. Roman-born master-carvers in marble were unknown in America, though the Churches had several fine examples of marble sculptures in their home. "Will it be a kind of portrait, then?"

He nodded with satisfaction. "Each gentleman is to be captured in the manner of an ancient senator, as is fitting for our republic," he said. "Ceracchi has arranged a makeshift studio in his lodgings, and I must go to him for sittings."

"That is fitting," I agreed. "You've borrowed the names of so many ancient Romans when you've written your various essays that you might as well pose as one."

He grinned, likely intrigued by the notion. Alexander had sat for the best painters from our country including Charles Willson Peale and John Trumbull, and his likenesses hung in several public buildings as well as the one by Peale that hung in our parlor across from my own by Mr. Earl. But in all of these he'd been shown wearing his customary dress.

"Must you wear a toga," I teased, "or some other heathen costume? Will he swaddle you in an old bedsheet before you strike a dramatic pose?"

"Oh, yes, imagine me striding down Broadway on my way to the Forum," he said, waving his arm in a grand oratorial style, "frightening every horse and chicken in my path!"

We both laughed heartily at that. However, when at last the carving was done and delivered to our house some months later for safekeeping (Mr. Ceracchi's original scheme of a collection of similar busts to be displayed to the public remaining as yet an unformed dream), I didn't laugh, but was instead moved to tears.

Mr. Ceracchi had in fact shown my husband as an ancient statesman, in a head-and-shoulders portrayal that Alexander said was called a bust. His hair was shown cropped short, a style I'd never seen him wear, but looked very noble and Roman, and which served to set off my husband's forthright profile to perfection. He looked steadfast and determined and confident, with the merest smile playing across his lips, exactly as I thought of him. Despite the blankness of the white marble, I judged it to be one of the best likenesses of my husband, and the most lifelike, too. Mounted on the column that Mr. Ceracchi had thoughtfully supplied, the bust had a prominent place in our parlor, and over time it became one of my most treasured possessions.

It was a good thing we were so pleased by the finished work, too, for our happiness helped ease the shock of Mr. Ceracchi's next delivery, a month later.

"My God, Betsey," Alexander exclaimed, coming to find me with a newly opened letter in his hands. "The audacity of the rascal!"

"Which rascal, my dear?" I asked, a reasonable question where my husband was concerned.

"Ceracchi," he said, his face flushed. "He has presented me with a bill for his services for making the bust, as a 'favor to me.' I ask you, what manner of favor costs six hundred and twenty dollars?"

I gasped with dismay, for that was a very significant sum to our little household. "Six hundred and twenty dollars! Will you pay it?"

"I fear I have no choice," he said, shaking his head. "There's no doubt that we accepted the bust, and that we were pleased by his workmanship, for we've shown it to every single person who's entered our house. No, I must pay him, though I shall consider it a lesson to myself to be less susceptible to Roman flattery, and to arrange all terms beforehand, especially with artists."

Most of our days, however, didn't include marble busts or audacious foreign sculptors. Instead we settled into a quiet routine that pleased me well. Each morning I'd be first at the dining table in our front room—my chair pulled back to accommodate my growing belly and the child within it—whilst Alexander finished dressing and preparing his papers for his day either in court at his office.

Our younger sons James and John, washed and dressed for the day, would join me, and while I cut and buttered neat slices of bread for their breakfast, they'd take turns reading aloud, a kind of informal lesson that Alexander had devised to begin their days in an educational manner. For John, who was still learning to read, a chapter from the Bible would be challenge enough, while James, who before long would be following his older brothers into Reverend Frazer's tutelage, would read a selection from Dr. Oliver Goldsmith's *History of Rome*. Angelica and Fanny would often appear then, too, and Alexander himself would soon join us to drink his coffee. Then everyone would be off to school and employment, and the day would begin in earnest.

Alexander and I were especially proud of our oldest son, Philip, who was to enter Columbia College in the autumn as a student, the same college that Alexander himself had attended when it had been known as King's College before the Revolution. I do not know who was made the happier, father or son, by this significant achievement, and Alexander was eagerly offering every kind of advice to Philip about how and what to study.

But despite this domestic contentment, and even though Alexander's role in the Federalist government had diminished, the Democratic-Republicans refused to believe it, and leave my husband in peace. They still considered him a dangerous adversary, one who needed to be destroyed, and that summer he and I both learned the depths to which his enemies would sink.

It began innocently enough. A small advertisement in the newspaper for a series of pamphlets caught Alexander's eye. It wasn't the title—*The History of the United States for 1796*—that attracted his notice, but the eager promise from the author that the pamphlet would include fresh revelations about the tenure of the last treasury secretary.

"I wish you would ignore it, Alexander," I said when he showed it to me. "You know as well as I that it's only going to be yet another version of the same old lies."

He'd continued to scowl at the page, as determined as any terrier.

"Most likely, yes," he did admit. "But ignoring the lies can also be perceived as being unable or unwilling to refute them, and therefore they become accepted as truth."

I handed the paper back to him. "You were investigated twice by Congress, and nothing untoward was found," I said. "I do not believe the efforts of this James Thomson Callender, whomever he may be, can rival those of a Congress filled with Democratic-Republicans."

"Callender is one of Jefferson's lesser pawns," he said. "I wouldn't be surprised in the least if Jefferson sponsored the entire series of pamphlets."

"Please, Alexander," I said. "You're no longer in office. They can't hurt you now."

"It's better to be certain," he said doggedly. "I'll send a clerk to buy them tomorrow so that the publisher won't know of my interest. Most likely the pamphlets will be exactly as you say, nothing new, but I cannot in good conscience make that assumption."

The pamphlets were duly purchased the next day, and duly read by my husband, who studied them with far more care than they merited. There was in fact nothing new: the same old empty accusations of misconduct by the same men—James Reynolds and Jacob Clingman—that had led to the investigations by Congress. He was accused of financial speculation, of using his position to fill his own pockets, of taking bribes to fill that non-existent account in the London bank. There were also the equally tired hints of licentious behavior, doubtless added to titillate readers and beguile them into their purchase.

Despite my pleas for common sense, Alexander was unable to ignore this, and insisted on defending himself in a letter published in the *Gazette of the United States*. Nor could he resist adding a few lines to discredit the two men who were the sources of the inaccurate reports as being in the pay of the Democratic-Republicans.

"You know you've only made it worse," I said when he proudly showed me his letter printed in the paper. "Now people will be curious to see what has so inflamed you. You've likely earned Callender fifty more sales from this letter alone."

The letter gave Callender much more than mere sales. It gave him the confidence to make even more outrageous claims. He accused Alexander not only of professional misconduct, but of infidelity to me as well. He promised that in his next round of publications he'd prove his allegations in the form of confidential letters that he'd obtained from official sources. The letters were from James Reynolds, who claimed to be Alexander's agent in these same nefarious deeds.

And now I finally understood why Alexander had become so irritated. I didn't believe the accusations, knowing them to be lies, but like Alexander, I hated the idea that this rogue Callender could continue to play the gadfly in the public press. Yet the more Alexander railed against Callender, the more the man's accusations grew, so many that it became difficult to keep them straight.

A week later, Alexander stayed at his office longer than usual, having been compelled to work extra hours for a pending case. It was a hot, heavy July evening, the air so still that even breathing was uncomfortable. The children were already in bed, and I sat alone in the parlor beside the open window that overlooked our backyard, striving to ease myself as ever I could. I was regretting my decision to remain in the city until after my baby was born, and I longed for the relative cool of The Pastures.

I heard Alexander arrive in the hall below, and looked expectantly toward the stairs. As soon as he entered the bedroom, I knew from his expression that there'd been another salvo in the press. Without any greeting, he handed me the newspaper to read the latest remarks from Callender. I scanned them quickly, every sentence stinging with malice, while he stripped off his coat and waistcoat and tossed them on the back of a chair. He scarcely waited until I'd finished before he began his explanation.

"You see how it is, Betsey," he began. "The letters Callender mentions were highly confidential, and date from 1791, six years ago. Only three men had access to them, and I'd stake my life that the one responsible for giving them to Callender is Monroe."

"Mr. Monroe!" I exclaimed. "But why would he do this now, so long after the events?"

"Because he blames me for his recall from the pleasures of Paris," he said, beginning to pace the parlor before me. "There were many other voices besides mine offended by his inappropriate behavior as our envoy. You must recall it, Betsey: how the man was slavering over the Jacobins as much as Jefferson himself, praising their bloodthirsty actions when he was supposed to be stressing American neutrality. It was the president's final decision to do so, yet according to Monroe, Madison, Jefferson, and Burr, now it seems I am the one who must be punished with this outrage of lies against my honor and my name."

"Do you know that for a fact?" I asked, incredulous. He was sufficiently angry that he'd fallen into his courtroom manner, explanation laced with recrimination, which I always found extremely difficult to combat. "That the four of them have met to conspire against you over this?"

"I have heard such a meeting took place, yes," he said. "They all have a hand in this, and they're quite blatant about it. But it is Madison who has betrayed me the most, colluding with a low worm of a man like Callender."

"What is the nature of these letters that makes them so confidential?" I asked. "Or is it information to do with the government that I've no right to know?"

"They are—or were—confidential to me." He paused, obviously weighing his words. "They are the work of an insidious rascal named James Reynolds, who sought to inveigle me into a speculation scheme. He claimed to have proof that I enriched myself through abusing my position in the Treasury, and attempted to extort money from me to keep quiet."

I nodded. More lies, I thought unhappily, more lies, the heavy air made warmer still by these never-ending, hateful revelations of yet another conspiracy to tatter my husband's good name and honor.

"As a gentleman, Monroe swore to me to keep knowledge of the letters secret," Alexander continued, his pacing grown so heated that his shirt clung to his back in the hot room. "Instead he obviously had copies made, which he has now given to Callender for publication. For the sake of his party friends, Monroe has broken his word, and yet pretends ignorance. He is a scoundrel, and a villain."

"Oh, Alexander." I sighed, and rubbed my temples. I was eight months with child, and this was all more than I wished to endure. The entire situation had become exactly the morass that I'd feared it would, sucking everything in our lives into its greedy maw. "What have your friends advised?"

"They say the same as you, Betsey, that I should turn the other cheek and ignore it." He shook his head, and I knew he'd likely shaken away that advice in exactly the same way. "They say this is a battle I will never win, and only drive myself to madness by trying to answer all the claims they make against me."

"Then why don't you listen to them, Alexander?" I asked. "If you stop answering their accusations, the entire affair will fade away on its own. We could take the children and go to Albany, and stay there until this little one is born next month. By then, this pack of lies and ugliness will have collapsed in upon itself, and have been forgotten."

He stopped pacing and sighed, his head bowed.

"I wish that I were as certain that it would, my love," he said mournfully. "This entire affair torments me relentlessly, and I've no idea what course would be best."

"We can go to Albany," I said, pleading. "We'll stay there where it's green and cool, away from New York."

I could see him considering, and then slowly he shook his head.

"I must face this, Betsey," he said. "I can't run away. They've called me many things, but I won't let them call me a coward, too."

"My own dear husband," I said. "You've always been the bravest man I've ever known."

His courage, his honor, his integrity: these had always been the things that mattered most to him, and to me as well. Perhaps this had gone too far for him to back away now. Perhaps it truly was time he took a stand and defended himself.

He stopped before my chair with his arms hanging at his sides, his entire being so sadly tormented that it grieved me to see. I reached out and took his hand, linking his fingers into mine. My hands were swollen from the heat and my pregnancy, and my wedding ring with our two names was tight on my finger, yet to me it had never held more significance than it did that night.

Somewhere in the distance came a rumble of thunder.

"I'm lost, Betsey," he said again, his voice heavy. "I don't know any longer what is right, and what isn't."

"But you do know, my love," I said softly. "You always have. Do what you believe, and it will be right."

Finally he nodded, accepting. He didn't tell me what he'd decided, and I didn't ask. He was my husband, and that was enough.

Several days later, I was sitting in the backyard, half-listening to my two youngest boys squabbled over a ball. The day was already warm, but at least out of doors there was a shimmer of a breeze coming from the harbor.

The back door to the hall stood open, a clear passage through the house, and I heard frantic rapping on the front door. I frowned, wondering who could be so desperate at this hour, and as soon as the servant opened the door, my sister flew inside, demanding to see me.

"I'm here, Angelica," I called, and she ran toward me.

"Where is Hamilton?" she demanded, breathless and agitated. "When did you see him last?"

"When he left for his office after breakfast." Her wild manner had upset my boys, and I rose and put my arms around their shoulders to give them a reassuring pat. "Here, you two, go find Johanna in the house, and leave me with your aunt."

John trotted dutifully inside, but James, being older, hung back. "Is there something wrong with Papa?"

"No, dear, not at all," Angelica said with forced cheerfulness. "Go on now, so I might speak with your mamma."

Reluctantly he left, and as soon as he disappeared inside Angelica seized my arm.

"This morning John told me that he might not be back home to dine," she said, "that he'd an appointment to keep in Hamilton's company. I gave it no further thought, until I found a crumpled note from Hamilton that John had left on his washstand, asking him to accompany him to the interview at Mr. Monroe's lodgings at ten."

"An interview?" I repeated, my own dread growing by the instant. The only time that gentlemen spoke of interviews was when they were planning a duel. Of course, he would have asked Mr. Church, experienced in dueling, to be his second. Mr. Church's dueling pistols were infamous, London-made works of the gunsmith's art with long barrels and hair triggers, pistols that had already shot several men. The child in my womb quaked with fear, and I pressed my hand over my belly to calm it. "Oh, Angelica, he couldn't mean to do that!"

"The case with John's pistols was gone from top of the tall chest, where he keeps them safe from the children," my sister said. "We must stop them, Eliza."

"If they met at ten, it's already too late." My knees gave way beneath me and I sank back into my chair and buried my face in my hands. I remembered the last conversation Alexander and I had

had about Mr. Monroe. Had I unwittingly advised him to fight a duel? Was he even now lying wounded, or worse?

What had he done? What had *I* done?

I heard the door open again, and Alexander's voice. I looked up as relief swept over me. He was with Mr. Church, and he wasn't wounded and he wasn't dead, but it was clear that his mood was dark indeed.

"Thank God, you're unharmed!" Angelica cried, hurrying to the two men as I was still too overcome to do.

"Of course we're unharmed, my dear," Mr. Church said. "Hamilton asked me here for a glass of brandy, and I accepted."

All I saw was my husband. "You went to challenge Mr. Monroe, didn't you?" I asked unsteadily. "That's where you went this morning, wasn't it?"

"Nothing came of it," he said, his voice still taut with anger. "There was no need for you to worry."

Mr. Church waved a single hand dismissively through the air, as if that alone were enough to banish the tension among us.

"Words were exchanged, grievances acknowledged, moderation prevailed, and the peace was preserved," he said, purposefully bland. "There's nothing left to discuss."

So they had gone there prepared for a duel, which hadn't happened. My heart was still beating too painfully fast from what could have happened for me to be relieved.

I turned back to my husband. "Alexander?"

"It's done," he said. "We shall speak of it no further."

He kept his word, and we never did.

Whatever had occurred—and what hadn't—between my husband and Mr. Monroe was enough to inspire Alexander to make an important decision. He would cease the back-and-forth sniping in the press with James Callender. Instead, he would tell the entire story of these infamous letters himself, in a pamphlet that he would write and publish at his own expense. He vowed that he would omit nothing, and therefore leave nothing for Callender or Mr. Monroe or anyone else to misconstrue or misinterpret in the future. Honesty and truth, always among my husband's most sterling qualities, would finally put an end to this entire wretched conspiracy against him.

Two days later, Alexander left before dawn for Philadelphia to tend to some older business connected with the bank. Although I was always sorry to see him leave, I was to a certain extent relieved. President Adams was once again in Massachusetts, Congress was not in session, and Mr. Monroe was safely away from Philadelphia and visiting his wife's family here in New York. There was no one left in the capital to vex my husband, and I prayed that a week buried in the ledgers and records of the bank would help clear his head. While he was away, he was also determined to write his pamphlet. I applauded his resolve, and wished him well.

While he was away, I read the latest reply from James Callender in response to the last letter from my husband. Since Callender's work was first published in a Philadelphia newspaper, *The Merchants' Daily Advertiser.* I'm sure Alexander took note of this specimen of Democratic-Republican rubbish before I, though his letters to me made no mention of it. He would, however, have been properly gratified to have witnessed my indignant response, and the disdain with which I removed the newspaper from our home and deposited it with Mr. Church, who'd expressed a desire to read it as well.

It was particularly infuriating to me to think how this whole sorry spectacle, calculated and contrived by a cabal of Democratic-Republican scoundrels to discredit my beloved husband, must also have amused and entertained most of our fellow citizens during this long summer. According to Angelica, it had sadly become the favorite topic of gossip at her parties, no matter how much she tried to dispel it.

It was all the more reason for Alexander's pamphlet. By telling his side of the tale, he was convinced that he could rely on the wise eye of the public to see truth from lies—a most noble belief held by an equally noble man.

Yet to my disgust, it was exactly that belief that Callender chose to skewer in his own pathetic attempt at a closing argument:

Because it is your intention, shortly to place the matter more precisely before the public. You are right, for the public have at present some unlucky doubts. They have long known you as an eminent and able statesman. They will be highly gratified by seeing you exhibited in the novel character of a lover.

As angry as I was to read this, I believed, as did my husband, that soon the shining truth would prove to the rest of the world who truly had sinned, and who had been sinned against.

And soon, very soon, it did exactly that.

I gave birth to another son, our fifth boy, on August 4, 1797, five days before my own fortieth birthday. We named him William Stephen Hamilton, a fine, fulsome name in honor of two of his uncles. Alexander and I together relished anew that sweetly indescribable love for a newborn, and the wonder that such a charming little creature had been created through God's grace, and our love. I never tired of watching my husband care for our children, cradling each one in his arms with such unabashed devotion that it always brought tears to my eyes.

I was still in this blissful state some two weeks after William's birth when Alexander joined me in the parlor. To grant me a respite, Angelica had taken our older children with her for the day, and except for little William and the servants, Alexander and I were as alone in our house as we ever were. He'd a stack of pages in his hands, and I smiled in expectation.

"Is that your pamphlet?" I asked, patting the cushion on the sofa in invitation. "You cannot know how eager I am to read it at last."

I was surprised that he didn't smile in return. In fact he was unusually solemn, continuing to hold the manuscript.

"It's already been printed, and is with the binder now," he said. "I've just had my original pages returned to me."

"It's a good thing it's at the binder," I said, "considering you've already placed advertisements for its sale."

Yet still he hesitated. "I wished for you to be recovered from William's birth before you read it," he said. "I didn't wish to cause you any mishap."

"I've never been so fragile as that, Alexander," I said, smiling warmly at his solicitude. "If I've been strong enough to read Cal-

lender's vile letters, I'm more than strong enough to read your re-
buttal."

At last he handed me the manuscript.

"Everything I have written here," he said slowly, "adheres to the
most absolute truth, no matter how painful."

"Painful for Callender and that villain Mr. Monroe," I said,
glancing at the first page. "What a splendid title! *Observations on
Certain Documents Contained in N. V & VI of 'The History of the
United States for the Year 1796,' In Which the Charge of Speculation
Against Alexander Hamilton, Late Secretary of the Treasury, Is Fully
Refuted. Written by Himself.'* That sets it all out, doesn't it?"

"Almost," he said, and cleared his throat. "And recall, my dearest wife, that I love you above all others, and always have."

"As I love you, too," I said, smiling. His obvious nervousness as
I began to read touched me; clearly this work was so important to
him that he seemed almost desperate for my approval. He needn't
have worried. I always enjoyed his writing, the concise beauty of his
sentences and the clarity and brilliance that showed in every word.
The best way to alleviate his anxiety would be to read, and thus I
began.

His argument began much as I expected it would, linking the
Democratic-Republicans to the Jacobins, as was entirely accurate.
Then he systematically began to explain and refute every calumny
and slander that had been made against him, complete with affi-
davits and other letters for reference.

I will not paraphrase or copy the entire document here, for
surely over time it has unfairly become the most widely read of any
of my husband's writings, and a certain line the most infamous. It is
also known by a far shorter name now—*The Reynolds Pamphlet*—
and one that proves that prurience will always sell. Yet on that day,
unlike all later readers, I was completely unprepared for what it
contained.

> *The charge against me is a connection with one James
> Reynolds for purpose of improper pecuniary speculation. My
> real crime an amorous connection with his wife, for a consid-
> erable time with his privity and connivance . . .*

I caught my breath as if I'd been struck. *His real crime . . . an amorous connection. . . .* I could scarcely comprehend the words I was reading. I resisted the impulse to push away the pages, realizing too late that I did not want to learn what was contained in this writing. But having started, I had to continue.

> *Some time in the summer of the year 1791, a woman called at my house in the city of Philadelphia, and asked to speak with me in private. . . .*

I forced myself not to rush, to read each word with care, and to overlook nothing.

> *She told me the street and the number of the house where she lodged. In the evening, I put a bank-bill in my pocket and went to the house. I inquired for Mrs. Reynolds and was shewn up stairs, at the head of which she met me and conducted me into a bed room. I took the bill out of my pocket and gave it to her. Some conversation ensued from which it was quickly apparent that other than pecuniary consolation would be acceptable. . . .*

Without realizing it, I'd crumpled the edge of the page, my fingers had been holding it that tightly.

> *After this, I had frequent meetings with her, most of them at my own house; Mrs. Hamilton and her children being absent on a visit to her father. . . .*

The words were swimming before my eyes, and I had to blink for them to make sense.

> *My intercourse with Mrs. Reynolds continued. . . .*

I paused as the meaning of the words sank in: nearly a year, then, that this betrayal had gone on.

> *This confession is not made without a blush. I cannot be the apologist of any vice because the ardour of passion may have made it mine. I can never cease to condemn myself for the pang, which I may inflict in a bosom eminently entitled to all my gratitude, fidelity, and love. But that bosom will approve, that even at so great an expence, I should effectively wipe away a more serious stain from a name, which it cherishes with no less elevation than tenderness. . . .*

I compelled myself to read to the very last word. I hadn't looked at Alexander once from the time I'd begun, and I didn't now that I'd finished.

I was shaking with grief. I could scarcely breathe from the pain of it.

"Betsey," he said softly. Somehow he was next to me, his voice anguished.

I pushed myself away from him as I staggered to my feet. I let the pages drop to the floor, where they scattered on the carpet.

I rushed from the parlor, up the stairs, and into the room where little William lay sleeping. I gathered his tiny body from his cradle and held him close, seeking comfort in a love I could trust.

"My dearest," Alexander said behind me.

I didn't turn, and I didn't reply. Swiftly I began gathering a few of the baby's things to take with me.

"Betsey, please." He stood in the doorway, blocking my way. "I know I've no right to ask your forgiveness, yet . . ."

"Don't," I said sharply. The baby in my arms wailed mournfully, and at last I began to cry, too, hot tears of mortification and shame and hurt drawn straight from my heart. "Let me pass. Please let me pass."

At last he stepped aside from the doorway.

I slipped past him, and hurried down the stairs and away from the house, and from him.

CHAPTER 21

New York City, New York
August 1797

The distance between our house and the Churches' on Robinson Street was not far, and I had walked it countless times before without much thought. But on this day I was only a fortnight removed from childbed, and the child I'd carried for nine months in my womb was now squalling in my arms. The afternoon was hot, and in my haste to leave I'd neglected to pause for a hat, so the sun was full in my face. But most of all, I carried upon my shoulders the impossibly heavy weight of my husband's betrayal, and by the time that I climbed the white stone steps to my sister's house, I was gasping for breath. When the footman opened the door, I stumbled inside, my tear-filled eyes slow to adjust after the bright sun, and the servant caught my arm to support me and the child.

"Eliza!" exclaimed my sister, hurrying into the hall to me. "What is wrong? What has happened?"

"It's Alexander," I said, my voice choked with fresh tears. "Oh, Angelica, what he did, what he has done! I would never have thought him capable of such a thing. How could he have done this to me, to us, to our children!"

Angelica's expression softened with pity. "He has finally told you, then."

"You knew, too?" I cried. "How is it that everyone knew of this except for me?"

"Not everyone," she said, striving to calm me as she took my arm. "Come upstairs, and we shall talk. Let's give little William to Agnes to hold, and I'll help you the rest of the way."

Her children's nursery maid was standing beside her, and with a mixture of reluctance and relief I handed my child into her capable arms. Now I noticed that there were other servants here as well, hovering to one side, and that her two daughters, Kitty and Elizabeth, and my own Angelica were watching, wide-eyed and uncertain, from the doorway to the parlor. For their sake, I tried to gulp back my sobs, and failed.

Angelica slipped her arm around my waist. "Come upstairs to my room with me, my dear," she said gently. "We'll have a glass of lemonade, and we'll talk."

I sagged against her and let her lead me up the stairs to her bedchamber. It was cooler in here, with this corner of the house shaded by trees, and the windows thrown open and the shades drawn against the afternoon sun. I dropped onto the sofa in her bedchamber and buried my face in my hands, and she sat beside me, her arm around me. She said nothing, but let me cry, and cry I did, until my handkerchief was sodden and my eyes burned, yet still more tears came, drawn straight from the break in my heart.

A servant entered with a tray with a pitcher of lemonade, two glasses, and a plate of biscuits, as if I were making an ordinary call. Angelica murmured something to the servant, who curtseyed and left us again.

"I sent word to Hamilton that you and William are safe with me," she said quietly. "I didn't want him to worry."

I sat upright with a shuddering sob. "What does he care?"

"He cares, Eliza," she said, carefully smoothing strands of my tear-soaked hair away from my forehead. "No matter what you think at this moment, he loves you, and he always will."

"Do you know what he has done, Angelica?" I asked tremulously. "Has he told you and Mr. Church?"

"Why don't you tell me instead," she said. "That is, if you can."

I nodded, steeling myself. "He has written a pamphlet in which he confesses to having had an—an amorous connection—six years ago!—in Philadelphia with some coarse, wanton woman named Maria Reynolds."

Oh, how I hated saying even her name aloud, and from anger and shame I broke off, looking down at my crumpled handkerchief.

"My poor, dear sister," murmured Angelica. "How dreadful for you to learn of it like that."

"I remember when she came to our house seeking his assistance," I said, the painful words coming fast now that I'd begun. "I thought nothing of it and yet he—he went to her rooms later that night, and she offered herself to him, and he—they did what they did, and then he came home to me. And I didn't know, Angelica. I didn't realize any of it was happening."

"But how could you, sweet?" she asked. "You'd no reason to suspect him, nor reason for distrust."

My eyes burned with fresh tears. "That was when James was so sick and I took him to Albany, and while I was worrying over our child, he—Alexander—was bringing this woman into our home, into our own bed, many times."

Angelica drew in her breath. "He wrote that in the pamphlet, too?"

"He did," I said, my voice squeaking with emotion. "He says that he continued to—to be with her for nearly a year, and even paid her husband—her *husband*!—for the privilege of continuing with her, and keeping the secret."

I squeezed my eyes shut, wishing it were as easy to blot out the tawdry words I'd read. "There were other men who knew of it, too, including Mr. Monroe, who told that hateful man Callender. I understand that it is better for the world to know the truth, that Alexander wasn't compromising his—his integrity as the secretary. He was just compromising..." I broke into fresh sobs. "... our marriage."

I lowered my head, overwhelmed. I heard the clink of the silver pitcher against the edge of a glass, and then Angelica was pressing that glass into my hand.

"Drink this," she ordered, and I did, so broken by despair that I was as obedient as any of our children. The lemonade was sweet with sugar and orange-water, with the bite of mint: my sister's own recipe. From that day onward, I could never bring myself to drink it again.

"None of this is your fault, Eliza," Angelica insisted. "I know you will somehow blame yourself, because that is how you are, but it isn't. Not one bit."

"But why else would he have gone to her?" I asked miserably. "I've always loved him with all my heart, but if that wasn't—"

"Hush," she said, taking my hand in hers. "It's always the case that evil will do what it can to corrupt goodness, and break and reduce a noble spirit to its own base level."

"The Democratic-Republicans," I said, my bitterness undisguised. I couldn't forgive these fine gentlemen, nor did I wish to. "Mr. Jefferson, Mr. Burr, and especially Mr. Monroe."

"Exactly," Angelica said. "Your Hamilton is known for his generous spirit to those in need, especially to women in difficult circumstances. One of his finest qualities became a weakness to be exploited by his enemies."

"They would do that to him," I said slowly, remembering how often these same enemies had targeted him before, and how he'd gone before Congress not once, but twice, to defend himself. "Alexander is always kindness itself. No one in need has ever been turned from our door."

"Well, then, there you are," Angelica said with an emphatic nod. "It's clear enough that this slatternly creature was sent by Hamilton's enemies to seduce him into a scandal, with the hope that it would destroy him. But they did not succeed, did they? It didn't harm him six years ago, and it won't now, not so long as his friends stand by him."

"But even if they'd contrived this trap for him, Angelica, he didn't have to agree to it," I said, the raw pain bubbling back up inside me.

Angelica sighed deeply, her fingers squeezing around mine as she stared at the floor before her.

"There are things that men—even the best of men—do that make no sense," she said finally. "As much as I adore your Hamilton, I cannot begin to say why he would betray you for the novelty of this Reynolds strumpet. And yet he did."

"He did," I echoed forlornly. Even having read Alexander's words, even repeating them to my sister, I could still hardly accept this new truth about the one man I'd always loved.

"Yes." She was gazing past me, her dark eyes wide but unseeing. "Have you ever thought how different our lives would have been if there hadn't been a war, Eliza? Most likely we would have both married some dull Dutchmen, and led dull respectable lives within sight of the North River."

"Not you," I said through my sniffles. "You could never have been content with such a life."

"I would have had no choice," she mused, "and neither would you. Think of it, Eliza. If it weren't for the war, you would never have met your Hamilton, and I would never have met my John."

"I wish I never had met him!" I said vehemently.

"Hush, you don't mean that," she said. "You feel that way at this moment, but it will pass. You love Hamilton and he loves you. He is the father of your children. If it weren't for your Hamilton and my John, we wouldn't have known the pride, the pleasure, the endless satisfactions and frustrations large and small of sharing our lives with extraordinary men. They need us, just as we need them."

I nodded, blotting at my tears again. From the first time Alexander and I had met, he'd been the one I'd wanted, and the one I chose. And he did need me, just as I needed him; I'd never doubted that.

I wondered if Angelica were thinking the same of Mr. Church as she sat beside me, twisting and toying with the jeweled rings on her fingers.

"But then, everything in this life comes with a price, doesn't it?" she said, and gave me a small half smile. "If daring to love such men as we have means that we must forgive them when they stray, then . . ."

She let the sentence trail off unfinished, ambiguous and puzzling.

"Angelica," I said, turning to face her. "Has Mr. Church ever strayed?"

Her mouth curved upward, but it couldn't be called a smile. "In truth I do not know, Eliza. London and Paris have many temptations, and he has always been a restless man."

I nodded, and asked no more. Even between Angelica and me, there were lines that could not be crossed.

The tall clock in the hall chimed the hour: five o'clock. From downstairs I heard William crying, fretting, and I felt the answering twinge in my breasts, heavy and aching with milk.

"I must go to the baby," I said, beginning to rise, but Angelica placed her hand on my arm to stop me.

"You know you have a place with us as long as you require it," she said. "Tonight, a week, a month. Stay here until you know your heart."

I stayed the night in my sister's house. I slept but little, my thoughts still too much distressed by my husband's revelations. The next morning William roused me early, and to keep from waking the rest of the house, I took him with me into the garden. I found a bench beneath a tree and nursed him, relishing the quiet of the new day. Sun slanted bright over the brick wall, and dewdrops hung like diamonds in the lawn. My head ached and my eyes were swollen from weeping, but at least here, with my little son at my breast, I'd some semblance of peace.

Lost in my thoughts, I didn't hear Alexander enter the garden until he was standing directly before me, his hat in his hand. Despite the early hour, he was neatly dressed and clean-shaven, but from the shadows beneath his eyes, I knew he'd slept no better than I. We'd often been apart on account of his business and other journeys, but last night had been the first in our marriage when we'd been in the same city, yet had not slept together beneath the same roof.

I watched him warily, and I said nothing by way of greeting, leaving it for him to speak first. I hadn't wanted him here, not yet, and I felt almost trapped by his presence.

"Good day, madam." He bowed deeply. "How is your health this morning?"

"Not as it should be, Colonel," I answered. If he wished to keep that distance of formality between us, then so would I. "I slept ill, having received grievous news yesterday."

"I am sorry, deeply sorry, for that," he said, "For that, and for everything else. I've no right so much as to beg for your forgiveness."

His entire expression and posture showed his sorrow and re-gret, but it wasn't enough, not after what he'd done. I didn't an-swer, leaving the emptiness to be filled by the chattering of the birds in the tree overhead and the little mewling sound of content-ment from our son at my breast.

He nodded as if I'd answered, and I suppose by my silence I had.

"I have taken the liberty of booking passage for you and our daughter to Albany on tomorrow's sloop," he said. "I guessed that you would wish to be away from town with your parents when the pamphlet is published, and that you would find comfort in having our daughter with you."

I understood that he hadn't included our daughter simply for my comfort, but to remove her as well from the shameful uproar that would doubtless greet the pamphlet. It was meant to be thoughtful, the consideration of a father for his daughter's tender feelings. Yet where had that consideration and regard been six years before? What did it matter now, when the damage was al-ready done? My eyes stung with tears, and I blinked them back.

He nodded again and cleared his throat, and I thought of how rare it was for the great Colonel Hamilton to be without words.

William had finished his meal, sated and drowsy. I wiped the last milky bubbles from his lips with the corner of his blanket and put him to my shoulder so I could pat his back. Alexander watched, his expression full of the same love and wonder that he showed toward all our children.

"Might I hold him?" he asked humbly, as if he fully expected me to refuse.

After a moment, I held the baby out to him.

"Take care," I warned, offering him the same cloth I'd had over my shoulder. "You know how he can be after he's been fed."

He took little William and tucked him deftly against his chest without any concern for his fine dark silk coat. I watched as he walked the baby slowly around the yard, rocking him gently and saying the sort of soft, sweet nonsense that he always did to our in-fants.

He'd always been an admirable father, and in every way but one, he'd been an admirable husband, too. My heart swelled with love and anguish, a terrible combination, as I watched him with William.

At last he handed the now-sleeping baby back to me, lingering before me.

"Know that I love you more than ever, Betsey," he said at last, his voice at once both raw and contrite. "That has never changed. You are everything to me, and I could not bear my life without you beside me. I am so sorry that I have hurt you."

"So am I," I said, all I'd venture, or could say. I hurt too much for more. "Good day, Colonel Hamilton."

I do not know what he'd expected of me, but his disappointment was unmistakable as he settled his hat on his head to leave. "Good day to you, too, Eliza. I'll come for you tomorrow to accompany you to the sloop."

I watched him leave as he'd come, through the house, and only when I heard the servant close the door after him did I let myself cry again.

As he'd promised, Alexander saw me, our daughter, Angelica, and William on board the sloop to Albany. Our son Philip also came to bid us farewell, though I suspect more on account of his sister's urging than anything else. My two oldest children had remained close, and it pleased me no end to see how devoted Philip, fifteen, was toward his sister, thirteen, and she toward him. He now seemed more a man than a boy, taking extra care to keep at her side, while Angelica in her bright red habit flitted about the dock like a merry little bird, eager for amusement and attention.

As I waited to board, Alexander and I said little to each other beyond what was expected regarding the weather, the wind, and the provisions. As we watched our two older children, I thought proudly of how they both showed so much promise. Now taller than his father, Philip especially today struck me as thoughtful and solemn, and no doubt a bit preoccupied with the studies he'd left behind to tend us.

But as at last we prepared to board the sloop, I realized the reason for his somber mood.

"You already told Philip about the pamphlet, didn't you?" I said, my voice low so others would not hear. "He knows, doesn't he?"

He nodded. "It was better he hear of it from me than others at the college."

I grimaced. "I wish he hadn't had to hear of it at all."

"He's almost a man, Eliza," he said. "You can't keep him sheltered from the world as if he were an infant."

That wasn't what I'd meant. What I'd wished was that Alexander's own actions hadn't demanded the need for the pamphlet in the first place. Philip had always idolized his father, and to discover that Alexander had made such an unfortunate mistake in judgment and virtue must be difficult for him to comprehend. Now, too, he would be placed in the uncomfortable position of having to defend his father against his classmates' inevitable gibes.

But there was no time to explain that to Alexander, not with Philip and Angelica rejoining us to make our final good-byes. There was a final flurry of activity as the sailors prepared to cast off, waiting for Alexander and Philip to disembark so they could pull back the gangplank.

"You must go," I said, my heart suddenly racing at the thought of leaving him behind. "It's not fair to keep everyone else waiting while you tarry."

"I'm tarrying on account of you, Eliza." He smiled, squinting at me and into the sun beneath the brim of his hat. "Take care of yourself and my two little darlings, and carry my regards to your parents."

I nodded, unable to find any words that might express what I felt.

If he took note of my painful silence, he did not say it.

"Good-bye, my dearest." He swept off his hat and bent to kiss me, not on the lips, but on my cheek. Then like that he was gone and so was I, and the sloop was easing from the shore, and all that was left to me was the sight of him and Philip standing on the dock with their black cocked hats raised in salute and farewell.

When Angelica, William, and I arrived at The Pastures five days later, my parents welcomed us joyfully, believing that I'd come simply to present their latest grandchild to them. My second sister Peggy had not been well, and that, too, was another excuse for my visit to Albany.

As I had so many times before, I embraced the chance to walk in the gardens and across the fields and to be alone with my own thoughts. I'd time to let Alexander's words settle, and to consider my sister's wise counsel as well. I prayed for wisdom, and for understanding. Most of all, my wounded heart struggled to make sense of what had happened, and weigh it against the love I'd once believed entirely without flaw.

My husband had sinned six years ago. As I walked alone, I thought of all that had happened in those six years, of happy times and sorrowful ones that we had shared. We'd lost one child, but rejoiced at the birth of another. We'd survived an illness that had claimed a thousand other lives. He'd stepped away from the government for my sake, and we'd grown closer because of it.

That was our life together, and that was our love as well. Placed in the balance, how much did our marriage counter the "amorous encounter" with another woman? Was it sufficient to let me forgive him? Was our bond of love and trust strong enough to withstand this break, and be mended anew?

I'd only been at my parents' house for a few days when Papa sent for me to join him in his library. As soon as I did, I saw the pamphlet open on his desk, and my heart sank.

As can be imagined, he was furious.

"Did you know of this, Eliza?" he demanded. "Have you read it for yourself? Is that why you fled to us here, for sanctuary?"

"I have read it, yes," I said. "Alexander shared it with me before it was published, and I was—I wasn't happy."

"What decent woman would be?" he exclaimed. "That any Christian husband would dare to treat his wife with so little respect and regard, and then to boast of his sin in the press!"

"He is hardly boasting," I said, defending Alexander in spite of everything. "He simply means to present the truth, so that the public will know that he isn't guilty of all the treasonous misdeeds that the Democratic-Republicans have accused him of committing."

My father shook his head, and with each word thumped his fist on the desk beside the pamphlet.

"I do not know of any misdeed, Democratic or Republican or otherwise, that is more loathsome than the sin of adultery," he thundered. "I have always regarded your husband as another son,

Eliza, but to see what he has done to humiliate and betray my daughter makes me realize how misplaced my affection has been."

"Please don't think that way of him, Papa," I pleaded. "It was all a plot to discredit him by Mr. Madison and the others. That woman seduced him with the intent to create a scandal."

"No man is ever unwillingly seduced, Eliza," he said acidly. "Your husband admits that himself. This whore parted her legs for him, and he hadn't the strength to resist."

I blushed, for there really was no way even I could contrive an explanation for that particular act.

"I'm sorry I ever welcomed him into this house," my father went on. "I'm doubly sorry I trusted him as an officer and an honorable gentleman, and gave you to him as his wife."

"Papa, please," I said, my hands clasped tightly before me. "If I can forgive him his sin against me, then I pray that you can find it in your heart to forgive him as well."

At once I realized what I'd just said. Was I in truth able to forgive him? Was I ready to do so?

"You are under no obligation to return to him, Eliza," my father said sternly. "No one will fault you for it after this. You will do better to remain here, and send for the other children as well."

"Thank you, Papa," I said, but I knew it would be for my heart, not my father, to decide.

As I soon learned, there was little public sympathy for my husband, and less forgiveness. People were alternately shocked, appalled, or scornful. One or two of Alexander's oldest friends applauded his courage, but for the most part he was skewered and ridiculed. Few saw the malicious hand of the Democratic-Republicans at work, and concentrated instead only on the sordid affair with Mrs. Reynolds. Yet each word of mockery and criticism began to strengthen my resolve that Alexander and I would confront this together. Who would dare fault him if I were at his side?

But there was no such decency to be found in the Democratic-Republican newspapers. Echoing their malevolent masters, they attacked not only Alexander, but me as well. They accused me of being not his lawful wife, but only one more lascivious sultana in his harem. They chided me for tolerating what I hadn't known had happened. In language stolen from the Holy Bible itself, they chastised me: "Art thou a wife? See him, whom thou hast chosen as thy partner of this life, lolling in the lap of a harlot!"

Yet their harangues didn't shame me, so much as anger me on my husband's behalf.

The first week of September, I returned home to New York, and to him.

He and Philip were waiting on the same dock as when they'd bid us farewell. Although Alexander and I had agreed not to write to each other while I was in Albany, I had heard by way of my sister Angelica that he'd been thoroughly miserable, battered by his enemies, the newspapers, and even well-meaning friends over the pamphlet.

As the sloop pulled close to the dock, I stood on the deck beside the rail, rocking back and forth with little William in my arms. There'd be no missing me: I wore an extravagantly foolish hat that my mother had insisted on buying for me in Albany, with wide red silk ribbons like streamers that tossed around my face. The closer we came, the more I tried to gauge Alexander's humor. I could see he'd his customary half smile, but I sensed that he was as uneasy about greeting me as I was him.

He was the first up the gangplank, bounding on board to reach me with a younger man's agility. He came striding to me with purpose, and just before he reached me he swept off his hat, and stopped.

"Good day, Mrs. Hamilton," he said, his eyes searching mine. "Welcome home."

All I could think of at that moment was how glad I was to see him. I reached up, rested my free hand on his shoulder to steady myself, and kissed him awkwardly on the cheek. He smiled, and I smiled and for now that was enough.

Despite the trouble that Alexander's pamphlet had brought us, in the end it did accomplish what he'd set out to do. His reputation at the Treasury was again secured, and considered beyond reproach. If in the process he was now considered a libertine and an adulterer, then he (and I) accepted it, our heads high.

Others did not. President and Mrs. Adams were particularly

outspoken in their name-calling, practically hissing like snakes in their vehemence as they defamed my husband as the most lubricious and lewd rake in the country.

But likewise we learned who our true friends were: Robert Troup, Gouvener Morris, Rufus King, Robert Morris, Robert McHenry, and many more besides, from the Treasury, from Congress, from the legal profession, and even from his long-ago days in the army and at King's College. These gentlemen rallied about us and supported Alexander, choosing to value him for his many qualities rather than cast him aside for a single misstep. There were even rumors that, with relations between our country and France deteriorating, Alexander might be called back to service in the government, his talents and experience too useful to be ignored.

The greatest among these loyal gentlemen showed his loyalty to my husband in an unexpected way. From President and Mrs. Washington came the gift of a splendid silver cooler for holding wine, and a note with a pledge of friendship and regard that I treasured always:

> *I pray you to present my best wishes, in which Mrs. Washington joins me, to Mrs. Hamilton and the family, and that you would be persuaded that with every sentiment of the highest regard, I remain your sincere friend and affectionate honorable servant.*

Somehow we managed to escape the dismal days of that summer, and I could only praise God and His mercy that we had. In September I held a small dinner that was also a kind of thanksgiving, with the Churches, our own family, and several of our closest friends besides.

Yet even among the feasting and merriment and toasts, I fretted over my oldest son, Philip, who'd been included in the party. He was excelling at his studies at nearby Columbia, and there was every expectation that he would follow in Alexander's path and triumph in the law. As proud as I was of him, I worried that, also like his father, he worked too hard to the detriment of his health, and on this night he seemed quiet and pale, and thoroughly unlike his usual high-spirited self. He'd developed a hacking sort of cough as well, and as mothers will, after the cloth was drawn I drew him aside from the others to make inquiries and press my palm to his forehead.

"I'm perfectly well, Mamma," he said. "I've much to do for my recitations, but it's nothing that can't be completed in time."

"I don't like the sound of that cough," I said with concern. "I don't want to think of all you boys coughing away like that together in class."

He smiled, albeit too wanly for my tastes. "I assure you, I will be fine," he said. "But if you don't mind, I believe I'll beg off the brandy tonight, and retire for the evening. My head aches as well, doubtless from too much reading."

"Or too much stale beer in a tavern last night," I said. "Go upstairs to bed, and I'll make your apologies."

But by morning, he'd no interest in eating, and he'd a fever and soreness in his joints. I sent first for Dr. Bard, who then sent for Dr. Hosack, the professor of medicine from the college. He confirmed that a number of students had been taken ill with bilious fever, and immediately assumed the care of our son. Complaining and determined to continue his studies, Philip requested his books be brought to him so he might read in bed. Our other children were banished from his company for the sake of their health, though Angelica insisted on standing at the door of his bedchamber and singing foolish songs to cheer him.

Within two days, he'd worsened further. The ache in his joints had grown more acute, he'd chills along with the fever, and the window shades were drawn against the sun since bright light had become unbearable to him. Now there were no books read, nor foolish songs sung to him; instead we all whispered, and walked softly.

"I do not wish to leave the boy in this condition," Alexander said after he visited Philip to say good-bye. The carriage was already waiting in the street to take him to Hartford in Connecticut, where he was to represent the state in Federal Court; a long ride under any circumstances, but especially now. "You must make sure to send for me if there is any change."

"You know I will," I said, glancing fearfully back toward our son's room. "I trust Dr. Hosack's skill, but we both know how unpredictable fevers can be."

It was experience I wished we didn't have. I watched as Dr. Hosack tried different remedies to no avail, recognizing each of them in turn: the flannel cloths, the different medicines and elixirs, the brandy and the leeches and the cold baths and warm.

By the end of the week, our son was even sicker, and with a grim face, Dr. Hosack informed me that the fever had assumed a typhus character that was often fatal in young persons. He sent a courier racing to Hartford to bring Alexander home. He wouldn't have done that had there been any hope of our son surviving, and I grew distraught with fear and dread, and thought of how my sister Peggy had lost her two oldest children to fevers, too. When I sat beside Philip's bed, he no longer knew me. His handsome face was gaunt and ghastly, his breathing was ragged. His skin was covered with a ruddy rash, and was like fire to touch. When I begged for something to do to help Philip live, Dr. Hosack told me to pray.

In the evening, Alexander still had not returned. Philip was delirious, thrashing about and babbling incoherently about a dog we'd had when he'd been a boy, an old friend from Albany, a girl he'd met at last week's assembly. Then as abruptly as the delirium had begun, it vanished, and he became deathly still, without a pulse, and his eyes rolled back in his head.

I wept, distraught, so sure was I that he would die, and the doctor ordered me away from the room so that I wouldn't witness my son's agonized death. My sister Angelica came and sat with me, holding me as we prayed together for my precious boy.

From desperation the doctor tried one last cure, a bath not of cold water, but of warm, and infused with Jesuits' bark and rum. Philip seemed to improve, and the doctor ordered him removed and rubbed briskly with rough cloths, and the immersion repeated. He improved still more, and though he was so weak he could scarcely raise his eyelids, he recognized me, and smiled. Now I wept for joy, and praised the doctor as our son's savior.

It was well past midnight and I was still sitting drowsily beside Philip's bed when Alexander finally returned. I roused myself and met him by the stairs, where his steps were heavy and his shoulders bent with grief. He'd been delayed along the way by overflowing streams, and feared he'd arrived too late to bid farewell to our beloved son. When I told him that Philip not only lived, but seemed improved, he wept, and rushed to kneel at our son's bedside. He saw for himself that this was true, and when he learned all that had been done on Philip's behalf, he went to the room where Dr. Hosack lay resting and woke him, insisting on thanking the good doctor himself for preserving our child.

To Dr. Hosack's amazement, for the next fortnight Alexander put aside his legal cases, and instead devoted himself entirely to nursing our son back to health. I wasn't surprised, for I'd seen his tenderness and dedication in tending his sick family before, and even been the beneficiary of it myself. If he'd not chosen the field of law, I do believe he would have made a physician of the first order, and done even more good in the world.

When at last our son was clear of danger, Alexander and I sat beside his bed together one evening, watching over him as parents who've been newly reminded of the fragility of their children's lives, and the mercy of God's grace. Yet Alexander's thoughts were even darker, and in a way I'd never expected.

"All the way from Hartford, I grieved," he said, his voice low so as not to wake Philip. "I felt sure we'd lost him, and it would have been entirely my fault."

"No, it wouldn't have," I said. "You can't blame yourself. Dr. Hosack said there were several other boys in Philip's class ill as well, and they took the fever from one another."

"That's how it appears," he said, "but I would have known otherwise. It would have been fate, pure and simple. His death would have been my punishment, retribution for how grievously I'd wronged you."

"Don't even think such things, Alexander," I said, horrified. "It was the other boys who made Philip sick, and Dr. Hosack and God's will that restored him. There was no fate, no retribution, and I won't listen to you speak heathen nonsense like that again."

He didn't answer, content to watch our son instead, and uneasily I knew he remained still convinced of his blasphemous superstitions.

And from what befell us all later, perhaps in the end he was the one who was right.

Although in theory Alexander had retired from the government, throughout 1797 he continued to be an unofficial advisor in ways I didn't entirely understand.

When Mr. Adams had been sworn in as president, he'd planned to maintain the country's strict neutrality with the French government. But as the year progressed, this became an increasingly difficult position to maintain since the French government itself seemed to change as fast as the leaves on the trees. The leaders in Paris who welcomed American diplomats one week were fresh victims of the guillotine the next, and were replaced with another set of Frenchmen determined to scorn everything American. The American delegates were denied access to the true men in power, and were forced to make their negotiations through three buffoonish underlings— Jean-Conrad Hottinguer, Pierre Bellamy, and Lucien Hauteval, whose true names were replaced with the coded initials X, Y, and Z, men who extorted bribes and made other outlandish demands to the Americans. Like characters in some silly French opera, X, Y, and Z became universally loathed and declaimed in American newspapers, the only French names that ordinary Americans could both pronounce and despise. As if this all weren't enough, a powerful new general with no ties to past regimes had emerged, a man named Napoleon Bonaparte, who seemed to be the only leader in France with a definite plan of government, albeit one that had all the earmarks of a dictatorship.

French privateers plundered American merchant shipping, claiming their entitlement from the Jay Treaty with England. Merchants in the states of New England as well as in New York, New Jersey, Pennsylvania, and Maryland, that contained the home ports of much of lost shipping, were justly outraged, and demanded that the president take action, while the southern states, with less to lose and led by Mr. Jefferson, continued their infatuation with the French Jacobins, preferring them as allies, no matter how volatile or violent their actions.

Making matters even more difficult for President Adams was

the continued devious and underhanded behavior of the Democratic-Republicans, especially Mr. Jefferson. Not only did he illegally meet with French diplomats in Philadelphia, falsely representing himself as part of the current government, but he also sought to undermine President Adams and his cabinet by telling the French how weak the Federalists were, how they'd soon be out of office, and how if the French quickly declared war on Britain, America would come to their assistance.

Thus, while President Adams was attempting to maintain a neutral stance, he was also quietly creating an American military presence as well in the event that the country was finally drawn into a war with France. This, then, was where my husband proved so invaluable. He'd experience at building and supporting a military force that dated back to when he'd been an aide-de-camp for General Washington, and he'd continued his efforts through the Whiskey Rebellion. There wasn't another man in the country with this kind of expertise, nor one who possessed the organizational skills combined with the ability to negotiate the twisted layers of bureaucracy with ease. He also spoke, wrote, and thought in French.

As a result, Alexander's opinion was often sought by members of the cabinet and Congress, and his advice taken—likely far more often that President Adams himself ever realized. Alexander, too, being acutely aware of public opinion, wrote a fresh new series of essays called *The Stand*, in which he supported a standing army to defend the country. To accomplish so much would have been remarkable under any circumstances, but all this occurred during the same time as he was embroiled in his personal conflicts with Mr. Madison, composing the pamphlet regarding Mrs. Reynolds, and coping with the serious illness of our son.

The talk of war with France continued on with little or no resolution, and thoroughly agitating my husband in the process. I was grateful to see the end of 1797, and had hopes that 1798 would be much more fortuitous for everyone I loved most. I occupied myself with my family's affairs, encouraged my children's accomplishments, and cautiously rebuilt the love and trust with my husband.

But then in early May, the idle talk of war over suppers became a frightening reality. The afternoon was warm and sunny, that season when spring has just begun to cede to summer. The days were at last sufficiently warm to make the white muslin dresses that fashion demanded agreeable, and as my sister Angelica and I stepped from an apothecary shop, the straight skirts of our dresses fluttered around our legs and over the tops of our heelless slippers in the breeze. I don't recall what our conversation might have been—some idle foolishness—but in the pause between our words, I heard the first loud explosion in the distance.

We stared at each other, startled and unsure.

"Was that thunder?" asked Angelica, holding her hand on her straw hat as she tipped her head back to study the sky. "I'd think it too fair a day for a lightning storm."

"It's not thunder," I said slowly. It had been many years since I'd heard this distant, ominous, thunderous roar—all the way back to the Revolution—but once heard, it's a sound not easily forgotten. It was also a sound I'd hoped never to hear again in my life.

"It's gunfire, Angelica," I said. "Cannons. I recall it from the army."

Angelica's eyes widened. "Gunfire! How can that be here in New York?"

Even as she spoke, the sound came again, the rumbling roar of great guns in unison, echoing from across the water. It wasn't close—no ship was firing broadsides directly into the city—but it was still far too near for a country that claimed to be neutral.

Other people had paused as well, their conversations stopped and their business halted as together we all strained to listen, making the city strangely quiet and ill at ease.

It came again, echoing from the harbor to the east and the oceans beyond.

"The French," I said automatically. "It must be the French."

"But here?" Angelica said, her voice trembling with anxiety. "I cannot believe it."

My sister and I parted then, she returning to her husband and family, and I hurrying to Alexander's office. I didn't doubt that he would know about the guns, and as soon as I appeared, he ushered me quickly into his own room, and shut the door.

"Did you hear," I began, but he quickly finished my sentence.

"The broadsides." There was a renewed energy to him that I

hadn't seen for years, an animation to his gestures and brightness to his eyes. "Yes, everyone in the city heard them, didn't they?"

"But where were they from?" I asked anxiously. "Is it the French?"

"Who else would it be?" he asked. "This afternoon a French privateer of fourteen guns captured the ship *Rosseter* from this port, and the *Thomas* from Bristol. It was the privateer's guns we heard, for they were in our waters, less than a mile outside the harbor. Everything could be seen from the battery with a spyglass."

"But what does this mean, Alexander?"

He smiled slowly, confidently. "What it means is that the time for talking is done, Betsey. It means that Adams can no longer mince his words like an old woman, and must instead put some teeth into them. Because I'm willing to wager that before the summer's over, America will be at war with France."

CHAPTER 22

New York City, New York
May 1798

A lexander had predicted that America and France would be at war before the summer ended. Although usually astute in such political guessing games, this time my husband's prediction proved far too generous.

Only weeks after Angelica and I had heard the French privateer's cannon in the harbor, Congress authorized a new navy and commissioned a dozen frigates to be built, and further, had finally agreed to a provisional army of ten thousand men. Whilst all this building and recruiting and provisioning was taking place, American navy ships were encouraged to engage any French ships that dared threaten American merchantmen, and letters of marque were issued to enterprising American shipmasters who wished to try their hand at privateering against French ships. To be sure, no war had been officially declared, and so I suppose my husband's prediction was still correct, but the effect was much the same.

Almost overnight, war fever became the order of the day in New York. The city and harbor had suffered many indignities and losses at the hands of the French, so I suppose it was to be expected, but I still was not prepared for the sudden rush of patriotism and military fervor. The black silk cockades of the Federalists (for this was New York) appeared on every hat and bosom, the only music played by bands and orchestras were brisk marches, and even farmers in the market house made sure to drape a length of patriotic bunting above their stands of turnips and carrots.

Alexander was beside himself with anticipation. Nearly twenty years of time had burnished a fine and golden glow upon his memories of the army during the Revolution, and he chose only to remember the camaraderie and the glory of those days, and conveniently forgot the tedium and depravations, the squabbling, frustrations, and suffering that had played a much larger part in the Revolution. He was once again as eager for war as he had been at twenty, and I could not fathom it.

"It's not so much the possibility of war itself, Betsey, as the creation of a permanent military force," he tried to explain to me once again. "This country will never be regarded as a serious power without a permanent army and navy, yet the Democratic-Republicans have foolishly balked at their creation since the end of the Revolution. It broke Washington's heart to disband his army then, and if it now must take a pack of overreaching Frenchmen for Congress finally to restore it, then already this war has served its purpose."

"Either way, Alexander, it should no longer be of any personal concern of yours," I said firmly. "You served admirably enough in the Revolution, and there's no need for you to involve yourself once again."

"But that's the very reason I should," he argued earnestly, leaning forward in his chair. "Most of the generals from the Revolution are in their dotage by now."

I paused, thinking of how this entire foolish discussion was likely moot. Any military appointment that would draw Alexander from retirement would have to come from President Adams, who so despised my husband that I believed I'd sooner be granted a commission than he would.

"You're forty-three years old," I said instead. "You complain that a long carriage ride rattles your kidneys to an unbearable degree. How could you tolerate life in a rough camp?"

He swept his hand expansively through the air. "Forty-three is young for a senior officer, and the bracing rigors of camp life would restore me completely. Besides, there are few men in the country with my experience and knowledge. It would be irresponsible of me not to serve if asked."

I sighed, folding fresh shifts and dresses for me and for our daughter, Angelica, into neat stacks on the bed. I was packing my trunk for a short visit to my parents in Albany; my father had been unwell, with digestive difficulties as well as the old and ever-worsening malady of his legs, and he had reached the age when each time that I was summoned to his side, I was prepared for it to be the last. The trip would benefit Angelica, too. After nearly eleven years in our family, Fanny Antill had gone to live with an older, now-married sister, and Angelica missed her sorely in our house filled with boys.

I set the clothes into the trunk and turned back toward Alexander, my hands resting at my waist.

"You should also recall that you're a private citizen," I said, "with a profession that claims all your time, and six children to support."

"And a wife," he added. "You should not forget her, for I never will. I know it's your duty to go to your father, Betsey, but I wish it weren't necessary. You've no idea how much I miss you when you're away."

Despite my irritation over his foolish talk of the army, I smiled. I couldn't help it. Since the awful business last summer with his confession of the long-ago infidelity, he'd been even more attentive to me, and slowly, day by day, our marriage had been restored. Because of his renewed devotion and his determination to make things right once again between us, I'd grown to love him all the more, if such a thing were possible.

"I'll miss you, too," I said fondly. "I always do. At least you'll have the older boys here with you for company."

"Bachelor Hall, that's what this house becomes when you're away," he said dramatically. "Philip, Alexander, James, John, and me. Meals at all hours, and no order anywhere. You'd scarcely recognize the place when you return."

"Excellent practice for when you all run off to join the army," I said, closing the lid to the trunk. "It's late, Alexander. Come to bed."

"I'm not jesting, Betsey," he said, his voice again turning serious. "Congress will ask Washington to lead the new army as commander-in-chief, and he's already told me that he'll only accept if I'm his second-in-command."

"You would do that?" I asked, not wanting to believe him. "You'd give up everything again?"

It would be everything, too. He'd only now begun to recover his law career after letting it go for all the years he'd been employed at the Treasury, and we'd just begun to climb to some small degree of prosperity. He'd had more time to spend with our children, and with me. For the first time in our marriage, we'd begun to talk of building a house that would be our own design, in the country and away from the city—a dream that would abruptly end if he were to accept this commission with its likely diminutive salary.

And if he returned to the army, there would always be the chance that he could once again find himself at risk and in danger. It wouldn't matter that this time the enemy was French, not English. My fears for his safety would be the same as they'd been twenty years before against the British.

"You'd truly do that, Alexander?" I asked again, wanting us both to be sure of my question and his reply.

"If I were asked," he said, too promptly for my tastes. "I would, yes. Think of it, Betsey: I'd be a general. If Washington leaves Mount Vernon for the sake of the country, then I could hardly turn him down."

"You could for the sake of your family," I said. "If you wished your sons and daughter to have any memories of you as their father, you would not even let your name be considered."

He shook his head. "I can't, my love," he said solemnly. "My duty to my country—"

"No more," I said, my patience gone. "Not tonight, Alexander. No more."

We did not discuss it then, nor in the morning before I sailed. Instead the issue of the army remained like an unwanted specter between us, unseen and unmentioned but relentlessly present.

I understood the allure the army held for him, and always would. It wasn't only a question of duty. As second-in-command to General Washington, he'd once more have the kind of far-reaching power to organize and create that he'd held as secretary of treasury. He'd again be in the thick of the government, with the respect and responsibilities that went with it. And exactly as his desire for advancement had led him to risk his life at the siege of Yorktown, now, for the sake of being a general he was willing to risk his family and his marriage.

With all of this unsaid between us, I left New York and retreated to The Pastures. The distance made little difference. Through letters that came nearly daily, Alexander persisted, alternating declarations of his boundless affection with delicately worded hints regarding my health and the state of my mind. I understood: by my health, he meant he didn't want me to worry about him and the army, and the only real question about the state of my mind was whether I'd yet changed it to favor his hopes.

Nor did I find consolation this time at The Pastures. Despite my father's pain and suffering, he was still able to take great pleasure in Alexander's prospects. He'd already learned from his old friend General Washington of the plans for the new army, of how the general would again be commander-in-chief with Alexander his inspector general, and Papa was overjoyed by the prospect of another general in the family. The anger he'd felt last summer toward my husband had faded, and in its place he'd now only the highest praise for Alexander as an officer. Even my mother, who ordinarily cared little for politics, was delighted for Alexander.

In fact, I seemed to be the only one made unhappy by my husband's new prospects, and by the time I returned to New York in late June, the appointments were already in Congress awaiting approval. President Adams was not nearly so agreeable. He resisted Alexander's appointment as hard as he could, contriving all sorts of impediments to try to keep him from the office (including, in one particularly preposterous accusation, that Alexander could not qualify to be an American military leader because he was a foreigner, and not a citizen!). But in part because of General Washington's insistence and in part because Alexander truly was the most qualified gentleman for the job, his appointment was at last confirmed, and he was now officially Major General Hamilton. I'd no choice for the peace of my family but to swallow my objections and acquiesce to my husband's seeming good fortune.

As I'd expected, he threw himself headlong into his duties with his usual dedication and enthusiasm. There were few things my husband enjoyed more than creating systems and plans all the way to the smallest details, and inventing this army was no different. He devised everything from the most basic divisions of the planned army, the regiments, battalions, and companies, to the design of the tents, to the specifications of the weaponry, and even the most minute questions of military protocol. He lavished special care on the creation of the uniforms, and even before the army itself had been recruited, he was proudly wearing a uniform of his own design, lavished with gold lace and glinting epaulets that suited his military bearing.

Exactly as I'd feared, however, the corps proved a monumental task, though perhaps made more so by my husband's fastidious attentions to detail, and compounded by a federal bureaucracy that seemed to thwart him at every step. He'd had a sizable staff to do his bidding whilst secretary of treasury, but he'd only a single twenty-year-old aide-de-camp to assist him now. This young man was Philip Church, my sister's eldest son, and a well-bred, handsome young fellow he was, too. He was also thoroughly charming, as any son of Angelica's was bound to be, but it was clear that he was more attentive to the ladies of New York than to his duties. Not that Alexander would ever rebuke him, especially not to Angelica, but I did wish he'd a more conscientious assistant to help with his labors.

I was hardly surprised when our own son Philip suggested that he might also serve as his father's aide-de-camp: not surprised, but not pleased, either.

"He could be most useful to me, Betsey," Alexander said, after our son had approached him. "He'll also learn a great many useful things in the process."

"No, Alexander," I'd said firmly. "He is nearly done with his studies at Columbia, and then we'd agreed that he'd read for the law. The last thing I wish is for him to squander his talents in the army, toying with guns and squiring ladies about to balls."

Alexander had frowned. "You've a sorry impression of the career of an aide-de-camp."

"It's an entirely accurate one," I said, "formed from observing you in Morristown before you became attached to me."

He'd no argument to answer that, and Philip remained in college.

Yet even Alexander himself couldn't deny that he had spread

himself too thin. As he built the army, he'd attempted to retain a handful of his legal clients to help with our finances. As a lawyer, he'd been earning over a thousand dollars a month, an agreeable amount to support a household of our size. But as inspector general, his income was reduced to a quarter of what it had been, and once again our family's finances had tightened precipitously.

To me, the worst part of his numerous responsibilities was the one I'd feared from the beginning. He worked constantly, and by the time he returned home from his office he was exhausted, and barely able to topple into bed. He was frequently summoned to Philadelphia, and he could be gone for weeks at a time. The plain truth was that I missed him.

With Alexander so much absent and my children growing, I began to hunt about me for useful ways to keep my loneliness at bay. In the fall of 1798, I hadn't far to look.

New York was the country's largest port city, with scores of foreign strangers arriving on its docks every day. In most ways, this was a fine and prosperous advantage to the city, but toward the end of every summer, when the heat gathered most fiercely, it also meant that there was a higher risk of yellow fever. Much like Philadelphia to the south, New York saw some years with only a handful of cases, and then others when the fever was so widespread and severe as to become a veritable plague upon the citizens.

Thus was the case in 1798. The first cases began in the poorer neighborhoods near the docks, as was often the way, but soon spread north at an alarming rate. People took sick as they went about their work and collapsed in the streets, and died there, too, as all others fled. Because of the sweltering heat that lay so heavily upon the city this year, the fever took hold and progressed at a faster pace than was customary, swiftly claiming victims of every class of society.

Like every other person of any means, we, too, left the city to escape the risk of the fever, taking lodgings in the country in September. I couldn't forget how ill from the same fever Alexander and I had been in Philadelphia five years before, and I would do all that was necessary to preserve my children from such suffering. At least this time I prevailed upon Alexander to remain with us, and not venture back into the city as he foolishly had in Philadelphia, but he still continued to work, and through his associates reported to us that at the height of the sickness, a hundred people and more were said to be dying a day: a considerable number in a city of 60,000 souls.

Shops and other businesses were closed, courts shut, and streets were deserted. Farmers who usually brought their wares to the markets to sell kept away, and there were shortages of food among those who remained. Still the sun blazed down upon the suffering city, with no relief for the ill.

Finally, in late September, cooling rains came from the ocean, and at last the deaths began to subside. We returned to our home, and I had every inch of it thoroughly scrubbed with vinegar, just to be sure.

But for many other families, it would take far more than vinegar to clear away the effects of the fever. While illness most often claimed the very young and the very old, it was the special cruelty of yellow fever that it could devastate and kill even the strongest of men in a matter of days.

The city was filled with fresh widows of every age, their sorrowful faces and clinging, fatherless children everywhere. Most of these women were abruptly left without any support, and were now forced to contend not only with the dreadful grief of a husband's death, but the desperate realization that they'd no way to support themselves or their children.

It was the sight of these poor women that inspired me. I had always been involved in charitable works; my mother had instilled that virtue in me, as the duty of a Christian lady. But now I presented myself to Mrs. Isabella Graham, a Scottish widow who well understood the plight of her sisters, and had ten years before founded the Society for the Relief of Poor Widows with Small Children. Unlike many of the wealthier women who solely offered financial contributions (which were, of course, most welcome and essential), I gave myself over whole-heartedly to Mrs. Graham's activities, calling on the widows with packages of food, clothing, and medicine. I offered solace and prayer as best I could, and perhaps most importantly, I listened to their melancholy recollections of the husbands they'd lost.

"It's a good thing that you are doing, Betsey," Alexander said proudly as I described to him yet another sad case of a young woman with twin babies who'd never thought she'd be left in such a sorrowful state. "I've always known you to be kindness itself, and now the rest of the city shall see it as well."

"I don't do it to be recognized," I said. "You know that of me. Rather I've been so blessed in my own life that I feel it's my obligation to help others who haven't."

"As you do, dearest," he said, smiling warmly before he kissed me. "As you do."

It was in a way one more interest we'd always shared, for he himself was extraordinarily generous by nature, and his own sad situation as a child had left him with special sympathy for unfortunate women and children. But as much as I wished it could be otherwise, his own kindness was now restricted to making contributions—the names of "General & Mrs. Hamilton" were prominent on many of the membership rolls of city charities—and his countless responsibilities with the army meant he was almost never at home.

I suppose my loneliness would have been easier to bear if Alexander had himself been happy. But the grander his schemes for the army became, the less support from Congress he had to enact them, and most especially from President Adams. The first bloom of enthusiasm gave way to increasing frustration.

After over a month of inconclusive meetings in Philadelphia, he came home to New York in December, the tail end of 1798. I knew from his letters that he hadn't been well, but I was shocked by his appearance: he'd grown thin and weary-looking, and beneath the powder and pomatum in his hair, there was far more gray than there'd been before. He'd begun wearing his spectacles more often, too, their flashing lenses masking his eyes and making him appear older as well.

Our house was bedecked with greenery for the Christmas holidays and our children were wildly excited over the coming festivities, but for Alexander and me, alone together in the parlor the night he returned, there was little joy, and less cheer.

"I cannot help think that I am wasting both my time and my energies," he said, standing beside the fire. I'd poured him a glass of his favorite brandy, but instead of drinking it, he'd merely swirled it within the glass, staring into the amber liquid like an oracle searching for signs.

"Perhaps there will be more interest in the new year," I suggested. As much as I did not like the idea of the army, I hated seeing him like this. "People are often distracted by their own affairs in December."

"It's more than that, Betsey," he said. "Adams has no interest in leading, and shrinks from his responsibilities. He retreats to Massachusetts, and lets Congress run wild. There is no hint of civility, no respect, no decency. Senators openly brawl on the floor as if they were drunken sailors in a tavern, and debates deteriorate into shouting matches."

"Why doesn't anyone stop them?" I asked, genuinely shocked.

"Oh, occasionally they do," he said cynically. "But recall that they are all gentlemen, and in theory capable of regulating themselves. There will always be factions in any group of men, but the divide is so great now that I fear for the very government itself, let alone the army."

I'd seldom seen him in this black a mood, nor could I think of much to say that could dispel it. "Could General Washington be persuaded to return?" I asked. "No one would dare counter him."

"I would not presume upon his noble nature to ask," Alexander said. "You haven't seen him in several years, dearest. He's much altered with age, much diminished, and though nothing will change his innate civility, he no longer possesses either the inclination or the stamina for taming jackals."

"But he does still believe in the army, doesn't he?" I asked. Just as I knew how much the army meant to Alexander, I was also aware that without General Washington's leadership, it would be doomed to fail. "Surely you have his support."

He hesitated, clearly thinking how best to answer, his distinctive profile silhouetted against the fire's light.

"It's not so much that he has withdrawn his support," he said, "but rather he no longer perceives an army to be necessary. The antagonism that the French demonstrated earlier this year has faded to nothingness, and there are rumors that whatever differences may have existed will soon be resolved. With no threat of war or invasion, there's no need for an army. And that will be an end to it."

In this last year, I'd become accustomed to hearing him speak of the lack of support for the army with bitterness, even anger, but this resignation was new. He wasn't ordinarily given to despondency, and it worried me. I rose from my chair and went to stand behind him, slipping my arms around his waist and resting my cheek against his back. He covered my hand with his own, finding comfort in giving it.

"It seems that I'm no longer fit for the military life," he said ruefully. "To be here with you and the children suits me much better."

"I'm sorry, my dearest," I said gently. "I know how much you wished the military force to succeed, but even you cannot make an army by yourself."

"No, I cannot," he admitted with candor that was rare for him. "I still believe in the army, and I shall continue until I am released from my duties. I expect, however, that Adams will put an end to the endeavor as soon as he can from spite toward me."

The spite lasted longer than I ever expected. By sheer force of will, Alexander continued to push the army forward with less and less support from Congress. General Washington himself urged him to step away, but my husband would not quit. All his life he had succeeded by hard work and his own innate brilliance, and it was, I think, inconceivable to him that he should fail at this, a project that had held such promise to him.

Yet as was always the way with Alexander, the army was not his only endeavor. Just as the last severe round of yellow fever had inspired me toward more charitable works, the same vile disease had led to the search for a better, more healthy source of water for the city, impure water being considered the major cause of yellow fever.

A plan was devised to bring fresh water from Bronx River, and the various city committees and officials were so pleased that they granted all manner of incentives and allowances to encourage it. The plan was called the Manhattan Company, and was supported by many of the city's most illustrious gentlemen. These naturally included my husband and Mr. Church, but also Colonel Burr, who was the company's leader.

To my considerable surprise, this time my husband saw the colonel as an ally, not an adversary.

"It's a most welcome scheme," he said. "If Burr can bring it all to completion, then he will have accomplished at least one honorable act in his life."

For Alexander it was an honorable act, too, and he and I both viewed it as related to my work with the Widows Society. With his usual enthusiasm, he first produced a lengthy and detailed report on the region's water supplies that he and the colonel presented to the mayor for approval. Next, he brought an act before the state legislature for approval. I was heartened to see him so cheerfully employed, doubly so because I was once again with child, and to have Alexander happy meant my own spirits were more agreeable, too.

Thanks to my husband's persuasive talents, the act was easily passed by the legislature, and by April the Manhattan Company was a legal entity, signed into being by the governor. We all rejoiced, and I held a grand celebration at our house for all who had toiled so selflessly for the public good.

But before long, it became clear that the Manhattan Company had been designed primarily for the exclusive benefit of Colonel Burr and his friends, not the public. An over-looked clause in the act—carefully inserted by the colonel—permitted the Company to engage in all manner of business beyond providing water. Soon the Colonel announced the true plan for the Manhattan Company: to launch a bank that would cater exclusively to the needs of Democratic-Republican merchants, and rival both the Bank of New York and the Bank of the United States, institutions dominated by the Federalists, and initially conceived by Alexander. The new bank was launched, and the plan to bring fresh water to the city was abandoned entirely, and there was no legal recourse to undo any of it.

As can be imagined, Alexander was furious. He had not only succumbed to Colonel Burr's false promises, but he'd been duped into doing much of the legal work that masked the colonel's true purposes.

"The man has no conscience, no morals, no beliefs," Alexander stormed. "He has tricked us all, and displayed his complete lack of character by creating an institution that was completely unnecessary, and will serve only to extend him for credit for his own personal extravagances—which, being the worst sort of spendthrift, he most desperately needs."

The colonel's extravagances were widely known; his house, Richmond Hill, was one of the finest in the city, and he denied himself nothing (including, as Angelica informed me, a veritable parade of beautiful and wanton mistresses).

"Does this mean there will be no fresh water for the city?" I innocently asked, thinking of my widows and children whose lives had been so altered by impure water and yellow fever.

"None at all," Alexander declared with fresh outrage. "Piping in water was all a ruse, and I doubt from the first Burr ever intended it. He is a monster, Betsey, the worst sort of rogue who deserves to be publicly whipped for his audacity."

I heard the too-familiar edge in my husband's voice, enough to make me wary.

"Do not even consider it, Alexander, not even for a moment," I said as firmly as I could. "It is not your place to issue public whippings, even to Colonel Burr."

He sighed restlessly, enough to prove he had in fact considered doing exactly that. "Oh, I won't, Betsey," he said. "You have my word. He's insulted the entire city more than just me. But I wish someone would take Burr to task for what he has done."

Mercifully, he kept his word to me. But Colonel Burr did not escape entirely. When his actions became public, New York voters took notice, and the colonel lost his seat in the state legislature. That my husband helped this loss along with numerous well-placed conversations and letters in newspapers was most likely, but not to the degree that Colonel Burr blamed after the election. I believed it more a case of a wicked man finally being held accountable for what he'd done, and being punished for it.

But that wasn't all. Later that summer, at a private dinner attended by us, the Churches, and a number of others, Mr. Church boldly accused Colonel Burr of bribery and a number of other misdeeds. He made these accusations decisively, and loudly, too, on account of having had his share of wine. No one at the table thought much of his words, it all being the truth, but in some manner his comments were repeated to the colonel, who challenged Mr.

Church to an "interview" in New Jersey, where such affairs took place.

Needless to say, Angelica and I were not informed of any of this until after the event. Gentlemen will keep their secrets, especially the deadly, dangerous ones. I'm certain Alexander knew, but also knew better than to tell me.

But Mr. Church himself was not so reticent. I was with Angelica in her bedchamber, seeing a new hat that she'd just bought, when her husband came upstairs, his face flushed with high spirits.

"That was a good morning's work," he announced after he'd greeted us both. "You would've delighted in my marksmanship, Angelica. My shot clipped the button from the very breast on his coat, neat as can be, while his was so wide of the mark that it's likely still flying through the clouds."

Angelica frowned, the frothy new hat still in her hand.

"What nonsense is this, John?" she asked, though I suspected she might already have guessed, as had I. "What are you saying?"

His smile was wide with smug satisfaction. "That I met that scoundrel Burr on the field of honor in New Jersey, and easily got the better of him."

He had, too, though according to Alexander he also admitted afterwards that he'd no real proof that the colonel had accepted bribes. The duel and Mr. Church's superior marksmanship—as well as Colonel Burr's deplorable shot—were all the talk of New York for perhaps a week, and then forgotten, as they so often were.

In less than a month, thanks to Colonel Burr's greed, yellow fever once again returned to New York City.

CHAPTER 23

New York City, New York
September 1799

The end of one century and the beginning of another is a momentous thing, a special time that demands reflection and consideration. The papers were full of such discussions, of all that had happened in our country in the last hundred years, and what might lie in store in our future. Likewise the sermons from various pulpits could not refrain from imparting special significance to the coming century, with cautionary warnings balanced by rich promises.

Alexander and I were much the same, I suppose, for the final months of 1799 marked the end of some things in our lives, and the beginnings of others.

In September, Alexander learned that President Adams had gathered his cabinet together, and approved a peace settlement with France that went against all current Federalist policies. The latest outbreak of yellow fever had sent Congress scuttling away from Philadelphia, and the president and cabinet were meeting in a boardinghouse in Trenton.

Hoping to make one final plea for the necessity of the army (and in the process try to convince the president not to make peace with France), Alexander interrupted the cabinet meeting to demand to speak to the president. I do not know exactly what was said between them; I doubt that even the two men themselves did, for apparently tempers ran so high that those outside the room feared that they would come to blows. When Alexander returned home afterward, all he would admit was that the peace would be signed, and that the army would be shut down. Both those things had already seemed inevitable, and I wasn't surprised. But whatever was said on that autumn morning sealed their hatred forever with a bitterness that lingered between Alexander and Mr. Adams long past the grave.

In November Alexander and I were cheered by the arrival of little Elizabeth Holly Hamilton, our seventh child, but only our second girl. Angelica was overjoyed to have a sister after so many brothers, and I was, too.

But even the joy of a new baby could not combat the sad news that arrived only a few weeks later. General Washington had gone out riding to inspect his properties on a cold, wet day. He'd taken a bad chill, and had dined without pausing to remove his wet clothes. His developed a putrid quinsy of the throat, and died two days later.

His unexpected death shocked Alexander. I doubt there was any other gentleman in the present government who was closer to the first president than my husband, nor who grieved him more deeply. My husband had lost much more than a former commander, a president, and a friend. Over the years, he'd also depended on the great man as something of a second father, and certainly a mentor, even a protector. President Washington had been one of the first to see Alexander's enormous talents, and had been able to make the best use of them of anyone. We wept together when we learned of his death, for the man himself and for the times that were now forever gone.

Alexander traveled to Philadelphia to march in the funeral procession, and ordered the soldiers who remained in his army to wear black armbands in honor of their commander-in-chief. With that position now sadly vacant, he'd every expectation that he should fill it. As vindictive as ever, President Adams refused. By the middle of May 1800, he'd ordered the corps disbanded. Alexander reviewed them one last time, resigned his commission, and left off wearing the blue and gold uniform that he'd worn so handsomely. He'd given two years of his life and two years' worth of energy to the army, and all he'd gained from his efforts was disillusionment and unhappiness, and the empty title of General Hamilton.

There was further disappointment in May as well. New York decided its votes for presidential elections based on the results of the earlier elections for the state legislature. New York City had long been a Federalist stronghold, and Alexander worked hard to keep it that way, canvassing in the streets and making daily speeches to all who'd listen. In a similar capacity for the Democratic-Republicans stood Aaron Burr, who was likewise much in evidence before the elections. But the results were shocking, at least in our house: for the first time, the Democratic-Republicans easily won the majority. As a reward for his efforts, Colonel Burr became the Republican candidate for vice president, to run with Thomas Jefferson against President Adams.

For Alexander it was a hellish choice, and he could endorse none of the three, preferring a gentleman from South Carolina, Charles Coatsworth Pinckney, as the Federalist candidate. But instead of simply supporting Mr. Pinckney for president, he began a sustained attack upon President Adams, in essays, in newspapers, and in letters to friends. As can be imagined, the letters were far more personal and sharp, and when choice excerpts were anonymously shared and reprinted in the Republican newspaper, the result was sensational.

As talented as my husband was, he was not without flaws, and ironically his greatest could also be construed as a virtue. He could not refrain from telling the truth, no matter who or how that truth might wound. He had done it to me when he'd published the pamphlet with his confession regarding Mrs. Reynolds, and he did it again with another pamphlet. The *Letter from Alexander Hamilton, Concerning the Public Conduct and Character of John Adams, Esq., President of the United States* was fifty pages long, and revealed all of President Adams's weaknesses and missteps in stunning, critical detail.

He presented it proudly to me, the way he did with all his most important writings, and I sat with him to read it in his library. I was pleased that he sought my opinion, but wary because he hadn't asked for it earlier, while the piece was being composed. This would be entirely his work and opinion, without any tempering from another voice, and because I knew his hatred for the president, I was leery.

"Oh, Alexander," I said as I finally turned the last of the fifty pages. "You cannot publish this."

His brows rose sharply with surprise. "Can you deny that there's a single word therein that's not the truth?"

"But that's exactly why you can't publish it," I said. "It's too much truth, and not enough discretion."

"Betsey, my dear," he said indulgently. "There is no such thing as too much truth."

"In this there is," I said, tapping my fingers on the front page. "I know you believe that you're showing President Adams in his truest light, but that light will reflect back upon you, and not well."

"I believe I can withstand the glare," he said, smiling. "It's better for voters to benefit from my personal experience with the man, and judge for themselves exactly what manner of man they choose to lead them."

"Please, my love," I said seriously, and I didn't smile. How could I? "They'll judge you to be the petty and vindictive one, not him, no matter if that's the truth or not."

He didn't listen to me, preferring to trust the judgment of those faceless, noble voters over mine, and published it anyway in October 1800.

As I feared, the pamphlet was widely regarded as one of the most powerful and influential pieces in the presidential campaign, but not in the way that Alexander had intended. It secured the presidency for Thomas Jefferson, and the vice presidency for Aaron Burr. It also destroyed the Federalist Party from within, and any hope that Alexander may have himself harbored of obtaining another political position for himself.

He refused to see the connection, let alone admit it to me. Instead he felt evermore the outsider, and despaired that he no longer belonged in a world he'd helped create. The despair that I'd first glimpsed over the army's demise seemed to have deepened and taken a firmer hold upon his thoughts. I worried for his health, and his welfare.

Yet what he did soon after the election might have been perhaps a kind of apology. One afternoon he took me and the younger children, squeezed together into the chaise, on a long drive to the far end of Manhattan Island, in amongst the farmlands and forests of

Haarlem and high above the Hudson and East Rivers. There was still enough color, red and gold and orange, remaining in the leaves of the trees to make a brilliant contrast to the blue sky overhead and the steep stone cliffs of the Palisades across the Hudson in New Jersey.

I knew this to be one of Alexander's favorite places, and he came here whenever he could spare the time to hunt. We had rented a house here last fall when yellow fever had broken out in the city, and together we'd come to love the peace of the area.

He stopped the chaise near a walled pasture, telling the children that the farmer wouldn't mind if they ran about the land. They promptly climbed the wall and scattered into the field, running and wheeling about and bellowing with delight in ways that were not permitted on our part of Broadway.

Alexander and I sat on the wall ourselves, I with baby Elizabeth in my lap, and we breathed deeply of air that was free of the chimney smoke and soot of farther downtown. I shifted closer to him, and rested my head against his shoulder.

"I wish that we could live here," I said wistfully. "Away from the city, and away from the noise and racket."

He slipped his arm around my waist. "Do you think you'd be content here?"

"Oh, yes," I said. "I've always told you I've more the soul of a stout farmer's wife than a lady of fashion."

He chuckled, running his hand fondly up and down my arm. "Would you like to try?"

I glanced at him sideways, not considering his question with any seriousness.

"Oh, yes," I said. "We'll become that old couple we passed earlier down the road, each with a clay pipe as they sat on their stoop amongst the chickens."

"I'm not jesting, dearest," he said, though his eyes twinkled. "This week I bought this land, and I don't believe the farmer who sold it would be agreeable to returning my money."

"This land?" I repeated, shocked. "You bought this?"

"From this road, here," he said, turning to point, "to that stand of trees, there, and to those bluffs. It's all General Hamilton's property now."

I gasped, and pressed my hands to my cheeks. "We've never owned property like this. Oh, Alexander, can we afford it?"

"Well enough," he said. "It needs a few improvements, though. The farmhouse will do in a pinch, but I'd rather envisioned a fine country house, with tall windows and porches so we can sit outside and watch the boats on the river. A stable for the horses, and gardens. I've never had a garden, you know."

I flung my arms around him and kissed him, too overjoyed for words. I could envision a house for us and our children and our eventual grandchildren, too, far removed from the turmoil of the city, and it was a very fine vision indeed.

Once the Democratic-Republicans took possession of the government in February 1801, President Jefferson wasted no time in removing as much as he could of the Federalist legacy, especially anything that could be attributed to my husband. In his usual irksome manner, the new president claimed full credit for a peaceful nation and a happy economy. Neither were the result of his exertions or policies, but his inheritance from the previous Federalist presidencies that he had so desperately despised. Yet the common American seemed incapable of realizing these truths, and lavished President Jefferson and his party with the praise and reverence that their predecessors had deserved, but seldom received.

It was a bitter time for Alexander, who could not resist writing more taunting essays and letters attacking the new president. But to my relief he also spent considerable time on the law, and on the construction of our new house, called The Grange, after a country house in Scotland that had belonged to one of his distant ancestors.

He and I both took delight in our oldest son Philip's accomplishments, too. He had graduated from Columbia rewarded with prizes and praised as one of the brightest scholars in his class, and he was now reading the law with the aim of joining Alexander in his office.

At nineteen, Philip was tall and handsome and, like his cousin of the same name, a great favorite with the young ladies at balls and assemblies. I also guessed that he enjoyed himself with his friends in ways and places that young gentlemen his age often explore, and that on occasion he was party to certain small scrapes and misadventures that he and Alexander chose not to share with me. I was content to remain ignorant. So long as Philip dined regularly at our table, made sure his younger sister always had a partner at the assembly, and joined us for church on Sunday morning, I was content.

I suspected one of these misadventures on a chilly Friday evening in November, when he and another friend appeared very late at our house to speak to Alexander. There had been some sort of scuffle—I could tell that from the disarray of their evening clothes—and likely some sort of difficulty involving the watch, for both young gentlemen had long, somber faces before they disappeared with Alexander into his office. I was pregnant with my eighth child—one more proof of the new contentment between Alexander and me—and because I was forty-five years old and often tired, I was reluctant to sacrifice so much as a moment of my sleep. I went back to bed, and thought no more of Philip's mischief.

I did note, however, that he seemed especially devout at his prayers on Sunday, and that after supper, he praised my apple pie as exemplary, and embraced me with more open affection than he usually before he left.

"What's the meaning of this?" I teased, ruffling his hair back from his forehead with a mother's prerogative.

He shrugged, his shoulders working restlessly beneath his coat. Most of the time now he seemed a grown man to me, but I still could glimpse moments when he was a boy again, a bit awkward and uncertain.

"There's nothing to it, Mamma," he said solemnly, and swallowed. "Only that you are the best mother in Creation, that's all."

"And I the most fortunate of mothers, to be blessed with such a son," I said, touched by his words, "Now you'd best go, if you've so much more reading to accomplish today."

I hugged him again, and kissed him on his cheek so that he flushed. Then he loped down the steps two at a time, mounted his horse that the servant held for him, waved one last time to me, and departed. I watched him go, observing that he was riding too fast for the state of the road after last night's rain, and that I'd have to scold him on the subject when I saw him next.

On Monday afternoon I had just finished dusting the books in

Alexander's library (a task I never trusted to maidservants) when there was a frantic thumping on the front door. Because I was in the hall, I opened the door myself. One of the Churches' servants was on the step, breathing hard from running. He bowed quickly to me, and handed me a terse, swiftly written note in Angelica's hand.

> *My dearest sister come at once. Your Philip has suffered a Terrible accident.* ~ A.C.

I cried out with alarm and fear just as one of my servants appeared. I told her to fetch my cloak and then to watch the younger children whilst I was gone to my sister's house, and then left with the Church servant.

"Can you tell me what has happened?" I begged of the man. "Did my son fall from his horse? Was he struck by a wagon in the street?"

But the man only shook his head, his face wreathed with sorrow. "Mrs. Church told me not to tell you, Mrs. Hamilton," he said. "Only to bring you as fast as I could."

I didn't press him, but my fear grew with every hurried step. Angelica met me at the door, taking me firmly by the arm to lead me to a small bedroom at the back of the house.

"What has happened to my boy, Angelica?" I demanded breathlessly. "What is wrong?"

"My own dear sister," she said, supporting me as she spoke. "There has been a duel."

If she said more after that, I do not recall it, for I was already in the room where my poor son lay, on a plain open bed without curtains. His handsome face was ashen and contorted with pain, his eyes blank and unseeing, and if not for the painful wracking that each breath caused him, I would have thought he was already lost to me. Although some attempt had been made to bind the wound in his side, there was blood everywhere, on the sheets, on the mattress, in a puddle on the floor. Also on the bed lay my husband, tears streaming from his eyes as he cradled our shattered boy in his arms.

With a wordless cry of anguish, I rushed to them both, claiming my son's other side. Heedless of how his blood stained me, I curled beside my boy, his father and I holding him as tenderly as we could while his young life slipped away. I could not help but think of how Alexander and I would lie together with our baby Philip between us, how we'd pet and kiss him and dream together of the fine future we were certain would be his.

And now it had come to this instead.

We remained with him until he died early the following morning. I knew the moment his soul left this life, and he belonged no more to us, but to his Savior, yet this knowledge brought no comfort to me.

My grief was so black and consuming that I remember nothing more beyond that: not who else was with us in that little room, nor how I was conveyed home, nor how the awful news was delivered to our other children. I was too bereft to attend my son's burial, and there was considerable fear that I would miscarry the child within my womb. It was the most terrible time of my life, and my only comfort came from Alexander, whose bottomless sorrow equaled my own. No one else could understand the depth of our sorrow, or comprehend the pain of our loss.

But there was another.

When told of her brother's death, our daughter Angelica fell senseless to the floor with shock. All attempts to revive her failed, and instead she lay on her bed in a kind of twilight, neither awake nor asleep. When at last I was myself recovered enough to learn her plight, I crept to her side and did my best to rouse her, but failed, and I wept more bitter tears over her as well.

In time she improved so that she could sit and stand and be led about, and on her best days she would play her brother's favorite songs on her piano as if he were still in the room. But the bright and cheerful young woman she'd been before her brother's death had vanished forever. Like an inanimate doll, her lovely dark eyes remained wide and staring, her voice mostly mute, and her beautiful face without emotion. She had left us with Philip, and she never returned.

My husband was never the same again, either. In time he returned to his practice, but all his friends were shocked by the change that grief had wrought. He could now have been a man twenty years older than his true age, the change was that precipitous. He withdrew further from the wickedness of the political world, and turned to the Bible with a devotion that both surprised and pleased me.

Most of all, we turned to each other. No one else could comprehend our loss; no one else could share the depths of our despair, or feel the harrowing pain that had come from our son's senseless death. With Alexander, I didn't have to explain, or struggle for words that didn't exist. He felt the same, and shared the same unending sorrow and sadness.

Nothing would again be as it had been. We both knew that. But together we would continue for the sake of our other children. As each day somehow followed the next, we drew comfort from one another, and from the love we shared.

By the spring of 1801, our new house was completed, and we closed up the Broadway house and moved to Haarlem. Early each morning, Alexander would drive the chaise down Bloomingdale Road to his office on Garden Street, and each evening he would return to us at The Grange. We both found a melancholy peace there that was lacking in the city, and I'm sure that Alexander's old associates from the Treasury would have been stunned to see the interest he now took in planting trees and arranging gardens, his days of taxes and foreign tariffs forgotten.

Soon after we moved, in July, I gave birth to my final child, a boy. We named him Philip, and though he became Little Phil to set him apart, his older brother was never far from our thoughts.

And yet there was fresh grief in the years ahead. In early 1802, my younger sister Peggy sickened and died with little warning. My only solace was that Alexander, who had been in Albany on business, was able to see her in her final days.

In May of 1803, my dear mother was taken all of a sudden by a stroke, and her death left an emptiness at The Pastures that would never again be filled. Now that my father was alone, his health deteriorated rapidly. I spent as much time with him in Albany as I could, while Alexander remained at The Grange with our children.

Yet amidst all this, Alexander had still retained an interest in New York City politics, the only place where he felt he'd still be welcome. He'd also watched from afar—and with considerable satisfaction—as his old nemesis Colonel Burr had failed to find favor with President Jefferson and the other Democratic-Republicans in the new capital city of Washington.

To Alexander, it was a rare kind of justice, that a man who had turned his back on one party to join another for a better chance at victory had now been shunned by both. He would, I think, have respected Colonel Burr far more if he'd lost as a Federalist, than won, as he had, as a Democratic-Republican. For a man who prized truth and trust as much as my husband did, a perpetual turncoat like the colonel was a vile and loathsome anathema to him. It was difficult to recall how, at one time, the two had been friends, and how the colonel's daughter Theodosia had attended dancing lessons with our daughter Angelica.

With the possibility for another national post effectively blocked by the Democratic-Republicans, Colonel Burr announced that he would run for governor of New York, Alexander was livid, and all his old outrage at political indignities gathered again with fresh force. I urged him to ignore it, and reminded him that old quarrels were best left in the past. Yet at dinners with friends, and especially at the end of the meal when the bottle was passed around, he would launch into scandal-laden denouncements of Colonel Burr that often shocked others not with their detail, but with their vehemence.

Both behind the scenes and in the newspapers, Alexander worked relentlessly to make sure that the world remained aware of Colonel Burr's numerous faults and duplicities, of his lack of character and conviction, and of his deceitful part in the creation of the Manhattan Company.

"Burr must not win, Betsey," he argued when I found him at his desk late one night, composing yet another polemic against the colonel. "You know as well as I what an evil, ruinous man he is."

"But he cannot hurt you any longer, dearest," I urged. "Plotting another man's ruin, no matter how deserving, is never a wise course. You'll make yourself ill, and to what end?"

"I'd gladly suffer any illness in exchange for keeping Burr permanently from office and from influence," he said with fresh vehemence. "A man with as few scruples as Burr has no place determining the course of any government, large or small."

I sighed, placing my hands on his shoulders; I could feel the tension in his muscles, bundled tight beneath my palms.

"Why can you not trust to the will of the people in regards to the colonel?" I asked. "Surely the voters by now will recognize him for what he is."

"They will," he agreed, dipping his pen once again into the well. "Especially once they have been provided with a few more judicious facts."

Whether because of my husband's facts or not, the result of the election showed that the people did indeed possess a remarkably low opinion of the colonel. When the last votes were counted in April, he was shown to have been soundly beaten. His supporters placed the entire blame for the loss on my husband—which he happily accepted.

Nor was he done. At a small supper, Alexander and several old friends indulged in declaiming the colonel, the sort of conversation that gentlemen often have when the cloth is drawn and the bottle passed. But on this particular evening, one of the company was so exhilarated by what my husband had said that he repeated it to the editor of the *New-York Evening Post*. Soon all the city and most of the state had read that Alexander had called Colonel Burr "a dangerous man, and one not to be trusted with the reins of government," and a good many other things besides. It was all things I'd heard him say a thousand times before, but to have those same words in print was an entirely different matter. Printed words could not easily be explained away, and the fact that they were reprinted again and again in other papers only increased their power.

All this I knew, and it worried me no end. I couldn't imagine that the colonel would let such a slander pass unanswered. Disappointed in his career in Washington and his hopes of being the governor of New York crushed, I imagined him as a wounded animal, all the more dangerous on account of his injuries. Each day I pored over the various rebuttals and explanations in the newspapers, hunting in vain for word of his reaction. Even my aged father joined the fray on Alexander's behalf, accusing the original statement of being a complete fabrication.

Yet through it all, my husband himself seemed curiously unperturbed. I was the one who worried.

"You've said yourself that Colonel Burr is a dangerous man," I said, "and all his friends say he blames you for what has befallen him. This foolishness attributed to you must only confirm his darkest fears."

He smiled, that same sweet but maddening smile that he'd always possessed. "I won't deny it, Betsey," he said easily. "I've told you that before. I did say everything that was printed, and a great deal more besides. I am not ashamed of any of it."

"He could sue your for slander," I fretted. "He'd win, too, with proof like that."

"My dearest love," he said. "Surely you know by now how these things go. It's the way of politics. I've said far, far worse of him in my time, as I'm sure Burr himself has said far worse of me. By the end of the summer it will all be forgotten."

I shook my head, unconvinced. It was not my husband's way to be so blithe about personal insults, and I worried that the colonel would respond in print with something equally slanderous in regards to him.

"I cannot believe he hasn't answered you," I said uneasily.

"Perhaps he has simply realized that I spoke the truth." Gently he pulled me across his lap, holding me steady against the crook of his arm. "It's not worth your worry, Betsey. If this little incident serves to bring Burr's career to a permanent conclusion and remove him from the chance of any further harm, then I will have done the greatest service possible to the country."

I sighed again, and settled against his shoulder. I'd have to trust him, as I always had. What other choice did I have?

And in fact as the days passed, the entire affair did seem to dissipate, exactly as Alexander had predicted. The papers moved on to new scandals, new slanders, and even our closest friends seem to have wearied of the topic.

Snug in our home at The Grange, we often dined outside on the porch during the long days of summer, and as Alexander had once promised, we lazily watched the boats on the river while the younger children tried to catch fireflies on the grassy lawns below us. Each evening Alexander and I sat with our chairs close together and our hands loosely linked, and while the tragedies of our lives would never be forgotten, we were still able to find a contentment and peace, here in this place with the new moon shining on the river below us.

"My own dear Betsey," he said softly, turning toward me in the moonlight. I could scarcely make out his features, but I knew from his voice that he smiled, and I smiled in return.

"My own dear Alexander," I said. "How fortunate I am to have you as my husband, and my love."

He raised my fingers to his lips, kissing them fondly. "My love," he said. "The best of wives, the best of women."

He sighed, and turned back toward the river.

"I will be staying in town tomorrow night," he said. "I have an appointment early the next morning in New Jersey."

"Then come back when you are done," I said. "We'll expect you for supper."

"I will," he said with unexpected tenderness. "I will."

The weather changed late Tuesday night, and by Wednesday the morning dawned clear and almost cool for July. I opened all the windows high to let the breezes clear away yesterday's stale air. I made sure that Angelica was dressed for the day and that the little pet parakeets (a gift from Mr. Pinckney from South Carolina) that were kept in her room to amuse her were fed and their cage swept. The younger children were already in the barn, occupied with a new litter of puppies, and I carried my tea outside to sit on one of the porches and enjoy the blessing of the new day.

I heard a carriage come racing up the road, and leaned over the railing to look. It was likely too early for Alexander to be returning home from his appointment; whoever it was, however, was driving his poor horses at a breakneck pace.

To my surprise, the carriage drew into our drive, and Judge Nathaniel Pendleton, an old friend of my husband's, clambered from the seat and hurried up our steps. He looked uncharacteristically distraught, and his dark clothes appeared rumpled as well.

"Good day, Judge," I said, greeting him myself. "Isn't it a pleasant morning? I'm sorry to inform you, however, that General Hamilton is not at home, and if—"

"Mrs. Hamilton," he said, holding his hat in his hands. "I regret to inform you that the general is, ah, unwell with, ah, spasms, and requests you come to him at once."

I gasped with shock, immediately reminded of the messenger who had come for me after Philip had been shot. I glanced down, hiding my confusion and fear, and noticed that the judge's dark stockings and the hem of his coat were stained with blood.

"Tell me, Judge," I said, my voice trembling. "Has my husband been injured in a duel?"

He took a deep breath. "Yes, madam," he said. "He has."

"Who was the other party?"

Another deep breath. "Colonel Burr, madam."

Of course it was. It couldn't have been anyone else, not this summer. I remembered what Alexander had said, of how removing Burr from the opportunity to do further harm would be the greatest service possible to the country. But not like this, not at this cost.

Dear God in Heaven, never like this.

I ran into the house to tell the servants to watch the children and then left with the judge.

Although he drove the horses hard, the drive seemed interminable, with every minute another chance for me to fear for Alexander. I tried to concentrate and pray for him, but my fear was so great that my mind would not keep still. I thought of all the times that Alexander had almost come to this point, but hadn't, all the times he'd demanded satisfaction but had stopped before a fatal confrontation. My thoughts kept racing back to our son's terrible death, and I resolutely tried again to pray that I wouldn't find my beloved husband in a similar state.

At last we came to the home of Mr. Bayard, director of the Bank of New York and another of Alexander's close friends. We were shown to an upstairs bedroom, and at once I saw it all for myself, no matter what pretty falsehoods the men would tell me.

Alexander was dying. He had always preferred the truth in all
things, and this, then, was the most difficult truth he'd ever forced
me to accept. They'd cut away his clothes and bandaged his side,
but still there was so much blood, his very life spilling away. His
face was as pale as old parchment, his arms contorted and restless
with pain while his legs remained too still beneath the sheets.

Yet he knew me, and smiled as soon as he realized I was there.
At once I broke down and began to sob, sinking into the chair beside the bed.

"My own dear wife," he said. "Please, Eliza. Don't distress yourself."

"How can I not, my love?" I said, overwhelmed. "When I see
you like this . . ."

"I am sorry for that," he said. "It's not how I'd wish you to remember me."

"I'll remember you in more ways than I ever can say." I touched
my fingertips to his brow to smooth his hair back from his forehead, his skin sticky and warm with feverish pain. "Oh, my love, I
cannot bear to lose you like this!"

"You will," he said. "You will, for the sake of our dear children.
Remember, Betsey, that you are a Christian, and let that be your
comfort."

He closed his eyes and winced as fresh pain sliced through him.
I drew my fan from my pocket, and fluttered it gently over his face
to cool him, the only physical comfort I could offer. Dr. Hosack—
ah, another old friend!—was in attendance, and I looked to him.

"Is there nothing that can be done to ease his suffering?" I
pleaded.

Somehow the pity and sorrow in the doctor's respectful expression made everything worse, and fresh tears spilled down my
cheeks.

"I have given him sufficient laudanum to dull the worst of it,
Mrs. Hamilton," he said softly. "He has asked to remain lucid, and
I have obliged."

I nodded in agreement. Words had always been my husband's
joy, and he would want their use as long as he could.

"My love," he said without opening his eyes. "When we first
met, you said you'd pray for me."

"I did," I said, my voice breaking. "I still do. Oh, my dearest!"

But he'd drifted out of consciousness, or perhaps into the laudanum. It was like that the rest of that day, and all through the night. He'd rally and speak as clearly as if he were his old self, then the pain would pull him back. So many friends came to bid him farewell and many to pray, and he greeted them all by name, an agreeable host to the end. Bishop Moore from Trinity Church gave him holy communion for the final time, a solemn ceremony that brought my husband great peace. My sister Angelica came, too, so inconsolable that she could scarcely speak.

I never left Alexander's side.

On the second day, he weakened precipitously, and the periods when he drifted away were more frequent. He no longer possessed the strength to move, and he spoke only with difficulty. I had been reluctant to have our poor children here, not wanting this sorrowful sight to be their final memory of their father, but on this day I relented, and had them brought to us. It was as agonizing for them as I'd feared, and all seven wept bitterly. Each in turn bent to kiss him in farewell, and I held Little Phil so that Alexander's lips could press against his downy cheek. At last I bid them stand at the foot of the bed, clustered so that he might see them together one last time.

With great effort he opened his eyes again. He did not speak, but I knew from his expression—oh, most excellent of fathers!—that this was the most painful reminder of all he was leaving behind.

The day was so long, and yet time moved too fast. I'd never have guessed I'd so many tears to shed. For nearly twenty-five years, he'd been the other half of me, my constant support, my beloved husband, my dearest love, and I could not fathom what my life would be without him. I held his hand to the end, and told him again and again how much I loved him, and always would.

But love was not enough to hold him back, and at last, in the afternoon, he slipped away.

He was gone, and I was lost.

EPILOGUE

A nd now I've come back to where I began.
As much as I longed to die as well to join Alexander, I didn't. As broken as I was with grief and loss, I survived. For the sake of our children and my husband's memory, I continue.

Nothing has been easy. They tell me that the funeral was the most impressive in the city's history, and the public grief deeper than even for General Washington. My husband would have been surprised to see how well loved he was.

I hadn't the strength to go myself; my first raw grief was so harrowing that I feared I'd lose my wits. When I read the final letter that Alexander had written me the night before the duel, I did not believe I could bear my loss. But though God will test us sorely, He never gives us more than we can bear.

And I will bear this. I've too much to do for it to be otherwise. Already my husband's enemies have begun to take the luster from his memory, to use him as a scapegoat for their own flaws and errors. It's easy to blame someone who can no longer defend himself.

But they haven't reckoned with me. I will make sure my husband and his achievements are not forgotten. I will see that he receives all the honor that is his due, and that he will always be remembered by the country he loved and served so well.

I, Eliza Hamilton, will do that: for the best of husbands, the best of fathers, and the best of men: my Alexander.

AFTERWORD

In the days after Alexander died, Eliza was so overwhelmed with grief that those closest to her feared for her sanity. She was too distraught to attend the funeral or any of the other events honoring her husband's memory, and instead remained inside The Grange, shut away with her children and her sorrow. According to the few friends who did see her, her loss appeared unbearable, and she piteously longed for her own death as well so that she might be reunited with Alexander.

At the time of her husband's death, Eliza was forty-six years old, and considerably stronger than she realized during that grim July in 1804. She not only survived her grief, but lived on another half-century, dying in 1854 at the remarkable age of ninety-seven. Her long life spanned American history from the colonial era to the eve of the Civil War, and she died as the last remaining widow of a Founding Father.

The years immediately following the deaths of her oldest son Philip and Alexander were filled with more sorrow, and considerable challenges. Despite being lauded as a financial genius during his lifetime, Alexander left his personal finances in a shambles at his death. His years of low-paying public service and living beyond his means had combined with the large amounts borrowed to build the Grange, and when he died he was $60,000 in debt, which today could roughly translate to between two and three million dollars. The country estate that he'd so lovingly built for his family now faced foreclosure and public auction, and only the intervention and combined generosity of his many friends kept Eliza and the children from losing their home.

Those same charitable friends also contributed to a trust to provide a small income for Eliza, a fund whose existence was such a deep secret that it was not revealed until the 1930s. Even so, Eliza often scrambled to make ends meet, living on the edge of poverty, and was repeatedly forced to seek small loans from friends.

Alexander had believed that Eliza's father, Philip Schuyler, would look after her. But the old general's long history of ill health, coupled with the deaths of his wife and his favorite son-in-law, soon claimed him as well. He died in November 1804, only four months after Alexander. The enormous Schuyler fortune proved to be a myth. Like many wealthy 18th-century families, the family's wealth was tied up in land and credit, not cash.

The land that surrounded The Pastures was divided and eventually sold, with the profits going to the surviving children. The large brick mansion that had been the centerpiece of the Schuyler family for so many years was also sold. Eliza's share translated into an income of only around $750 annually. Perhaps more importantly, Eliza lost both the support of her father and the childhood home that had always been her retreat and respite in difficult times.

Her sister Angelica remained at her side throughout it all, sharing Eliza's grief for Hamilton, offering assistance with the children, and doubtless on occasion helping out financially. Angelica died in New York City in 1814, and is buried in Trinity Church cemetery, not far from Eliza and Alexander. Her husband, John Barker Church, returned to London, where he died four years later; at the time of his death, his mercurial fortune had been reduced to a mere £1,500.

Through the years, Eliza persevered. Two things drove her: her children, and her husband's memory.

Despite her precarious finances, Eliza was determined to do her best for her children. While none of them achieved their father's rare stellar fame, all grew to be men that clearly carried Alexander's heritage. Four of the surviving sons became lawyers, and were active in state and federal politics and government. The fifth was a soldier who attended West Point and fought in the Black Hawk Wars on the western frontier.

Tragically, Eliza's older daughter Angelica's mental instability deteriorated to the point that she could no longer be kept at home, and lived out her life under the care of a private doctor. The younger daughter, also named Eliza, married Sidney Augustus Holly, and Eliza lived with them in the later years of her life. Eliza was justly proud of her children, and Alexander would have been so, too.

But while Alexander lived on through his children, Eliza was determined that posterity would not forget him in other ways as well. In New York City, that would never be the case. The entire city was swathed in black after his death, and he was mourned by people of every rank. The shock of his sudden death at a relatively young age made New Yorkers remember only his best qualities, and remember, too, all the good he had done for the city, from his commitment to the merchant and banking communities, to his involvement in promoting education and civic matters, and to the countless small charities and good works that benefited from his care and attention. With his death, he had become their martyred hero.

One New Yorker did not mourn, however, and was in fact stunned and a bit disgusted by the vast outpouring of grief. From the instant he fired the shot that killed Alexander Hamilton, Aaron Burr showed no remorse, let alone guilt, for the duel or its aftermath. Already realizing the possible consequences, he quickly left New York for Philadelphia. Publicly he believed that he had acted entirely by the established codes of dueling that Hamilton had agreed to as well, and therefore was not at fault, nor deserved any blame.

The courts did not agree. A coroner's jury handed down a verdict that Burr was guilty of murder, and arrest warrants were issued in New York. A grand jury in New Jersey did the same. Gambling that in time the warrants—and the sensation—would fade away, Burr returned to Washington, where the country was stunned by the sight of the current vice president presiding over the Senate while under indictment for murder.

But Burr's political career was done, and he'd become a pariah to both parties. He was also bankrupt, and when he'd fled New York, his creditors had seized his house and belongings. As soon as his term as vice president was completed, he went to Europe. In time, as he'd predicted, the murder charges were dropped, and he was able to return to America. A misguided scheme to recoup his fortune in the west led to him being charged with treason. He was eventually acquitted, and returned to his law practice in New York, where he remained a social outcast, if not a legal one. Nor was he spared personal tragedy, either: his only grandson died as a child, and his beloved daughter Theodosia was lost at sea. Late in life, he married a wealthy widow, only to have the marriage end in a scandalous divorce after he'd spent much of his new wife's fortune. He suffered a debilitating stroke in 1834, and finally died alone in a Staten Island boarding house in 1836.

What would perhaps have been most galling to Burr is that he is remembered today primarily as the man who killed Hamilton. The majority of his personal papers were lost at sea with Theodosia, and with them vanished much of his legacy. There are many modern, scholarly volumes devoted to the collected writings of other men of his generation. Jefferson's work requires thirty-three volumes, while Hamilton's papers fill twenty-seven. The entirety of Burr's surviving writings are contained in just two. The man who believed in keeping his thoughts to himself has ironically done exactly that.

In the capital city of Washington, Hamilton's death was met with shock, and perhaps less than genuine sorrow. His old adversaries— Thomas Jefferson, John Adams, James Madison, James Monroe— began almost at once to polish their own legacies at the expense of Hamilton's. Finally free from any retribution from Hamilton's razor-sharp pen, they made him a convenient scapegoat for their own mistakes and errors in judgments.

Jefferson served two terms as president, and died at Monticello on the Fourth of July, 1826; except for his contradictory and often despicable views on slavery, he has over time become one of the best-known and most important of the Founders. John Adams famously died on the same day as Jefferson, July 4, 1826, and he, too, has been treated well by posterity. James Madison also served two terms as president, steering the country through the War of 1812, and died in 1836 at his Virginia plantation Montpelier; he is remembered today as the framer of the Constitution, and the husband of the much more personable Dolley Madison. In one of those inexplicable quirks of history, James Monroe also died on the Fourth of July, in 1831, after serving two terms as president; he was the last of the Founders to occupy the White House, and the last veteran of the Revolution.

But none of them counted on Eliza, who outlived them all, and refused to fade away as widows were supposed to do. She fought for, and eventually received in 1809, the military pension and bounty lands owed to her husband for his lengthy service as an officer during the Revolution—the pension that he had long before so nobly renounced so that he might be perceived as a completely impartial member of the government. Quite simply, she and her children needed the money—around $10,000—to survive.

For the rest of her life, she dedicated herself to organizing Alexander's voluminous papers and correspondence, determined to see them fashioned into a lasting testament to her husband. A woman who'd never enjoyed writing letters now wrote them constantly, seeking reminiscences from anyone who'd known Alexander and appealing to old friend and acquaintances from the earliest days of the Revolution onward. For the rest of her life, she worked relentlessly to create a truthful portrait of the man she had loved so well. She enlisted her sons in her efforts, and it was John Church Hamilton who finally completed the monumental biography she'd envisioned—seven years after her death.

Eliza was a vocal advocate for Hamilton in person, too. In 1848, she and her daughter Eliza moved from New York to Washington, D.C. At the age of ninety-one, she became both a political celebrity and a venerable connection to a glorious era of the country's past, a tiny woman clad in the same old-fashioned style of mourning clothes that she'd worn since 1804. Still sharp-witted and clear, she received countless visitors including President Millard Fillmore. They came to hear her stories of the early republic, to drink a "merry glass" from George Washington's punchbowl, and most of all to hear her speak about her husband. The marble portrait bust carved by Giuseppe Ceracchi stood near to her chair, and she'd often address it directly, as if it truly were her husband.

One visitor who was not welcome in her parlor was James Monroe. In 1820, during an earlier visit to Washington, D.C., Eliza was stunned to learn that Monroe had come to call upon her to make amends. Eliza wanted none of it. Three decades after the Reynolds affair, she still blamed Monroe for his part in the scandal. Finally, she decided to receive him, but refused to make him welcome, standing the entire time of his visit so that he, too, was forced to stand. When he tried to make a conciliatory speech about how the past should be forgotten and forgiven, she tartly rebuffed him. Her nephew, who witnessed the encounter, preserved her words as family lore:

> *"Mr. Monroe, if you have come to tell me that you repent, that you are sorry, very sorry, for the misrepresentations and the slanders, and the stories you circulated against my dear husband, if you have come to say this, I understand it. But, otherwise, no lapse of time, no nearness to the grave, makes any difference."*

That was apparently too much for Monroe, who took up his hat and left without another word.

Throughout her long life, Eliza continued her own charitable work. It didn't matter that she herself was often on the brink of insolvency. She never forgot her husband's grim childhood, and devoted herself to helping orphans and other helpless children. She was one of the women who founded the New York Orphan Asylum Society in 1806, and sat on their board for many years. Beginning in 1821, when her own children were grown, she served as the asylum's first directress, and oversaw every aspect of the children's care as well as assuming many of the financial and administrative aspects of running the asylum. She continued as directress until 1848 when she finally, reluctantly, stepped down at the age of 91, yet she never lost interest in the children she had grown to love as an extended second family.

The Orphan Asylum Society that she helped found continues today. Now known as Graham Windham, it has evolved into an organization that supports hundreds of at-risk children and their families in the New York area. Times have changed—the nineteenth-century orphans are today's youth in foster care—but the mission remains true to Eliza's original goals. If Eliza was proud of everything that Alexander had done in his life, then Alexander in turn would have been equally proud of what she achieved—and her legacy continues to achieve today—on behalf of her orphans.

Yet although Eliza was married to Alexander for only twenty-four of her ninety-seven years, he remained the shining centerpiece of her life. In an era when most widows and widowers remarried for security and companionship, she stayed constant to his memory, and his love. There could, quite simply, never be any other man after her Hamilton. At the time of her death, she was still wearing a tiny cloth packet on a ribbon around her neck, and close to her heart. Inside the packet was the sonnet he'd written for her long before in Morristown, the paper so worn from unfolding and rereading that she'd been forced to carefully stitch the fragments together with sewing thread.

As she wrote forlornly to a friend soon after Alexander's death:

I have had a double share of blessings and I must now look forward to Grief. . . . for such a husband, his spirit is in heaven and his form is in the Earth, and I am nowhere any part of him.

They were at last reunited with Eliza's death in November 1854, when she was buried beside him in Trinity Churchyard in New York City.

I've enjoyed the time I've spent in Eliza's company, and I feel privileged to have told her story. I can only hope that she—and Alexander—would approve.

Susan Holloway Scott
March 2017

ACKNOWLEDGMENTS

A novel of this scale is not undertaken lightly, or alone. Many, many others shared their knowledge and eased my way, and helped me bring both Eliza and Alexander to life not just as characters, but as people.

For all details both large and small about life in 18th-century America, I rely, as always, on my friends at Colonial Williamsburg: Neal Hurst, Mark Hutter, Michael McCarty, Janea Whitacre, Sarah Woodyard, and Christina Westenberger.

For sharing some of the most personal surviving artifacts related to Eliza and Alexander Hamilton (including Eliza's wedding ring!): Jennifer B. Lee, Rare Book & Manuscript Library, Columbia University.

For keeping Eliza Hamilton's legacy alive today, and offering wise suggestions for how I could best help spread the word myself: Jess Dannhauser and Harry Berberian, Graham Windham.

For my wonderful tour of the Hamilton Grange: Jamie DeLine, who answered all my questions and somehow miraculously arranged for me to have the house (and the ghosts) entirely to myself.

For answering my questions about the Schuyler Mansion and the fascinating family who lived there: Danielle Funiciello, who also obliged my requests for photos.

For teaching my long-ago undergraduate self how to turn the most complicated American history into prose that was researched, succinct, and readable: William G. McLoughlin (1922–1992), Professor Emeritus of History, Brown University.

For helping me bring this book into being, and not laughing (or screaming) each time I said "It's almost done": my amazing editor Wendy McCurdy, Kensington Books, and the best agents in the universe, Annelise Robey and Meg Ruley, Jane Rotrosen Agency.

Additional thanks to the staffs of the following historic sites, libraries, and other institutions:

American Revolution Museum at Yorktown
Brandywine Battlefield Historic Site
Colonial Williamsburg
Columbia University Rare Book & Manuscript Library
The Earl Gregg Swem Library, College of William & Mary
Independence National Historical Park
Morristown National Historical Park
Museum of the American Revolution
Museum of the City of New York
The National Constitution Center
New-York Historical Society
The New York Public Library
The Pennsylvania Historical Society
The Rockefeller Library, Colonial Williamsburg
The Schuyler-Hamilton House
Washington's Headquarters State Historic Site, Newburgh
Valley Forge National Historic Park
Yorktown Battlefield, Colonial National Historical Park

DISCUSSION
QUESTIONS

- What did you know about Alexander Hamilton as a founding father before you read this book, and how has your perception changed?

- Eliza was very much a woman of her time in her devotion to her family and her husband. What do you think were her greatest strengths? Her weaknesses?

- Eliza was the second of the three older Schuyler sisters. Do you believe being in the middle between her brilliant older sister Angelica and her beautiful younger sister Peggy influenced her? How?

- Do you think Eliza ever truly regretted marrying Alexander?

- Some historians believe that Angelica and Alexander had an affair. What's your opinion?

- Why do you think Angelica married John Barker Church? Do you think their marriage was a happy one?

- After George Washington's death, Alexander admitted that Washington had always been his "aegis"—his protector. Had Washington lived, do you think Alexander would have fought the duel with Aaron Burr?

- If you were Eliza, would you have forgiven Alexander after he published the details of his affair with Maria Reynolds?

- At the time Alexander proposed to Eliza, cynics believed he was marrying her only for her money and family position. What do you think?

- Why do you think Alexander constantly courted physical danger and social disaster?

- Alexander always believed in the truth, no matter the consequences. Do you agree, or not? Why?

- Over the course of his life, Alexander was involved, either as a primary or secondary participant, in at least eleven duels or near-duels. Why was his honor so important to him?

- Eliza strongly objected to dueling on both moral and religious grounds, yet not even she was able to persuade Alexander to stop. What could she have done or said differently to change his mind?

- During the duel with Burr, Alexander apparently fired in the air, purposefully avoiding injuring Burr. Why do you think he did this?

- Burr was said to have taken the duel very seriously, and reportedly practiced his aim and shooting for days beforehand. Do you think he intended to kill Alexander? Why?

- Abigail Adams loathed Alexander. At one point, she wrote: "O I have read his Heart in his wicked Eyes many a time. The very devil is in them. They are lasciviousness itself, or I have no skill in Physiognomy." What do you think she meant by this?

- Alexander supposedly advised his son Philip before his duel to fire into the air as a way to satisfy his honor, but avoid murdering a man; this strategy led directly to Philip's death. Do you think Eliza ever learned her husband's advice to their son? Do you think he told her himself? What do you think her reaction would have been?

- What aspects of eighteenth-century American politics reminded you of modern politics?

- It's easy to take American democracy for granted. Did it come as a surprise to you to realize how much of what holds the U.S. together was created and put into practice by Hamilton? Did it change your perception of the United States, and what makes it different from previous forms of government?

- Was Alexander Hamilton a hero? Was Aaron Burr a villain?